just another SUMMER Romance

NEW YORK TIMES BESTSELLING AUTHOR

J.S. COOPER

Coconut Beach Island

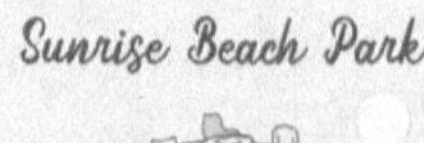

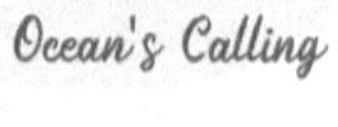

Municipal Airport
Sunrise Chapel
City Hall
Hidden Cove
Paws & Claws
Coral Moon BOUTIQUE
Art Gallery
Seashell DINER
Salt & Sand Spa
Rusty Anchor BAR
Seaside Bed & Breakfast
Scoops & Loops Ice Cream
Tide & Table
Grand Palm of Coconut Beach Resort
Dayton and Summer's House
Sunshine Surf
Coconut Bay Pier
Coconut Bay
Live the sweet life in Coconut Beach

Copyright © 2026 J. S. Cooper
www.jscooperauthor.com

Just Another Summer Romance
Coconut Beach Series

Editor: Jovana Shirley at Unforeseen Editing

Illustrator: goldenmushroom_
Cover Design: Covers by K. Webster

All rights reserved. No part of the book may be used or reproduced in any manner without written permission from the author, except to include brief quotations in a review. This book may not be used to train AI models. Names, characters, establishments, organizations, and incidents are products of the author's imagination or are used fictitiously to give a sense of authenticity. Any resemblance to actual persons, living or dead, events, or locales is entirely coincidental. No part of this book may be used to create, feed, or refine artificial intelligence models for any purpose without written permission from the author.

dedication

To Sebastian and Poppy who went on countless beach trips with me for inspiration for this book.

prologue

Luke

From: Miaisaprincess@googly.com
To: Lukehaverbrook@Haverbrookmoney.com
Luke,
I was thinking if we both turn 40 and are still single, we should get married. Not for sex or anything, but just so we both have someone. What do you think?
Mia

From: Lukehaverbrook@Haverbrookmoney.com
To: Miaisaprincess@googly.com
I think not. Is this a way for you to get me to support you for the rest of your life? I thought you wanted to marry for love and not money?
Luke

From: Miaisaprincess@googly.com
To: Lukehaverbrook@Haverbrookmoney.com
Wouldn't you support me if I was old and broke anyway? Isn't that what best friends do?
Mia

From: Lukehaverbrook@Haverbrookmoney.com
To: Miaisaprincess@googly.com
Is this your way of asking me to take care of you in your old age? I suppose I can do that without us getting married, Mia. I think a wife and no sex kinda defeats the purpose, don't you?

Luke

From: Miaisaprincess@googly.com
To: Lukehaverbrook@Haverbrookmoney.com
Luke, do you care more about sex than love? I want to marry for love. For unbreakable, soul-shattering love.

From: Lukehaverbrook@Haverbrookmoney.com
To: Miaisaprincess@googly.com
You mean in the case that you don't marry me for my money? Or are you expressing your undying love to me?

From: Miaisaprincess@googly.com
To: Lukehaverbrook@Haverbrookmoney.com
You are my best friend, and I love you, Lukey.
But if I am lucky enough to meet my soulmate, I want it to be earth-shattering. I want him to make me feel like the only woman in the world.

From: Lukehaverbrook@Haverbrookmoney.com
To: Miaisaprincess@googly.com
Not asking for much, huh? I guess I understand why you want me as your backup now. But isn't 40 a bit early to give up on your dreams of fictional love?

From: Miaisaprincess@googly.com
To: Lukehaverbrook@Haverbrookmoney.com
I still want to have kids. So, if we hit 40 and are still single, it's you and me, baby. And before you ask, we will do IVF, thank you very much.

From: Lukehaverbrook@Haverbrookmoney.com
To: Miaisaprincess@googly.com
So romantic, Mia. I feel so honored to have been chosen to be your life partner if we both crash out and burn in trying to find real partners! 😀
But time for me to get back to work. Speak soon.
Your maybe soon-to-be hubby,
Luke

chapter one

Mia

LUKE

Call me now.

"Demanding much, Luke?" I mutter under my breath as I smile at the message on the screen.

I tuck my phone into the back pocket of my favorite faded blue jeans. Luke will have to wait ten minutes. I've just gotten to work, and I need to help my best friend Juniper set up our mobile bookstore, Salty Pages, for the day. The sun already feels warm on my face, and I'm thinking that I should have worn shorts instead of pants. I already know it's going to be one of those hot Coconut Beach summer days that the tourists love to complain about.

Beep.

I pull my phone out of my pocket again.

LUKE

I need to talk to you. It's important.

MIA

Give me ten minutes. Just got to work.

After I text him back, I start putting up our store signs.

"It is so hot today," I mumble to Juniper as she writes a welcome message on our black chalkboard sign.

"You can say that again." She waves her hands in front of her face and grins.

"If it's slow in the afternoon, I'm going to take a swim in the ocean to cool off." I laugh.

"You just wanna stare at the hunky lifeguards as they sit in their huts," Juniper says, and I just grin back at her.

Nothing beats jumping around in the waves while watching hot men with six-packs contemplate whether or not you need rescuing.

Beep.

LUKE

Mia Bishop, you have five minutes.

He really thinks he runs my life.

"What's our song of the summer this year?" My best friend, roommate, and fellow business owner, Juniper, lowers her knock-off Ray-Ban sunglasses and peers at me with her knowing brown eyes. "And if you give me the title of another sad country song, I will scream." She leans back against the side of our mint-green mobile bookstore and wiggles her fingers at me before humming my favorite achy-breaky tune of the last year.

The sun makes her skin glow, illuminating her freckles like specks of gold. I take a deep breath of the salty ocean breeze and allow the familiar feeling of calm to overtake me. The cries of the seagulls make me smile, even as the humidity flattens my fine hair against my neck uncomfortably.

It almost feels like being on vacation, coming out here every day. Even though I'm here selling books, painting kids' faces, and taking photos of happy couples and families on vacation who are trying not to kill each other, it is still fun.

"I don't know yet. Why don't we write our own and perform it for all the tourists in town?" I grin at her and shimmy back and forth. "You can sing, and I'll be your backup dancer." I spin around, my long blonde hair flying across my shoulders as I do my little dance. That slightly resembles a wonky two-step move.

"Is this the mobile bookstore I've heard so much about or auditions for *American Idol*?" a voice whispers softly behind us.

We both still and turn around slowly. I let out a loud laugh as I see Wendy standing there with her sister, Josie, both gazing at us with amused expressions on their faces.

"How's it going, Wendy?" I ask her.

Josie giggles and immediately enters our renovated VW van to check out what new books we've gotten in stock.

"I'm good," She nods, and I see her checking out her phone. "Just waiting on Summer and Silvie, as we're all going to do some yoga."

I am not a yoga girl, and I don't enjoy it, but I decide to keep that information to myself.

"Yoga on the beach sounds like a good way to start the day." I tuck some loose wisps of hair behind my ears. My plethora of colorful bangles jangle with the movement, and I look down at my wrists in pleasure.

Beep.

LUKE

Two minutes. I'm waiting.

I grin at the text. I kinda like him waiting on me for once.

"Yeah, Summer says yoga on the beach and then a swim in the ocean is like becoming one with nature." Wendy shifts her beach bag against her hip.

"I feel the same way about sex on the beach," Juniper adds in slyly, and we all start laughing, though I know I have to call her out.

"You've never had sex on the beach, Juni," I tease her and wiggle my eyebrows as a cool breeze brushes past us. "Or are you keeping secrets from me?"

"Would I do that?" She adjusts some of the *Greetings from Coconut Beach* postcards on the tall rack to the left of the van and starts unpacking the box of bookmarks that arrived the night before. "Oh, I forgot to give you the mail."

Juniper hands me a stack of letters, which I idly sort through, only expecting to see bills.

"Ooh, what's this?" I say, spying an elegant linen envelope with my name written in calligraphy. I notice the name at the top is Rex Haverbrook.

I'm about to open it when my phone rings with the song "Baby Got Back," which my best friend, Luke, programmed in years ago. Nerves are now entering my stomach. Luke is never this insistent about getting in contact with me.

"What's up?" I say as I answer the phone. "Everything okay?"

"It's fine. I needed to talk to you," he says in his smooth, dry voice.

Luke Haverbrook has been my best friend since we were four years old and we met in pre-K. And even though he left Coconut Beach right after high school for college, we've remained close. It's crazy to me that we haven't seen each other in five years. Other than a late-night video call every few weeks when we watch a movie or something together. I miss my friend, but he's happy in the city, working his very lucrative job.

"Did you know your brother sent me a letter?" I rip it open eagerly, wondering if it's some sort of declaration of love. That would be weird, but kinda exciting.

"About that ..." Luke clears his throat, and he sounds awkward. Which is weird because he never sounds awkward. "That's why I've been trying to get in contact with you."

"What is it?" I feel an internal flicker of something like hope or anticipation, swiftly followed by dread, and I'm not sure why.

"I'm actually working right now, and I can't talk for super long, but ..." he says, his voice dropping dramatically, which is so unlike Luke. He's the least dramatic person I know. And the least likely to gossip, which I find quite annoying.

"But what?" I ask eagerly, and both Wendy and Juniper look up at me with questioning eyes. "Luke, stop being coy! Tell me what's going on!"

"I'm nervous to tell you, Mi-Mi."

He almost chuckles as I growl at his pet name for me, which delights him. Luke loves to annoy me.

"Why are you nervous to tell me?" I ask, my eyes narrowing as I think about what he could have to tell me.

"Did you open the envelope?"

"I just did. Let me take out the letter. Wait, what? It's an invitation?" I stare at it in confusion.

"Rex is getting married." He says the words like they mean nothing, but my heart stops beating for a couple of seconds. "Are you there?"

"Yes, I thought you just said Rex is getting married," I whisper into the phone and quickly read the invite. "Please tell me if I'm hearing and reading this correctly. Is this for real?" My earlier joy evaporates and is replaced by shock.

"Rex is getting married." His voice is amused and yet worried. "You didn't fall to the ground, did you?"

"No." I roll my eyes. "Not at all."

"Are you okay?"

"I'm fine," I say, though I feel slightly breathless. "Is this for real?" My heart drops.

"It's for real."

There's silence on the phone while I process everything.

"Mia, are you there?"

"I thought you were calling 'cause you got a girl pregnant or something," I joke because I just don't know what else to say. I just need to think.

"Really, Mia?"

"True. You'd have to be having sex for that to happen." I can't help but tease him, even though I'm closer to being a nun myself.

"You can't talk, queen of romance and empty beds," Luke snaps back, and all I can do is laugh. "Are you okay?" he asks again, his voice soft this time.

I don't answer immediately. Luke knows me better than I know myself. He knows that when I'm joking, I'm actually processing. And this is a lot to process.

Instead, I look past the book truck to the white sand, swaying green reeds, and turquoise-blue water of Coconut Bay and take three deep breaths. The water always calms me down when I feel anxious or overwhelmed or just taken aback.

"What's going on?" Wendy asks, concern in her eyes as she stares at me. "Is Rex your ex?"

"No," I say, shaking my head. "He's Luke's older brother. My first crush. The man I told everyone I was going to marry." I wrinkle my nose and laugh loudly, even though the merriment doesn't reach my eyes. "I guess that proves I'm not a psychic." I stare at Juniper, who rubs my shoulders.

All I can think is that the entire town will be there for the nuptials.

"That and many other reasons," Luke says in my ear. "He was never worthy of your crush, you know."

"I know, but I still can't believe it."

The truth of the matter is that I always thought Rex Haverbrook was going to be my one. Even though we'd never kissed, never dated, never anything. We'd just had one moment when I was a teenager, where he carried me to my room after a party I'd gotten drunk at and put me to bed and then whispered in my ear that he'd never let anything happen to me. And that was it. I spent the rest of my teenage years attempting to get his attention, but he never really noticed me. Everyone would stare at me, wondering if I was heartbroken.

"You and me both," he sighs. "Did you read the actual invitation? It's ridiculous."

"No, let me read it now." I stare at the words and read them out loud.

Ms. Mia Bishop,

You are cordially invited to the wedding of Rex Haverbrook and Andi Maggiano on the eleventh day of July at the Coconut Beach Cathedral. The wedding party festivities will begin on June 27, and we invite you to take part in a two-week celebration that will culminate in a coming together of our love. The festivities will center around the Grand Palm Resort of Coconut Beach, and we are delighted to offer every expected guest free accommodation and transport across the island to partake in the activities.

Please RSVP within the next week, as the festivities are soon to begin. We do understand this is short notice, but we hope you will be able to join us.

Rex and Andi

"Wow, that's fast." Juniper's eyes search mine, and I just shrug. "Wait, I think there's something on the back."

I turn the invite over and stare at the note scribbled in bright red ink.

There's a handwritten note, in neat cursive and I can't believe what it says.

You're invited to the wedding of the summer. We hope you can join us. Mia, it's a pity you don't have a date.

"Oh, hell no," I blurt out loudly, and I hear a low groan on the phone.

My entire body suddenly feels cold, like I just landed in the North Pole and I'm only in my underwear.

People will stare at me, wondering why I'm alone, feeling sorry for me. Coconut Beach loves a good gossip session, and I will be the top headline.

"I take it, you got a rude note as well?" Luke asks as I feel fire burning in my cheeks.

"Your jerk-off of a brother said it's a pity I don't have a date." My jaw drops in shock as I read the note again.

Now this has made me mad. I will not allow myself to become upset. Rex Haverbrook has never been mine. And we've never been close friends, but this note is next-level rude. Now I know why Luke called me. He must have known about the note.

I take a deep breath and allow the cool salt air to calm me. I may be single, I may not have any options, but I'm sure as hell not going to show up to the wedding festivities with no one. Even if that means going out that very evening and finding a guy at Cocktails & Chaos to play the part. The truth of the matter is that I don't want Rex. I just don't want to always be the girl who's never chosen.

"You okay, Mi-Mi?"

"I'm fine."

"You don't sound fine."

"Yes, I do."

"Your voice dropped in that way it does when you're upset but hiding it." His voice softens, and he sighs. "Don't do anything reckless, Mia." His familiar tone washes over me and comforts me. I hate that it sparks a warmth in me that has nothing to do with my new idea.

"I'll show him."

"What does that mean?" Luke's voice is oddly sober, and there's silence on the line for a few seconds. "You're not going to bring some idiot from the bar, right?" There's something in his tone that makes my stomach flip, and I strangle out a laugh. "Mia, you have nothing to prove to him."

"I know that."

"Mia."

"What?"

"You deserve better than a revenge date." He pauses, and I wonder what he's going to say next.

My heart thuds in anticipation. If I closed my eyes, I could almost picture his bright blue ones staring at me.

"Mia."

"Fine, I won't find someone at Cocktails & Chaos."

"You deserve someone who wants you. Who chooses you first. Who knows how special you are."

"That would be nice, if only he existed." Sadness fills me, and I blink rapidly. I will not cry.

The weight of being alone hits me like a dump truck. It's not even that I really care about Rex. It's that if he—the one guy I thought would be single forever—is getting married, it means that I may truly be unlovable. There's a voice in my head telling me I'm overreacting, but his note has stung me to my core.

"There's another option, you know."

"What?"

Silence fills the line. I watch as a pelican walks along the sandy white beach, looking for some scrap of food. The waves crash into the rocks near the lighthouse, pounding as hard as my heart is.

"You can take me."

My stomach flips in a way that has nothing to do with Rex and his engagement. Heat fills my cheeks, and a fire ignites in my stomach. I brush my hair away from my face as my throat constricts.

Luke Haverbrook has been my best friend since we were four. When we were thirteen, after we almost kissed, we made a promise to never cross that line.

Now, suddenly, it feels like that promise and our friendship could become dangerously complicated.

If I took him and it went wrong, I wouldn't just feel embarrassed in front of everyone; I could also lose my best friend. The thought sobers me. The thought of risking my friendship with Luke makes losing Rex mean absolutely nothing. But the thought of him pretending to be my boyfriend in front of everyone fills me with a pure shot of excitement. Everybody would be shocked, and I wouldn't mind just a little bit of positive attention on me.

chapter two

Luke

"Wait, what?" Mia's familiar tone sounds just as shocked as I feel.

I can imagine her standing there with parted pink lips. I bet anything that her blonde hair is in a messy ponytail, and she's twirling a few strands of hair between her fingers.

"What did you just say?"

"You can take me," I say again softly. "Want to be my girlfriend?"

She's quiet, and I laugh loudly so she knows it's a joke. If she needs a reason to believe I'm not being deadly serious, I will give her one.

"Luke, what are you saying?"

"I said, do you want to be my girlfriend?"

I quickly FaceTime her, and she answers immediately.

"Hey." I grin and smile when I see I was right about the ponytail.

"Hey."

I watch her nostrils flare as her eyes narrow. Mia wears her emotions on her face, and I can always tell what she's thinking. It's been that way since we were four years old and playing in pre-K. Back in the days when she stood up to bullies for the both of us.

I can still remember when Kenny took the last two cookies off of the plate in first grade and she went up to him and demanded he give me one of the cookies.

When he ate the first cookie right in her face, she pushed her little shoulders back, glared at him, and then said, "You give Luke his cookie, or I will pull your pants down."

She then turned to me with a crooked little smile, which was missing a front tooth.

Seconds later, Kenny gave her the cookie, which she ceremoniously brought over to me.

"You didn't need to do that, Mia," I mumbled, though I happily took the cookie from her.

"Best friends stick up for best friends." She beamed at me and hooked her little arm in mine, and we found our seats and read our books.

That was the moment I definitively knew that Mia—though she was bossy, goofy, and far too direct for me—was someone I'd be best friends with for the rest of my life. And here we are, twenty years later, and she is still my number one everything, even though I haven't actually seen her in person in years. But there were reasons for that.

"Be your girlfriend?" She enunciates each word like she's practicing speaking in a foreign language. "Is this about my emails? We're not forty yet, Luke."

She licks her lips nervously, and I can't stop from laughing. Mia looks absolutely clueless, and I wonder what's going through her head right now.

"Not my real girlfriend, you doofus."

Her face relaxes slightly, but I can see that she still looks super confused.

"My fake girlfriend. It will solve all our problems."

"All our problems?" she repeats.

I'm about to call her a dummy, but I hold back. Even as a joke, I know she wouldn't find it funny.

"We both want dates for the wedding. And Rex left me a rude note as well. You weren't the only one he chose to diss. Let's be real; it's unlikely that either one of us is going to find a date in the next couple of weeks. So, I say we go together. We're best friends; we can easily fake it. We'll just pretend we've been secretly dating."

"It was a secret to me as well." She giggles, understanding in her expression finally. Though there's a look in her eyes that seems thoughtful. She plays with her hair and starts braiding it, which is something she does when she's nervous or thinking. "I guess, it's not a bad idea." She grins into the phone. "It's a huge lie, and I don't know if anyone would believe it, but I don't hate the idea." She tilts her head to the side. "Do you think anyone would actually believe us though?"

"Why wouldn't they, if we made them?" I shrug, not really having thought the idea out properly. Which is unlike me.

I normally don't suggest an idea until I've thought it through from every possible angle. But this isn't work, and I don't have to worry about Mia twisting what I said to make it work for only her.

Mia is the one person in the world I trust above everyone. Even my own brother, who has time and time again shown me that he cares more about money, women, and being the favorite son to our parents than he does about our brotherly relationship. It is one of the reasons I left Coconut Beach and decided to step away from the family business. I've made a name in New York based on my work ethic and intelligence. And the multiple millions I have in my bank account have been earned by me and not from my trust fund, which I've never touched. Unlike Rex, the golden son.

"So, what exactly would we do?" she asks curiously.

I watch as she leans back against her van and brushes some loose tendrils behind her ears. I smile as I stare into her brown eyes, even though it's through a screen.

Mia looks just the same as I remember her looking in high school. She's still got that innocent, skeptical, questioning air about her, even though she's always been the most fun-loving and gregarious person I've ever met. I miss her friendship daily and just being in her presence.

The calls are a great way to stay in touch, but they're not the same as grabbing a coffee in person or even just hanging out at the beach on a starlit night and telling each other ghost stories, which was something we did monthly when we were seniors in high school. Even when we were in relationships, we still made time for our friendship, much to the chagrin of the people we were dating. But I think we both knew that our friendship was special, and we just loved being in each other's presence—oftentimes with Juniper, Josie, and my friend Tom, who was on the baseball team with me.

"Each other?" I joke and then stick my tongue out, lest she think I am being serious. "We'd just say we had been secretly dating because we didn't want the gossip mill talking about us, but we wanted to attend this wedding together."

"But how long have we been dating? And when did we see each other last? And …" She wrinkles her nose. "What if people expect us to be all touchy-feely?"

"You are always hugging me anyway, Mia. Or at least you used to when I was still in town."

"I don't mean hugs. I mean, kisses and stuff."

She pretends to gag and shudders like she's having a stroke. I won't admit that I don't find the idea as abhorrent as she does.

"Really, Mia?"

"The thought of having to kiss you is just … gross." She clears her throat and starts giggling. "GROSS."

"Tell me how you really feel." I roll my eyes and then wink. "At least I know how to kiss, Ms. Slobbery Lips."

"Luke Haverbrook, I told you that story in confidence. And I was thirteen at the time. I didn't know what I was doing."

I try not to think about that time, when she asked me to help her learn how to kiss. How I wanted to, but then we decided our friendship was more important.

"And you know what you're doing now?" I chuckle and try not to stare at her lips too hard. "When's the last time you kissed a guy anyway?"

"A few months ago, and, yes, I know what I'm doing. I think I could win a kissing competition if I wanted to." She licks her lips and then blows a kiss into the camera. "I could make millions off of these lips."

"So, why don't you plan on doing that at forty instead of marrying me then?"

"Funny. But anyway, back to your idea. I don't hate it, but I just don't know if it will work. Would anyone really believe we were dating?" She makes a face. "Plus that we've been keeping it a secret?"

"If you prefer we go to the wedding alone, like the losers Rex thinks we are …" I stare at her and purse my lips. *"Pity you don't have a date, Mia. And pity you had a crush on me, but I was a jackass to you. But, yes, please come to my wedding and my two-week festivities by yourself and watch me and my bride be all lovey-dovey in your face."*

Her face contorts, and she lets out a long, low sigh.

"He's such a jerk for what he wrote, but he's not all bad." A hopeful, reminiscent smile crosses her lips. "I still remember the boy who took me home from that party and tucked me into bed and whispered that he wouldn't let anything happen to me."

"But did you actually see his face?" I ask casually because I hate that she still tells this story to excuse the fact that Rex is a jerk. The story I know isn't exactly as she remembers it to be.

"No, but I remember him saying he was going to wear that costume."

"Yeah."

I don't tell her that he and I changed costumes at the last moment. I don't tell her that I saw her getting drunk and noticed other guys circling in on her like crows to dead carcasses. I don't tell her that I was worried that someone would take advantage of her and that it was me in that costume who got her home and tucked her into bed. I don't tell her that her grandma knew it was me and thanked me and gave me cookies. I don't tell her because I didn't tell her all those years ago because I wanted her to hold on to a glimmer of hope that her crush on Rex wasn't for nothing. I didn't want her to feel completely rejected, but now I wonder if I should have told her the truth. It's too late for me to admit that it was me, but every time she brings up that night to excuse Rex's poor behavior, I cringe inside because I know the truth. And I hate that she still holds out some sort of hope that he is a good guy inside.

"But his note was rude," she continues, and I can see her thinking hard. "I'm going to speak to Juniper in a few minutes and get her take on it, okay?"

"Sure," I say softly, knowing it's pointless to ask her to keep it a secret from her other best friend.

I'm not as close with Juniper as I am with Mia, but I still trust her and consider her a good friend.

"Let me know soon though because if we do decide to do this, we'll have to figure out the details."

"Or maybe you could come into town early and we could spend time together, figuring it out." She looks excited. "That would be fun."

"Mmhmm," I say, without formally committing to that idea because I know based on my current work schedule, that will be hard.

In fact, part of the reason the idea appeals to me is that if I go as Mia's date, I can pretend we're spending quality time together while I'm actually working. I'm in the middle of a 2.8 billion-dollar deal that could elevate me to the next level of my career. If I secure this deal, I will make equity partner at the hedge fund. I will be the youngest financial analyst at the firm to have secured multiple billion-dollar deals. I will be able to write my own ticket. I will show my parents and Rex that I was able to make it without having to use the Haverbrook name.

"Luke, is that a yes?"

"Let's see," I answer and try not to laugh as she groans and shakes her head.

Mia, for all her wonderful qualities, doesn't have the same head for business as I do. She's more about laughing, enjoying life, and having fun, and I'm more about studying the stock market and international trade. On the surface, our friendship shouldn't work, but beneath the surface, it is the most prized possession that I have.

"Anyway, I'm going to go back to work. Call me later tonight or tomorrow and let me know what you decide."

"Okay, Luke." She nods and smiles at me in that familiar way that reminds me of home—walks on Coconut Bay Beach, hikes to Hidden Cove, swimming in the waterfall, grabbing a bite at Iggy's Grill, taking ice cream cones and biking to the lighthouse, listening to Mia sing as we swim in the ocean, hoping to call the dolphins to her as she pretends to be a mermaid. "I'll call you later," she says and hangs up.

I walk over to my floor-to-ceiling windows and stare out at the glittering city in front of me.

I love living here in New York. I love the hustle and bustle, the bright lights, the tall buildings, the millions of people from all over the world walking the streets and going about their business. Living here makes me feel like I'm a part of something big. Like I'm important. Especially from my view in this office. Which is picture-perfect. My life here is fantastic. And yet there's still a part of me that misses that small island desperately.

I shake my head to clear it. I hate feeling nostalgic about a past that I want to remain in the past. I'll go back to Coconut Beach for the wedding. Then I'll be on the first plane back to the city, and I will never look back. I love my friends and my family back home, but I am always the second-best Haverbrook in my hometown. Here, I am somebody making a name for himself, not having to stay in the shadows. The only thing missing is Mia.

And I don't know if I'll ever get over that fact.

I'm about to start working again when my phone rings, and I see that it's my nana, Bitsy Haverbrook. I answer on the first ring.

"Hi, Nana. How are you?"

"Lucas Haverbrook, why haven't I heard from you in over two weeks?" She sounds annoyed, but I know she's just teasing me. My grandma is one of the busiest women I know.

"Sorry, I've been busy with work and making millions. You know how it is."

"All work and no play makes Luke a dull boy, dear."

"I thought it was Jack?" I tease her affectionately.

I love my nana and have always known that I was her favorite. Though I've never been quite sure if it is because of me or because she wants to make up for the fact that my parents quite obviously adore Rex more than me.

He has always been the golden boy. Handsome, sporty, charming, a kiss-ass. Whereas I've been more thoughtful, studious, introverted. It is one of the reasons why my friendship with Mia has worked so well. She brought me out of my shell. Showed me that there was more to life than studying. And even though I am now very different to the young boy I was, he still exists somewhere inside of me. Life just looks different for me now.

Back in middle school and even high school, girls never paid attention to nerdy Luke Haverbrook. Everyone was about Rex, the jock, but now I am muscular and look the part of a leading man. Women gush over me when they see me out. I get compliments on my blue eyes, my silky hair, my bulging biceps. I am the package that women want now, but it doesn't take away from the insecurities I grew up with, being tall, skinny, and full of acne. Though that didn't matter to Mia and our friendship. She always validated me, always made me feel seen.

"Now, now, Luke. Did you hear that Rex is getting married?"

"I did. In fact, I received his invitation today."

"Ooh, really?" She pauses. "That's nice. The invitations were so classy, weren't they?"

"I suppose so. I don't know much about invitations. Just like I don't know much about his fiancée, Andi. How long have they even been dating? Mom and Dad haven't mentioned her before, and she wasn't in the annual Christmas newsletter that Mom sent out either."

"Well, I can't say that Lucille or I know much about her, dear. I know she works at the mayor's office as a receptionist. I suppose I could ask Mayor Sharkey Smith what he thinks about her, but if she and Rex are in love, then what can I say?" She pauses again, as if she's waiting on me to tell her what to say, but I know better than that. Bitsy Haverbrook needs no help in any of her conversations. "I was just calling to see if you'd gotten the invitation and if you were going to partake in all the festivities."

"Two weeks is a long time for me to be away from work. I've never even heard of expecting people to spend two weeks together to celebrate a wedding."

"Well, it's also a way for us all to get together with family and friends," she says softly. "It was actually my suggestion to Rex that it be that long so that everyone can celebrate. Not every guest will be there for two weeks. Just family."

"But Mia got invited for the festivities as well."

"She is family, Luke. She's your best friend, and she's Lucille's granddaughter. And you know Lucille and I have been best friends for decades, since before I met your grandfather. She and I are thick as thieves. She's like my sister."

"I know, Nana." I laugh. "No need to remind me. I just think it's late notice for such a celebration when so many of us are busy."

"You will come though?" Her voice is hesitant. "You don't want Rex to think that you're upset that he has someone and you don't."

"Who says I have no one?" I don't know why I say that. Maybe it's because I don't want my nana to feel bad for me as well. Maybe it's because I want to force Mia's hand.

"You're dating?" She sounds shocked. "Who? Does Mia know?"

"Nana, I can't talk about this right now, but …" I chew on my lower lip. I don't want to say too much because what if Mia doesn't agree to the plan?

My stomach churns at the thought. What if she doesn't agree to the plan? A part of me is nervous that she will say no, though I know that is a stupid feeling. I literally have nothing to lose either way.

"You have a girlfriend, and you haven't told me." She sniffles, and then I hear her whispering to someone. "I don't know," she mumbles, and I frown.

"Who are you with, Nana?"

"Lucille and I were just going to bingo. She was curious if you'd gotten the invitation. We know that Mia got hers and was a little upset about a note." She sounds dazed. "Not sure what it said exactly, but supposedly, Rex was a little rude, and we just wondered if you'd perhaps received something similar."

"Yeah, maybe." Something seems off, but I don't question her. "Mia and I were just on the phone actually."

"Oh, really? One sec." There's an odd noise on the phone and then I hear her talking as if in the distance. "Mia and Luke were just on the phone." She is obviously talking to Lucille again. "Well, I didn't want to disturb you, darling. Give me a call this weekend, and we can catch up. Granddad and I were talking about flying out to see you next month, if you don't happen to make it to the wedding."

"I'll be there, Nana."

"Oh, great, great. I can't wait to hold you and hug you. Oh, I'm so excited you'll be back home." She sounds delighted, and I feel guilty for having not returned home for so long. "We will all be super excited to see you and to hear about your girlfriend, of course."

"Who knows? You might even get to meet her." I am not sure why I add those words. I must be out of my mind. "I'll send you my trip details soon. Give Lucille a kiss and a hug from me. Love you, Nana. I'll call you soon."

I hang up and stand there, wondering what the hell I just did. I must be out of my mind. Why am I going so hard with this narrative?

I don't have time to ponder my thoughts though because my phone pings with a text from Mia.

MIA

Spoke to Juniper, Josie, and Wendy about your idea. And they think it is ingenious. So, I'm in. But we need to set some ground rules. 😀

LUKE

Sounds like a plan to me, girlfriend.

MIA

Don't be goofy, boyfriend. I'll call you tonight to plan, if I'm not too sloshed.

LUKE

Great. I can't wait to see Rex's face when he realizes we're together.

MIA

He's going to feel like a fool.

LUKE

I know. This is going to be perfect. Have fun tonight and stay safe.

I drop the phone onto my desk and take a seat. There's a huge grin on my face, and for the first time in a long time, I feel excited about heading back to Coconut Beach and seeing my old friends and all the new friends that Mia has told me about.

I'll still have to do a shit-ton of work while I am there, but Mia will understand. She can cover for me when I need to be in meetings or on calls. That is what is so great about this arrangement. She isn't my real girlfriend, so she won't expect me to be with her one hundred percent of the time. I'll just have to show up to key events, and that will be enough. I will be able to close this deal and show up for the wedding. It will be perfect. And it will wipe that cocky smile off of my brother's face.

He's always thought he's better than me. He's always known my secret. Well, this time, I'll show him. I'll finally come out on top.

chapter three

Mia

I read the front of the cream linen invitation out loud again and try not to roll my eyes. I'm still mad about the note that Rex wrote.

"Who invites someone to a wedding with a two-week celebration two weeks before it's meant to happen?" I shout out to Juniper, who is in the kitchen, making us an easy chicken fried rice dish for dinner before we go out for the night. "That's absolutely ridiculous."

I drop the invitation on the bed and head out to our cozy little kitchen. I stop next to the small pinewood table my grandma Lucille gave us when we moved in, along with four uncomfortable chairs. They are the reason we usually sit on our couch to eat instead of at the table, but the one time I complained to my parents, they told me that was why God had invented cushions. When I told them the cushions didn't help, they told me to be grateful and not to upset my grandma with complaints, and so that was that. Thankfully, Juniper's parents allowed us to choose the couch we wanted, so that is deep and comfortable.

"Have some cucumbers, Mia." Juniper looks up from cutting onions. "It's still going to be about twenty minutes." She frowns. "Are you hangry? Or still upset over Rex?"

"I am neither hangry nor upset. I am still pissed about the rude note on my invitation." I wave it in the air in front of her face.

"The invite sounded perfectly polite, but I agree his note was rude as hell. But at least you and Luke have that plan."

"The note was tacky and rude."

"The note was rude, but that doesn't surprise me. Rex has never exactly been Mr. Nice Guy." She makes a face like she wants to gag.

I've always known that neither she nor Josie liked Rex. But I also knew his mean persona was a front. The true Rex was the guy in the bear suit who carried me home and to my bed like I was a damsel in distress and whispered in my ear. I was so drunk that night, and I knew that most other boys would have taken advantage of me.

"I know he has that jackass front, but he's not all bad." I sigh because I don't really want to defend him, given the note on the invitation. "I don't want to partake in two weeks' worth of wedding festivities, even if Luke is there as my pretend boyfriend, but I know I'm going to have to. Grandma Lucille and his nana, Bitsy, are best friends. They will expect me and Rafe to be there." I mention my older brother, who also still lives in town. However, because he runs the local vet clinic, I'm sure he will find plenty of excuses to not have to spend much time partaking in *all the fun*.

"How is Rafe?" Juniper asks casually as she minces some garlic cloves. "Haven't seen him in a while."

"He's busy with Paws and Claws and training Cherie. Oh yeah, I saw her at Salty Sirens this morning, and she said to remind you that Lani needs to come in for her rabies shot soon."

"Oh yeah, I'll make an appointment." She looks up at me. "Want to open a bottle of red wine and grab three glasses?"

"No, what I'd like to do is tell Rex off." I groan and cover my face as I think about everyone staring at me while he's all lovey-dovey.

The worst part is the fact that I know half the town knows about my stupid teenage crush. I literally performed a one-woman play in the town talent show one year, talking about two fated soulmates who lived on an island off the coast of Florida, called Ria and Mex. I still cringe when I think about it. That wasn't my finest work, but I was fifteen, with my head in the clouds and under the mistaken belief that Rex felt the same way for me as I did for him.

I no longer had feelings for him, but the embarrassment is still as bad as if I did. His note hurt me. Did he really think I was sitting around, pining for him, unable to get a man? Would he believe that Luke and I were dating?

"I just hope no one figures out that Luke and I are lying and I look like a loser."

"You're not a loser. Many of us will be there as singles." She shrugs like it's not a big deal, like we didn't spend our teenage years detailing exactly what we wanted in a future partner and how we both expected to be in some sort of relationship by now. "Though I guess I didn't get invited to the two-week long festivities." She laughs. "I guess that's what you get for your grandma being one of the Busy Bees." The Busy Bees are the nickname we gave to the group that refers to themselves as the Bees, in town, on account of how much time they spend discussing other peoples business.

"That's what I get for my grandma being best friends with Bitsy Haverbrook."

I think of my grandma Lucille and her best friend, Luke and Rex's grandma. They have been best friends since they were young girls and are now members of a small group of retirees who loved to gossip, crochet, and read books. Juniper and I call them the busy Bees because they always seem to be everywhere.

"Though I suppose that means Wendy, Josie, Summer, and Silvie will all be at the events as well, seeing as Gale, January, and Birdy are all part of the Bees as well." I mention the other members of our friend group. Josie was a good friend from school, Wendy was her older sister, Summer had gone to school with us as well, but then had left Coconut Beach and Silvie was her good friend, who'd just moved to the island recently.

"Yep, and we're all single, so it won't just be you." Juniper pauses with her knife up in the air, and her expression changes to one of contemplation. "I sure hope that Silvie is okay though, what with her just running away from her own wedding."

"True. I didn't even think about that." Guilt courses through me as I think about our new friend, who came to Coconut Beach as a runaway bride. "Hopefully, she's not regretting her decision."

"Her ex sounded awful, so I doubt it. We shall all be the beautiful and happy singles at the wedding." She starts chopping again. "Trust me, no one is even thinking about our status. Plus, didn't she say she was going to try and work some deal out with Cal?" Cal was the manager at our favorite local bar, Cocktails & Chaos. He was tall, dark, and handsome and many a woman had fallen under his spell. Asides from me, of course. He was cute, but totally not my type.

"Yeah, that's true."

"Do you think Rex was trying to be funny?"

"Maybe, but if that was meant to be a joke, it was a fail." I'm about to start bitching and moaning again, but I can tell from the look on Juniper's face that she doesn't want to talk about this for much longer.

"I'm excited for tonight though. I hope Cal has some discount cocktails tonight. I want to party my ass off and not worry about spending all the money on my credit card." I giggle and grab some cucumber sticks and take a bite. "This is not hitting the spot."

"Make yourself busy. It'll be a while."

I step into the living room and look around. A feeling of contentment fills me. I love our little apartment. It's not fancy, nor is it large, but we've decorated it to the best of our ability with the meager bank account funds that we have. There's a large white sectional couch that occupies most of the floor space in the open-plan living area. The floors are a light pine wood, and we have one large colorful Moroccan wool rug in the center of the room. The walls are adorned with photos of us throughout the years, along with our families, and different paintings and photos we've taken of the island. A candle burns on the circular table, and a lemony scent fills the air. My phone vibrates just as I'm about to take a seat on the couch.

"It's Luke. I'll be right back." I hold up my phone and hurry into my bedroom. "Lucas Haverbrook, are we crazy?"

"Yes." There's silence on the line for a few moments, and then he continues, "I'm going to video-call you."

He clicks off, and then my screen lights up with a new call. I answer immediately, looking up into the phone. His blue eyes look tired and amused as he gazes at me. I watch as he holds up the invitation in his hand. It is exactly the same invitation that I received.

"Yep. I'm still mad," I mumble, still annoyed, though I'm trying to process why I'm so upset. Is my hurt radiating from jealousy or bitterness or loneliness? I'm still not one hundred percent sure.

"Not as mad as me, I'm sure," Luke says dryly and flips the invitation around.

He's sitting in the living room of his apartment, which I've only ever seen on video, and he's dressed in a nice button-up shirt. Which is unusual for him in the evenings. He normally goes to the gym after work, so he's normally in a shirt and sweatpants when we talk.

"Wait, what did your note say? You never told me."

"Oh, listen to this." He clears his throat. "*Hey, bro. You're invited to the wedding of the year. Yeah, baby, your big bro is getting married. Can't wait to see you at the festivities. Pity you're a workhorse and have no one to bring, but, hey, hope you're still happy for me. The best Haverbrook son.*" He stops and rolls his eyes.

"Holy smokes, Batman," I growl. "Your brother is rude as hell. I just don't know why he would do that."

"Yeah, he's an ass. I don't care about my note, but yours was intentionally hurtful … given your history." Luke frowns, and his boyish, handsome face contorts into one of anger.

One of the nicest qualities that Luke possesses is that he hates it when anyone hurts me. He's always been protective over me and my feelings, which oftentimes feels annoying, but I've always appreciated how he's been there for me.

"Do you want me to say something to him?"

"No way," I answer him quickly. "Don't you dare say anything. I don't want him to think that I care. Because I absolutely don't."

There's nothing worse than being rejected by someone who never really noticed you. I'm sure that Rex thinks that he's being funny, but that almost makes it worse.

"Okay then." Luke puts down the invitation, and I see his jaw clench as he stares at me.

For a moment, my heart softens because I think he's genuinely concerned with how I'm taking everything. The note, while rude and mean, is extra hurtful to me due to my youthful crush. The thought stings that Rex could be so cruel, but it doesn't surprise me. Not deep down.

"I'll be okay. No need to worry or look so concerned. I'm upset, yes, but I'm not crushed or anything. It's not like we ever dated and …" My voice trails off as I see Luke scrolling through something on his iPad and frowning. "Um, Houston, are you there? What's going on? Are you even listening to me?"

"Sorry, Mia." He sounds aggravated, and it's at that moment that doubt creeps in. Maybe he no longer wants us to pretend to be dating. "I was looking through my work calendar. I can't believe that he thinks I can just take off two weeks to come and spend time in Coconut Beach, partying with him and his fiancée, who I've never even heard of before."

"That's why you're upset?" Understanding courses through me, followed by slight disappointment. It was nice, momentarily thinking that Luke was that hurt for me, but I should have known that work always comes first for Luke. Always. "Can't you take a vacation or something? It's not like you've been to Coconut Beach or anywhere for years. If I made your sort of money, I'd be taking epic vacations every couple of months."

"I make epic money because I'm here, brokering deals and investing, not because I'm jet-setting around the world." He sighs, and I watch as he runs his fingers through his slightly overgrown, dark hair. "And I seem to remember that you like the fact that I make epic money"

"I do?"

"Isn't that why you wanted to marry me at forty?" He chuckles, and I watch as his face comes closer to the screen. His blue eyes are twinkling as his lips twitch. "Or was it because of my devastating good looks?"

"You're hardly Ben Affleck." I scoff, and he bursts out laughing.

"I thought you preferred Matt Damon?"

"Have you seen Ben lately?" I lick my lips and picture the handsome actor. "He is looking absolutely scrumptious."

"I didn't realize you'd met him in real life." Luke leans back on the couch, and I watch as he picks up a glass of something and takes a sip. "Are you holding out on me, Mia?"

"Yeah, he came to Coconut Beach, and we had two very hot and steamy nights, and I just never told you about it." Sarcasm drips off of my tongue. "Seriously, Luke, like Ben Affleck would ever come to Coconut Beach." I laugh loudly and derisively. I like our small, close-knit, and highly gossipy town. "The busy Bees would be all over me if any movie star came to town and gave me the time of day."

"How are our grandmas?" Luke asks curiously. "And the rest of the Bees?"

"Grandma is fine. She is loving the new book club they started. She told me your nana Bitsy wanted to start a poker night, but she was nervous because, supposedly, Gale has been spending too much money, and the bed-and-breakfast isn't doing well, and Grandma is nervous Gale will spend every last penny she has, and Wendy and Josie will have a hard time keeping the business afloat. January did a psychic reading on her though and said not to worry 'cause Wendy will save the day and fall in love with some rich, blond-haired dude, though Gale didn't tell Wendy that because Wendy is not into psychics." I pause and take a breath. "Bored yet?"

"Could I ever be bored of hearing about all the island gossip?" He winks at me. "You want to watch a movie tonight? I've got some work to do, but maybe around eight? We can also discuss our plan."

"No can do." I grin at him. "I'm going dancing with the girls at Cocktails & Chaos. I'm hoping Cal will hook us up with some drink specials. And maybe some hot guys as well. Kill two birds with one stone, you know? Help me forget my pain."

"Hoping to find a date for the wedding that isn't me?" He stands up and starts walking down a corridor. "Just remember that you want a good guy. Not someone who's going to steal your wallet."

"Shut up, Luke." I glare into the phone as he reminds me of a tourist I met the previous summer and went on two dates with. Only for him to steal my wallet as we took a moonlit stroll on the beach. Cal and Benny, one of the bartenders, had to chase him down for me to retrieve it. That was embarrassing. "I have more discerning taste now."

"I hope so. A crush on my idiot brother and a thief aren't exactly great indicators."

"And who are you seeing? Miss Universe? Why don't you bring her?"

"I'll have you know, I go on dates." He smirks. "Plenty of them, in fact."

"Uh-huh. So, why don't you take one of them to the wedding?"

"I think not." He shakes his head vehemently. "The last thing I need is for some woman to think I'm trying to get serious with her just because I invited her to my brother's wedding."

"That would be awkward, indeed." I laugh. "What you need is someone who just gets it. Like me." I stretch out on my bed. "So, I guess we are doing this then?"

"I think it's the best idea for both of us." Luke's expression changes to one of deep concentration, then ponderance, and then he grins widely. "Pity we can't seal it with a kiss."

"Yeah, right." I stick my tongue out at him, and he bursts out laughing. "Neither one of us would want that."

My heart skips a beat as my eyes flicker to his lips. For a brief second, I wonder what it would be like, kissing Luke, but I immediately banish the thought from my mind.

chapter four

Mia

The sky looks like a painting with its purple, pink, and orange hues. The sand tickles my toes as I make my way down the sandy white beach toward my grandparents' house for our weekly dinner. I stop to pick up a perfect pearlescent-hued shell and brush the granules of sand off of it. I drop my flip-flops to the ground and make my way to the water, so I can dip my toes in for just a few moments before I continue on my way. The cool water makes me shiver for a few seconds as I watch the sun make its final descent on the horizon. A couple of plops in the water to the right of me makes me swivel my head, and I'm happy to see two dolphins swimming.

Coconut Beach has always felt magical to me, which is one of the reasons why I've never even thought of leaving the island to live elsewhere. Though there is a part of me that would like to explore other parts of the world. Just to see what's out there. Maybe one day. When I've got money. Maybe Juniper and I can take a trip somewhere. Or maybe even me and Luke, if he ever takes time off of work.

"Am I crazy?" I call out to a circling pelican, who is looking for scattered food left by tourists on the beach. "Am I making a mistake, trying to pretend like Luke and I are in a relationship?" I speak out loud and then look around me quickly to ensure that nobody is nearby, listening to me talk out loud to myself like a crazy person. I really don't need word going around the island that Mia Bishop is a nutcase.

"Hey, Mia. Is that you?"

I look behind me and see Wendy in a pair of jogging shorts and a sports bra. Her dark hair is on top of her head, and her face looks sweaty and focused.

"Going for a swim in your clothes?"

"No, just headed to my grandparents' house for dinner with my brother, Rafe." I giggle as I step back from the water and head over to her. "Been jogging?"

"Yeah, trying to stay fit after all our nights partying it up at Cocktails & Chaos." She wipes her forehead. "Thanks for including me. I know, sometimes, I can be a bit of a grouch when you girls are talking about men." She smiles ruefully. "I hate that my ex has turned me off of love, but I don't want to make you girls hate it as well."

"Your ex sucked and was a fool for dumping you." I stick my finger up in the air. "Screw you, jackass, for dumping Wendy. Mark my words: he will regret it."

"I know he will." Wendy nods. "But suffice it to say, right now, I'm just concerned with keeping Seaside Bed-and-Breakfast open." She looks stressed out. "And trying to get my grandma to spend more time figuring out how to get her spending under control and less time in everyone's business."

"Ha-ha, girl. I know what you mean. Those busy Bees are in everything." I wrap my arm around her shoulders. "I have faith in you though. You are more than capable of turning the business around, and I bet you end up meeting a hot guy who will make you forget your ex."

"I'm not interested, thank you very much."

"Not even for a hot one-night stand?"

I start humming the words to "WAP" by Cardi B, and Wendy just looks at me in shock. I burst out laughing at her expression and she just shakes her head.

"Nothing wrong with getting some. There are going to be some hot men at the wedding, I bet. Maybe even staying at your place. You wouldn't want to have hot sex with some tall, dark, handsome stranger?"

"No," she says quickly, but I notice her face goes red, and she's looking away.

My brain immediately starts ticking. Has she already met someone? I'm about to pry and ask her a question when she speaks again.

"What about you? Are you planning on having a hot love affair with a gorgeous wedding guest? Oh, wait, did you decide to go with Luke?" She lowers her voice, and I grin.

"I mean, I wouldn't say no to a hot guy." I move my hips back and forth. "But I'm not sure that's going to work, to be honest. Now I officially have a fake boyfriend."

"So, it's on?" She grins at me, and I nod.

"Luke and I are going to the wedding together. As a couple. We're going to pretend to be in love." I giggle and twirl around. "*My heart beats for you, Luke.*" I stop and wink at Wendy. "At least, that's what I'll be telling everyone in a couple of days."

"Oh, hmm." Wendy smiles ruefully, and I see her gazing at me before speaking again. "Is it all a ruse or …"

"Or what?" I frown and stare at her. "It's just a ruse, trust me. There is nothing between Luke and me in real life, other than being best friends. Nothing at all. You know this, Wendy." My tone sounds slightly too high, and I frown.

Why would Wendy even ask me that question? There is absolutely nothing between Luke and me. Nothing at all but years of friendship.

"Rafe, can you have a seat, please?" I ask my brother as he hovers over the table, grabbing warm chocolate chip cookies and stuffing them in his face. "I have something important I want to announce to everyone." I glare at him as he goes to grab another cookie. At the rate he's eating them, there won't be any left for me. "Please save some for the rest of us." I grab my fork and take another bite of the lasagna my grandma made for dinner. "I would like some cookies as well."

"You snooze, you lose, Mia."

"You sound like you're five." I grab two cookies and place them next to my plate just in case.

"I don't know any five-year-old vets." He chortles as he takes a seat across the table from me. "What's the deal? What's the big announcement?" He looks over to our grandparents and then our parents. "Does anyone know?"

"I have no idea." My mother looks slightly miffed that she's not in on whatever I'm about to divulge to everyone, but I hope she will understand why.

"Everyone, I'm about to impart on you a huge announcement, something I can no longer keep to myself."

I look down at the table, my face bright red. To everyone else, it may look like I'm blushing with anxiousness or embarrassment, but the fact is, I'm doing my best to look like I'm struggling to tell them this information. I need for them to believe that this is real. My grandparents, parents, and brother are all upstanding people, and I love them, but they like to talk. And while I don't think any of them would deliberately tell my secret, I am not so sure that it wouldn't slip out. Especially from my grandma's lips. So, I have to ensure that they all believe me.

"What is going on, Mia?" Rafe checks his watch and then taps his fingers against the table in a grating way. "And how long is this announcement going to take? I have beach volleyball later tonight, and I have to go to work tomorrow. Unfortunately, the animals are not going to understand that I spent the night listening to you whine about how …" His voice drifts off as I give him my best death stare.

"I'm sure all of you have heard that Rex Haverbrook is engaged and getting married in a couple of weeks."

"Oh, boy, are you heartbroken?" Rafe's voice is teasing, but I can tell from the concerned look on his face that my big brother is worried.

For all of his moaning and groaning, I know that Rafe would do anything for me. He's always been an overprotective big brother. He just doesn't know that I know about all the times he stuck up for me in school.

"No, I'm not heartbroken. Far from it." I hold my head up high and burst into a wide smile.

I channel my inner Viola Davis from *How to Get Away with Murder*. I channel my inner Meryl Streep from *Sophie's Choice*. And then I desperately try to recall every memory of Kate Hudson from *How to Lose a Guy in 10 Days*. My fingers play with my hair nervously, and then I look down in a demure fashion, like I'm giddy but nervous to speak. I tilt my head up, pretending Steven Spielberg himself is directing me, and then I look each one of them in the eye and blink rapidly. The goal is to tear up in happiness, but unfortunately for me, my skills aren't that profound.

"Do you have an eyelash stuck or something?" Rafe leans forward. "You need to stop wearing so much eye junk."

"I do not have an eyelash stuck." *Calm down, Mia. Do not go off on your brother.* I offer him a sweet smile instead. "I am in love."

"You, what?" He starts coughing and spits out a piece of the cookie he was chewing. "With who?"

"I have been waiting to tell everyone the news, and we've decided that it's best to let everyone know now." I lick my lips.

Everyone is staring at me intently now.

"I don't want anyone to be upset that we've been keeping this secret."

"Oh shit, you're not sleeping with Captain Smitty Johnson, are you?" Rafe cackles and slams his hand down on the table. "I knew you were desperate for love, but you can do better than him, sis. He's, like, sixty-five." He grins at me. "I suppose it's because Ocean's Calling is right there near your book truck, isn't it? Did he promise you a free boat ride to see the dolphins and you couldn't resist?"

He laughs like he thinks his joke is funny, and I want to go off on him and his single status, but now is not the time to be sidetracked.

"Very funny, Rafe." I look down my nose at him, and he just rolls his eyes in response. "My boyfriend—and, yes, I said *boyfriend* because we have been official for about a year now. Well, my boyfriend and I want everyone to know about our love because he will be at the wedding." I'd have to remember to tell Luke that we'd been dating for a year. All of these small details would bring us down if we weren't on the same page.

"You're bringing some random dude to the Haverbrook wedding? Yikes." Rafe stands up. "Look, if you want an internet date, that is up to you, but I'm sure everyone at this table can agree that we don't want to meet your cyber boyfriend—"

"Everyone knows him," I cut him off. I am done with Rafe and my demure act. It's getting me nowhere fast. "Luke and I want the world to know about our love and our relationship. It is finally time for everyone to know that we are soulmates."

"Luke?" Rafe's jaw drops in shock, and on the inside, I'm screaming in delight. "Like Luke Haverbrook, your best friend?"

"No, Luke Skywalker from *Star Wars*." I giggle and then look over at my grandparents, who look absolutely delighted. "Does anyone else have anything to say, or is Rafe going to dominate the conversation?"

"Me, dominate anything in this family?" He chuckles loudly, as if that could never be a possibility—which, to be fair, may be true. But I can't help it that I am the baby of the family and much more dramatic than he is. "But seriously, sis, when did this happen? Luke hasn't even been back on the island in years."

"As far as you know."

I give him a small wink, and he frowns. My stomach twists slightly because I know that frown. It's the frown of him thinking deeply. Overanalyzing and trying to figure out facts of the situation and then parse them into a manner that makes sense to him. It's why he's such a good vet. But at this moment, I don't want him thinking too hard about what I said.

"Grandma, Grandpa, are you happy for me? Grams, I know that Bitsy is your best friend. Will she hate the fact that we're dating, or will she be happy?"

"I can't speak for Bitsy," Grams says slowly as she studies my face. "But I do think she will be intrigued to find out more. I had no clue you were seeing Luke, my dear. What caused you to reveal this new status of your relationship with us tonight?"

"We just thought it was time," I say dreamily. "We got the invitations, with some fairly rude notes about dating statuses, and we decided to let everyone know that we'd been secretly dating and falling desperately in love."

"How did this happen?" My mother looks happy but confused. "I'm just so surprised you never let anything slip. You've been such a good actress. I truly didn't even suspect that you were seeing anyone. You let nothing slip that you were dating at all."

"Yeah, you're constantly bitching about not finding any good guys." Rafe stares at me. "Just last week at Cocktails & Chaos, I heard you telling Juniper that you were thinking of leaving the island to meet a man." He raises an eyebrow. "And Cal and I were teasing you, and you said that …"

"Well, I was just pretending, Rafe." Since when has he listened to my conversations that closely? "And if you were paying closer attention, you'd know that Juni and I were actually talking about how we wanted to go traveling."

"Why don't you and Luke go traveling then? He has loads of money." Rafe is annoying me. "And what's the plan? Is he moving back to Coconut Beach, or are you planning on moving to New York?"

"Hmm?" Shit, I didn't anticipate that question.

"How often have you guys seen each other in the last year?" my grandma asks. "Bitsy will feel saddened to hear that Luke has been on the island and hasn't been in touch to see her."

"Oh, well, I mean …" I lick my lips nervously.

"Where did he stay?" My dad frowns. "I hope not with you and Juniper."

"I, um, well, you know … he, um …" I don't know how to answer any of these questions, and I suddenly realize how hard it is going to be to sell this relationship. I have two options at this moment. I can pretend this was all a joke and just end the ruse now. Or I can go all in and make sure that everyone believes me.

"And what note are you talking about?" Grandma asks as she grabs her cup of tea and sips. "You got a note from Rex?"

"Kinda. It was a little rude." I shrug, but that feeling of hurt and discomfort fills me as I think about his dig. I do not want to go to all those wedding festivities alone. I am not going to tell my family that this was a joke.

"But I, um, need to call Luke right now," I say quickly, feeling overwhelmed. "I will—"

"Call him in front of us," Rafe demands. "Let us congratulate him as well."

"I, uh …"

"Yes, do it, Mia." My mother sounds miffed, and I know I need to appease her for keeping the secret.

I grab my phone and dial his number, praying to God that he won't answer. The last thing I need is Luke revealing the truth to my family before he even gets to town. As the phone rings, I hold my breath.

Do not answer, Luke. Please do not answer.

chapter five

Luke

"Hey there, girlfriend. What are you—" I stop as I notice the petrified look on Mia's face.

For a few seconds, my heart stops because I'm scared she's in danger, but then I notice her background, and the expectant faces behind her. Shit! From the look on her face and the shocked expressions on those of her family, I deduct that Mia has told them we are together. This is not something we planned to do right away, but I know Mia. Once she gets an idea into her head, she runs with it.

I am taken aback by the faces that I see on the screen, even though I recognize everyone who is staring at me. Mia's practically gawking, and her eyes are bulging so much that she reminds me of an owl. I can see the fear in her eyes, and it takes everything in me not to burst out laughing. Mia is the last person to be speechless, and yet at this moment, I know she has absolutely no clue what to say.

"Hey, everyone. I am guessing, the cat is out of the bag?" I grin and think fast. How do I convince these folks, who have known me since before I could walk, that I am telling the truth?

"So, it's true?" Shock is in Rafe's voice as he gazes at me.

Mia's older brother has always been friendly to me, if not particularly warm. He's around the same age as my brother, Rex, but they were not in the same friend groups. Rex was popular, a jock, and always going on dates. Rafe was intellectual and thoughtful, and from what I know, he didn't have many girlfriends—which was surprising because, for all intents and purposes, he was probably the better-looking of the two. Something that annoyed the shit out of Mia, growing up, as almost all her girlfriends wanted to know about Rafe. All but Juniper.

"Well, I'm not really sure what Mia has told you," I say, keeping a cheerful expression on my face and trying to read their expressions for some sign of how to play this. None of them are giving me anything. "But if she's told you that we're desperately in love, then yes."

"See? I told you it was true." Mia blushes a bright red, and I want to tease her and say that Rudolph's nose is jealous of her cheeks, but I don't dare. She glances back at Rafe, who still looks quite disbelieving.

"So, tell me, when exactly did this happen? And how come no one has seen you in town, Luke? I know for a fact that you haven't gone anywhere, Mia."

He's firing questions like he's an attorney and not a vet, and I know for a fact that both Mia and I are panicking inside. He raises his eyebrows and looks at her with skepticism. Rafe does not believe us.

I watch as she puts her hands on her hips and glares at him.

"How would you know that for a fact? Are you spying on me, big brother?"

"No, but Coconut Beach is a small town, and everyone knows everyone. I see you several times a week."

"But you don't see me every single day, just like I don't see you every single day. So, if you left town, you wouldn't actually know."

She glares back at him, and I realize that no one else in the family is saying anything. I notice that Mia's nana, Lucille, is looking particularly entertained, and I know that this entire conversation will be regaled to the busy Bees within the next two hours.

"I would know because we meet up with the family almost every weekend."

"Rafe, stop being jealous," she says. "Just because I have someone and you have no one." She holds her head up high. "It's not my fault you don't have a date for the wedding."

Rafe just rolls his eyes. "I don't need a date for the wedding. I don't want a date for the wedding." He shakes his head and then leaves the screen. "Something smells fishy, and it's not coming from the ocean," he calls out as he leaves the room.

"It's your upper lip, jerk," Mia calls after him, and her parents just shake their heads, not saying anything.

They are used to Mia and Rafe fighting like cats and dogs. It's been that way for years. The Bishops are loud, argumentative, loving, and always there for each other. Unlike Rex and me. We didn't argue like that. He was more subtle in his digs, and I was more introspective. We didn't love as hard, nor did we fight. I kinda wish that we had. But that was the past. We had no real relationship now. Past hurts and jealousies had caused a wedge between us that even a wedding couldn't fix.

"I'm looking forward to explaining everything as soon as I get to town," I say brightly. "I'm sure Mia is as well. We are so happy to finally let the cat out of the bag. Aren't we, darling?"

Mia stares into the camera, and her eyes are twinkling.

"Oh, definitely. We have been counting down to this day. Haven't we, Lukey Wukey?"

I try not to cringe at her nickname for me. As I listen to Mia, I realize there are a lot of things that we need to figure out. While the idea seemed like a good one at the time, I am fast beginning to think that neither Mia nor I has thought this through properly. She is my best friend and always has been, and I know her like the back of my hand. But this is brand-new for both of us. I don't know her on a romantic level, and I'm certainly not sure how we are going to convince people that we've been together for over a year. I can feel panicked thoughts moving through my brain toward my heart, but I keep my expression cheerful. We'll figure out the kinks when I get to town.

"Anyway, I need to speak to my boyfriend in private, please?" Mia says and turns to the rest of her family.

"Grandma, Grandpa, hi," I say, waving. "Good seeing you both." I use the old familiar terms that they'd asked me to use when I was young. They'd always been loving and gracious to me. I missed going over for Sunday dinners.

"Hello there, Luke." Lucille speaks up, beaming at the screen.

Mia's mother looks pissed, which makes sense because I have a feeling that my parents and grandparents are going to be pissed too. I haven't been home in a while, and they're going to wonder if I've been sneaking onto the island to see Mia and not them.

Shit, this is already murky.

"So, Lukey, I want to just ask you something private," Mia says in a singsong voice. "I'll be right back."

She hurries quickly through her grandmother's kitchen toward the backyard. I watch as she opens the door and then runs around to the side of the house. Her hair is wispy and loose, and she's breathing heavily as she leans back against the white exterior of her grandparents' home.

"Oh my God, Luke. I think we fucked up," she says, staring into the phone. "They had so many questions, and I didn't know how to answer them. And then, of course, Rafe wouldn't believe me because he sucks, but he's right. How do we explain all of these things? Ugh, this was a mistake."

"Take a deep breath, Mia. Breathe in. Breathe out. Breathe in—"

"Jeez, shut up!" she says loudly. "I do not have time for meditation techniques. I don't even like meditation when I am not feeling anxious, let alone when I'm feeling anxious. Who thought breathing was a good way to calm down? It's not. It's absolutely not."

"Mia, you're losing it," I say patiently. "And actually, breathing techniques are known to be—"

"Shush." She glares into the phone, but she stops speaking and just breathes for a minute. "What are we going to do, Luke?"

"What do you mean, what are we going to do? We've already decided what we're going to do."

"But it was a mistake. Should we come clean? I can just go in there and be like, *April Fools*."

"It's not April."

"I can be like *June Fools*."

"Really? And then what do you want Rex to think? *Oh, I was right. You two are losers who couldn't get dates.*"

"He really sucks—you know that, right?" She stares at me, her light-brown eyes as open and endearing as they've been since the very first time I met her.

"I know, trust me. He's my brother, and he's sucked for a long time. I've told you that."

"I suppose you're right. I mean, it's not my fault that he was charming to me once." She nods slowly.

"And about that … Mia, I think there's something that you should—"

"Anyway," she says, cutting me off, "I have an idea."

"I was just about to say something to you." I frown at her interruption.

"You can say it to me after I tell you my idea." She gives me her impish smile, the contagious one that makes me smile in response, even though I'm slightly irritated.

"I'm listening."

"Can you come early?"

"What do you mean, can I come early?"

"Can you get home early? Maybe a good week early so that we can go over everything and get our story straight and practice acting like a couple who's desperately in love." She makes a face like that grosses her out. Her long blonde hair falls past her shoulders and I watch as she twirls it in her fingers delicately. I can still remember when we were fifteen and she'd asked me to brush her hair a hundred times a night. At the time, the task had felt tedious, but now, I missed touching those silky locks.

I can't help but laugh.

"Because I'm not that good of an improv actress, and I don't think you're that good of an actor period."

"It's going to be that hard for you to pretend you're in love with me?" I pretend to be wounded.

"Luke, we have to pretend we're in a relationship." She practically gags. "We have to pretend that we kiss and we touch and ... oh my, even thinking about it makes me feel sick to my stomach." She shudders. "Can you imagine us kissing?"

My heart sinks slowly at her words. I'm slightly offended by what she's saying, but I'm not going to tell her that.

"It makes you sick to your stomach to think about kissing me? Well, that's good to know."

"What? I'm just being honest. I'm sure you feel the same way." She grins and leans back into the wall and brushes her hair back behind her ears. She's got a dark blue headband on, and I notice she's got her bikini top on under her blouse. "Can you imagine your lips on mine?"

"Ew." I pretend to gag as well. "Not at all. I'm pretty sure you suck as a kisser."

"I'm pretty sure you suck as a kisser too, Luke."

"I'm pretty sure that Beatrice—who I kissed a couple of weeks ago—thinks I'm a pretty fine kisser." I smack my lips together. "In fact, she moaned like I—"

"Gross, Luke." She blinks rapidly. "And who the hell is Beatrice?"

"No one important. So, who have you kissed recently that thought you were a pretty fine kisser?" I don't know why I ask the question because I don't really want to know who her Barbie-pink lips have been smooching.

"Well, I wouldn't say anyone recently." She runs her fingers through her hair. "So, maybe I'll go to Cocktails & Chaos tonight, and I'll practice with a hot tourist. That way, it can't get back to Rex, but I can get my flirting skills on because, honestly, I'm not really good at flirting and pretending I'm in a relationship because it's been so long." She takes a deep breath. "So, maybe tonight will—"

"Really, Mia?"

"What? It's a good idea. I'm going to get all dressed up tonight, and then Juniper and I are going to flirt up a storm with two hot surfers, and I'm going to make out and—"

"Ew. I do not want to hear this story. You're going to go and pimp yourself out just to practice for when I get to town?"

"I'm hardly pimping myself out, Luke. That's rude." She shifts the phone closer to her face, and I can see her skin is glowing. It must be a hot day in Coconut Beach. "We also need to figure out the parameters of this contract."

"Of what contract? What are you talking about, Mia?"

"I mean the contract between us—obviously not a *Fifty Shades of Grey* contract or anything," she says, giggling. "That would be disgusting. But we need to figure out exactly what we will and won't do to sell this story."

"I kinda wanna know what a *Fifty Shades of Grey* contract would consist of, but you can tell me that in person." I wink at her. "You tell me, Mia, what are some things that you will do to sell our love story?"

"I guess I'll allow you to kiss me on the cheek."

"I already kiss you on the cheek."

"Yeah, but not in a passionate way."

"There's a passionate way to kiss on the cheek?"

"Maybe not." She giggles. "Maybe I'll allow a quick peck on the lips."

"Ooh, salacious. Are you sure you can handle being that scandalous, Mia?" I smack my hand to my mouth. "We'll be on the front page of the newspaper."

"Shut up, Luke."

"I'm just saying, if we're going to sell this, we're going to need more than a peck on the cheek or on the lips. We're going to need some making out." I pucker my lips to the phone. "No slobbering though."

"No way."

"I'm just saying, have you ever been around a couple that's never made out?"

"No, but I'm also not around couples when they make out or are groping each other."

"I'm not talking about groping you. I'm not telling you to go without a bra. I'm not telling you that my hands are going to be down your pants." I stiffen slightly as I think about touching her in those ways. I cannot allow my mind to go into the gutter.

"Ew, Luke, really?"

"Mia, we need to discuss these things. Because if we're doing this, then we need to figure out our boundaries and exactly how far we're going to go." I pause. "And how far we want people to think we've gone. Have we as a couple had sex?"

"Ugh, I didn't even think about that. Okay, you can kiss me on the lips. I don't want tongue though. Tongue is a step too far."

"No tongue it is."

"And your hands are to stay above the waist at all times."

"They can stay above the waist." I smirk.

"And not on my boobs either."

"What? You don't want me to have a quick grope?"

"This was such a bad idea, wasn't it?" She giggles. "A quick grope, Luke, really?"

"Would you rather me say, *Can I fondle your bosoms, Mia?*"

"No. I would rather you not say that. We're not in eighteenth-century England."

"Would you rather me say, *Can I suck on your titties?*"

"Oh my heavens, Luke Haverbrook. What did you just say?" Her jaw drops in shock.

"Okay, so we're not going R-rated. Agreed. I'm just checking what things are going to work and not work for you."

"You don't even speak like that anyway." She rolls her eyes. "Just because I haven't seen you in person in years doesn't mean I don't know who you are and your character. And you don't say things like *suck on titties.*"

"You got me there. But you don't know how I am with the guys."

"True. And you do live in New York now." She wrinkles her nose.

"Hey, what's so wrong with New York?"

"Nothing, I suppose. Maybe one day, I'll visit."

"Are you going to come and visit me in New York before I come to town?"

"I would love to come and visit you. I mean, if you ever extended me an invitation."

I keep my mouth shut. I'm not going to tell her why I haven't extended her an invitation.

"It's going to look really weird that I haven't come to visit you," she says, "and you haven't come to visit me."

I stare at her and nod. "It is going to look very weird."

"So, do we pretend that it's happened? No one's going to believe I left Coconut Beach. And if you say you've been back home, your entire family's going to be mad at you."

"Then we're going to have to say that we fell in love chatting on the phone and the computer."

"Oh my God. I feel like such a loser."

"Mia, you are not a loser. I will say I came to town a couple of times," I sigh. "My grandparents and my parents will be upset, but that's better than us looking like internet geeks."

"Yeah, you would hate that, Mr. I Program Computer Games for Fun."

"That was when I was sixteen."

"Yeah, you still did that for fun."

"And you played the games and enjoyed them."

"That's because I was a good best friend."

"The very best," I say. "Anyway, I should get going."

She wrinkles her nose. I watch as she plays with her long blonde hair. The bangles on her arms clink and clink as she moves her hand back and forth.

"Everyone in my family's probably talking about me right now, wondering how they didn't know. Wondering how I kept this a secret."

"Well, you do have a big mouth."

"Thank you."

"What? It's not like I'm going to tell your parents and your grandparents and your brother—who already looks like he wants to kill me—that you have a big mouth because you like going down on me."

"Luke Haverbrook. I have never gone down on you."

"But if you were my girlfriend for real, isn't that something you would do?"

"We're putting that in the contract," she says, laughing. "That is not happening. No way, no how. I don't care who finds out it's a lie."

"Of course not. Just like I'm not going to go down on you." I start laughing.

"Of course you're not," she says, blushing. "I feel weird even having this conversation with you. This is either going to be amazing or it's going to be the worst decision we've ever made in our lives."

"Let's stay positive, Mia. It's going to be amazing. Oh, and, Mia?"

"Yes, Luke?"

"Don't go to Cocktails & Chaos tonight and get into any trouble."

"What do you mean?"

"Leave those poor tourists alone." I hang up to her laughing.

I sit there at my desk and frown. I really don't want to think about Mia making out with some random tourist—and not just because she's meant to be my secret girlfriend. I don't want her lips touching another man. I don't want her doing anything with anyone else. The thought of her kissing someone else makes me pissed. The thought makes me want to puke, and that's not something I want to think about too deeply.

There's a knock on my door, and I rest my phone on the desk.

"Come in," I say, looking up.

"Hi, Mr. Haverbrook. Johnson would like to speak to you."

"You can send him in. Thanks, Rebecca."

"You're welcome, Mr. Haverbrook." She gives me her sweet, sexy little smile and backs out.

I know for a fact that my assistant, Rebecca, would love to go on a date with me. She's let me know in no uncertain terms that she's willing to accept anything that I'd offer her, including a one-night stand. She'd love to go to the wedding with me as well, but there is no way I'd ever ask her. I sit there, holding my gold fountain pen in my hand, and watch as Johnson—my boss—walks in.

"Haverbrook," he says.

"Good afternoon, sir." I stand up. "Everything okay?"

"Yes, and no." He closes the door behind him and looks around. He walks over and takes his seat in front of me. His bald head looks especially shiny today as he gazes at me sternly.

"We've got a problem."

"Oh? Big problem? A small problem? A problem with me?"

"A problem for you. We've got a problem with the Equinox deal."

My heart sinks. The Equinox deal is the largest deal our hedge fund has ever been a part of. In fact, I've been working on it for the last year, and it's set to close within the next couple of months. I know—and he knows—that if I make this deal happen, I will be the next equity partner. I will run this town. And that's saying a lot.

"What's up?"

"Burlington was at the Seminole Club the other evening, and he was having a conversation. I don't know with who—it doesn't matter. He was speaking with one of the waitstaff there, who overheard a conversation between TCO and Ricardo from the Equinox team." He pauses. "And it looks like they may have another offer on the table."

"But we have the best offer. They've already agreed to sign with us. They've already agreed to this merger. It's the highest amount per share that they will get."

"Apparently not. It looks like the Brazilians are now coming to the table with a huge offer."

"The Brazilians?" I frown. "But I thought the Chinese were the only ones interested."

"Turns out, the Chinese and the Brazilians have decided to work together. This could blow everything up. You do understand what I'm saying, Haverbrook?"

"Of course, sir."

"I need you working on this night and day until it closes."

"Of course."

And then I remember Mia. And the wedding. And her desire for me to come a week early.

Shit.

"I will be out of town for two weeks, possibly before the deal closes. But I'll be back in plenty of time."

"This is not the time for you to be going on vacation, Haverbrook. Are you out of your mind?"

"My brother is getting married," I say firmly. "I have to be there."

"Not a good idea."

"Johnson, how long have I worked here?"

"I don't know. Multiple years."

"Exactly. How many vacations have I taken in that time?"

"I don't know."

"Zero. How many days have I missed?"

"I don't know."

"Zero." I fold my arms and lean forward. "My brother is getting married. I have to go back to Coconut Beach for the wedding celebrations. This is my family. This is important. The company has always come first for me. The deal will not suffer. I will work from Coconut Beach. However, I cannot and will not miss this."

"I didn't even think you were close with your family," he says, shaking his head.

He knows he can't threaten me. That I'll walk away. He also knows I'm the best guy he has working for him—probably even better than him. That if I walk now, the deal is definitely done.

"My family and I are as close as most families are. This is very important. I will be there."

"So, you say it's for two weeks?"

"Two weeks," I say.

I know I should mention the third week. I need to get to Coconut Beach early so that Mia and I can discuss all the plans. But I also know that three weeks would be pushing it with Johnson—and also with the deal. I need to be hands-on. I need to find out what's going on with Equinox. I'll have to take some people out for lunch and dinner. I'll have to get to the root of the issue.

I have to make sure that I do not lose this deal.

The one thing I have above my brother is the fact that I am making it on my own. I am making a name for myself. This isn't just important for the hedge fund. This is important for me. This is important for me to show my family that I am a son worth paying attention to, that I am a son worth caring about and nurturing. Rex might have everything else, but I will not let him take this from me as well.

Jonathan stands up. "Fine. Two weeks. But I'm warning you, Haverbrook. If you have to get back here at midnight on a Wednesday, I don't want any excuses. If you can't catch a commercial flight then I want you chartering a plane."

"Don't worry. The flight is five hours. If you need me back here at the office for anything, I will be here. This deal means everything to me. I will always be accessible via email as well." I offer him my hand. "I have to be there for family, but my job comes first, as it always has."

"Good" he says, shaking my hand firmly. "Well, have fun, and let's close the deal."

"Done, sir." I watch as he walks out, and I lean back in the chair.

Fuck, I think to myself.

I have no idea how I'm going to balance this merger with the wedding. I have no idea how I'm going to plan with Mia and make sure we're both on the same page—and sell the fact that we've been in a relationship for the last year. Especially not after I just told her I would come to town early to make sure we could sell it. She'll be mad at me, but she is my best friend. She, more than anyone, knows how important this deal is to me. She, more than anyone, will understand. I will just have to make it up to her when I get to town. I'll buy her a necklace or another bracelet or something that will make her happy. And then we'll sell our relationship, break up, and I can come back to New York and live my life the way I have been for the last few years.

I try not to think about the fact that I've missed Mia. I try not to think about the fact that I look forward to kissing her. That I've always wanted to kiss her.

I try not to think about the fact that a part of me, deep down inside, wishes that this weren't a fake relationship. A part of me, deep down inside, wishes that we had truly fallen in love.

chapter six

Mia

It's seven p.m., the sun has set, and I'm feeling slightly buzzed as I sip wine with my girlfriends. The night is still early, and we're all at the apartment Juniper and I share, getting ready for the evening. Music plays through the small Bose speakers in the corner of the room, and I watch as my friends Summer and Silvie bop their heads to Bruno Mars. I'm so glad to see them with smiles on their faces, as they've both been through a rough time recently.

"Who wants another glass of wine?" Juniper holds up a bottle of cabernet sauvignon and looks around. She's always a gracious host.

We all rush over to the kitchen with our glasses to get more wine.

"Thanks for inviting us tonight," Wendy says gratefully. "I needed a girls' night, where I could just decompress." She runs her fingers through her dark hair and shakes her shoulders, as if shaking off her money woes.

"You're telling me." Summer lets out a light sigh. "I love Coconut Beach, and it's been great being back, but renovating a house is not for the weakhearted."

"I'm so glad you girls were able to rally with me tonight because I really needed girl time." I look over at Juniper, Wendy, Josie, Summer, and Silvie and beam at them. "And doesn't my new candle smell just like butter popcorn?"

"Yes, and it's making me hungry." Juniper fake growls at me, which delights Lani, who starts zooming back and forth on the rug. She loves it when we have company.

"She's so cute." Summer's green eyes light up as she takes in Lani, who is now rolling on her back and yelping. "I love dogs."

"She's a keeper," I agree and clear my throat. "Attention, everyone. I have an announcement. Most of you already know, but my best friend, Luke, and I are going to Rex Haverbrook's wedding together, and we will be pretending that we are madly in love."

"I don't know that it's the best idea you've ever had," Juniper says, tilting her head to the side, "but I fully support you." Her brown eyes shimmer under the glittery silver eye shadow she's applied, and she looks absolutely gorgeous.

"Now, that's a good best friend," Silvie says with a warm smile as she takes a seat at the dining table and applies some blush.

"Yes, she is. But remember, everyone, it's a secret." I glance at Josie and issue her a warning look.

I love Josie, but sometimes, she gets so excited that she has loose lips.

"My lips are sealed. Trust me, I won't tell a soul." Her lips are pink and glossy as she leans back on the couch. She looks over at Wendy. "I've been good at keeping secrets."

Summer brushes through her long blonde hair, and I watch the way it shines with a tinge of jealousy. "You don't have to worry about me. I've got my own issues going on right now with Dayton second-guessing every decision I'm trying to make for this renovation. It's infuriating." She puts the brush down and takes a couple of deep breaths. "He is driving me crazy."

"Oh, I'm so sorry. It's that bad?"

"Worse than bad. But enough about me right now. I don't even want to think about him right now." She looks over at Wendy. "How have you been doing?"

"Let's just say that I'm trying my best to ensure that we don't lose the bed-and-breakfast, and Grandma is so busy in everyone else's business, but her own." She lets out a frustrated sigh. "I'm scrambling to get as many guests as possible."

"But we did get someone. A very hot someone," Josie adds, making an *ooh* sound.

"A very, very hot someone," I say, giggling and moving back and forth. "Or as some would say, sexy."

"We have a new guest who is staying with us. His name is Carter, and he is handsome to some," Wendy explains to Summer and Silvie.

"I will totally make out with him tonight if he's at Cocktails & Chaos." I lick my lips.

"You and me both," Juniper says.

"No, you guys won't," Wendy says quickly, and I see her blushing slightly.

I wonder if she has a thing for him. I'm almost positive that he has a thing for her because the last time I saw him, we were all at Salty Sirens, and I was pretty sure he had lust in his eyes, though I didn't tell her that. Wendy's the sort of woman who doesn't want to hear about hot men wanting to seduce her. She doesn't understand how beautiful she is and how men are drawn to her. If I had a man like Carter gazing at me like caviar, I'd be sure to let him have a nibble. Maybe that's why I don't have any men after me.

"Well, I'm not going to say anything either," Silvie says. "Especially not now that I'm entering my own fake relationship with Cal."

"Yeah, that's going to be interesting." I stare at her, wondering if she knows what she's getting into.

She doesn't know Cal that well, as she hasn't been on the island long, but apparently, they hit it off right away.

Cal is the owner of Cocktails & Chaos, and he is a really nice, good-looking guy, but I've never known him to be the sort of guy who would be great in a fake dating situation. I wonder if Silvie has a thing for him. Even though she did just run away from an almost marriage. Silvie's love life is even more of a hot mess than mine. Mine is just nonexistent.

"Plus, he's really hot," I say loudly. "How are you going to fake date a really hot guy? You're going to want to date him for real."

"Are you going to want to date Luke for real?" she shoots back at me.

"Oh, no way. He's been my best friend since before I could do multiplication. I do not want to date him." I gag.

"But he's cute," Summer says, teasing me. "I remember him from high school. He's tall, dark, and handsome, and those baby blues of his are to die for."

I frown at her words. She's gushing far more than I like.

"Yeah, he's okay. But, my gosh, I'm kind of nervous, guys. I realize that we may have to kiss."

"What do you mean, you may have to kiss?" Juniper giggles loudly. "You're definitely going to have to kiss."

"But I'm not going to French kiss him. I'm just going to give him a peck. That's what I told him."

"A peck?" Wendy raises her eyebrows in surprise. "What are you, twelve?"

"Why do you sound like Luke right now?"

"I bet he'd totally want to go all the way with you," Josie says, winking at me. "And, girl, you should go for it. Luke has always been a stud muffin."

"No, he hasn't," I say, staring at her. "Do you have a thing for him?"

"No, I don't. Why would you ask me that?" Josie looks at me and bursts out laughing.

"I don't know. I just thought you said that kind of weird, like you wanted to make out with him."

"Are you acting jealous?" Juniper's eyes narrow, and my heart races. There's no way I'm jealous of any woman who wants Luke.

"I'm not. At all. Let's finish putting on our makeup." I take a long gulp of wine and try not to think of kissing Luke.

"My parents were kind of gobsmacked when I told them, my grandparents were cool with it, and Rafe was acting like an absolute jerk. I don't know that he believed me, but Luke and I are going to sell it so that he'll have to eat crow."

"Well, you know he is very smart." Juniper walks around with the bottle of wine and tops us all up.

I stare at her. "Since when have you thought that Rafe was smart?"

"Since always. He's always been smart. You know that."

"He's book smart. He's not emotionally intelligent. He's my brother, and he is so freaking annoying. All the questions he kept asking me, I was like, is he trying to ruin this for me?"

"Have you heard what Rex has said?" Silvie asks. "Because he's the reason you're doing this, right?"

"I have no idea what Rex thinks," I say softly. "And I am not doing it because of him per se. I'm doing it because of the note he left on the wedding invitation. *It's a pity you don't have a date*. Excuse you, Rex? I have a date. Your brother. Your very eligible brother. Your much better-looking brother."

"You think that Luke is better-looking than Rex?" Juniper asks, and my heart thuds.

"What are you talking about?" I blink rapidly.

"You just said that Luke is much better-looking than Rex."

"No, I didn't. I mean, Rex is gorgeous, and Luke is just Luke."

"Girl, you just said that," Summer says, grinning at me.

"I heard you say that," Josie adds.

"Me three," Silvie says with a wry smile.

"Slip of the tongue. I really like that eye shadow that you're wearing, Silvie. It really stands out."

"Thank you. I want Cal to see why it's a good idea to fake date me."

"Are you *into him*, into him?"

"No. Of course not," she says a little too loudly. "How's your brother, by the way, Summer?"

"Oh, Dayton is not my brother. Do not call him that," she says, blushing bright red. "He's my stepbrother and I can't stand him. He's more like my enemy."

"Ooh, sorry," Silvie apologizes and glances over at Wendy. "And what about you? Are you seeing anyone?"

"No one," she says a little too quickly. "No one at all."

"And I know you're not seeing anyone, Juniper. Are you down to find a hot guy with me tonight and make out?" I ask my friend.

"Sure," she says. "Do you know if Rafe is going out tonight, by the way?"

"I have no clue. Why?"

"Well, you don't want to be making out with some strange guy when you told him that you and Luke are in love," she says quickly as she slips on some heels.

"I guess I kind of forgot that he goes out sometimes. He's such a bore."

"He's not a bore," Juniper says.

"Why are you sticking up for my brother so much?"

"I'm not. I'm just saying that he's not an absolutely awful guy."

"Girl, if you saw him the other day when I was on the phone with Luke at my grandparents' house, you would know he is as awful as I say he is—and maybe even more." I apply red lipstick to my lips, stand up, and twirl around.

I'm wearing a short white skirt that emphasizes my golden tan and a silver top that clings to my breasts and exposes my taut belly.

"How do I look?" I say, spinning around, my long blonde hair bouncing against my back.

"Stunning," Juniper says, her brown eyes warm. "You're gorgeous.

You know that, right? If you really wanted a date—a real date—for the wedding, you could have one."

"I guess. It's not like any guys are really banging down my door. It's hard, living here."

We don't have many new guys who move to the island. The tourists come and go, and while there are locals, it's such a small community that it's hard to date.

"I get it, girl." She lets out a long, deep sigh.

"Hey, don't be down on yourself." I reach over and rub her shoulders. "You'll meet a good guy. Maybe there'll even be someone at the wedding."

"Maybe."

"Girls, what if we vow to have the best summer of our lives?" I jump up and hold my glass in the air.

"I'm in," Josie says.

"Yeah. I mean, I wouldn't mind some good sex and some hot kisses," Wendy says, grinning wickedly as she stands up and spins around.

"I guess I wouldn't mind some fun," Silvie says with a wry smile.

We all turn to look at Summer, who is looking down and blushing.

"Hey, you already know that I fucked up and sent my stepbrother those pictures," she says quickly, waving her hand in front of her face. She's now bright red. "I think, right now, I just need to concentrate on the reno."

"Or wickedly send him even sexier pictures?" I tease.

"Really, Mia?"

"What? I'm just saying, this is going to be our summer. We're all going to have the best sex of our lives."

"We're all going to be wooed," Josie says.

"We're all going to fall in love," Juniper says.

"I just hope to save the bed-and-breakfast," Wendy adds.

"I just hope to get over my broken heart and succeed in business," Silvie says.

"And I just hope to get the beach house looking as beautiful and wonderful as I've always envisioned it could be," Summer says softly.

We all grow slightly quiet then because Summer recently lost her parents, and we all know that she's still getting over that deep trauma. I know that grief is something that never fully leaves you, but I want Summer to know she will always have us supporting her.

"Here's to a summer of fun. And to you fooling the world into thinking Luke Haverbrook is your gorgeous boyfriend." Juniper grins. "Cheers, girls."

We all hold our glasses up and clink them.

I sit back down on the couch and look over at my friend group. I'm so happy to be in Coconut Beach with them. I haven't known them all as long as I've known Juniper and Luke, but they all mean something to me. It's friendships like this that make small towns worth it.

"Do you think we'll grow up to be the busy Bees?" Juniper asks, laughing slightly.

"Never. We don't gossip," Josie says. "As much."

"Just all the time," Wendy adds, and we all start laughing.

My phone rings and I stare at the screen. "It's Lukey," I say, waving it. "Should I answer or let it go to voicemail?"

"Answer," Summer says, giggling. "And does he like it when you call him Lukey?"

"I think he absolutely hates it." I start giggling. "But it is what it is."

I answer the phone. "Hey there, darling lover boy. What are you up to?"

"Are you drunk already, Mia?" His voice is dry, and I just start laughing.

"No, I've only had one glass. I'm here with the girls, and we're getting ready to go to Cocktails & Chaos."

"Oh." His voice changes slightly. "So, you're going through with that plan then?"

"I don't know. I haven't gotten there yet. We'll see."

"I just don't think it's a good idea, Mia, especially if—"

"My gosh, Luke. Let me have some fun. I mean, you and Beatrice had fun recently, didn't you?"

There's silence on the phone.

My friends look at me with questioning eyes, and I whisper, "I'll tell you after I get off the phone."

"What did you just say, Mia?"

"Nothing. Hold on. Let me FaceTime you."

I press FaceTime on the screen, and wait for him to pick up. He answers after a couple of seconds, and I can see that he's still in the office.

"Hey." He glances at me, his eyes narrowing as he takes in my outfit. "Are you wearing a belly top?"

"It's called a crop top."

"But it's showing your belly."

"Yes, Dad. It's showing my belly. I live in a beach town, where most of us show our bellies."

I move the phone around so he can see how the other girls are dressed.

"Hey, everyone. Say hey to Luke."

"Hi, Luke," they all chorus.

"Hey, girls," he says. "Have fun tonight."

"We will," Juniper says. "Can't wait to see you."

"Yeah, you too, Juniper. So, I kind of have something to tell you."

He sounds nervous, and all of a sudden, my heart drops.

"Oh shit. What is it, Luke?"

"Hey, I haven't even told you yet. No need to sound like that."

"It's fine," I say as a million different thoughts pass through my mind. Has he found a real date? Is he about to tell me that he doesn't want to go with me? Is he about to tell me that he's changed his mind?

All of a sudden, I feel low. I feel bleak. I've been having so much fun, talking about and getting ready for this fake summer relationship that I didn't realize that it was taking the place of a real relationship.

All of a sudden, I wonder what it would be like to really be in a relationship with someone who chose me—someone who wanted to go to this wedding with me as my partner, not just as my best friend.

I'm desperately single, and I hate it. I don't even want to think about what it's going to be like, being at the wedding by myself with Luke actually there with someone.

"Hey, what's going through your mind, Mia? You look miserable."

"It's fine. What is it? Are you going with Beatrice or something?"

"What are you talking about?"

"Why are you calling? You're not changing your mind, are you?"

"Why would I change my mind?" he asks, looking genuinely confused. "You mean because it's not going to be a *Fifty Shades of Grey* contract?"

"Did I just hear him say *Fifty Shades of Grey*?" Juniper squeals and comes running over to me. "Mia, what have you held out on us?"

"Nothing," I say, laughing. "He said it's *not* a *Fifty Shades of Grey* contract."

"Oh," Juniper says, laughing slightly. "I thought he said you guys had a *Fifty Shades of Grey* contract, and I was like, *Whoa, how do you go from kissing on the lips with no tongue to anal and whips and chains?"*

"Whips and chains, eh?" Luke sounds amused. "You didn't tell me that was on the table, Mia."

"It's not, Luke. Now tell me why you were so nervous when you called me. You've got me worried."

"So, you know how we said I'd be there a week early?"

"Yeah."

"It's not going to happen right now." He looks nervous. "I'm so sorry. I really wanted it to happen, but my boss came into the office, and I'm in the middle of this big deal, and I just can't get away for that long."

"It's fine," I say, though disappointment courses through me.

I love Luke. I've always loved Luke. He's been my best friend forever, but sometimes, I feel like he takes my friendship for granted. Sometimes, I feel like I come last to everything else in his life. Sometimes, I just want to be a priority. But I don't want to be that girl. It's not like we're really dating. I don't want to be the girl who gives ultimatums to her best friend like some sort of loser. I want him to choose our friendship above his job because that's what he wants, not because I make him.

"You're not mad at me, are you? You're not going to kill me?"

"Of course not," I say. "Why would I kill my fake boyfriend?"

I pretend to laugh and shrug it off, and he grins into the phone.

"Thank you. I knew you would be understanding. We'll figure it out when I get there."

"Yeah. It'll be fine. I'm sure no one's going to ask lots of questions that we won't be able to answer. It will be cool."

"You're mad," he says, his eyes narrowing. "Mia, tell me the truth."

"I'm fine," I say. "I have to go now though because Summer is really excited to get to the bar, and so is Silvie because she's going to see Cal."

"Why did you say that?" Silvie says quickly with a defensive tone. "I never said I was excited to see Cal."

"I think you protest too much, girlfriend."

She blushes again, and I wonder just how fake this relationship with Cal really is.

"Anyway, I got to go. I'll speak to you later."

"Okay. Have a good evening. And, Mia?" he says softly.

"Yes, Luke?"

"Don't do anything I wouldn't do."

"Okay, I'll try not to," I say and hang up.

I throw the phone onto the couch and let out a low yelp.

My friends all look at me.

"Hey, what's wrong?" Juniper looks up from applying mascara. "Mia?"

"I'm just annoyed he's not going to be able to come the week early anymore and we have nothing fleshed out. Rafe is already suspicious. What's going to happen when even more people ask us questions that we can't answer?"

Juniper nods slightly. "You guys will figure it out. You always do. You're Luke and Mia. I swear you can read each other's minds."

"I guess," I say. "I mean, I guess we're just going to have to see what happens."

"Hey," she says, giving me a look. "It'll work out. I promise. It's going to be the best fake summer romance you've ever had. And who knows? Maybe you'll actually meet a really cool guy at the wedding, and then you'll have a real romance come out of it."

"I don't really know how that's going to work, but, yeah, maybe." I feel slightly deflated, but I don't want to let Luke and his change of plans affect me. "How about we all have shots of tequila before we go out dancing?"

"I am down," Wendy says. "Trust me, I need a shot for the week I've had."

"Great," I say. "I've got a bottle of some top-shelf tequila in my closet that I was saving for a special occasion, and I think tonight is that special occasion."

I head to my room to grab the tequila, and Juniper gets a bunch of shot glasses. I pour the tequila and fill each one up while Juniper cuts some lemons and grabs the salt.

"To tonight," I say, holding up my shot glass. "To the wedding. To summer. To hot sex. To friendships. May we all be blessed with fun times and fun guys."

"Cheers," Juniper says, and we all down our shots.

As the warm liquid ripples down my throat, I start to feel myself perk up a little bit, but for some reason, I'm still a little deflated. I shouldn't be. But all the years of Luke choosing his job and everything else above me come crashing into my head.

I've always been the faithful friend. I've always been there for him—

supporting him through high school, college, grad school, when he got his job at that hedge fund. Even when he stayed in New York City summer after summer and Christmas after Christmas. I even downplay how hurt I am that I haven't seen him in years. But now I can feel my anger threatening to bubble over. I know I can't let it bother me though. Not until we get through the summer.

But once the summer romance is done and the wedding season is over, I am going to tell him how I really feel. He is my best friend, but I am fed up with him not treating me like his.

I feel like an option and not someone he is choosing. I feel like the friend who is always there that he takes for granted and not the friend that he is going above and beyond for.

chapter seven

Luke

LUKE

My plane just landed. I will see you soon.

MIA

Okay.

LUKE

Cat got your tongue or in the middle of baking me a welcome-home cake?

MIA

You wish.

LUKE

Another short response from my talkative bestie. Still mad at me?

MIA

Getting ready to go to the engagement party with the girls. Crazy level: 99/100.

LUKE

Not due to our love match, I hope?

MIA

Nope. We're all just trying to look hot for all the men tonight.

LUKE

Um, did you forget you're taken, Mia Bishop?

MIA

Ha-ha. Doesn't mean I can't look for when we break up.

LUKE

Ouch, already planning on the end, eh?

MIA

No, but I am looking forward to finally meeting my Mr. Right. Not my Mr. Fake Right. :P

LUKE

BRUTAL!

MIA

Just being realistic. I hope we can pull it off for even the two weeks, seeing as we haven't been able to discuss in person ... yet ...

It is apparent to me that Mia is far more pissed than I initially thought when I spoke to her previously. Staring out the window at the familiar structure of the Coconut Beach Airport makes me smile. I am back home. Even if it is for Rex's wedding. I am still excited to see everyone, especially Mia. I'll have to buy a bunch of books from her mobile bookstore to make it up to her.

The sky is a clear cerulean blue, and I can smell the salt in the air as I deplane.

MIA

BTW, I got an anonymous note in the mail today. We need to discuss.

LUKE

Oh? What did it say?

MIA

Some sort of treasure hunt.

LUKE

Are we going to be Goonies?

MIA

Maybe. 😜

I smile as I make my way to baggage claim. I knew she couldn't stay mad at me forever.

The Goonies was one of our favorite movies as kids, and we used to take my dad's old metal detector to the beach and search for hidden treasure. We never found anything valuable, but it was a lot of fun. Maybe we can have some movie nights while I am back in town—if I have time after working and participating in the wedding festivities.

My phone pings with alerts, and I know that I will have to work tonight. My mind immediately goes to the merger and all the work I have to do, but I dismiss the thoughts. I will work after the engagement party.

It seems to me that it is an odd thing to have an engagement party right before a two-week pre-wedding celebration, but I am no expert. I am not even close to getting married. There hasn't been one girlfriend I've ever thought about marrying, but then I've never had a strong relationship with anyone other than Mia. There were times in my teenage years when I wondered if she would ever be interested in me, but it has been clear to me that she's never even entertained the thought.

I grab my suitcase and head toward the rental car station, rolling up my sleeves as I walk. The heat is brutal, and I already regret packing so many slacks. I am definitely going to wear shorts to as many activities as I can. Knowing Rex, I bet most of the planned fun will revolve around the beach so that he can show off his muscles, so I am pretty sure that isn't going to be a problem.

"I'm home," I whisper to myself as I pull my rental onto the highway that takes me toward the beach and my grandparents' house. I wonder if I should buy a car and keep it at Mia's so that if I start coming to town more frequently I don't have to keep renting.

I'm going to stay with them for the first two nights and then check in to the hotel room that Rex has booked for all of his guests. He has spared no expense and booked a number of rooms at the Grand Palm of Coconut Beach—the nicest and only five-star hotel on the island.

I make my way down the coastline, my eyes taking in the beauty of the island. The ocean is a turquoise blue and calm today, though I can still see some paddlers out in the water with their surfboards. Coconut trees line the streets as I take my exit and pass Oceanside Market. I think about stopping at Salty Sirens for a coffee, but I know my grandparents are waiting for me.

I will barely have time for a quick shower and change before we head out to the party at Cocktails & Chaos. Though I'll head to Sunrise Beach Park first to meet Mia under the gazebo. Excitement buzzes in my veins as I think about seeing her in person for the first time in years.

My grandma is waiting outside as I pull up the driveway and that familiar tug of love pulls at my heart strings as I gaze at her waiting there for me with some happiness. I feel guilty for not coming home often enough. I feel guilty for not keeping in better contact. I know she has a full life, but I know she misses me something horrid. I park the car, turn off the ignition and jump out eagerly. I feel like I did when I was a little boy and going to visit her.

"Luke Haverbrook, you are a sight for sore eyes." She looks just as I remember her, with her shrewd blue eyes, white-blonde hair, and bright-colored dress. She hurries over to me with open arms, and I give her a big hug.

"How I've missed you, my boy."

"I've missed you as well, Grandma." I kiss her on the cheek and allow her to look me over with her curious eyes.

"You've lost weight." She frowns, her lightly lined face telling me that she is going to do her best to fix that. I see lots of freshly baked cookies and pies in my future, and I am not mad about it at all. "Do they not feed you in New York?"

"They feed me plenty."

"Is the boy here yet, Bitsy?" I hear my grandfather's voice before I see him, walking around the side of the house. His white shirt is muddy, and I know he's been planting something in the ground in his good clothes. "Oh, Luke." His impassive face splits into a wide grin, and I meet him halfway for a big hug. "Why, look at you, Lucas."

"Luke, Granddad." I laugh and correct him. "It's always been just Luke, Granddad—you know that. Unless Mia's trying to get on my nerves."

"And I've always been just Joseph, but people call me Joe."

"What are you saying, Joe?" Grandma walks over and stares at his dirty clothes. "Oh, Joe, you can't wear that. You need to change."

"Again? Hmmph." He looks at me, a twinkle in his eyes, and wraps an arm around my shoulders. "Shall we go inside and get ready?"

"I want to hear all about you and Mia Bishop," Grandma interrupts. "Lucille and I were shocked to hear you were in a relationship. Why didn't you tell us?"

And it starts. I should have known the questions would be rapid-fire. I feel utterly unprepared, even though I came up with so many different responses. Now that I am here, I have no idea what to say. All of a sudden, I understand what Mia went through and why she was so peeved with me. This is not going to be easy.

"We wanted to see how the relationship panned out before we announced anything, but when Rex invited us to the wedding—which was very sudden, I will add …" I look to my grandparents to see if they are going to offer any information as to this sudden wedding. "What is Andi like, by the way? I don't really know anything about her."

"Neither do we." My grandfather looks clueless. "I can honestly say I never even heard her name until three weeks ago."

"Joe, shh!" My grandma pats him on the shoulder. "It's not our business. We're just happy that Rex has met the love of his life."

"I suppose so. Wasn't he interested in that Summer girl as well? I remember him talking about her." He looks at Grandma, and she nods, eyes wide, a small smile on her face as she looks at him.

"Yes, I was talking about it with the busy Bees the other day." She lowers her voice and presses her finger to her lips. "But neither of you are to say anything about that. I don't know if Andi knows that Rex was also trying to date Summer, Silvie, and Wendy earlier this summer. Well, at least, that's what the other Bees and I think."

"How do you know this information?" I cock my head to study her as we walk onto the wraparound porch of my grandparents' grand white beach house.

Memories of sitting on the wide wooden porch swing, rocking back and forth, while eating grapes with Mia flood my mind as we walk through the open doors into the wide foyer. I can see the ocean through the floor-to-ceiling windows that make up the entire back of the home. The air is chilly as I make my way through the open-plan house and toward the back, where the oversize gray sectional couch sits, right next to the French doors that lead to the back porch.

"Grandma?" I look back at her and wait for an answer.

"We Bees know everything." She offers me a secret smile. "Would you like some iced tea before we get ready? The festivities start in an hour, but I'm sure you can't wait to see Mia."

"You've got that right." I laugh, though she doesn't know why we need to see each other right away. "And I'd love some tea, please."

I push open the French doors and step onto the white woven rug that sits on the wooden floor. The fine white sand beckons to me, and I slip my shoes and socks off and head down toward the water. I pass the tall, towering hibiscus plant that Mia loved as a kid and smile, thinking about the time we attempted to crossbreed different hibiscus plants to make our own variation.

My feet sink into the cool sand as I look down the long stretch of beach. The houses on this side of town have fairly private beaches, as the tourists prefer to spend their days on Sunrise Beach, as that is right next to the food trucks and the pier. It is also were they can charter a boat from Captain Smitty at Ocean's Calling and go swimming with dolphins—an activity that Mia and I both loved, though we'd go in my parents' boat. Those were the days.

I am looking forward to the next two weeks. I am more pleased than I realized at being back. Coconut Beach is home, even if I now live in New York.

"Tea's on the kitchen table, Luke," my grandma calls from the porch, the wind blowing her skirt back and forth. "You should get ready, Luke. We will need to leave soon."

"All right, Gran," I call back, though I allow myself to take in the clean ocean air for a few more moments before I go back inside. I feel at peace, standing here. I feel happy and even a teensy bit excited.

I am looking forward to this holiday and charade. I only hope that Mia and I will be able to pull it off. I am not sure why I am so excited about pretending to be madly in love with her, but I'm not going to question it.

The sounds of a string orchestra fill my ears as I make my way toward the park. The beach party is already packed, and I am ready for one of Cal's fine cocktails and a couple of beers, but I need to find Mia first. I walk past Iggy's Grill, surprised to see the crowds of people hanging out outside. My heart races as I make my way past the playground and toward the gazebo. Someone attached string lights to the canopy, and they sparkle in the night sky.

I pull out my phone to let Mia know I will be there in a few minutes when I realize there's a group of six women standing there, laughing and chatting about something. I stop next to one of the palm trees and just stand there, watching them. The women don't notice me, so I allow myself the time to observe them.

I gaze at each of their faces quickly. I recognize Juniper immediately, her long, dark hair hanging in waves down her back as she talks to another brunette next to her, who I'm pretty sure is Wendy. My eyes keep moving, and I see Josie standing next to Wendy. She's laughing at something while texting. Next to her is a blonde, who looks vaguely familiar. I'm pretty sure that's Summer, though we didn't really hang out much in high school. She's chatting with another blonde, who, at first, I think is Mia, but I soon realize it's not. This is a lady I don't recognize. I rack my brain to try and remember the names of the new women Mia told me about, but I can't place it. My eyes move to the next woman, but I know she's not Mia.

I frown as I decide to call her. Did she stand me up? Her phone rings three times, and then she answers breathlessly.

"Hey, Cool Hand Luke." She giggles into the phone, and I immediately know she's already had a few drinks. She always sounds happy when she's drunk.

"Hey, Mia Farrow. Where are you?" I scan the women under the gazebo again and then realize there's another woman at the back that I didn't notice before.

"I'm here. Where are you?" I hear laughing in the background and realize that the seventh woman, the woman who has her back to me, must be Mia.

"I'm here." I'm about to step forward when my breath catches.

I watch as the woman moves toward the front of the gazebo. She's wearing a simple, short silver dress and heels. Her blonde hair hangs past her shoulders, silky and shiny. Her brown eyes survey the park as she looks for me, a sweet, sexy smile on her face. My eyes wander down her body to her long, slender legs and the anklet that clings to her right ankle. My eyes move back up her slinky, shiny dress to the V neckline that shows off a generous amount of cleavage. I feel like I'm seeing her for the first time. That is definitely Mia, but this is a grown-up version. Somehow, I didn't realize that my best friend had grown from a tomboy to a sex kitten. I shift back, watching as she continues to look for me in the crowd.

"Where exactly? I'm looking for you." She looks back, and I watch as her hair bounces across her bare golden shoulder. "Hey, Juniper. Do you see Luke? He says he's here, but I can't see him."

"I see you," I say as I step away from the tree. "I'll be right there."

I grip the phone in my hand tightly. I should not be noticing her curves or the way her breasts have blossomed from A cups to what looked like Cs. And those legs … I never knew that Mia had legs for days. Legs like that could drive a man wild. And I am very much a man.

"Look to your right."

I take another step toward her and watch as she swings around, her eyes searching. And when she sees me, it's like time stands still. Our eyes meet, and her lips turn up in a wide smile, transforming her entire face into one of beauty and wonder.

"Lukey," she calls out, hanging up.

I watch as she runs toward me, happiness in her every stride, and for the first time since landing back on the island, I wonder if I've made a mistake. Mia Bishop is my best friend, but she's also the hottest woman I've ever seen in my life. As I wait for her to reach me, I wonder what she would do if I let the wicked side of my brain take over and I pressed her up against the tree.

I'm here for my brother's wedding. I'm here to play a fake boyfriend, but there's a part of me that wants Mia in all the dirtiest of ways. Though there's no way I'm going to tell her that. Mia has grown up into a stunningly sexy woman, and I am a man who wants to teach her all the ways of the world.

"Lukey, you're here," she shouts in pleasure, and I step forward to take her into my arms.

chapter eight

Mia

Oh, my giddy heart.

My heart races as I run toward Luke, my best friend, my *boyfriend*. Ugh, even the thought of our summer charade has me feeling tense. Not just because I'm nervous we're not going to pull it off, but I'm also concerned that it's going to end up being far more complicated than I initially thought.

Because why is he standing there, looking like a tall, delicious snack that I very much want to devour?

His white cotton shorts and loose blue shirt cling to his body, showing off a muscular physique that I didn't know he had.

Shit! When did he get so handsome and so mature-looking? When did he get tan and grow muscles? And silky, slightly too-long hair? And when did his boring blue eyes become mesmerizing and seductive?

Apparently, my best friend is now a stud, and he hid it from me.

Shit, I'm in trouble.

"Lukey."

I stop in front of him and jump into his arms because I am so happy to see him. I'm still mad at him for not coming early, but I can't stop my excitement at seeing him. He picks me up and spins me around, his azure-blue eyes warm as he welcomes me.

"You're finally here."

My hair flies in the wind as he spins me around, and I know that my silky tresses will now be wild and frizzy, but I don't care. He finally puts me down, and I wrap my arms around him in a big hug. He hugs me back tightly, and I rest my head on his decidedly much-more-muscular-than-I-remember shoulder. I breathe in his familiar scent and smile. He still wears Acqua Di Gio cologne, only this time, for some reason, it not only smells fresh and ocean-like, but also slightly hypnotizing.

I must have had too many shots with the girls before we came out because I am positively buzzing, standing here.

"I am finally here." He nods, a tinge of amusement in his tone. "I like your sparkles. Are you going to a disco?" he teases me.

I look him up and down before spinning around. "If I'm going to a disco, then you're going to a retirement home, dressed like one of the busy Bee's husbands."

I giggle as he looks down at his attire and frowns. To be fair, his outfit is similar to something both of our grandfathers would wear, only he's pulling it off much better. Most likely due to his biceps and quads, but I'm not going to tell him that. I don't want him getting a big head.

"Ouch, don't let my grandma hear that." He grins. "Or she'll sign you up to be a part of the club in a heartbeat."

"No thanks." I giggle and grab his hand. "Come and say hi to the girls real quick, and then we need to chat because I've been fielding a billion-gazillion questions, and I have no idea how we're going to pull this off."

"Lucky for you, I've prepared a billion-gazillon answers."

He winks at me, and I can't help but notice how juicy his lips look. I wonder if he's a good kisser and immediately blush at the thought. I do not want to know if Luke is a good kisser. God forbid we actually have to kiss. I can't even imagine his lips on mine in that way.

Liar, a voice in me screams, mocking the thoughts I'm trying to convince myself of.

"Seriously though, Mia, don't worry; we've got this. Rex is going to regret the day he sent us those rude messages."

"I know."

I drag him to the gazebo, and I notice that all of my friends are staring at us with expectant expressions on their faces. All of them know that this is a ruse, and I also know I can trust them to keep it to themselves.

"Luke is here, guys. My oldest best friend in all of the world." I beam as I push him forward. "Luke, I'm sure you remember Juniper, Josie, Wendy, Fallon, Silvie, and Summer."

"Oh, yes." He nods dutifully, and I can tell from his expression that he's lying, but I won't ask him who he doesn't remember. He steps toward Silvie and offers her his hand. "I'm not sure we've ever met before." He's so polite and formal and I've never been so grateful to have someone back in town in my life.

"No, we haven't. I'm Silvie." She smiles as she shakes his hand. "Nice to meet you."

"Silvie's dating Cal," I explain to Luke.

"Fake dating," she says quickly. "Well, we're going to get fake married." She blushes and shakes her head as she looks around. "It sounds so strange to say that out loud, but it's for a good cause," she says quickly, lest we think it was for a bad one.

"Cal Bennett?" Luke looks at me in surprise. "As in Cal from Cocktails & Chaos?"

"Yep." I nod, laughing loudly at the shock in his eyes. "Guess he's not just mixing up sweet concoctions of alcohol to please our throats."

"I guess not." He bites down on his lower lip and then reaches over to give Juniper a hug. "How are you, Juni? I heard the business is doing well."

"We're trying our best. You'll have to come down to the book mobile and buy some books. I bet Mia can find you a good one."

"I did help Carter choose a good book." I catch Wendy's eye, and we both burst out laughing. "I bet I can help you as well, Luke."

"I thought you sold mainly romance books?"

"We do. Sweet and steamy. And some are downright erotic."

"I say you get an erotic one, Luke." Josie nods enthusiastically. "Teach yourself some new skills."

"Who says the skills I have aren't erotic enough?"

"Me." I hit him lightly in the arm, and his eyes catch mine. "As your fake girlfriend, I'm going to need you to step up your game in the bedroom. And you can do that by buying as many erotic romances as you can fit into your suitcase."

"I'm to take them home with me?" His lips twitch, and I watch as he runs his fingers through his dark hair and pushes it back. "I should be offended that you all think I need help in the sack. I can assure you that I don't."

"I don't think Carter needed it either," Wendy says and then immediately blushes a deep red. "Not that I know, of course."

"Of course not." Josie teases. "And when I say *of course not*, I mean, yes, you do."

"Josie!" Wendy glares at her, and we all burst out laughing.

I move back over to Luke and reach up to grab his face. He looks down at me in surprise at my touch, and there's an unfamiliar warmth in his gaze that makes me shiver.

"Are you thirsty?" I ask him, trying to ignore the butterflies in my stomach. "Want to grab a drink and have a quick talk before we head down to the beach to meet up with Rex and his blushing bride?" I don't bother to mention our parents because I know he is aware that all four of them are ready to bombard us with questions.

"I am thirsty. And I would love to chat before we feed ourselves to the wolves."

We share a smile, and I turn to Juniper.

"You okay if Luke and I go and grab a drink and chat before we head over to the engagement party?"

"Of course." Her brown eyes are warm and comforting as she nods. "I think we'll walk over in about ten minutes. If I see anyone, I'll tell them you guys are on the way."

"Thanks! And if you see Rafe, tell him to just ignore me," I joke. "Or hold him hostage, please. I have a feeling he's going to be acting like frigging Hercules Poirot, trying to solve a case."

"You got it." Juniper laughs. "If I see Rafe, I will try and keep him occupied. Operation Keep Rafe Away is officially in effect."

"Thanks, Juni. I'll see you girls later." I offer the others a quick wave, and Luke and I head toward the other side of the park.

He walks in his normal fast fashion, and I reach out to grab his arm.

"Hey, slow down, Usain Bolt. I'm in heels, remember? I can't walk that fast."

"Sorry, Mia." He stops dead and looks down at my feet. "I almost forgot you're a klutz in heels."

"I am not a klutz. I just can't walk fast." I see that he's about to burst into laughter, and I swat him on the shoulder. "Just because I couldn't walk in heels in high school doesn't mean I can't walk now." I glare at him. "Do not laugh. It's not funny."

"I'm not laughing." His tone is light, but I can see his nostrils flaring. "And I'm totally not thinking of the night we went out with Juniper, Josie, and my two friends from Chess club Sam, and Mark to Seashell Diner for burgers, and you pretended you were a supermodel walking on the runway and tripped and fell over a penny on the ground."

"My heel broke, Luke." I cross my arms, trying not to laugh at the memory. "It wasn't funny. I could have broken my ankle."

"It was your fault for wearing four-inch heels. Where were you going, Mi-Mi?"

"I was trying to practice for when I walked the catwalks in Milan and Paris." I giggle and shake my head. "I thought I had a future career as a model." I fold my arms and glare at him. "I didn't know that my lack of balance would stop that career in its tracks."

"I had to carry you to my car, which was five blocks away, because you didn't want to walk barefoot." He laughs. "Even though you walk barefoot almost every day of your life."

"Maybe I just wanted you to carry me. Ever think of that?" I wink at him, and he takes a step closer to me, his eyes bright as he gazes down at me.

"Then you should have just asked," he says softly, and my heart races.

The mood between us has shifted slightly. It's still lighthearted and fun, but there's a heaviness in the air that's making it hard for me to breathe. My eyes shift to the expanse of his chest showing through his shirt, and my mind wanders to thinking if he has a six-pack. It's not that I care if he has one; I'm just curious. For practical purposes, of course. I only want to know if he has abs so that I can answer any questions that may come up.

Who's going to ask you if he has abs, Mia? The devil inside of me rears its ugly head, and I ignore it.

"Shall we grab a drink at Cocktails & Chaos first and then head to the beach party?" I say quickly as I try to get us back on track.

Going down memory lane is the last thing we need to be doing right now.

"First round's on me."

"All rounds are on you, Luke. You're the rich one, not me."

"I see you're only dating me for my money." He grabs his heart. "Oh, do I feel used now."

"I can make you feel even more used if you want?"

"How is that?"

He bites down on his lower lip, and I notice his eyes flicker to the top of my dress. Which is particularly boobalicious. Maybe too boobalicious? Is Luke checking out my boobs? I don't know, and I don't know if I want to know.

"We can go shopping, and I can make a huge dent in your bank account." I give him my most wholesome smile. "Don't you want to spoil me, oh darling boyfriend?"

"Nah." He grins and grabs my hand. "I think you'd be a terror if I spoiled you too much. Come on, Mi-Mi. Let's get you that drink and talk about how we're going to fool everyone into thinking we're madly in love."

"Or just mad," I groan under my breath. "I'm sure people would need no convincing as to that fact."

"Are you ready to take the stage, Meryl?" Luke asks me as we head back to the beach for our first public performance.

"Of course, Brando." I spin around, loving the feel of my silk skirt against my skin as it brushes past. "Let's get this party started. Just remember the rules, Luke." Meryl Streep and Marlon Brando were two of our favorite actors and we'd always pretended to emulate them whenever we needed to fake something.

"How could I forget? Rule one, we will pretend we're soulmates and destined to be together."

"Yes, and rule two is that we won't cross any physical lines," I say pointedly, as a reminder to him and myself. "We will have to be slightly touchy-feely in front of others, but we won't do more than pecks on the lips and hugs."

"Like every normal couple," he adds with a chuckle, and I glare at him.

"And rule three, we break up immediately after the wedding," I add. "That way, no one expects either one of us to make life-changing decisions for the other."

"Makes perfect sense." He nods, and then his eyes widen. "Ten o'clock," he says suddenly.

"What?" I look down at my watch. "It's not ten. It's—"

"Rex at ten o'clock," he hisses.

I look to the side. Even though he just gave me a warning, I'm still surprised to see Rex headed toward us, an intoxicatingly handsome look on his face as he makes his way. His eyes rove over me in pleasure, and I'm satisfied to know that he likes what he sees, even if it does make me feel slightly uncomfortable.

"Mia, you look gorgeous. Long time no see." He stops in front of us, and he pulls me in for a long, lingering hug before stepping back. "And, Luke, dear brother, thanks for making it."

He grabs his brother and pulls him in for a hug as well. Luke doesn't seem to be too receptive though.

"I still can't fucking believe that the two of you are banging." Rex glances at us with narrowed eyes. "When Grandma told me that you were coming to the wedding together, I nearly fell to the floor. You sly dog." He hits Luke in the arm. "Never woulda thought you had it in you."

He cackles and then looks back at me.

"Who knew you would have a glow-up, eh, Mia?" He lets out a low whistle as he checks me out. I don't bother reminding him that we both live on the same island and that if he'd had any interest whatsoever he could have dropped by the bookmobile or Cocktails & Chaos to say hello. But Rex lived in his own world. A world that didn't frequent the same small-town establishments as my friends and I. "If I had known that you'd become this sexy little thing, I might have paid more attention to you when you came over all the time." He chugs his beer and throws his head back. "Mighta let you sneak into my room a couple of the nights you stayed over."

He grins at me, and I try not to make a retching sound. Rex is even more obnoxious than normal tonight.

"That's enough, Rex."

Luke wraps his arm around my waist and brings me into him. It's not an unwelcome feeling, but the way he touches me seems way too familiar. I am not used to us being in close proximity like this. I notice that the movement is soft, lingering, and possessive. It's nice, but weird. Way too comfortable. But I suppose that's the only way we're going to sell this.

Rex's eyes narrow, and he appears to be inspecting us for any indication that this might not be a real union. Luke shifts and is now even closer to me, and my stomach flips. I've never seen him like this before. And I've never felt this heat spreading at his touch before either. What on earth is happening?

"I must say that Luke is the man I've been dreaming of all my life. Who knew that he was under my nose all along?"

I snuggle next to him, and he holds me closer. Rex presses his lips together, and his eyes meet mine for far longer than feels comfortable. I wonder if he's going to call us out right here and now. Is he going to tell us our acting sucks and he knows we're only doing this because of his notes?

"Can't lie. If I had known you were going to grow them big ol' titties, I woulda let you hit it." He throws his head back and laughs loudly. "When you were chasing me around, you were just a string-bean, tomboy-looking thing. Never thought you'd grow up to be a banger, Bishop." He licks his lips. "Play your cards right, and I might still let you—"

"What the fuck?" Luke steps forward, and for a moment, I think he's going to hit his brother. In all that is good and holy, I've never seen him look so threatening in all my life. "Who do you think you're talking to, Rex?"

"Can't you take a joke, golden boy?" Rex pretends to hit Luke in the jaw. "You go to New York like some crybaby in the night and hide your gal. I'm just saying we all know that …" His voice trails off as Mr. and Mrs. Haverbrook approach us with glasses of champagne in their hands.

"Hey, Mom, Dad." Rex's voice changes, and his expression becomes friendly.

He really is a chameleon, and I wonder what I ever saw in him.

"I was just telling Luke and Mia how happy I was that they were able to make it and participate in all the fun." He grins and looks back at me. "And to think, Mia, if you'd played your cards right, this could have been our celebration." He chugs more of his beer, and his expression changes slightly. "But who knows what could happen, right?"

chapter nine

Luke

"Sorry about that Mia." I offer my apologies as soon as Rex and my parents walk away to entertain some of the other guests.

I am furious at how my brother spoke to her, and even more so, I was angry at the way he was looking at her. Like she was a juicy steak and he was a hungry dog. He was practically drooling over her. I had to resist the urge to thump him in the eye. He was close to walking up the aisle with one blue eye and one black one.

"That's okay."

She runs her fingers through her hair, and I watch as she grabs a hair tie and wraps her hair into a bun on top of her head. Her slender neck is elongated now, and the new hairdo draws more attention to the top of her dress. I will my eyes to stay on her face and not on her chest. I will not be one of those pervy guys, checking out her breasts.

"I will forgive him. I guess he was just drunk."

"I guess." I study her face to see if there are twinges of jealousy or regret there. "How are you feeling? I'm sure that tonight—"

"I'm feeling fine." Her voice is a little too high.

As I try to make eye contact, she looks away. I'm not sure what that's about, but I'm not going to push it. The evening has already taken me on a roller-coaster ride.

"I'm surprised your parents didn't ask us more questions though. Do you think they suspect anything, or are we in the clear?"

"I'm not sure."

I was also surprised at their lack of questioning about everything. They didn't ask about our relationship, they didn't ask about New York, they didn't even ask about my job. Though I had a feeling Dad was still peeved that I'd walked away from the family company to make it on my own, but there was no way that I was going to play second fiddle to Rex. In any aspect of my life.

She shifts closer to me and lowers her voice. "So, you're staying with your grandparents tonight?" She giggles girlishly and places her right hand on my chest, all the bangles clanking together as she runs her fingers down.

I look to the right and notice Talia Robber is standing there, arguing with Andi about something. Talia is the wedding planner of this extravagant wedding, and I remember her being one of the mean girls from high school, even though she was a few years ahead of me.

"Luke Haverbrook, is that you?" Andi sees me standing there and rushes over to me with wide-open arms. She's overly friendly, considering I think we've only spoken a few times in our lives, but I dismiss that as excitement that she's marrying my brother.

"Hi, Andi. So good to see you. And let me offer my congratulations. I saw Rex earlier, but I guess you're making the rounds separately."

I study her face to see if she's upset that Rex is going around without her. Also, I wonder if she knows he's flirting with all the guests. I wonder if she'd be as upset as I was about the way he'd spoken to Mia, but it's not like I can bring it up.

"Oh, you know Rex," she says, staring me deep in the eyes, like she's searching for life's meaning in my brain. It's slightly uncomfortable, and I wonder if she realizes how she's coming across. Her green eyes are vibrant and streaked with black from her mascara and eyeliner. I hope the streaks are from sweat and not tears, but I wouldn't put it past my brother. "He is the consummate bachelor, loves entertaining a crowd."

"But he's not a consummate bachelor any longer," Mia interrupts, her tone one of confusion. Tendrils of her hair are falling from her bun, and she brushes them back without thinking. I notice her hot-pink nail polish and try not to smile. She always did like bright vibrant colors. "He's marrying you. So, shouldn't he be acting the exact opposite right now?"

Mia looks to me for confirmation, and I nod dutifully.

"I suppose so." Andi looks annoyed at her comment. "But he's also Rex Haverbrook, the most eligible bachelor on the island, so he's likely still behaving that way because that's in his DNA. I'm sure he'll change when we get married." She presses her palms against the leather skirt she's wearing and turns to Talia. "Right?"

"Of course, though he wouldn't have been the most eligible bachelor if Luke still lived in town." Talia grabs my arm and squeezes my biceps. I jerk back in response to her touch, and she winks seductively at me. "So, how have you been, Luke? I've heard that you're making a name for yourself in the Big Apple."

"I have been working hard. It's really nice to be back home here in Coconut Beach with—"

"I'd love to take a bite of that apple one day," Talia says, running her hand down my arm as she moves closer to me, and I notice Mia staring at her, frowning slightly. "A very big apple," she whispers in my ear, and it takes everything in me to not laugh before pulling away from her.

She looks slightly taken aback as I distance myself, but I'm not interested in whatever she's trying to sell. I watch as Mia's eyes narrow, and she takes a step closer to me. She's not happy. I'm not sure why that elates me, but a throb of energy pulses through me as she takes a step closer and clears her throat.

"I dunno if you heard, but Luke and I are kind of dating." She says the words casually, a polite look on her face, but I know Mia well enough to know that she's pissed. I'm only glad that it's not with me this time.

Talia looks at her, and then at me, then over to Andi and sniffs loudly.

"You don't say?" The words drip off of Talia's tongue in disbelief. She stares at Mia's dress and recoils, her angular face tight as she processes her distaste. "Cute dress. Get it at the boutique in town?"

Her words let us all know that she thinks the dress is anything but cute. I personally think the dress is sexy as hell, but I'm not going to bring that up now.

"I did actually. Thank you." Mia beams at her in her best *I know you're a bitch, but I'm going to pretend you're being nice* way. I know that if Talia keeps going down this path, Mia will then get to her *I'm going to warn you once before I shut you up* stage. "Is yours from the boutique as well?"

"Ha! This?" Talia looks down at her black sequined dress. "This is couture, darling," Talia says, disdain drifting from her tongue.

"Designed by Oscar de la Renta. Have you ever heard of him? Do you even know what couture is? Can you spell *couture* even?"

Shots have been fired, and I'm about to say something when Mia shoots me an *I can handle this* look.

"I own a bookstore." Mia's head goes higher. "I think I can spell *couture*."

"Well, it's not really a store, is it? Can you call a converted van with a couple of bookshelves in it a store? What do you think, Luke? In Manhattan, if someone were to say they were going to a bookstore, would they be saying that they were going to see a converted, dilapidated van?" Talia purrs as she rubs her hand across the back of my shoulder. "So thick and strong." Her eyes stare into mine with open lust.

"My van is not dilapidated," Mia says, snapping. "And if you don't mind, please keep your paws off of my man."

She grabs my hand, and I jump slightly at the shock that runs through me at her touch. I'm surprised she's acting this way. The Talias of this world don't normally bother her.

"Your man?" Talia laughs, the sound reminiscent of a witch around a cauldron. "Really?"

"Yes."

"And how long has this been going on for? I thought the two of you were just friends." She looks over at Andi. "You never told me that your future brother-in-law was dating *her*."

"Well, I didn't know," Andi says, looking uncomfortable. "And Rex didn't know either." She shrugs as she looks at me, as if I'm going to give her an explanation here and now. "I guess they're just a family of secrets."

"Mia and I wanted to keep it under wraps until we were ready to go public. We've been best friends for such a long time that we didn't want to out ourselves until we were able to see if the relationship was going anywhere."

"And you just figured this out, huh? Or has Mia been hoeing around?" Talia looks over at Mia and smirks. "Because don't I remember seeing you at Cocktails & Chaos about two months ago, all over that surfer from Hawaii? And weren't you saying how you'd love to go to Maui, and he was saying he was from Kauai, and didn't you make some comment about how he could show you all the islands?"

"No," Mia says loudly and blushes. "It wasn't like that. I was just being friendly." She looks at me with wild eyes. "Luke, I was just being friendly."

"It's fine. I already knew about that night." I give Talia and Andi a huge grin, letting them know the story doesn't bother me. "Mia has no secrets from me."

The truth of the matter is, I did know about that night. Mia always tells me about her nights out, even the details I have no interest in hearing.

"So, what is this then? Some sort of open relationship?" Talia throws her head back and runs her fingers through her sharp white-blonde bob. "Because if you guys are open, I'll throw my hat in the ring." She licks her lips and purrs, "They don't call me Talia Robber for no reason."

Oh boy, I did not see this offer coming my way. I'm not interested, and I'm even more surprised to see Mia giving me a dirty look. I wipe the smile off of my face immediately.

"What's that supposed to mean?" Mia says.

I've never seen her look so pissed off in her life—at least not recently and never over me.

"It means if your relationship is open, I want in with Luke. I'm not a jealous type, and I'm in New York every other month." She winks at me. "I can save money on hotels."

I press my lips together because I don't want to be rude and I'm curious to see what Mia will say next.

"Like I just sad they don't call me Talia Robber for no reason. Emphasis on robber. When I want a man, he is mine. I say to women quite openly that they should just be prepared to lose their man if I want him. Don't think you've got a man that can't be taken from you," Talia says, coquettishly licking her lips again before sipping her glass of champagne. "Because just as easily as you get them, I can take them. I'm a robber of the heart."

She looks me dead in the eyes, and if she had magical powers, I know my clothes would be gone. I've met women like her before, and they think that heavy flirting and sexual innuendos will get them an in every time, but I'm just not that guy.

"Talia," Andi says, shaking her head and grabbing her friend's arm. "Don't mind her. She's just a little bit drunk. She would never steal your man, Mia."

"The Haverbrooks sprang for top-shelf liquor and Moët & Chandon champagne. Hell yeah, I'm going to get drunk. Not like the typical beach parties, where it's all, like, twenty-dollar vodka." Talia takes another sip and Andi grabs her hand roughly and whispers something to hear. Talia flinches and then lets out a low sigh. She seems to realize that she's overstepped. "I love planning weddings where expenses are no cost."

"Well, I'm glad you're enjoying it, but I see Wendy and Juniper over there, and it looks like they're calling out to us, so maybe we should see what they want."

"Yeah, we should see what they want." Mia nods enthusiastically, and we hurriedly walk away. "And then tonight, we need to have some hot, passionate sex," she says loudly and looks back at Talia.

"So, she's a bitch," Mia says as soon as we're out of earshot, and she turns to me. "What the fuck was that?"

"Don't let her get to you." I want to ask her why she got so upset, but I suppose it's because it ruins our acting job.

"I'm not letting her get to me. But what the hell was that? How dare she offer to hook up with you? As if I would share my man."

She trips slightly, and I reach out to grab her arm and steady her.

"Slow down. She's not worth getting a broken ankle."

"She'd love that. She'd be like, *Let me take care of you, Luke, now that Mia is down and out*. Well, keep your hands off, Talia. Like she could steal my man anyway."

"Are you jealous, darling?" My lips twitch as I tease her.

Her face and voice are super animated, and I can tell she's still pissed. I also can't help but notice how hot she looks with her flushed skin and heaving bosom, which fills out her dress a little too nicely.

"No, I'm not jealous." She rolls her eyes, like it's the most ridiculous comment she's heard all day. Which I would find quite hurtful, if I actually cared about her answer. "I would hope that even if we weren't fake dating, you wouldn't give her the time of day."

"I certainly wouldn't."

"Yeah, right. You think she's hot, don't you?"

"To be honest, she's cute, but she's not my type."

"Yeah, right." She rolls her eyes again and stomps toward Wendy and Juniper, obviously annoyed. "That fucking bitch Talia Robber was just coming on to Luke, saying she could steal him from me."

"No way." Juniper's jaw drops, and she looks over at Talia in shock. "Do I need to go and slap her?"

"Maybe. Just maybe," Mia says and then laughs as she sees my expression. "Don't worry, Luke; I'm not actually going to slap her."

"Take some deep breaths," Wendy says softly, always the voice of calm. She's slightly older than us, but I always remember her being the one to reason with Mia and Josie when we were in high school and they were upset. "One, two, three. One, two, three."

I watch Mia breathe in and out, and then she starts giggling.

"Thanks, Wendy. I feel better now. That was literally crazy. Absolutely crazy." She turns to me, and her brown eyes are sparkling as she shifts closer to me. "Also, why are Andi and your brother not walking around together? Why is she just going around, saying hello to people by herself? That's so weird."

"I know," Juniper says. "If I were getting married and this was my engagement party, my hands would not be off of my fiancé. I mean, if I ever have a fiancé."

"You'll have a fiancé," Mia says, touching her friend softly on the arm. "I mean, hopefully, we'll both have fiancés soon."

"Hopefully not before you and I officially break up." I give her a look, and she just smiles.

I know Mia wants to be in love. She's talked about it her entire life, but sometimes, I wonder if she's more in love with the idea of it than actually experiencing it.

"So, Wendy, is Carter here tonight?" I look around at the thinning crowds.

The DJ is still pumping music outside of Cocktails & Chaos, and people are dancing and drinking under the twinkling lights, but I don't recognize most of the people.

"I don't know. I definitely invited him." She smiles at me. "Thank you for saying that was okay."

"Of course. Any friend of yours is a friend of mine—and the family's. When Mia asked me if it was okay, I knew it wouldn't be an issue. So, is he a close friend of yours? I'd love to meet him."

"Well, I wouldn't say he's my friend." She blushes a bright red and shifts nervously in the sand. "He's just a very well-paying guest, and God knows we need them at the bed & breakfast.." She lets out a low groan. "We're one summer away from having to shut down."

"I'm more than happy to go over the numbers with you if you would like me to."

"Oh, I got it. But thank you. I may not be as successful as you, but I know a thing or two about business." She smiles graciously, and I nod, hoping she didn't think I was overstepping.

"I know, and you're doing a great job. Mia has told me all about the advice that you and Josie have given her over the years for the bookstore, and I know that's been really well appreciated."

"It really has," Mia says, reaching out to grab Wendy by the arm. "You are such a good businesswoman."

"Please tell Grandma Gale that." Wendy moans loudly. "She wants to spend every penny that we have, and when I tell her we need to be saving and paying off bills, she just makes comments like, 'Don't worry; the earth will provide.' And I'm like, 'No, Grandma, the earth is not going to provide if we can't pay our mortgage.' "

"I feel that," Juniper says excitedly. "The earth hasn't provided me millions, nor has it provided me with a man."

"I'm sure it will," Mia says, looking around and tapping her feet in time to the music.

I wonder if I should ask her to dance, if that's what our families expect, even though everyone knows I hate dancing.

"Oh shit, I think Rafe is coming." She quickly turns her face. "No one look around."

"Oh." Juniper stills. "Where is he?" Her tone sounds slightly excited as she turns her head, and I wonder what that's about.

Is it the heat, or is she blushing?

"Please, everyone, no one look in his direction. I really do not want to speak to—"

"Hey, Meow-Meow," Rafe says in his jovial tone as he joins us. "There you are."

"Oh, hi, bro." She turns to him with a fake smile. "I didn't see you there."

"We just made eye contact about twenty seconds ago, but you didn't see me?" He scoffs, his blue eyes laughing as he stares at his sister.

Rafe never has put up with her bullshit, much to her chagrin.

"Well, you know how it is. My contacts are kind of dry."

"Luke, so good to see you again." His voice doesn't sound like it's so good, but I know it's my turn to put on a good show.

"You too. How's the vet practice going? How are the animals?"

"Can't complain." He nods, and I watch as he looks over at Juniper. I notice his eyes widening for a few seconds as he takes in her sexy dress and her long, silky hair. “Hi, Juniper.” This time, his voice is deep, throaty, gruff.

There is definitely something there. I’ll have to ask Mia what was going on there.

“Hey,” she says, her voice oddly tight. “I didn’t know you were coming tonight.”

“I couldn’t miss the hottest party in town. Especially when our families go back so many years. And who knows?” he says, turning back to me. “Maybe there’s going to be a future engagement between you and my little sister.”

His eyes narrow as he stares at me, and I just smile congenially back at him. Rafe looks almost menacing, standing there in his white shirt and dark jeans.

“Rafe, really?” Mia glares at him. “This is not the time or the place to—”

“To what? To question the man who has been secretly dating my sister for a year and hasn’t thought to tell anyone in the family or ask if it’s okay?”

“He does not have to ask if it’s okay, Rafe. How antiquated are you?”

“I’m your big brother. I’ve got to make sure that you’re not dating a loser. That’s my sole role.” He looks at me. “Have you even thought this through properly? I would hate for your friendship to be ruined because you all of a sudden figured out the other was good-looking.”

“I think they are old enough to make their own decisions,” Juniper says, rising to Mia’s defense, her brown eyes flashing at him.

“You may think that, but I know my sister. I know she doesn’t always think things through, and she’s been so desperate for—”

“Rafe!” She punches him in the shoulder.

“Sorry, but it has to be said. Sometimes, just because we’re attracted to someone doesn’t mean that a relationship is the right way to go.” He crosses his arms and then looks back at Juniper again before his eyes widen at seeing a grinning Wendy, who’s just been observing the entire conversation. “Oh, hey there, Wendy. Please forgive me for being rude. I didn’t even see you there.”

“No worries. How are you?”

“Good. I actually saw your guest at the front, drinking some beers with Dayton.”

“Oh, yeah?”

She looks surprised and pleased at the same time, and I notice she's now patting her lips. Interesting.

"What's his name? Carter?"

"Yes, I didn't know he'd come."

"Yeah, he looked like he felt slightly uncomfortable, but I guess he knows a couple of people here." Rafe shrugs and glares at Mia as she stands closer to me.

"Yeah, I should go and look for him, I guess. Thanks for letting me know." Wendy grabs her bag and looks around.

"No worries. I'm sure he'll be grateful for the company because Dayton was looking for Summer and asking where she was."

He looks at Mia. "What's the deal with them?" He lowers his voice as he nods over at Summer.

"What do you mean?"

"Are they together or what? Every time I see him, he's looking for Summer or asking about Summer or arguing with Summer, and I swear he has a thing for her."

"I mean, we've always thought he had a thing for her since high school, right?" Juniper says softly.

"Yeah." Mia nods. "But Summer has never really seemed that interested, though I have kind of noticed that she's been a little bit more flirtatious with him recently."

"I've kinda seen him checking her out at yoga as well," Wendy adds. "I'll see you guys later. Let me see if I can find Carter and, uh, figure out if he needs help finding anything."

She walks off with a wave, and Rafe just starts laughing.

"Next thing you know, everyone in Coconut Beach is going to be falling in love," he says, shaking his head and raising an eyebrow at me.

I'm not really sure what to say. I just stare at him because I realize that Mia was correct. Rafe is definitely suspicious of our relationship. I don't know if he just disapproves of it because it has come from nowhere or if he has real doubts, but the looks he is giving me tell me that she and I are going to have to stay up late tonight and come up with several stories to satisfy both of our families.

"I think I should figure out where my grandparents are so I can get a key from them because I forgot to get it from them before I left." I look down at Mia as I glance around.

"Everyone's going to the hotel after this. They're handing out the room keys tonight," Rafe grunts. "They want everyone at some special breakfast tomorrow."

"I didn't know. I guess I'll be staying at the Grand Palm tonight then."

"I didn't know either. I haven't even packed my bag." Mia frowns.

"Well, I guess you can pack your bag tomorrow, sis. I just heard Mr. and Mrs. Haverbrook telling some of the other guests. They asked me if I was sure I didn't want a hotel room as well, but I still have quite a lot to do at the veterinarian's office. And even though Cherri has been helpful, I still have a lot of dogs and cats coming in tomorrow. Even a couple of bunny rabbits."

"Aww, I love bunny rabbits," Juniper says.

Mia gives her an odd look. "Since when have you loved bunny rabbits? Didn't you say they have, like, a million babies?"

"I mean, I think they're cute." Juniper gives her a look, and Mia just shrugs.

"I wonder if they're going to give us rooms next to each other or if that's too close," Mia says, laughing. "I wonder if they're going to put us on completely different floors."

"Yeah, I wonder."

"There you are, Mia and Luke."

I look up, and I see Lucille Bishop, Mia's grandmother, standing there.

"Luke, so good to see you."

She walks right over to me and gives me a big, warm hug. I hug her back and breathe in her familiar scent of jasmine.

"Good to see you as well, Lucille."

"I was so happy when Mia told me that you two were together."

"Well, I'm glad to hear that you don't disapprove."

"Your grandmother and I have actually been talking about it, and we convinced your parents to get you one room."

"What?" Mia says loudly and then lowers her voice. "Wait, what? Grandma, what are you saying?"

"Well, these are new times. You guys have been dating for a year, and you haven't seen each other for who knows how long. I know you have something special, and you've probably been missing each other terribly. So, we've got you in the same room. I mean, you are boyfriend and girlfriend. Who are we to stop young lovers in love?"

"Really, Grandma?" Rafe looks shocked. "I cannot believe you're going to let them—"

"Let us what?" Mia turns to him with her hands on her hips.

"I'm just saying"—Rafe looks at me—"do you think this is a good idea, Luke? Is this really the way you want to present your relationship to my parents and your parents and the rest of the world?"

"It's already done, Rafe." Lucille looks at him with a stern glance. "And part of the reason was because there were no longer any hotel rooms left, and I suggested it would be okay if Mia and Luke stayed together. That's not going to be a problem, is it?"

"Of course not," I say, shaking my head. "Right, Mia?"

"Of course not," she says, looking at me with panic in her eyes. "I mean, we've spent plenty of nights together."

"Exactly. We have," I say. "We've watched movies ..." And I suddenly realize that I can't talk about all the platonic nights we've spent together. "And other stuff."

"I don't want to hear this," Rafe says, cutting me off. "In fact—"

"Can I speak to you for a second, Luke?" Mia says, grabbing my hand. "We'll be right back."

We head over to two tall palm trees, and she leans back and slips her heels off and holds them in her hands.

"Shit, what are we going to do?"

"What do you mean, what are we going to do?"

"We're in the same room, Luke."

"Yeah, and?"

"Do you think there will be two beds?"

"Unlikely, but maybe."

"Luke, we can't sleep in the same room."

"Why not? We've done it plenty of times."

"The last time we slept in the same bed, we were, like, sixteen. And we're not sixteen anymore."

"It'll be fine, trust me." I lean toward her and kiss her on the cheek.

"What are you doing?"

"I think I saw someone walking by. Plus, we're going to have to act a lot more lovey-dovey if we're going to sell it to everyone."

"I mean, I guess," she says, wrinkling her nose. "You're right; we have a lot to figure out. We need to stay up late tonight because we need to figure out some more rules."

"What do you mean, more rules? We've already got three."

"And that's not nearly enough. We need to figure out a much better backstory." She sighs. "I don't know, Luke. This might not have been the best idea in the world."

"Are you regretting it?" I ask her quietly, hoping she won't say yes because for the first time in a long time, I'm feeling really excited, and I'm enjoying the farce, and I'm not one hundred percent sure why. Other than the fact that it means we have to spend a lot of time together.

I'm also not mad about the fact that we're going to be sharing the same room. In fact, I'm actually quite pleased, and I don't know what that says about me—but I also know I'm not going to tell Mia what I'm thinking because I just don't know if she feels the same way.

"Nah." She grins and reaches over to give me a tight hug. "We're going to kill this," she whispers.

I only hope she's right.

chapter ten

Mia

"That's one hell of a bed." I try not to gawk as I stare at the single bed. If that bed could talk, I bet it would spill a lot of salacious secrets. I blush at the thought. Sexy, sultry, and salacious. This is a room where babies are made.

Get your mind out of the gutter.

You are not here to make any babies.

I sneak a peek at Luke

Luke and I stand in the middle of our hotel suite and stare at the king-size bed that takes up half the room. It certainly looks comfy, with its oversize down pillows and plush comforter. The room itself screams luxurious and smells like vanilla pods. Although it's a pleasant scent to my nose, it also makes me want to eat something delicious, like a cupcake.

"It sure is." Why does his voice sound like that? Has it always been that deep? That smooth. Like some old time crooner sitting in a smokey bar and playing a piano. And why does his shirt fit him so tight, like it's ready to be ripped off.

I want to have a seat, bounce up and down, and see if it's as relaxing as it looks, but I daren't do that while I am still wearing this dress. I know it will ride up my thighs and expose my panties as soon as I lie back. And who knows what the top would do? I was already close to having a nip-slip scandal, and that is the last thing that I need right now. I also barely made it through the night without getting into an argument with bitchy Talia.

"So, how are we doing this?" I turn to Luke, who I suddenly realize has been watching me keenly for the last few minutes.

His blue eyes look intense, with a slight twinge of humor in his irises. There's a hint of a five-o'clock shadow on his stubborn jawline, and he's undone the top button of his shirt.

"Ah jeez, I just realized you'd traveled all day. You must be tired."

I suddenly realize that he must be exhausted; it's been a long day, and he's likely out of it. I'm likely out of it as well because he is very much looking like a man I wouldn't mind taking a nibble out of, but I'm almost positive it's because of sleep deprivation and that I am also tired. And now I am hungry, for actual food. Darn that delicious vanilla scent filling the room.

"I'll live." His lips twitch as he continues to gaze at me.

It's weird how much his stare is affecting me. It's unsettling, and it feels like his gaze is penetrating every fiber of my being.

I wonder if he's a mind reader and trying to infiltrate my brain. Wouldn't that be a cool trick? *Hey, Mia. Just came back from NYC, and now I can read your brain.*

I will myself not to think about how hot he looks in his crisp light blue shirt and how silky his dark hair looks, falling in front of his eyes.

Oh shit, my mind was wandering again.

"What am I? An amoeba under a microscope? You're looking at me like you're trying to find my nucleus." I push past him and take a seat on the edge of the bed. Partially because my feet are killing me. I was not made to wear high heels for hours. And partially because being too close to him was making me think thoughts I absolutely did not want to think about Luke.

"Find your nucleus?" He laughs.

I wonder if he's going to remind me of how poorly I did in our Biology and Chemistry classes in high school. He still randomly teases me about crying for Kermie, the frog I nicknamed right before we had to dissect it. I knew then and there med school was never going to be seeing me.

"It's not funny." I can't resist leaning back on the bed. It is even more comfortable than it looked, and my body is rejoicing in pleasure at the soft cushioning. "I'm hungry." I look around the room. "Do they have any snacks in here? I need something to eat. With all the drama tonight, I didn't remember to grab any actual food. Just drinks." I yawn suddenly. "And before you say anything, yes, I should just go to bed first, but I don't want to wake up hungry."

"Noted." Luke takes a few steps forward until he's looking down at me, lying on the bed.

His expression is amused, and I'm taken back to our teenage years—when we'd go camping in his vast backyard, watch movies on his iPad, and I'd moan and groan for him to get me snacks to munch on while we watched B-horror movies that he loved and I hated. It was the popcorn and chocolate that made the movies palatable to me; I'd spend half the time eating, half the time burying my head in his shoulder, trying not to see the gruesome bloody scenes of multiple people being beheaded and eaten. I hated those movies with a passion, and yet those movie nights were one of the best parts of our shared relationship.

"Popcorn, chocolate, ice cream, or Pop-Tarts?"

"I'm not fifteen anymore. I need more sustenance right now."

"Like?" He takes a seat next to me, and I roll over to look at him, feeling my skirt rolling up as I shift on the bed. He leans down and casually brushes my hair back out of my face, his eyes crinkling as he smiles at me. "I'll go out and grab you something now."

"No, you don't have to do that." My heart races a million miles a minute. Why is he looking at me like that? "You should get ready for bed. Seeing as you were traveling all day, I will let you have the bed tonight, and I'll take the couch, but from tomorrow on, I'm taking the bed, and you're taking the couch."

"Really, Mi-Mi? Neither one of us needs to take the couch. We've shared a bed many times."

"Yes, but never as a fake dating couple."

"So?" He rolls his eyes at me. "What does that have to do with anything? We have the rules, right? Plus, it's us. It's not like we're suddenly going to be all over each other ..." He pauses, and his eyes search mine, a sneaky expression on his face. His blue eyes appear to be laughing at me. "Right?"

"Well, duh." I sit up suddenly and groan as my stomach gurgles. I brush my hair back and attempt to straighten my dress out. "There is no way that anything is going to happen." I jump off of the bed and head to the side of the room. "Ooh, look, they have a menu. We can order room service." I grab it up, my eyes surveying the list of options. "I think I'm going to get a cheeseburger and fries. You want anything?"

"I'll have the same." He looks around the room. "You know what I just remembered?"

"What?"

"We don't have any change of clothes." He frowns. "My luggage is at my grandparents' house, and all your stuff is still at home, right?"

"Yeah, I didn't bring anything. I wasn't even thinking about it. I thought we weren't getting our rooms until tomorrow afternoon." My stomach growls again, and I look down at the menu again. "Maybe I'll add some onion rings as well."

"Onion rings?" Luke doesn't look impressed. "I guess that means we're not having a practice make-out session tonight then, sexy Mia?"

"Very funny, Luke." My stomach flips at his words. I try not to look at his lips. "I don't think we need to have any practice sessions. I think we're both adults who know how to kiss. Now let me order this food before I fall to the ground from hunger."

"I think you'll be okay for an hour." He shifts closer to me and then stops. "But if not, I can head down to the lobby and grab you a bite from the deli. I think it is twenty-four hours."

"You don't have to do that, but thanks." I shake my head. "Though do you think they have clothes?"

"You want to go clothes shopping now?" He raises an eyebrow at me. "Really?"

"No, but I want to sleep in something other than this dress." I look down at my frilly smock. "It's cute, but I can't imagine it will be comfortable to sleep in. Nor do I think your outfit is going to be comfortable to sleep in."

"Oh, I'm not sleeping in this." He laughs, and I watch as he undoes all the buttons on his shirt and takes it off, so he's now standing there shirtless.

This isn't the first time I've seen Luke shirtless. And not even the first time I've seen him shirtless in a bedroom, but it has never felt like this before.

"What are you sleeping in then?" I pick up the phone and push the button for room service so that I don't have to look at him. It's not that I don't want to look at him, but I don't want to stare and ogle him.

Luke went and got himself a lean, muscular physique in the last couple of years. He is built, and he has abs, and my brain is appreciating them far too much. I feel like a sad sack, staring at my best friend like that. I suppose it is the consequence of not having a boyfriend for ages.

"I was going to sleep naked."

"What?" My tone is loud.

He bursts out laughing. His eyes twinkle as he takes a seat at the edge of the bed.

"Ain't no way you're sleeping naked, Luke."

"But I'll be on the couch. It's not like I'll accidentally touch you with all my naked bits and pieces."

"I said I'll take the couch, but if you want the couch, I don't mind taking the bed. It looks comfy."

"It sure does." He eyes me. "Remember when we shared a book as teens and no-one had to take the couch? And we'd watch movies and fall asleep telling stories and then in the morning you'd wake me up by hitting me with a pillow."

"We didn't share the bed that often, but yes."

"I think best friends can share a bed and not worry about it, don't you?"

"Really Luke?" I place my hands on my hips. "Is this your way of saying you don't think anyone should be on the couch?"

"This is my way of saying we've slept in beds together, plenty of times. Why not on this trip as well?"

Because you've never looked this sexy before.

"Luke, you can sleep in the bed with me. It's large enough, and we can just build a pillow fort between us."

"A pillow fort?" His lip twitches. "What is the fort keeping in or out?" He stands up and I watch as he walks over to the large French door and opens it. He steps out onto the balcony and I follow behind him. We both stare out at the ocean in the distance and the swaying fronds of the palm trees that run down the side of the property. It's a beautiful night.

"I don't know." I shrug as I lean back against the wall and then my eyes catch the hammock. "Ooh, look." I head over to it and glance back at him. "Want to give me a push?"

"Right now? He steps toward me and I feel his fingers on the slight of my back. "You want to sleep there tonight?"

"No, of course not."

"It would protect you from my morning wood." He winks and all I can do is blush. "Better than even a pillow fort."

"Really, Luke?"

"Isn't that what you're worried about?"

"No."

"I mean it would be awkward if there was no pillow fort and you work up and I was pressed up against your ass, all hard. Or maybe that's okay? Makes it all the more real right?"

"Luke, really?" I swallow hard. I know he's just joking, but I'm starting to feel hot. I'm about to make a joke to cut through the sexual tension when the phone inside the room rings, and I hurry back inside to answer it. It rings off before I can answer it, but I decide to call down to order some food instead of going back onto the balcony. A pleasant-sounding lady answers within seconds.

"Room service. Can I help you?"

"Hi. This is Mia in—"

"You're in the Lincoln Suite, correct?"

"Yes, yes. I was wondering if I could place an order for room service, please. I'm kinda hungry." I don't know why I'm telling her this information, but maybe I'm just trying to stop my mind from thinking about Luke sleeping next to me, naked. He has to be crazy because there is just no way.

"Sure, Mrs. Haverbrook. What would—"

"It's Bishop." I interject quickly. "I'm Mia Bishop. My, uh, well, my friend—boyfriend, I mean, is Luke Haverbrook. He is also staying in the suite, but we aren't married. I mean, not that we won't ever—"

"Mia." Luke gives me look.

I let out a low moan. I am blowing it. Thank God it's only with the room service lady.

"Sorry, I'm sure you don't care about our relationship status. I'd like to get two cheeseburgers, two fries, a portion of onion rings, a Coke, and a side salad."

"You never eat the salads, Mia." Luke gives me a knowing look. "And I know I don't want it."

"I will eat it tonight. I actually always eat my salads now," I lie smoothly. "You don't know everything about me, Luke. You've been gone, and I've changed."

"Haven't changed your habit of picking the wrong guys though."

"Anyway, sorry about that, ma'am. I would like two cheeseburgers, two fries, a Coke, and a large salad with ranch dressing, please."

I give Luke a pointed look, and all he does is laugh as he turns around and heads into the bathroom. I already regret my decision to add the salad, but I'm going to make sure to eat it.

"So, four cheeseburgers, four fries, two Cokes, a side salad, and a large salad with ranch? What dressing would you like with the side salad?"

"Huh? I just want two cheeseburgers, please. With two fries, one Coke, and a salad with ranch."

"I see. And you're charging it to the room?"

"Sure, thanks."

"You're welcome. That will be up within forty-five minutes. Thank you."

We hang up, and I once again look around the room. Luke is doing something in the bathroom, and I'm glad to have a moment to myself while I wait for him to come out.

I grab my phone to text Juniper so I don't think too much about what I've gotten myself into.

MIA

I'm thinking I may be crazy. What do you think?

JUNIPER

What happened?

MIA

Luke and I had to check in to the hotel room tonight, and we have no change of clothes or anything, and I'm just like, can we do this?

JUNIPER

You two have shared beds for years. It'll be fun.

MIA

Yeah, true. I just ... well ...

JUNIPER

Well, what?

MIA

He has abs now, Juni.

JUNIPER

Abs? Wow. Who knew he'd start working out? Good for him.

MIA

I guess.

JUNIPER

Wait ... are you admiring his abs?

MIA

NO! Of course not.

JUNIPER

Okay, so then what's the problem?

MIA

What are we going to sleep in?

JUNIPER

Underwear.

MIA

I suppose. :(

JUNIPER

Do you want me to bring you some PJs?

MIA

Aren't you in bed though?

JUNIPER

No, I just got home from Hidden Cove. Rafe and I were talking, and he just dropped me off.

MIA

Rafe, as in my brother?

JUNIPER

Do you know another?

MIA

Why did you go to Hidden Cove?

JUNIPER

He offered me a ride home, and then we decided to go up to see the stars. I guess there was some unique constellation that we could see tonight or something.

MIA

Weird. He's such a nerd.

JUNIPER

So, you okay? You going to stay the night?

MIA

Yeah, ordered room service, and maybe I'll watch a movie. I'll see you at Salty Pages after the breakfast activities tomorrow, okay?

JUNIPER

Sounds good. Have fun.

I grab the remote control and make myself comfortable on the bed, curling my legs up under me as I turn the TV on. I settle back against the pillows and flip through the channels, not looking for anything in particular, but hoping for a rom-com. The bathroom door opens about ten minutes later, and Luke walks out with damp hair, a towel around his shoulders, and only wearing a pair of black briefs.

What on earth? My eyes immediately fly to his crotch, and I feel heat rising in my face. He's not hard or anything, but the outline of his business is very easy to see.

The bulge sits comfortably in his briefs as he makes his way over to the bed and towels his wet hair.

Stop looking, Mia. Are you out of your mind?

"What are you watching?" he asks innocently.

My eyes fly to his. Did he notice me staring at him in a totally not innocent way?

"Huh? What do you mean?" I frown and grab my phone. "I was just texting Juniper and was thinking about her messages. I wasn't watching anything."

"Oh, okay. So, I can grab the remote then and change the channel?"

"Wait, what? No." I squeeze the remote control close to me. "I want to watch a rom-com."

"Oh, no," he groans loudly and drops onto the bed beside me, his eyes beseeching as he gazes up at me. "Not a rom-com, Mia." He pouts like a cute little puppy dog begging for a treat and love. "Anything but a rom-com."

"What? We haven't watched a rom-com together in years. Like, maybe not since we were fifteen." I continue to flip the channels. "And then I seem to remember you falling asleep after about ten minutes."

"I mean, I figured a movie called *Sleepless in Seattle* gave me permission to also get some sleep." He moves up the bed until he is seated next to me.

"Sleepless, Luke, not sleeping."

"Aw, yes, well if we're remembering things, I seem to remember you falling asleep as well."

"How can you remember me falling asleep when you were asleep, Luke? That doesn't even make sense."

"I woke up because I was going to watch the movie, but then I saw you snoring your little ass off, so I figured it was fine for me to go back to sleep."

"It was a good movie. Maybe I can even find it now, and we can watch it."

"Oh, no." He makes a face and then chortles as I hit him in the shoulder. "I mean, oh, yay, I really hope you can find it."

"Yeah, right." I try to ignore the way his smile is making me feel. Like I'm in a cozy cabin, in front of a fireplace with a hot chocolate in my hand. "We should talk about our plan before the food comes. I don't know what you think, but I'm not sure that tonight went amazing."

"Because my brother is a huge douche?" He shakes his head, and his eyes survey my dress. "You keeping that on all night?"

"I have nothing to change into."

"You have on underwear, right?"

"Yes, but ..."

"And we're doing a pillow fort, so it's not like I'll accidentally wake up in the middle of the night, feel your almost-naked body, and think to myself, *Ooh, a warm, sexy piece of meat for me to snuggle up with.*"

"Really, Luke? I take offense to that."

"To which part?"

"Being compared to a piece of meat." I giggle, though I kinda want to ask him if he finds me sexy. Or if he was just saying that generally. Not that I would ask him that. "Do you think I'm sexy, or was that just a general statement?" I ask seconds after my brain told me not to ask.

Who cares, Mia? He's your best friend. You can ask him these questions. It doesn't mean anything.

It doesn't mean that you care about his answer.

"Do I find you sexy?" He bursts out laughing. "What sort of question is that?"

"You just said—"

"Is this you needing me to validate that you're beautiful and sexy and that every man on this earth wants you?" He cocks his head to the side and grins. "I mean, we both saw that Rex was trying to get his flirt on, though I wouldn't be shocked to find out that was because we said we're together and he wants to take what's mine."

"I'm not yours. I'm not a piece of property." I poke him in the chest. "Even if we were dating. Also, what do you mean, he only found me attractive because—"

"That's not what I said, Mia." He sighs. "I'm sure every guy there tonight noticed you, including Rex. But let's be real; his sudden admiration and crude comments coming now? Sus. He just wants what he can't have." He frowns suddenly and looks me up and down. "You don't still want him, do you?"

"No. Ugh, of course not." Though I can tell from the look on his face that Luke doesn't believe me. "Do I want him to want me so that I can make him take back the rude words from the invitation? Why, yes, but not because I actually wish I were his blushing bride."

"If you say so." He peers at me. "So, what's the plan? We just act lovey-dovey and hold hands?"

"Sure." I nod, thinking hard. "We can hold hands. That's not going to cross any personal lines."

"And I guess we can hug as well," he says. "You're always hugging me anyway."

"That's true."

"And cheek kisses?"

"Sure, forehead as well." I grin at him. "And hand kisses and caresses. That's sweet and romantic and not too intimate."

"Yeah, that's not intimate at all."

He grabs my hand and kisses it three times in a row, and I giggle. Then he turns my wrist over and kisses my palm and the soft skin of my wrist lightly as if I'm a delicate figurine. I swallow hard as his eyes don't leave me. I feel his tongue on my skin for a second before he pulls away.

"Not intimate at all," he repeats.

I just nod because what on earth was that? And why do I feel so weird inside?

"What about pecks on the lips?" he asks after a few moments.

"We said that's fine, right? Just no tongue." I quickly lip my lips. "We established that."

"What if there comes a time when we need tongue to really prove the point that we're together?"

"We'll cross that bridge when we come to it." I shift on the bed and sigh as the skirt rides up. "Can I borrow your shirt?" I ask him, trying not to stare at his rugged chest. "I can sleep in that. It will be more comfortable than this dress."

"Sure." He points to the couch and the stack of folded clothes, and I get off of the bed.

As much as I feel self-conscious, being here, I am also really happy. Luke has always been my closest friend. He knows things about me that I can't even remember.

"Do you remember the time I came over to your house and forgot my PJs and had to sleep in your Spider-Man suit?"

"I don't think you had to sleep in it." His lips twist up in a smirk. "You chose to sleep in it out of all the clothes I had offered. I was so annoyed."

"I know you were." I laughed. "You were glaring at me the whole time."

"I thought you were going to take away my powers."

"What powers? Climbing up the side of buildings?" I giggle as I grab ahold of his shirt. "Close your eyes. I'm taking my dress off."

"Close my eyes? Would a boyfriend have to—"

"Luke!"

"They're closed." He lies back on the bed. "So, as you change, let's discuss our backstory. How did we figure out we were in love?"

"One night, we were watching a movie on the phone together, and you said, 'This love story reminds me of us,' and I said, 'What do you mean?' and you said, 'It reminds me that I love you and want you and think you're the best woman in the world.' "

"Nope," he grunts from the bed. "I am not going to sound like a simp. There is no way in hell that I would say any of those words, and my family knows it."

"I think it sounds so romantic."

"Mia Bishop, could you ever imagine me saying that?" He laughs loudly. "*This love story reminds me of us*? Um, no."

He pretends to throw up, and I can't help but laugh as I button up his shirt. It's not super long on me, as it stops mid-thigh, but it is big, loose, and soft. It also smells of Luke, like the ocean and lemon mixed together.

"Maybe not the old Luke, but the new super-romantic Luke, yes."

"Let's not get carried away, Mia." He yawns loudly, and I head back to the bed. "Where is this food?" he asks.

I notice his eyes are wide open. Did he even close them? Did he see me taking off my dress? His eyes follow me as I walk, and I can see the way he's looking at my thighs as his shirt lifts up every other step. Thank God I have on underwear. Never have I been happier about the fact that I am not one of those girls who likes to go commando. I can't even imagine what would happen if Luke were to see the jungle growing down there. He'd probably laugh. Which reminds me that I need to shave or get a wax. Just in case.

Just in case what, Mia? the Goody Two-shoes in my head demands to know.

For swimming at the beach. In a bikini. I don't want to find myself renamed as Mia, queen of the Amazon.

"Earth to Mia."

"Oh, sorry. I was just thinking that it should be here soon. Anyway, if you don't like my backstory, what do you suppose we tell people?"

"I was thinking something along the lines of you calling me in the middle of the night with a secret and begging me to call you, even though I was at work and—"

"You're always at work."

"Exactly, and I stop in the middle of a meeting and—"

"How would you be in the middle of a meeting in the middle of the night?"

"Touché. Okay, fine, you call me in the middle of the day while I'm in a meeting, begging me to call you."

"That sounds like a you move, Luke, not a me move."

"Anyway, Mia. You beg me to call, and I walk out of the meeting, worried that something has happened to you, and you tell me that you can't hold it in any longer, and you absolutely must tell me what's on your mind."

"I absolutely must tell you?" I burst out laughing as I sit on the mattress and grab my phone to see the time. "And what do I tell you?"

"You tell me that you've secretly loved me for years and that you can't live another day without letting me know." He grins at me. "And then you send a photo of yourself topless to me, and I—"

"Oh, hell no, Luke. I am not telling anyone that story. Are you out of your mind?"

"No, but that would have been kinda fun to receive."

"You want to see me topless?"

I turn to him and push him back. His skin is warm to the touch, and I can't help but notice how broad his shoulders are. His skin, a golden-olive complexion, is smooth and silky-looking. There's a light smattering of dark hair across his chest, and he twitches his pecs so they jump back and forth. Heat radiates from his body to mine, and soon, his thigh is pressed against mine as he shifts closer to me.

"What do you think, Mi-Mi?" he whispers next to my ear, tickling my sensitive eardrum and making me shiver.

"You're such a perv." I tuck my legs under me and turn toward him. "I'm not a stripper. You're not about to see these goodies."

"Ah. jeez, my lifetime dreams have been shattered. Call the police."

"Very funny." I punch him lightly on the shoulder, and he grabs my hand and pushes me back slightly. "You would be so lucky, Mr. Haverbrook."

"Rex would be so lucky, you mean." He winks at me and grabs my wrist and holds it up to his lips and lightly kisses it. I quickly pull it down. "Or maybe he still thinks it's a pity that you didn't have a date to his wedding."

"Well, he thought you were a loser as well." I grab ahold of his arm with my other hand, but he grabs that as well, pushing me back slightly.

"Thus the position we find ourselves in now." He grins as he reaches down to tickle me. "Two lonely losers who couldn't get a date to a wedding."

"Don't." I giggle as I fall back on the bed, my hair a tangled mess on either side of my shoulders. "I'm sure I could have found someone, Luke." I attempt to push him back, but he's much stronger than he was when we were fifteen and constantly engaged in tickling and teasing fights. "Stop." I attempt to bring my arms down to prevent him from tickling me. "I can't." I giggle uncontrollably as he continues to tickle me, giving no mercy.

"I suppose you could have found some surfer, and I could have found some socialite who wanted a vacation." His fingers run down the side of my body toward my legs before caressing the skin on my thigh as he makes his way to my ticklish knees.

"Luke."

I push him to the side and quickly roll on top of him. I grab his wrists and push them back toward his head as he falls back onto the mattress, his dazzling ocean eyes laughing at my attempt to get him back. My shirt rides up slightly, and I shift on top of him to try and bring it back down without letting go of his arms. This just proves to bring the shirt up higher, and as I sit back, I realize I'm straddling his lap. In fact, I'm now sitting firmly on something very hard.

I swallow as I realize that what I'm feeling is not a rock. Or his knee.

Oh shit, I'm sitting on his cock.

I gaze down at him, my brain suddenly clouded as I feel him pressed up against my panties. There's a heady feeling of desire rising through me as his cock suddenly twitches, grinding against me through the thin material of our underwear. I move forward, attempting to move off of him, when he suddenly grabs me, and I fall back, bouncing down hard on his cock. I bite down on my lip, trying to ignore the wetness that fills my panties. I'm really hoping that Luke is too tired to feel what I'm feeling, but as I look down into his eyes, his expression has changed slightly. His eyes are darker, more intense, and he's biting down on his lower lip. An overwhelming feeling of want courses through me. I want to suck on his lower lip. I want to grab his face.

Get your drunk mind out of the gutter, Mia, you fool.

I quickly avert my gaze and squeeze his wrists, pushing down hard, my hair brushing past his face.

"Can't touch this, baby," I tease him as he suddenly shifts, grabs both of my arms, and rolls me onto my back. "Ooh." I glare up at him. "No fair."

"You didn't think you'd really beat me, did you, Mia?" He lowers his face closer to mine, and his lips brush against my cheek softly before lightly kissing my nose.

I am barely breathing now. Is he going to kiss me? And if so, is it for real? Or is this just practice?

I reach up, grab his bicep, and try to shift him off of me, but he's just too strong. He sits back lightly on my thighs and grins as he looks down at me, licking his lips slowly as he gazes at me.

"Nice bra."

I look down and notice the top buttons of his shirt have come undone, and he can see the tops of my breasts in my mid-cut bra.

"Perv."

"Not quite. A perv would take advantage of this situation."

"And how is that?" I don't know why I ask him that. Maybe I'm stupid. Maybe I just want to know what he'll do. Maybe I've just lost my mind.

And because Luke is Luke and he doesn't give a fuck, he grabs the front of the shirt and tugs on it, and half the buttons go flying off as the shirt falls open.

"I'd do that." He cocks his head to the side and laughs. "That was a two-hundred-dollar shirt as well."

"Luke!" I see his eyes falling to my exposed bra, stomach, and the top of my panties.

I swallow hard as he stares at my body. I think he's about to touch me, but instead, he jumps off of the bed and shakes his head.

"Where is this room service? I'm starving." He walks over to the phone and grabs it. "Let me check and see."

He turns his back to me, and I take a couple of deep breaths as I close the shirt and grab the remote.

"Tell them to hurry." I feign a lightness I don't feel. "Or I'm going to run down and raid the kitchen."

"Okay." He turns back to me with a small smile and nods.

The room is tense with sexual chemistry that neither one of us wants to address. I'm still in shock at how quickly the tension has built up between us. It was never like this before. Yet, now, I can barely look at him without thinking of how hot he looks.

The bulge in the front of his briefs wasn't helping either though.

Luke is my best friend, but I can't stop thinking about how hard and thick he felt between my legs. Shit! The last thing I need is to fantasize about my best friend.

chapter eleven

Luke

The stack of pillows pushed against my body does nothing to quell the desire I feel for Mia as I wake up. I roll onto my back and try not to groan as a wisp of Mia's scent floats through my nostrils. She's whimpering slightly in her sleep, and I can't stop myself from turning onto my side to watch her sleep. Her face looks peaceful, and there's a smile on her face. I wonder what she's dreaming about.

I look over at the bedside clock and groan when I see that it's still three thirty a.m. Far too early to wake up, though there is work that I need to get done. I think about grabbing my laptop and going through some emails when Mia rolls over. I freeze and wait to see if she's also going to wake up, but she doesn't.

My shirt has come open, and I stare at her silky black bra. The sheet has slipped down to her waist, and I go to pull it up to cover her so she doesn't get cold. As I lean over, I accidentally bump into one of the pillows, and it bumps into her stomach.

"Huh?" Her eyes slowly open, and she blinks sleepily as she gazes at me. "Oh, hey, Luke. Is it morning?"

"Yes, but no," I whisper. "It's only three thirty a.m."

"Oh." She yawns and stretches her arm, hitting the pillow and sending it flying. "Oops."

"It's fine," I say, picking up another pillow and throwing it to the ground. "It's not hurting them."

"It's our fort." She points at me. "You destroyed the fort."

"We'll survive the night."

"I suppose." She yawns again and tugs on the shirt. Before I know what's going on, she tugs it off and throws it to the ground and offers me an impish smile. "I'm too hot."

"That's okay," I say, trying not to look back at her body. "Get some sleep. We have a big day tomorrow."

"Yeah, we do." She giggles as she moves closer to me in the bed. It doesn't seem like a good idea, but I'm not going to stop her. "Lots of people to fool."

"Hopefully, they believe our chaste kisses are real," I murmur as her eyes flicker open and close. "Do you think they will?"

"I suppose so." She stretches her arm out so that it's resting on my chest. She lazily strokes my stomach. "I mean, I would believe us."

"You would?"

I roll over so I'm facing her and move my face closer to hers. Her eyes are open now, and she smiles sweetly, reminding me that she is the girl I've known almost all my life. The girl who called me after her first kiss, losing her virginity, and her one and only pregnancy scare. I should not be looking at her and feeling the things I am feeling.

"Yes." She runs her fingers up my chest and moves her face closer to mine so that her nose grazes against mine. " 'Cause we are amazing. We can practically read each other's mind."

"So, what am I thinking right now?"

"You're thinking this." She leans forward and kisses me lightly on the lips, and I almost freeze.

Can she really read my mind? The fact of the matter is that I have been thinking of kissing her. Granted, I wanted it to be more involved than this brief peck, but shit.

"Not bad." I touch the side of her face tenderly, brushing back her blonde hair. It's grown longer since I last saw her. It's almost halfway down her back now. "But I don't know if that's going to convince anyone."

"Oh?" She wrinkles her cute little button nose, and I can see the smattering of freckles on her cheeks. "We can practice tomorrow when I wake up."

"You're up now."

"Barely. I'm going back to sleep." She closes her eyes, but doesn't move.

I lean forward, almost without thinking, and kiss her again. This time, my lips press against hers in a firmer way, but I don't attempt to slip my tongue inside her mouth.

"Oh." She's breathing heavier now as I move back.

"Oh?" I grin at her, running my finger down her shoulder and toward her waist. I lightly touch her skin, and her eyes fly wide open. "Oh, as in *that was a kiss that will fool Rex*, or oh, as in *you suck at kissing*."

"Oh, as in *I wasn't expecting that*." She licks her lips and moves onto her back.

My fingers glide across her stomach lazily and play with her belly button.

"What are you doing, Luke?"

"I'm touching you casually." My heart is racing as my cock throbs in my briefs. "If we've been dating for a year, we will be used to touching each other casually."

"I suppose so." She shifts on the bed and parts her legs slightly, shivering slightly. Her head is still turned toward me and I'm glad to see her reactions as I touch her.

I move my fingers up past her belly button and stop beneath her bra. She's breathing heavier now. Then I run my fingers up between the valley between her breasts and along her neck. Her skin feels smooth, like velvet, and I can barely breathe as I touch her and wait for her to stop me.

"Are you still practicing your touch?"

"Yes, just tell me when I go too far," I say almost clinically.

"How far are you planning on going?" she whispers into the air.

"Not too far."

I brush my fingers back down and over the top of her bra, moving rapidly. I lightly brush her hard nipples, but I don't stop, even though I feel her large intake of air. My fingers move back down across her stomach and to the tops of her lacy panties. She stills as my fingers run across the lace pattern at the top of her panties. I daren't slip my fingers inside of them. I daren't actually touch her, though I'm dying to.

"That's good," she says, her voice barely recognizable as her body stiffens.

I run my fingers back up toward her bra and rub my thumb across her nipple, slower this time. I don't move my fingers away, but instead slip my finger into her bra. Her eyes widen as I lightly graze her nipple and then pinch it between my thumb and finger. She gasps and shifts on the bed, and I try not to groan as a light moan escapes her lips. My fingers slip back down, and I run my fingers all the way down her panties, tracing her mound as I get to the apex between her legs. She closes her legs in on my fingers, and I move my fingers back up to her belly button.

"I can play that game as well," she moans as she stares at me.

"What game is that?"

"The testing game."

She leans over and runs her fingers across my stomach muscles and then further down so that her fingers are grazing my cock through the thin cotton material. I stiffen as I wait to see what she will do next.

"I mean, just in case we're somewhere and I feel like I need to be comfortable touching you anywhere," she breathes.

"If the act requires it, you have to do it." I nod, my voice deep with desire.

"Exactly," she breathes as she shifts closer to me.

"Just like I would have to do this, if it required it." I reach my fingers to her stomach again.

"Do what?" she asks.

Her mouth is a wide O as I slip my fingers into her panties and down between her legs. She spreads her legs slightly, and I rub her clit for a few seconds, the wetness between her legs telling me how turned on she is. I shift next to her and allow my fingers to slide down her slit before gently rubbing her again. Her thighs clench my fingers for a few seconds before she moans.

"I don't think you'll have to prove that, Luke."

"Maybe not," I croak out as I pull my fingers from out of her panties. "But you never know."

"I mean, do you think I'll have to prove this?"

She slips her fingers down the front of my briefs and strokes my cock. I grow against her touch, and her eyes widen as I twitch against her.

"Probably not." I grunt and I try not to feel too despondent as she pulls her fingers out. "It's likely I won't have to do this either," I say as I roll over on top of her and kiss her hard.

She reaches up and strokes my back, and I gyrate against her, simulating sex as she spreads her legs. My cock strains against my briefs as I grind against her panties. She kisses me back and wraps her legs around my waist. I reach down and pull my cock out and slide her panties to the side. I reach down and rub the head of my cock against her slit and clit. She's moaning loudly now, her chest heaving as she whimpers. She's so wet. I want to slide inside of her. One thrust, and then I'll be inside of her.

"Test is over, Luke," she moans against my lips. "I think we've proven that we can both act if we need to."

"Yes, of course." I pull my cock back and readjust her panties, giving her clit a few strokes as I move back to my side of the bed. I lie back and look up at the ceiling, not knowing what to do with my stiff cock.

"We're both tired, and we drank a lot last night," she whispers.

I nod. "You're right. We're not in our right minds."

"Are you still horny?" she whispers a couple of minutes later, and I laugh loudly.

"What do you think, Mi-Mi?" I roll over and gaze at her and watch as she rolls over onto her side. My cock flops against the front of me, and I quickly tuck it back inside my briefs, so it doesn't get any ideas. "I'm hard as hell."

"I'm pretty wet." She makes a face at me. "We totally can't cross that line though. Friends don't fuck."

"Friends with benefits do."

"Best friends do not become friends with benefits." She touches the side of my face. "It would ruin our friendship." We're talking about this lightly, like it's not unusual for us to be in this situation. Like I am used to almost fucking her. Like it's normal for two people to practice fake dating by almost fucking.

You've dreamt about this though, Luke.

Shut up.

"But talking about my hard cock and your wet pussy won't?"

"Luke!" She presses her finger to my lips. "You can't say that." She is so red that she could camouflage in next to a firetruck, but I don't say anything. I want to reach over and thrust two of my fingers inside of her. I want to get her off. I want her begging me to fill her with my cock. I want her screaming for me to take her.

From the front. From the back. From behind.

Now, is not the time, Luke.

I let out a long sigh. "We're just going to pretend that—"

"We should go to sleep," she says softly and gives me a quick peck on the cheek. "I bet you in the morning, we'll wake up and think this was all a dream." I can't believe she's trying to gaslight us both but I understand why. We'd gone from zero to a million miles per hour and she was likely confused.

"I think not," I mutter under my breath. "In my dream, we wouldn't have stopped."

I stare into her eyes, and she smiles softly at me. Her eyes flutter closed, and I don't know if she's really falling asleep or just pretending, but I know that it's for the best. It is all for the best. I'm glad she stopped me. She was right. If we'd fucked, we would have crossed a line neither one of us wanted to cross. She is too important to me to become a fuck buddy. Though the hardness in my briefs wants to disagree.

I can still feel her wetness on my fingers. I bring them to my mouth and suck her juices off. The taste of her sweet pussy is intoxicating, and I know I need to forget what just happened. I need to forget and not let it happen again. The last thing we need is to make this situation even more complicated.

The sound of banging on the door awakens me, and I groan as I wake up. My eyes fly open as I remember where I am and what went down the evening before. I turn to see if Mia is upset with me, but she's no longer in the bed. Another knock on the door makes me sit up, and I slowly clamber out of the bed. I have no idea who could be at the door, unless it's Mia and she forgot her key, but then I hear the sound of water running in the bathroom, and I realize that Mia is in the shower.

"I'm coming," I yell as I head toward the door.

I look down at my watch. It's nine a.m. I can't believe I slept so late, and for once, I'm grateful that Rex and Andi scheduled a late breakfast at ten a.m.

"Hello?" I open the door suspiciously, expecting to see Rex, but it's Juniper's smiling face I see standing there.

"Morning, Luke." She beams at me as she steps into the room and looks around. "I brought a bag of clothes for Mia." She holds up a black duffel bag and whistles as she looks around the room. "Wow, this is amazing." She looks around, exploring the room. "Rex really sprang for the expensive rooms."

"My parents did, you mean," I say dryly and study her face to see if she's looking at me awkwardly.

Did Mia tell her what had gone down between us the night before?

"Well, that was very nice of you to drop by, Juniper. I'm sure Mia will be thrilled to have some real clothes. I don't think she wanted to sleep in her dress last night ..." My voice trails off, and I casually observe her face for a reaction to see if Mia mentioned anything.

Juniper places the bag on the ground and continues exploring the hotel room.

"She ended up taking off her dress and sleeping in my shirt," I add to see if she's going to respond scandalously or give me a knowing wink. I pause to see if she's going to react.

I'm curious what Mia thinks about our actions from the previous evening. We definitely crossed a line. And I know Mia well enough to know that she'd want to talk about it with someone.

"That's cool. I was wondering what she was going to sleep in." She walks over to the window and looks outside at the view. "Wow, you've got an amazing view of the ocean here. I wish I lived in a condo right next to the beach." She then turns back to look at me with a wry smile. "But, wait, I forgot; you're a Haverbrook. You have multiple houses at the beach."

"I wouldn't say that I have multiple houses, Juniper." I laugh slightly. "My grandparents live at the beach."

"And your parents have an enormous mansion on the beach. I've been there multiple times, remember?"

"I know. Those were the good old days."

I think back to barbeques in my backyard with Mia, Juniper, Josie, and some of our other friends. Mia was the glue of our group, always bringing people together to hang out on the weekends. We'd swim, have bonfires, go stargazing, play board games all night. She'd sing and dance and cheer me up whenever she thought I was working too hard.

It was hard, growing up as a Haverbrook, especially as the youngest son. My parents funneled every dream into Rex. He was the golden boy, the jock my father boasted about to all of Coconut Beach. Sometimes, I thought my dad lived vicariously through Rex. He was proud of every move Rex made. From the cheerleaders he dated to the business classes he took at the University of Florida. Rex was a Gator, a star football player, a handsome all-American son to be proud of.

I was the geek, too skinny when I was younger, always studying, getting ready to take over the family business and grow it. I had my eye on an Ivy League university and then an MBA, and I achieved my dreams, but they were never enough. I was always overlooked, and that was why I stayed away from Coconut Beach. I didn't want to be in Rex's shadow any longer.

"I mean, you could always move back and buy your own mansion on the beach, and then Mia and I could come over every weekend, and we could have epic parties." Her eyes glaze over as she thinks about that possibility. "That would be so cool. Then Mia and I could meet hot guys who aren't in town for a week. Oops." She quickly covers her mouth with her hand, her eyes widening as she stares at me. "I guess we would meet hot guys after the summer's over and you guys break up though."

I don't respond to her comment. It's only day two. I'm not ready to think about Mia and me breaking up, even though this entire situation is fake anyway.

"So, how's it going? Is it totally weird, pretending that you guys are in love and in a relationship?"

"I don't know that I would say it was weird. It's definitely different though."

Like the fact that I was on top of her last night, touching her in ways that I shouldn't have been touching her. Listening to her moan in ways my ears should never be privy to. I can still taste her on my lips.

I need to speak to Mia. I need to make sure she's okay. That she's not obsessing over what happened.

Juniper heads to the couch and takes a seat. "Did you and Mia figure out the treasure hunt map that she got in the mail?"

"No, we were both caught up with trying to convince our families that we're together. I bet she'll show me today."

"Makes sense. Did you have a good night last night? You must have been exhausted, getting off the plane and then having to party."

"It was a lot, but I managed. Thank you for asking. Did you have fun?"

I wonder what she's thinking as she looks down and then back up at me. Her brown eyes are open, and I think about how I was first jealous when she became good friends with Mia. I was nervous Mia would drop me, but she navigated being friends with us perfectly.

"I did have fun. The girls and I enjoyed all the free food and drinks and, of course, dancing." She leans back into the couch. "It was a magical night. Almost surreal, you know?"

"So, did Mia say anything about ..." I pause, not wanting to be too blunt. I'm almost positive that she hasn't said anything because I don't think Juniper would be acting so casually. "I mean, I was wondering if …" My voice trails off as I hear the bathroom door open.

"Who are you talking to?" Mia sashays out of the bathroom with a fluffy white towel wrapped around her body. Her long blonde hair is damp and sits in a bun atop her head.

She looks at me with a shy smile, but then she spies Juniper, and her lips twist into a wide grin.

"Yay, you made it." She rushes over to Juniper and practically jumps up and down.

Her towel clings to her body in all the right ways, and I try to ignore the dip of her curves and her long, slightly wet legs.

"I can't stay long, as I have to get to the beach so I can open the bookmobile, but I wanted to make sure you had some clothes. You sounded kind of desperate in your text messages." Juniper points to the duffel bag on the ground. "I packed some dresses and skirts and stuff for you."

"Thanks, girl. I didn't want to leave here, doing the walk of shame. Though maybe that would have really sold the relationship to everyone."

Mia giggles loudly, and my eyes fly to her to see if she's losing it. She looks at me, and for a couple of moments, I search her face, trying to see what she remembers, trying to see if she's upset, mad, happy, excited. I can't tell from her expression what she's thinking, but I don't think she's mad at me, which is good. I'm not getting a tense vibe, which is what I was worried about when I woke up.

"Maybe some of the tourists would have thought I was a hooker, slinking away in my cheap dress."

"Nah, that dress was too hot to ever be anything other than fabulous." Juniper jumps off of the couch and picks up the crumpled dress that Mia took off the evening before. "It is so pretty, and, wow, this room is absolutely stunning as well. I love the wallpaper and all the decor." Juniper walks around, her fingers touching the linen wallpaper, filled with seashells, pearls, and sand dollars. "This is so pretty."

"Isn't it?" Mia says. "If I had a mansion, I would definitely have a room that had wallpaper with seashells and maybe dolphins. That would be so cool."

"What do you mean, if you had a mansion? You can do it now in your bedroom if you want. I can help you while I'm in town."

"My room is small, Luke. I wouldn't put it in my bedroom, but I would definitely put it in a guest room or something. But Juni and I are poor, and we don't have a guest room."

"You're not poor, Mi-Mi." I suddenly realize that I'm still in my briefs. "I should get myself ready as well. Can't go down to breakfast in my briefs. I don't want to scandalize anyone."

"Just me and Juni?"

"You weren't so scandalized last night," I tease, but then I wonder if I've gone too far.

Mia shoots me a look and then just shakes her head.

"Ignore Luke. You know he's just trying to show off that he has abs now."

I notice that her eyes linger on my chest, and as I take a step back, her eyes meet mine and then dart away quickly. So, she's thinking about my body as well. The idea that I'm also in her head pleases me.

"Juni, we're about to head down to breakfast. Would you like to join us?"

"I wish, but I really do have to get to the beach and open up Salty Pages. I think a couple of tourists are coming by to grab some psychological thrillers for their boat ride later today. So, I need to go through and see what we have."

"Ooh, awesome, I think we have some books by Steve Cavanagh. I loved his book *Fifty Fifty*." Mia gazes over at me as she grips her towel.

I can see that her body is still damp. I try not to look at her legs or her exposed shoulders. I try not to think about her naked body under the towel.

I will not let my mind swim in the gutter. I will not think of her ample breasts.

"I think you will like it as well, Luke."

"Like what?"

"The book I was just talking about."

"Oh, okay." I'm not going to tell her that I wasn't paying attention to what she was talking about.

"On that note, I should be going." Juniper spins around. "I'll see you guys later." She heads to the door and waves her goodbyes before she leaves. "See you guys. Have fun. Don't do anything I wouldn't do." She closes the door behind her.

I turn to look at Mia, who is staring at me with a guilty expression on her face.

"What Juniper doesn't know is that we already have, right?" Mia says, staring at me, gripping her towel to her body tightly.

"What are you talking about?"

"Well, Juni just said, 'Don't do anything I wouldn't do,' but I feel like we already crossed that line, don't you?" She licks her lips nervously and shakes her head, and her hair falls down her shoulders.

She stands there, looking beautiful and sexy, and I feel like I'm seeing her as a woman that I can't resist.

"I wouldn't say that exactly." I shrug and take a step forward. "Do you think we crossed a line?"

"Luke, don't play dumb with me. We're best friends for a reason, and I can read your mind."

"What am I thinking?"

"You're thinking what I'm thinking. We both remember what happened early this morning."

I can't stop the smirk that crosses my face as I gaze down at her parted lips. "I might remember some of it. So, what do we do? How do we approach this, moving forward?" I run my fingers through my hair as I wait for her answer. "Do you think we crossed lines that—"

"Luke, we were drunk. We were tired. We got a little carried away. You haven't been with a woman in a while, from what I can remember, and you know I haven't been with a man, and I guess we were in close proximity …" She shrugs and looks down. "These things happen." Her voice trails off.

I narrow my eyes as I take another step closer to her to observe her better. She's taking this way too cool. In fact, I'm kind of annoyed by how unbothered she seems. She's just going to play it off as us being drunk?

"So, you're okay with the fact that we were practically naked and—"

"Luke," she cuts me off, "we don't need to talk about it. We can just move on from here."

She touches me on the arm, and I want to pull her into me. I'm annoyed that she is brushing this off. Not only is it irritating, but it's also making me wonder if she regrets it. Or if I just wasn't good enough for her.

"You don't want to talk about it?" I ask her, pushing it. "You always want to talk about everything." Which is an understatement.

Mia talks as much as anyone I've ever met in my life. She analyzes almost everything that anyone ever said or did to her. Yet she doesn't want to discuss this? Why not?

"No, I don't want to talk about it. I don't always want to talk about everything, and I don't want to talk about this either. It happened, and we can just ..." She plays with her hair, curling some strands between her fingers. "We can just pretend it never happened."

"We nearly had sex, Mi-Mi, but we're going to pretend that didn't almost happen?"

She blushes a bright red and looks away again before hurrying away to her duffel bag.

"We just got caught up in the emotions of the night." She opens the duffel bag and mumbles under her breath, "These things happen."

"Not between us."

We'd never been in that position before in our lives. I had never touched her intimately. She had never touched me intimately. This was a path we'd never gone down before in our lives, and I am kind of astonished that I am the one who wants to talk about it and not her.

"So, we're not going to discuss what happened then?"

"I don't really think we need to, Luke." She sighs as she looks up at me. "Don't you think this summer is complicated enough as it is?" She rifles through her clothes.

She looks cute, standing there, half naked, bent over.

Get your mind out of the gutter, Luke.

"Fine. If that's what you want. What did Juniper bring you? Anything that might work for me to wear?"

"Not unless you want to wear a skirt." She giggles, her eyes finally meeting mine again. "Or a bikini."

"What would Talia say if she saw me in your bikini?" I tease her. "Maybe she'd be impressed if I said it was couture."

"She's such a bitch. And, yes, I would say it to her face."

"Would you really though?"

"Maybe I wouldn't." She grins. "She looks like she can fight, and I don't want to ruin my flawless face."

"No, you don't." I take a couple of steps over to her, which I know is a dangerous thing to do, seeing as I'm still standing in my briefs and she's just in a towel, but I need to look her in the eyes. I need to make sure that we really are okay. "So, last night—"

"Luke." Her voice is choked up as she glances up at me, her eyes wide. There's a small smile on her lips, and she grabs my hands and squeezes. "We're okay, trust me."

"Are you sure?"

I cock my head to the side and look her up and down. Her towel looks like it's about to fall off.

"I'm sure. I mean, it might have been a different story if you had accidentally slipped it in, but you didn't." She giggles and looks at the front of my briefs and then grabs a skirt from the bag.

"True, I also think you should get changed because I don't want an accidental slip to happen right now."

"What?"

"I'm just saying that your towel's about to slip off." I point to the top knot that is starting to unravel. "And if your towel slips off and you're naked and then you accidentally trip and slip on top of me, well, who's to know what could happen?"

"You're funny," she says, grabbing the knot quickly, "but not that funny. I'm going to change." She heads off to the bathroom with some clothes.

"Thank you for asking though. I know last night was kind of weird. This whole thing is kind of weird, but … I love you. You're still my best friend, and we had a little fun, and we stopped it before we went too far, and that's the main thing." She walks into the bathroom and closes the door.

I stand there, just staring for a couple of moments, wondering what she would do if I headed into the bathroom behind her and ripped her towel off and said I wanted to make another mistake with her. Only it wouldn't be a mistake. I don't know what she'd say. From the sounds of it, she also enjoyed the moment, but it didn't seem to mean anything to her, which fucking pisses me off because it meant something to me.

I can still smell her. I can still taste her. I groan as I feel my cock twitch. I push my hand down and adjust myself.

"I do not need this right now."

I think about going for a jog, but stop when I hear my phone ringing. I grab it, surprised to see Rex's name on the screen.

"Hello?"

"Hey there, bro. Just want to make sure you're going to make it down to breakfast on time."

"We'll be down."

"What do you mean, we?" He sounds surprised.

"Me and Mia."

"She spent the night with you?"

"She's my girlfriend. Of course she spent the night with me."

"Lay off it, Luke. What's really going on? We all know that Mia's always wanted me."

I stay silent.

"You guys didn't even look like you'd banged. Last night, you looked like two goofy-ass friends, just hanging out, not touching each other, not doing anything with each other."

I press my lips together. Was that really how we came across? I'll have to ask Mia's friends to see what they thought.

"Was there something you wanted, Rex? Because Mia's getting changed right now, and then I'm hopping into the shower."

"So, you didn't have shower sex this morning?"

"Excuse me?"

"I mean, you haven't seen your supposed girl in how long, and you didn't think to have shower sex with her?"

"You know what, Rex? I'm not a pig, and I'm not going to discuss with you the intimate details of my relationship with Mia." I don't bother to tell him that if she really were my girl, I'd be in the shower right then, letting her feel the full length of me.

"You know if it were me, she'd want to hit it."

"I'm going to go, Rex."

"Well, I also wanted you to know that it was really uncool of you to just walk out on the family business the way that you did."

"Excuse me?"

"Dad was counting on you to take over some of the accounts when I became CEO, and you kind of bailed."

"The plan had always been for us to be joint CEOs," I say. "And Dad made you CEO. I did what I had to do."

"You're still fucking upset about that? I'm the oldest son."

"I know you're the golden boy, Rex. You're the Haverbrook who will inherit it all."

"You've always been jealous of me, haven't you?"

He hangs up, and I just stand there, staring at the phone, wondering if he's right.

Have I always been jealous of Rex?

I must have spaced out for a little bit because the next thing I know, Mia's walking out of the bathroom in a long, flowy cream skirt and a midriff green top. Her hair hangs straight down her back, and she's got a glittery headband on. Her brown eyes are warm as she gazes at me. As she comes closer to me, I notice her expression change.

"What's wrong? Who was on the phone?"

"Rex."

"What did he want?"

"He doesn't seem to believe that we are really together, and he just made some comments about the family business."

"He sucks." Mia presses her lips together.

"He does."

"You know you should have become the CEO yourself. You shouldn't even have been joint CEO. You've always been the one with the business prowess."

"Yeah, well, I surmise when you're not quarterback of the football team, you're just not a good enough Haverbrook."

"I'm sorry," she says. "Your parents—well, your dad …" She wrinkles her nose. "He just seems to value the wrong things."

"It's okay. I am over it. I'm an adult now."

"Yeah, but childhood hurts, and slights can still hurt."

"Yeah, they can. You look pretty this morning. I like your skirt."

"Thank you. I got it at a thrift store." She spins around, and it flows back and forth across her ankles. "You like my top too?"

"It's revealing." I frown slightly. It's sexy, but maybe too sexy for a morning breakfast.

"It's not like it's showing my boobs, Luke. It's just a little midriff."

"I can see your belly button."

"It's cool."

"I know. I'm just saying, in New York, this would be a very daring outfit."

"Well, I don't live in New York, do I?"

"No, you don't."

"Are you going to shower?"

"I guess I should do that, but unlike you, I do not have clothes to change into, nor do I have clean underwear."

"So, you can go commando."

"I suppose I can." I grin. "Unless—"

"You're not about to ask me if I have a pair of panties you can wear." She bursts out laughing. "Because you totally can. I have a thong."

"I'm not that sort of guy. I do not want to wear your thongs, though I wouldn't mind seeing you in one."

"Ha-ha, Luke," she says, hitting me across the shoulder.

As her fingers touch my skin, I grab her hand and pull her into me. She looks up at me. She's breathing slightly hard, and I can see that she doesn't hate my touch. Her heart races slightly, and her eyelashes flutter down as I continue to stare at her.

"We have to up our game in front of Rex and everyone else. He didn't think we were touchy-feely enough. He didn't believe us. I don't know if he's just saying that, if he's just jealous or what, but he said we just looked like regular old friends. So, we need to play the part a bit more."

"I can do that," she says, biting down on her lower lip and nodding. A flush of heat rises in her cheeks, and I wonder if she's thinking about last night. I wonder if she's thinking about the way she rubbed my cock or the way my fingers stroked her clit.

"We should get ready. You want me to go down to get you a pair of shorts? I'll get some from the surf shop."

"Yeah, that sounds great."

"Anything else you want? A T-shirt?"

"Yeah, why not get me a Coconut Beach T-shirt? Really make me feel like I'm back in town."

"I'm glad you're here," she says, squeezing my hand. "It's been too long since we've seen each other."

"I know," I say. "And I'm sorry about that."

"Yeah, me too. And I'm sorry about your brother and your parents. They kind of suck."

"Joke's on them. I'm about to close the merger of my career, and it's going to be amazing."

"Well, good for you, Luke," she says softly and heads toward the door.

I stand there and think about all the emails I likely have waiting for me, and my mind immediately shifts into business mode. I have work to do. I pull out my phone and bring up my emails. I'm here on vacation, and I'm meant to be enjoying this wedding, but this deal is really big, and now that Rex is being even more of a jerk than usual, I have to ensure that I close it. I have to ensure that everyone knows that I am a far better businessman than Rex will ever be.

"Hey, Luke. Did you hear what I said?"

Mia stands there in the open door, and I gaze up at her.

"Sorry, I was just thinking about work."

"It's okay. I'll be back." Something flashes in her eyes, and she shakes her head, looking annoyed.

She closes the door, and I stand there, wondering why she sounded so upset.

I head toward the window, and I look out at the beautiful blue water and the white sand in the distance. The beach isn't too busy right now, save for maybe about five people.

I can't believe I'm back in Coconut Beach, and everything is so familiar and yet so very different. Everything about this trip is making me question who I am and where I'm going. Not for the first time do I wonder if it was a good decision to play the part of Mia's boyfriend because what I'm beginning to realize is that my best friend, Mia, the girl who captured my heart when I was just a teenager, blossomed into an even more gregarious and beautiful woman, and the teenage crush that I once had has not only remained, but it has grown, and I want her badly.

I want to know every inch of her inside and out.

I know I can't have her though.

She is the best friend I've ever had, and I can't risk that, and I have a feeling that is why Mia didn't want to discuss the night before either. She was clearly into it, but I'm reminded of what she said when we were teenagers and going to have our first kiss together.

"If we get too physical or too intimate, it will make things complicated, and when relationships become complicated, they're far easier to break. And I don't want to lose you, Lukey. You're the best friend a girl could ever have, and a kiss is not worth losing that."

Her words reverberate in my brain, and I feel the sting of them just as much as I did back then. If a kiss could ruin our easy friendship, then sex could break us.

I'm not going to push the issue, even though my cock is aching with need. I can ignore my cock, though I am not sure what I can do about my heart. Mia let me know in no uncertain terms that we are never going to be anything more than friends, and I am going to respect that because the truth of the matter is, I can't lose her from my life.

She is the only constant that makes me feel like I am good enough and smart enough and funny enough, and I know she does it because that's just the way she feels and not because of the way I look, or the money I have, or the power I have at my company, and that is worth a lot more than some hot sex.

chapter twelve

Mia

The Coconut Beach Boys, a local band that sings Beach Boys songs, performs in the lobby as Luke and I make our way back to the hotel room after breakfast. We stand there for a few moments, watching the older gentlemen rock their hearts out in their bright Hawaiian shirts and shorts.

We're standing next to a couple of kids, who are obviously on holiday, as they chow down on watermelon spears. Luke and I exchange a glance as the young boy drops his spear on the ground, quickly picks it up, and stuffs it back into his mouth. Luke grins at me, and we share an unspoken memory of when he was twelve and stuffed his face with so much watermelon one summer that I had to give him an ultimatum—share it with me or I'd not share my cookies.

"Shall we head up?" he asks after a few minutes when the band finishes "Good Vibrations." He drops a twenty-dollar bill into a top hat sitting atop a small table in front of them.

"Sure."

We make our way to the elevator and wait for it to arrive. A group of tourists in sun visors and *Life's a Beach* T-shirts walks past us, and I lean forward to whisper in his ear.

"Juniper designed those shirts," I say proudly as I nod toward them. "Aren't they cute?"

"Real cute." He watches the tourists as they walk past and turns back to me with a smile. "She's always been so artistic."

"Yes, she designs most of the postcards that we sell as well."

"Outstanding. Today went okay, don't you think?" His familiar blue eyes gaze into mine, questioning me in such an earnest way that I smile at him as I nod my confirmation.

I'm trying to ignore the way my heart is racing and the fact that my body is more aware of him than it has ever been in my life. I'm noticing things about him I've never noticed before, like the way his bushy eyebrows are silky but could do with a slight waxing, or the way his blue eyes are so deep and vibrant, or the way his lips are just that perfect touch of pink, and his hands—they're elegant, slender, and soft. I tremble, just thinking about them on my body. What they did to me the evening before still has me trembling. I felt like I was floating in the air in a state of perpetual bliss, and I very much wanted to feel the ground beneath my feet again. This is a new level in our relationship, and my overanalytical brain isn't sure what it meant. I loved feeling so happy, but I wanted to know what it all meant.

"Earth to Mia. What did you think?"

"Oh, yeah, it went really well, I think. Rex was giving us odd looks, but thank God for Andi and her being so touchy-feely with him."

"She definitely wanted his full attention."

"Well, it was the official breakfast to start off the two-week festivities."

"I cannot believe that my brother is having two weeks' worth of festivities for his wedding. Like, we're not the royal family, and we're not—" Luke groans as his expression tightens. "I still can't believe he never told me he was seriously dating someone."

"Hey, it's okay," I say, touching his arm, enjoying the ripple of his muscles beneath my fingers. "We can both still work if we really have to, and we'll just take part as best as we can. Plus, we get to stay in that really gorgeous hotel room." Hopefully he wouldn't have to work too much though. We hadn't spent much time with each other in ages.

I bite down on my lower lip. Why? Why did I bring up the hotel room? Will he think all I want to do is spend nights in bed with him, practicing and exploring? Why didn't I think before I spoke?

"How did you sleep last night?" he says as we step into the elevator.

My heart flips at his comment, and I feel my face flush as I press the button for our floor. I look up at him through lowered eyelashes. I really hope he will not ask about what went on again. I don't want to discuss it—not because it wasn't amazing and not because I am upset, but really more because I am confused about how to process everything. I am confused about what we did. Not because it didn't feel amazing, but more so because I found hit touches to be achingly sexy and sweet. And I'd never expected to experience passion and lust for Luke. He is Luke. My Lukey. My best friend forever. He was the first boy to see me cry. The first boy to hold my hand. The first boy to tell me I was pretty. He was the boy I spent nights on the phone with, talking about other boys.

And now ... now I've done things with him that made me blush.

I'd never looked at him like that before, though as I gaze at him, standing there with his muscular, lithe body, all I can think is, *Why not? How have I never noticed how gorgeous he is?* I know if I'd seen him at Cocktails & Chaos on a night out, I would definitely have tried to get my flirt on.

"So, before you forget, I'm going to go to my apartment in a little bit and grab more clothes because Juni didn't bring me PJs. Nor enough underwear ..." My voice trails off as his lips twitch. I know exactly what he's thinking, and I blush. "So, I'll get all that good stuff ..."

"Important pieces of clothing." His expression is serious as he nods. "Don't want to forget your panties."

"Luke, never say *panties* again. It sounds so pervy."

"Panties sound pervy?"

He takes a step closer to me and gazes down into my eyes. There's mischief in his gaze, and I wonder what he's going to do next. My stomach curls in expectation, but he just stands there, looking dashing.

"You know it does when you say it like that. Anyway, after I grab some new underwear, I'm going to head to the beach and help Juni for an hour or so and then take some photos of some tourists. I should be back by late afternoon, and we can go to Cocktails & Chaos tonight with everyone. Does that sound good?"

"Sounds like a plan to me," he says in a dry voice. "You seem like you have a busy day. Already had enough of my presence back in town?" The elevator pings before I can respond, and he holds his arm out. "After you, my lady."

"Thanks. When did you become such a gentleman?"

"I've always been a gentleman. I guess you just didn't notice."

"I guess not," I say as I step out into the hallway. I am acutely aware of him as we walk toward the bedroom, and I groan as I realize I left my door key inside the hotel room. "Don't suppose you remembered your key, did you?"

"Would I forget?" he says as he pulls his key out of his dark leather wallet and opens the door. "Who woulda thought that your hero saves the day again."

"My hero?" I giggle as I step inside and decide against asking him what that word means to him.

For all I know, he'll pick me up and carry me across the room, pretending he's Tarzan and I'm Jane. While I've always enjoyed our playful antics, it feels different now.

It is different now.

Not that I'm going to dwell on that fact.

I'm surprised to see that the housekeeping service has already made our bed. I'm reminded of the evening before as I stare at the lush pillows and the silky sheets. Memories of delicate touches, sultry moans, and illicit heat fill me.

It was just some fun, Mia. Get a grip. It was practice. You and Luke are consummate professionals, preparing for the role of a lifetime. Get it together now!

"I should get going now. Do you want to come with me, or are you going to stay here and work?"

Or do you want to take me real quick so we can make sure we have the right amount of passion flowing?

Get your mind out of the gutter, Mia.

"I think I'd like to see your place," he says. "I can bring my laptop with me, and then I'll work at Salty Sirens afterward. Hopefully, there aren't too many tourists there."

"We are in peak season, Luke. You know tourists love to come here for the summer. It will be busy."

"I know. I thought it just used to be snowbirds, but I guess word got out, and now everyone from all over the country comes for the summer as well."

"You know the surf contest is coming up, and there are—"

"Don't tell me. Lots of hot surfers you want to say hello to." He rolls his eyes. "You upset you can't flirt with any this summer?"

"No, why would I be upset?"

He's giving me a weird look, and I don't want to ask him why he's looking at me like that. I also don't want to talk about flirting with other men right now. I need to break the awkward moment, so I change the subject.

"Don't you need to go to your grandparents' house and pick up your suitcase?"

"No, my grandfather told me my luggage was in his car, so he's going to give it to the concierge, and they'll just bring it up for me."

"Oh, nice. Did you notice that our grandmothers were giving us a look?"

"I did notice how they were staring at us. Everyone was paying attention to us, almost more than they were Rex and Andi."

"Do you think everyone bought we are together?"

"I don't know, but what I do know is that our grandmas love puzzles and trying to figure stuff out. By the way, what's the note that you got for the treasure hunt?"

"Oh, I forgot to show you. Let me grab it."

I dig into my pink-and-purple cotton bag and dig through the numerous contents. My fingers brush past Tic Tacs, lipstick, my wallet, goggles, dried tissues, a small notebook, some random shells, until I feel the stiff envelope that contains the note card with the treasure hunt information. I slide the card out of the envelope and stare at the colorful, illustrated map.

"So, it has this map, and there's a typewritten clue on the back." I hand it to him. "I'm not really sure what it means or how to figure it out."

"Who sent it to you?" He looks at the front of the card and then turns it over, scanning it quickly.

Luke has always been the smart one. The analytical one. When we played board games, he always won, but I didn't really care. I wasn't competitive like that.

"I have no clue. It was anonymous."

"Let me see if I can figure it out."

He scrunches up his face, and I know he's in deep thought. He runs his fingers along the top of the card, like he's feeling for some extra clue. I can't help but notice how neat and manicured his fingernails are.

"Let me read the clue."

A treasure awaits on an island.
The island is big; the island is small.
A treasure awaits somewhere rocky.
Don't trip, or you'll fall.
Gold, silver, bounty aplenty.
Do your very best to come and find me.

"I have absolutely no clue what that is meant to tell me," I admit with a hearty laugh. I'm not embarrassed to admit that none of those words are resonating with me in any way.

"No clue whatsoever?" He heads to the dark gray linen couch and takes a seat, adjusting the fluffy cream throw pillows behind him. He stretches his legs out and leans back. "Wanna have a seat?"

I head over to the couch and take a seat next to him, careful not to sit too close. I don't need his legs pressed up against mine. I don't need my body reaching one hundred twenty degrees because it gets too excited. I also don't need to find myself in the middle of a therapy session, questioning why I'm all of a sudden thinking of my best friend naked.

"I'm kind of wondering if this is like some hidden bounty somewhere or something." He taps his fingers against his thigh. "Or something that relates to riches."

"What? Like missing gold?" My voice sounds far too excited. "Like hundreds of millions of gold bullion bars that were hidden by pirates and now it's our opportunity to find the missing treasure?"

"Mia, you watch too many movies." There's warmth in his gaze as he shakes his head. "You're not Mikey, and I'm not Chunk."

"I'm not talking about *The Goonies,* though that would be cool. Man, we watched that movie so many times in sixth grade."

"Only, like, two hundred times." He shifts on the couch and faces me. "What do the Goonies never say?"

"Die." We both whisper at the same time, sharing a smile that takes us back to our childhood.

He holds his finger up, and I press my finger against his, like we did when we were younger. Suddenly, I'm eleven years old again, sitting with Luke on his grandparents' couch, eating popcorn, watching a movie, while our grandmas sit at the dining room table, playing cards and gossiping with the other busy Bees. A memory of him pausing the movie, turning to me, and asking me if I would ever want to go on an adventure with him hits me.

I can clearly remember my answer. *"Anytime of day."*

And I can remember his responding happy grin.

Warmth hits me as we finally move our fingers back.

"I wasn't talking about *The Goonies,*" I say finally. "I was talking about that show on Netflix about those kids who were looking for gold."

"You're going to have to give me more than that."

"*Outer Banks*. You didn't watch it?"

"*Outer* what?"

The expression on his face tells me he's never heard of the show, and I vow then and there that I will make him watch it with me. A twinge of despondency hits me when I realize it will likely have to be over the phone. We don't have enough time with all the festivities to watch the show in its entirety. Not if we want to sleep.

"*Outer Banks*. It's set in the Outer Banks of North Carolina, and it's about these kids—"

"You'll have to tell me another time." He frowns as he looks at his watch and jumps up. "We should get going. Sorry, I have a call in an hour. Let's go to your place first. I'll have a look, and then I'll head to Salty Sirens. They still have that spot in the back to work in quiet, right? I can't miss this call."

He pulls his phone out and starts typing something rapidly. I've lost his attention.

"You have a call in an hour, Luke? Really? This is your first day here."

I'm annoyed. We haven't even finished discussing the treasure hunt clue.

"Technically, it's my second." He looks up from his phone. "You're headed to work today as well, right? We'll both get shit done."

"I know, but I'm not on vacation. I live in Coconut Beach."

"And I used to live on the island too."

"But you're on holiday, Luke. You haven't been back home in ages. We haven't spent real time together in years. I thought you'd want to see what I do at the bookmobile, catch up with Juni in a meaningful way, check out our old spots again."

"I wish I could, but I still have a job." His voice sounds pained. "I'm working on a really big deal, Mi-Mi. This is the deal of my life. I close this, and I am officially a big deal. I close this, and I can show everyone that I—"

"I know," I sigh as I cut him off.

I don't want to continuously go on about him having to work, but I really wanted to spend some quality time with him. I wanted him to say that he'd left his job back in the city and was once again on island time. I just wanted us to hang out by the beach. I wanted him to sell books with me. I wanted him to take me up on the offer of finding him a romance book. I wanted us to read steamy romance scenes together and laugh at some of the crazy sex positions that authors wrote about. I just wanted to spend time with him in person, doing nothing and everything. And more than that, I wanted him to want that as well. But I overestimated his ability to walk away from his job for even a day.

"So, this looks like an old map of Coconut Beach," he says, his eyes narrowed as he holds up the card. "Notice that the mark appears to be the waterfalls at Hidden Cove."

He points to the right of the card, and I nod. He's good at changing the subject when he doesn't want to argue or is just ready to move on from a topic. It irritates the heck out of me, but I don't want to argue with him. Plus, I'm not sure if I'm being unreasonable or not.

"Where the big *X* is?"

"Yes, and you notice there's a number one, two, three, and four on the map?"

I grab the card from him again and survey it. "I didn't before, but now I do. What do you think it means?"

"I think it means that we go in order. We have to find whatever's at number one first, and I think it will give us a clue how to get to number two."

"But how do we find where number one is?"

"That I don't know." He shakes his head. "I'm curious who sent this to you though."

"Do you think I should even bother trying to figure it out or just forget it, seeing as we're already super busy?"

"No, we have to do it. We've always loved a challenge. It's fun, right? Plus, we have two weeks. We'll find the treasure."

"Yeah, that would be cool." I don't remind him that he was always the one that loved a challenge and I was the one who just went along with them because our adventures were always fun. Being with Luke was always exciting and we always had each other laughing. Our temperaments just seemed to fit each other. "I mean, if you can take time away from your job."

"I'm sure I'll find some time. Can I hold on to this?" he says. "I feel like there has to be a clue in the actual message at the back. It's not just a fun poem. I want to study it a bit more."

"Sure, maybe we can also talk about it tonight at Cocktails & Chaos with the girls. Maybe one of them will have some ideas."

"Sounds good to me. Shall we get going? We just need to pick up my rental car. I can get the keys down in the lobby."

"Ooh. What did you get? A Mercedes, Lambo, Rolls-Royce?"

"No, Mia, a Jeep."

"Oh."

"Disappointed?" His eyes crinkle as he bends down to grab his leather satchel and places his laptop into it.

"Jeeps are fun." *Not as fun as Lamborghinis though.*

"Yeah, they are. Especially if we go off-roading."

"We're not going off-roading, Luke."

We head back out of the hotel room and toward the elevator, and I can't help, but notice that he moves with such a confident gait. He's really grown up. He is all man now. I swallow hard at the thought. He's all man in all ways.

Not that I care. Or even really notice.

"Not even once? I promise I won't feed you to any gators or snakes."

"You're not fooling me again, Luke." I giggle as we step into the elevator and head down to the lobby. It must have just been cleaned because it smells like Lysol, and I rub my nose. "I still remember when we were in high school, and we used to spend our days together doing every harebrained idea you came up with. It's really good, having you back here, but I'm the big boss now. You're my sidekick now, hon."

"I'm meant to be your sidekick?" He chuckles, like he knows that I know there's no way that's going to happen. "What's that supposed to mean?"

"I'm just saying that it's nice, having you to do things with."

"You mean, like you're the boss, and I'm just your manservant to do what you want with?"

"That's not what I'm saying, Luke." I giggle. "But, yes, I'm the boss."

"I see. So, is this some sort of subservient relationship? Am I your sub, Mia?"

"My sub?" Cue my racing heart. These conversations are different from when we were younger. But then we never explored in this way before. Even if it was for a performance. "You mean, my submissive?" I burst out laughing at the quizzical look on his face. Luke always knows how to make me laugh. "In what world would anyone think that you were my submissive?"

"Maybe in the world where everyone knows that you're a bossy boots who wants to have her wicked way with me while also—"

He stops as the elevator beeps again, and Rex and Andi enter, looking like they were just arguing.

"Why, hello, Mia." Rex immediately steps next to me, then glances over at his brother in disdain. "Hi, Luke." Then he looks me up and down like he's trying to undress me with his eyes. "Where are you guys off to?"

Andi stands to the front, looking uncomfortable.

"We're just going to head over to Mia's place and then to the beach and to her bookstore." Luke sidles next to me and wraps his arm around my waist.

I can see Rex staring at his hand and then smirking. I make eyes with him while leaning back into Luke.

Rex runs his hands through his short blond hair, and once again I'm reminded of how different they are in terms of looks. Both of them are gorgeous, of course, but Rex is the typical surfer type with his dirty-blond hair and his bright blue eyes. He resembles their mother, except for his build, which is strong and muscular, like his father. Mr. Haverbrook was also a football player and was quarterback of the football team at the University of Florida when he was younger, which is why I think he gravitated toward Rex more than Luke, even though Luke resembled his father more.

"So, what's the plan for tonight?" Rex asks. "Are you guys going to go for a special dinner to celebrate not having seen each other in a long time?"

"We're going to hang out with some of our friends." I frown.

Rex looks at me and laughs. "Weird flex, bro."

"What does that mean?"

I can hear the tension in Luke's voice and feel it in his touch as well.

"Not what I'd be doing tonight if I hadn't seen my girl in a really long time. No way I'd want to go and hang out with her friends instead of banging the living daylights out of her."

"Rex"—Andi presses her hand against his side as she turns around —"that's really rude and uncalled for."

"What? If we hadn't seen each other in a long time, wouldn't you want to bang me?" He reaches out and slaps her ass lightly. "You know you can't get enough of tiring me out."

"Well, yeah"—she giggles slightly—"but we're not like everyone. Maybe they are saving themselves for marriage and not into going all night long like we are."

"What is that supposed to mean?" Luke says, gazing over at her, looking pissed and offended.

"It doesn't take someone with superhuman vision to figure it out. We've all noticed that you guys don't seem like you're super affectionate with each other." She shrugs.

"In what ways?"

"I don't know. It's not like you're desperately in love and you can't keep your hands off of each other. Not like me and Rex."

Rex grabs her and pulls her into him. He pushes her back against the elevator wall and kisses her hard. I watch in horror as he reaches down and gives her boobs a quick squeeze and then pulls back. She giggles like a schoolgirl and taps him on the shoulder.

"Oh, Rex, honey, you're so naughty."

"What? I'm just saying, if you're really into your girl, everyone knows it. And when I look at you two"—he sniffs and sneers—"I'm not feeling it." He stares at me. "There are two types of men in this world. The kind you want to ride all night long and those you want to chitter-chatter with. I don't care about idle talk, but I'll have you panting like a motherfucker."

He waggles his tongue back and forth, and I try not to gag. Has Rex always been this crude?

"I don't manhandle my woman just to make a point," Luke says as he pulls me in tighter to him. "But let me make this very clear to both of you. Mia is mine, and whether or not you think she's mine because of the way we handle each other in public doesn't mean anything because we know the way that we interact in private. Don't we, darling?"

He looks down at me with adoration in his eyes, and I swallow hard because he's looking at me so intensely and my body is shivering, and I think he might be about to kiss me.

I glance over at Rex, and then I look at Andi. They just stand there, looking like they're judging us. Like they think Luke and I are asexual and boring. There's no way I'm letting Rex get away with that diatribe, trying to put us both down. Like he thought I wished I could ride him.

I have no interest in riding you, prick, nor do I need your tongue anywhere near me.

I stand on my tiptoes, and I grab Luke's head. I press my lips against him and kiss him hard. He wraps his arms around me and holds me tight, and he kisses me back passionately. I feel his tongue pressing against my lips, and I part my lips, pressing myself into him when Rex slams his fist against the elevator. The sound makes us both jump.

"Get a room, guys." Rex sounds pissed, and we spring back from each other.

I feel slightly off-kilter, and my heart races rapidly.

"What? We couldn't resist," Luke says, smirking at him. "Don't tell me you have a problem with our need for touch and contact now."

"I don't have a problem with anything." The elevator dings, and Rex pushes past everyone to exit in a huff.

"Sorry about my brother. He wasn't raised like that," Luke says and allows Andi to head out of the elevator before us.

I step out next, and then Luke follows behind. We make our way through the almost-empty lobby in silence. I suddenly remember that Luke has to get the key to the Jeep from the lobby.

"You forgot to get the key," I say to him, breaking the silence.

"Ah, yes." He looks at me, but he doesn't head back inside. "That was pretty intense," he says, gazing at my lips.

"It was definitely intense, but I think the kiss was definitely needed to make Rex and Andi realize we are really together." I nod slowly.

"I agree," Luke says solemnly. "I think we played the part well."

"Yeah, we could be up for a Golden Globe soon."

"I don't know about that." He grins. "Maybe one day."

"Well, hey, I don't know that I could have done it much better."

"I don't know about that," he says with a grin. "It wasn't bad, but I could tutor you to make your kisses just a little bit better."

"How generous of you, Luke. You'd lower yourself from hedge fund manager to kissing coach? I'm sure I can find someone else—"

"There will be no one else touching those lips right now. Just me."

His gaze darkens, and I swallow hard as I think about our kiss. It felt so sweet, so real … almost like we were really together.

You don't want to be with Luke like that, Mia. This is just an act.

"Do you think that we are making a—"

"Don't ask me again if you think we are making a mistake. I don't want you to ask me that again for the rest of the summer, okay?" He frowns. "We're already in this, Mia. We've already committed to this relationship for the summer. We can handle Rex."

"But, Luke—"

"We've already made our decision, Mia. We said we are going to do this, so we do it right, and we stop second-guessing everything, okay?

We do what we've got to do. Let's make sure that Rex knows his place."

"I suppose you're right. I just ... I just don't want the lines to become so blurred that we get confused ourselves."

"Not going to happen. We're Luke and Mia. We know each other better than most married couples."

"In some ways, but not in all ways ..."

"We could learn each other in all ways as well." He winks, and I flush.

"Very funny, Luke."

"I'm just joking." He checks his watch, and I know he's thinking about work again. "Just remember, we need to make sure that everyone believes that this relationship is real. Rex can't get away with treating us like shit."

"I wonder if people are buying it or not though."

"They're buying it in droves. Trust me! That's why Rex is getting so mad."

"Are you doing this because you can't stand him?" I already know the answer.

"Uh, yeah." His expression darkens as he thinks about their history. "Mia?"

"Yeah?"

"We want to one-up him, right? We both want to walk away from this, feeling like we showed him, right?"

"Yeah."

"Good." He looks pleased. "Do you know what I was thinking about the other day?"

"No clue. Wait, let me see if I can guess. You were thinking about watching a boring horror or sci-fi movie?"

"Hey now, I love a good sci-fi movie."

"Trust me, I know. I've watched far too many with you and fallen asleep."

"I wasn't thinking about my awesome taste in movies. I was thinking about those emails that you sent me when you were, like, eighteen."

"Which emails?" I know exactly which emails, but I'm not going to admit I remember. The embarrassment is still high.

"You know, the ones where you said if we're both single when we're forty, we should get married."

"Oh, I forgot about them." *Liar!*

"I was thinking that if we are single at forty and we have to get married, at least we know we won't absolutely hate kissing each other."

"I suppose that's true, but I really hope I'm not single at forty."

"Oh?" He gives me an odd look, and I feel my heart racing.

"Why? Do you think I will be?"

"Not at all," he says softly. "A good woman like you … any man would be happy to snatch you up." He nods slowly. "And I'm sure one will. Stay here. I'll be right back," he says, and he does an about-face and heads back into the hotel lobby.

I stand there next to the tall planters and vases and admire the bright pink bougainvillea that is directly next to the white wall. It's tall and beautiful, and it provides a welcome burst of color next to the row of tall palm trees that stand proudly on each side of the expansive driveway. The wind has picked up today, and I watch as the leaves sway back and forth, like they're bowing to the cars entering the grounds. I take a deep breath of the ocean air and let the fresh air free my mind from focusing on the last twenty-four hours of interactions with Luke. I can almost hear the wind calling out to me, asking if I've lost my mind.

Don't think about it, Mia. Don't question anything. Just go with it.

I don't want to think about the kiss in the elevator. I don't want to think about why we're really doing this.

Are we really doing this because of Rex and his rude notes? Deep inside, I don't know. But I also know I don't want to fixate on the change in our dynamic. I just want to enjoy the next two weeks of summer with my best friend. I just want to enjoy being with Luke one-on-one, and as far as I'm concerned, that's all that really matters—having fun and making everyone believe that we're in love. I don't question that we've already done things that purely platonic friends would never do, but then we have a special friendship. We both know our experimenting means nothing.

It's not like we actually want each other or anything like that.

Not at all.

chapter thirteen

Luke

"I think everyone's already here," Mia says as we make our way down the beach toward Cocktails & Chaos.

She's still slightly miffed that I spent the entire day working and not hanging out with her and Juniper at their store.

The bustling tiki bar greets us with open arms as we head past the stools toward the bar. It's always been one of my favorite spots on the beach, with its wide-open seating and casual vibe. I can hear the ocean waves lapping against the rocks in the distance as we make our way to grab some drinks and meet up with her friends.

"Ready to put on a show?" Mia beams at me, her eyes sparkling from the silver eye shadow she applied abundantly to her upper eyelids.

I'm glad she's not going to give me the silent treatment.

"I am ready," I say, following behind her as she looks around for her friends.

She's wearing a short red dress that amplifies her slender calves and her shapely ass. I try not to stare at her body too much, even though I'm pleased to note that if someone does catch me checking her out, they'll think it's because we're dating.

"Oh, look, there are Wendy and Juniper." She rushes across the bar toward her friends. "Hey, guys, we're finally here."

"Hey, Mia." Juniper gives her a quick hug and then looks over at me. "Looking mighty handsome there tonight, Luke."

"Now, now. Anyone would think you're hitting on me, Juniper."

I give her a quick hug, and she giggles before turning back to Mia.

"You look gorgeous. That dress is stunning."

"Thank you. I had to step it up now that I have a boyfriend." Sarcasm drips from her tone, and I reach over and poke her. Her eyes flash at me as she grabs my hand to stop me.

She looks over at Wendy. "How are you doing, Wendy? How's the bed-and-breakfast?"

"We're surviving one day at a time." Wendy looks hopeful as she leans forward. "Right now, our top guest is proving to be quite challenging."

"Oh," I ask her, "is there anything you need my help with?"

"She doesn't mean challenging in that way, Luke." Mia shakes her head, her eyes shining.

"What does she mean?" I look over at Wendy, who is now blushing, while Juniper grins.

"I'll explain to you as we grab a drink. Do you girls want anything?" Mia asks them as she grabs my hand.

"We're good," Juniper says, holding up a fruity pink cocktail in her hand. "You should get one of the pink flamingo specials now while Cal isn't so busy." She takes a long sip. "It is soo good."

"Will do," Mia says. "Come on, Luke."

She squeezes my hand, and I look over at her in surprise.

"Who knows who could be spying on us?" she whispers. "Your brother, my brother—they could be here. Or their friends. They both know so many people in town who would happily tell them that we're here, and they will report everything that they witness."

"True." I frown slightly. "By the way, what's up with Rafe? Why is he acting so annoyed with me?"

"You mean, why is he such a jackass?" she asks, rolling her eyes.

"Well, I wouldn't have put it in those words, but, yeah, what's his problem?"

"I'm not really sure," she says, though she looks down.

There's something more there, but I'm not going to push it.

"I think he's just taking his role as my overprotective brother too far, you know?"

"You think so? He seems overly harsh."

"I guess maybe it has to do with something that happened two summers ago." She nibbles on her lower lip. "But I don't know."

"What do you mean? What happened two summers ago?" I stiffen as I gaze at her.

She blanches and recoils for a few moments before plastering a smile on her face. There's something there, but I'm not going to push it. Now is not the time or the place. I can't help but feel disappointed though. Why hasn't Mia shared that with me before? Is this something I missed because I no longer lived in Coconut Beach? Has she not told me because she forgot, or has she not told me because she doesn't trust me enough to know? The thought makes me sad while also making me realize that even though we are still the best of friends, we've lost something in the long distance. Something I never realized before. But I know in the past, Mia never kept anything from me. She was more open than an open book.

"Nothing to worry about. We can talk about it later."

"Mia? Is there something that—"

"We'll talk about it later, Luke." She gives me a look, and I just nod, though now my heart is beating, and my mind is racing, and all sorts of things are crossing my mind. What could have happened two summers ago that had Rafe being so overprotective over Mia?

"Hey, guys." Cal offers us a wide smile as we approach. His golden-tan skin is the envy of every man on the beach, along with his silky jet-black hair. "Looking like a male model still, Cal," I joke.

"And you're looking like a rich tourist, Luke." He shakes his head and laughs. "Actually, I'm joking. You look rich and cool, but not like a douche, like most of the tourists who come to town." He whips a towel over his shoulder and grabs some glasses. "I'm totally jealous that you're making so much money."

"You have nothing to be jealous about. How are you doing?"

"I'm good. You heard I'm getting married?" He cocks his head to the side. "Want some drinks?"

"Heard something about you and Silvie." I nod and look over at Mia. "I'll have a beer. What would you like, Mia?"

"Yeah, Silvie needs to get married and needs it to happen soon." He fills a glass with beer. "And I'm the lucky bachelor who gets to make that happen."

"You are lucky." Mia smiles. "I'll have a strawberry daiquiri, please."

"Really, Mia?"

"What? I love them."

"I know, but I just thought you would've grown into a more sophisticated drink."

"Do I look like the sort of girl that wants to grow into a more sophisticated drink?" she says, giggling.

"No, I guess not." I look around the bar. "It's busy tonight. I don't know that I've ever seen it this busy."

"It's summer," Mia says by way of explanation. "It's always busy in Coconut Beach in the summer."

"I guess I just forgot," I say, still thinking that it's even busier than I ever remembered.

"Yeah, I guess because you haven't been back home in ages."

"Touché." I frown slightly at her tone.

She still has a smile on her face, but there's something in her voice that makes me think she's not joking one hundred percent. Is she upset that I haven't been back to town recently? We still speak on the phone all the time, and yet she keeps bringing up my absence.

"So, Luke, tell me how the big city is treating you," Cal says as he hands me the beer. "You know, my mom was reading the paper the other day, and she saw your name mentioned in some article."

"She saw me?" I ask in surprise, not that I've been in the paper. I am always in the paper for brokering deals, but more so that his mom saw one of the articles.

"She read an article about you and I guess the company you work for." He shrugs. "Can't remember the details."

"Oh, it's no big deal."

"Aren't you one of the players in one of the biggest mergers that has occurred in the last twenty years?"

"I wouldn't say that I'm personally in it, but I am brokering the deal for the hedge fund I work with." I shouldn't really say too much. "It's outside my normal scope of work, which generally consists of investing billionaires' funds in the international and domestic markets."

"What is it exactly that you do?" he says as he hands me her fruity, bright red drink.

She takes it eagerly, and I watch as she takes a gulp and gets frosted ice all over her top lip. I'd love to lick it off.

"Well, I'm just a numbers guy." I look away from her lips and back to Cal. "I make sure the numbers make sense while also working with legal to ensure any kickbacks or deals are in within the realms of the law."

"Sounds complicated." Mia offers me a sweet little smile before taking another sip. "I get it though, your job has to be important because you're always working."

"I'm not always working."

"Let's be for real here, every time I talk to you, you're usually at work."

"Sometimes, I'm at home."

"Yeah, that's true. Sometimes, you're at home, having just got off of work. And we'll chat for a bit before you have to get back to work."

"Are you upset that I have a job?" I question her.

Her tone is light, but the comments seem pointed.

"Why would I be upset that you have a job?" She shrugs.

"I don't know. I just—"

"Hey, I'm not causing trouble in paradise, am I?" Cal holds up his hand and bows his head. "It's the evening, and it's a nice night. Enjoy the ambiance."

"Thanks, Cal. Do you know if Silvie's coming tonight?" I ask him, curious what was going on there.

Mia gives me a look like I just got her in trouble, and I just chug some of my beer in response.

"I think she is. I know Birdy wanted to talk to her about something, so I'm not one hundred percent sure she's going to make it. I can call her and ask her if you want."

"No, that's okay. If I see her, I see her."

"I did see your brother earlier," he says. "He was looking for you and Luke."

"He was?" Mia makes a face. "Do you know why?"

"No idea. He just asked if I'd seen you. I said no, but then I told him that Juniper was here, and you'd likely be here later, and he kind of just hurried off. Is he with her?"

"No, he's not." Mia looks back over to Juniper. "She didn't even mention seeing him actually."

"You want to start a tab, Luke?" Cal looks at me.

I hand him my credit card. "Put the drinks for all the girls on this tonight."

"You don't have to do that," Mia says, shaking her head.

"It's my treat," I say. "What good am I if I'm not the sort of boyfriend who will buy you and your girlfriends drinks?"

"True," she says. "I don't want a cheap-ass boyfriend."

"I'd hate to be a cheap-ass boyfriend." I look across the bar, and I see a couple of women looking over at me intently. My eyes move past them until I register that one of them is Talia. "We've got company," I say, lowering my voice. "Play lovey-dovey."

"Huh?" Mia puts her arms around me and presses herself against me. She gazes into my eyes and sways back and forth. "Don't tell me it's Rex," she hisses against my lips.

I kinda want to pretend that it is. I want to see what she'll do if she thinks it's him, but I don't lie.

"No, I haven't seen him, but I do see Talia."

"Of course she would be here tonight." Mia rolls her eyes. "I can't stand—"

"I know you can't stand her."

"She's just horrible. You want to dance?" Mia asks as she takes another sip of her strawberry daiquiri before placing it down on the bar top.

"I don't think so," I say, shaking my head.

I've never been much of a dancer—not when we were ten and she wanted to do breakdancing, not when we were fifteen and she wanted to practice twerking, not when we were eighteen and she wanted to learn how to slow dance, and certainly not now.

"Come on, Luke. Why won't you dance with me?"

"Because I don't have rhythm and—"

"Oh, I thought I saw you there, Luke." Talia's sultry voice is suddenly beside us.

I turn to the side and give her a warm smile, like we weren't trying to avoid her.

"Hey, how are you this evening?"

"Good. Tired, of course. I've been putting a lot of work into the planning for Rex and Andi's wedding. They just demand so much, but I suppose when you're a Haverbrook, you want the finest?" She sniffs and gives Mia a judging look.

"I guess that's true," I say. "Though I have no idea what Rex is demanding from you for this wedding."

"Hopefully he's not demanding anything. He's such a good guy. He said Andi can have whatever she wants because she's the love of his life." She looks over at Mia. "Does that hurt to hear that?" Her tone is full of fake pity. She's as fake as her double Ds.

"Why would that hurt?" Mia's tone is stiff and obviously pissed.

"Well, you know, because you were *pining* for him for so long."

"I wasn't pining for him. I don't know what you're talking about."

"We all knew you wanted him, and he didn't want you."

"I don't even know what you're talking about, Talia." Mia presses her lips together, and I hold on to her hand tightly before rubbing her lower back in a circular motion.

"What? Like you didn't have a crush on him in high school? Like you didn't tell the whole world that you thought he was going to be your husband?"

"I was a teenager then, and now I have Luke."

"True. I guess when you can't get the first prize, you settle for second."

I press my lips together at her words. I'm not going to let Talia offend me. I don't care what she thinks, but the words still sting.

"I'm not settling for anything," Mia says and squeezes my hand back, her eyes searching mine. "You know that, right, honey?"

"Yeah, of course."

My heart aches though because I know the fact of the matter is that it's true. Mia always had a thing for Rex, not for me. She wanted to be with him. She talked endlessly for months about how she could attract him, about how amazing it would be if she married him and if she became my sister—which, at one point, made me want to gouge out my ears and my eyes, but of course I didn't say anything to her. How did you tell your best friend that you didn't want her to become your sister? How did you tell your best friend that the last thing on your mind was helping her to catch the attention of the brother you couldn't stand? There was no way on earth I wanted her with him. The very thought of it made me feel sick.

"So, anyway, Luke," Talia says, almost purring, "do you remember that time when you were in college and you came back one summer and we all went skinny-dipping down at the beach?"

Fuck, why is she bringing that up now?

"What?" Mia suddenly steps back, her expression pissed. "What are you talking about?"

My back stiffens as I see the hurt in her eyes.

"Oh, he didn't tell you?" Talia says, giggling and touching my arm, like she's trying to claim me. "Luke, you didn't tell your girlfriend about *that* night?" She speaks seductively, and I can tell that she's trying to rile Mia up.

"I guess not. I don't even remember." I look over at Mia to

nonverbally tell her that it wasn't a big deal. It wasn't a big deal, though I know, to Mia, it will be.

"Really, Luke? You don't remember us skinny-dipping?" Talia giggles and looks down at the front of my pants. "I certainly haven't forgotten one moment of that night."

"You went skinny-dipping with Talia?"

"To clarify, it wasn't just Talia there. There were some other people." It's how I know she doesn't naturally have double Ds, but I'm not going to say that.

"Where was I?" Mia presses her lips together. She looks furious now.

"Um, I'm not sure where you were. Maybe you and Juniper were hanging out and doing something."

I don't tell her that I knew exactly where she was. I don't tell her that I knew she went on a date with some surfer from California who was in town for the surf competition. I don't tell her that his name was Jake and that his dad worked in Silicon Valley. I don't tell her that I can still remember how blue his eyes were and how blond he was. I don't tell her that I can hear the way she went on and on about what a great surfer he was. I don't tell her that I saw the way that he stared at her, the way he played with her blonde hair, the way she wrapped her arms around him as she sat in his lap and kissed him on the cheek. I don't tell her how she ignored me when I wanted to chat with her about college because she had her summer dalliance with some surfer she probably wouldn't even remember now.

I am certainly not going to tell her that when I was invited to go to the beach party that night, I went because I just wanted to forget about her and what she was doing. I don't tell her that Talia and some of the other girls jumped on me naked and that they tried to entice me, but I wasn't even interested. I don't tell her any of that because I don't even want to think about it. I don't want to acknowledge that the entire night, I thought about her.

"It was fun. Wasn't it, darling?" Talia strokes her fingers down my forearm and eyes me in a way that would make anyone watching think that we had been intimate, even though we never had. "We were naked and … well, I don't know that you want to know everything that happened." Talia giggles coquettishly and looks at Mia. "We almost had a threesome, but I suppose he didn't tell you that either."

Mia looks more pissed than I've ever seen her. "No, he didn't. I'm going to go and speak to Juniper. You can find me over there."

She stomps off, and I let out a low sigh.

"Really, Talia?"

"What? It's not my fault your girlfriend is jealous. But why didn't you tell her?" she says, gazing at me. "Is it because you wish that something had happened that night? Maybe you're looking at me right now, wishing that it could still happen?"

"No, Talia." I shake my head. "That's the furthest thing from the truth."

"It still can, you know?" She licks her lips slowly, the tip of her tongue darting like a snake slithering in the sand. "I've always wanted to have a Haverbrook brother. And to be honest, I'd rather have you than Rex. You know, you've always been the talk of the town."

"I'm not sure what you're saying." I frown.

"Everyone knows Rex. He was the football star and the tall, blond god. But really, we all wanted you, Luke. You had to know that, right? With your dark hair and your blue eyes and those muscles, and you were so quiet and demure. No one wants the big, brash, loud guy who's fucking every woman he can get. We all want the sexy man with secrets in his eyes. At least, I know I always did."

She leans forward and blows into my ear. "I'd love to suck that big cock of yours. Just let me know, and I'd be down." She sucks on my earlobe and tugs gently before stepping back.

"Your girlfriend looks like she wants to kill me right now." She runs her fingers through her short blonde bob and laughs. "But let me know, Luke. I'm yours whenever you want me."

She steps back and disappears into the crowd, and I just stand there, chugging on my beer.

"Holy shit, what the fuck was that about?"

I look up and see Cal standing there, observing me.

"You okay?"

"I just feel like I am in the middle of something absolutely crazy," I say as I step toward the bar and look around to make sure that no one's listening to us. "What is with the women in Coconut Beach?"

"I think there's something in the water," he says, laughing. "I just don't understand why they've all gone mad."

"Oh, why? What's going on with you?"

"It's just Silvie. She's gotten under my skin."

"In a good way or in a bad way?"

"Fuck if I know." He shakes his head and chuckles. "Hey, you want another beer?"

"Sure. You want one as well? On me."

"Thanks, Luke. You know what? I think I will have one." I watch as he pours IPAs into two frosted glasses and hands me one. "So, what's really going on with you and Mia?"

"Silvie didn't tell you?"

"Not really, I heard a little bit. You guys are pretending to be together for the wedding, right?"

"Yeah. Rex left some really rude notes on my and Mia's wedding invite, and we decided, why let Rex think he's better than us? So, we're pretending we're together."

"You think that's smart?" He gives me a look.

"What do you mean?"

"Let's just say, she's a cute girl. I know you know she's a cute girl."

"What's that supposed to mean, Cal?"

"You don't think all these years of you guys coming to the bar, I haven't noticed?" He leans toward me with a knowing look.

"Notice what?"

"You want to play dumb? I can play dumb, but I'm just saying, she's a hot girl. She's not just going to be single forever, you know." He chuckles. "Playing these lovey-dovey games ... well, they can lead to complications. Trust me, I've got my own." He shakes his head. "These hot blondes are going to drive us crazy." He looks to the side and then starts laughing. "Those girls are trouble, aren't they?"

"What do you mean?" I turn my gaze from him, and I notice that Mia and Juniper are now standing on the bar top at the far end of the bar and dancing in time to the music that is playing.

"She's crazy. She's going to fall." I shake my head as I watch her effortless dancing.

She looks like she's having the time of her life in her sexy red dress, and I can't help but think what it would be like if she were dancing on me.

"You know she likes to dance on a bar top. She does this frequently."

"How frequently?"

I gaze at him, and he holds up his hand.

"I plead the Fifth, Your Honor."

"I'm not an attorney, I'm not a judge, and we're not in court."

"Let's just say, she likes to have fun. All the girls do."

I watch as Juniper and Mia dance around while Wendy is standing there, laughing. They all look like they are having fun.

"I'm glad she has good friends here. I think it makes me feel less guilty about not having been back home in a while."

I know Mia misses me. I miss her as well. I just couldn't be around her, couldn't always be wanting her, knowing I couldn't have her. Even now, being here with her for two weeks feels like the sweetest pleasure and the sweetest torture.

Mia spins around, the skirt of her dress clinging to her ass. She's laughing at something that Juniper said, and I watch as she throws her head back and then takes too long of a sip from her drink. I love watching Mia dance.

I watch as Juniper gets down and says something to Wendy, and both girls giggle. However, Mia stays on top of the bar and continues moving back and forth. I'm about to head over when I see that Rafe is suddenly standing next to me.

"Hey." I offer him a friendly smile, but he eyes me and just nods.

"You want a beer or something? I've got a tab with Cal, and I can get you one."

"Thanks." He doesn't move. "We cool, Luke?"

"I don't know. Are we?"

"I think so. Don't hurt my sister, okay?"

"What are you talking about?"

"Your brother broke her heart when she was a teenager, and you know as well as I do that Mia likes to get carried away. She's in love with love, and I just don't like her keeping these secrets."

"What do you mean?"

"You guys have been dating for a year, and she didn't even tell me." He frowns like he still can't believe it. "And that's not good. She shouldn't be hiding shit like this. It's not healthy."

I don't know what to say.

"Look, I'm just saying, sometimes, when things are born out of lies, that's a bad sign."

He looks over, and I see him watching Wendy and Juniper as they dance back and forth.

"Look at Mia. She's going to fall and break her ankle. Then she's going to wake up tomorrow, and she's going to wonder how she did it."

"I won't let her fall," I say.

He looks at me and chuckles.

We head over to the other side of the bar, and I look up at Mia, who is eyeing me with a half smile. She's still annoyed with me, but she's trying to let it go. For now.

"Join me, Lukey."

"No thank you. You already know I don't like dancing, let alone on a bar top."

"You're no fun."

"Well, that's not what you said last night."

"Whatever." She giggles.

I look over at Rafe, and he's frowning.

"It was just a joke," I say quickly.

"Uh-huh. Hey there, Juniper, Wendy. Good to see you both."

"Hey, Rafe." Wendy offers him a wave and looks back at her phone.

Juniper eyes him and blushes slightly. "Hey," she says, her voice slightly high-pitched.

He grunts as he stares at her. I see his eyes narrowing as he looks her up and down in her sexy black dress. If I'm not mistaken, Rafe thinks Juniper is hot.

"You into her?" I ask him softly.

His eyes fly back to me as he frowns. "What are you talking about?"

"Are you into Juniper?"

"Don't be crazy. Of course not." He looks at his watch. "I'll be back." And with that, he's gone.

I wonder what that was about, but I'm the last person to be questioning anyone else.

"Tonight is the night. I'm going to have some fun," Mia sings loudly and continues dancing. She's shaking her hair back and forth now and getting completely carried away.

"Be careful, Mia."

"I'm fine. I'm having—oops!"

She screams as her clumsy ass trips suddenly, and she goes flying. I step forward and reach my arms out to catch her. Her drink spills everywhere, including on my shirt, but I'm glad I'm able to catch her in my arms before she falls to the ground. She hits me with a thud that leaves us both winded as I slowly let her down to the ground.

"You saved me. I thought I was going to fall to the ground."

"I guess I'm just your regular knight in shining armor."

"I guess so," she says, grabbing the sides of my face and pressing her lips against mine. "You're just amazing, Luke. You know that, right?"

My heart thuds slightly as she looks at me and strokes the side of my face and then runs her fingers through my hair. She presses her body up against mine and wraps her arms around my neck. I feel her breasts pressed up against my chest, and I wrap my arms around her waist.

"I guess you're really thankful, aren't you?"

"I'm so thankful," she says as she presses her lips against my cheek and then my neck.

I feel her fingers running down the side of my body, and I feel my cock growing hard in my pants. I run my fingers down the small of her back and squeeze her ass, and she giggles slightly as she presses into me. She grabs my face and kisses me harder, and for a few moments, the world is still, the bar is quiet, and all I can feel and think about is our two hearts as they beat in simultaneous connection.

I deepen the kiss, and my tongue slips into her mouth. She moans against my lips as she sucks my lower lip. I can smell the jasmine of her scent, feel the softness of her body. I pull her tighter to me so she can feel the hardness in my pants, and she moans against my lips.

Fuck. This is why I came back to Coconut Beach. For all of this. I don't know if the kiss is because she's grateful that I caught her or what, but this was a moment I'd been waiting for—a real connection.

"My gosh, that was close," she says as she suddenly pulls away from me.

"What?" I stare at her in confusion.

She grins and nods to the side.

"I totally saw Andi and Rex come in, and they were glancing at us. Did I do a good job?"

I nod slowly as I realize that entire thing was fake. She wasn't kissing me because she wanted to. She was kissing me as part of the act.

"Oh, yeah. You're a really good actress. I saw them as well," I say quickly. "That's why I slipped you the tongue so that it would be more believable."

"Well, great. Good job." She licks her lips and swallows hard. "A-plus for effort." She giggles slightly.

"A-plus for effort?" I raise an eyebrow. "Are you saying the kiss itself wasn't A-plus?"

"Would I say that?" she says. She gives me a quick hug and then kisses me on the cheek. "I'm going to grab some water. I'll be right back," she says, and hurries away.

I stare after her, my heart thudding in confusion. All I can do is shake my head. I look over at Wendy, and I see that she's still checking her phone, texting quickly. Juniper is standing there, looking at me with wide eyes. I'm not sure what she's thinking. I'm not sure what she just witnessed, but she looks as flustered as I feel, and I don't know if this has been the worst decision of my life.

I'm about to go after Mia and ask her if she thought we were pushing things a little bit too far when I notice that I have a missed call from Rebecca and ten text messages. I scroll through them quickly and curse under my breath. There's a problem with the merger. One of the Chinese companies has offered a lot more money and to release the mining rights to be shared between everyone. This could absolutely sabotage my deal. The Brazilians also had another offer on the table, but I needed to read through all of the new sub-clauses.

"Fuck, I need to make a call." I know I shouldn't be working this late at night, but I can't let this deal fall through.

I clench my phone, hold it up, and call out to Juniper, "I just have to take a work call if Mia asks. I'll be right back, okay?"

"Okay." She nods.

I hurry out of the bar and toward the beach. When I reach some of the palm trees, I stop and take a couple of deep breaths.

I'm feeling out of my element, which is something that I don't normally feel. I'm not sure what I'm going to do, but right now, I need to concentrate on what's really important—and that's this business deal and not the ache in my heart or the hardness in my pants.

chapter fourteen

Mia

My head feels like it's spinning, and it's not just because of the two strawberry daiquiris I've already had tonight. For some reason, I can't get the thought of Luke skinny-dipping with Talia and some other unknown random women in the ocean out of my head. I'm not jealous per se because he can do what he wants, but the fact that he hadn't even told me about it hurt more than it should. It had been years ago, and it shouldn't matter, but I always thought that we didn't have any secrets from each other.

As I glance at Rafe heading toward me, a twinge of guilt hits me as I realize I can't be super upset because I haven't always been truthful with Luke about everything either. Rafe stalks toward me, his blue eyes looking annoyed and concerned at the same time. I look around, seeing if I can find an escape from the bar without him catching up to me, but I know it's no use.

"Hey," he says, stopping in front of me.

The brotherly look of concern in his eyes makes my heart warm, even though I want to tell him that I'm not a little kid anymore. I don't need his protection.

"Hey, you're still here?" I'm surprised, as it's past eleven and the music is loud and pumping.

Crowds of locals and tourists fill the bar, and there's barely room to move around. Juniper and Wendy are dancing near the entrance, where I left them, enjoying the beats of Ed Sheeran and Justin Bieber while I take a quick break.

"Yes, I'm still here. I like to party as well."

"Could have fooled me. You've never liked it that much before."

"I'm just trying to make sure that everything is okay with you."

"Why wouldn't it be okay, Rafe?" I say as I look down. I realize I haven't seen Luke in over an hour.

"What's wrong?" Rafe asks, touching my shoulder lightly.

"Nothing. I was just looking for Luke. I'm not sure where he is."

"Juniper said he had to take a work call."

"A work call? Really? At this time?" I can hear the annoyance in my voice. I close my eyes and take a couple of deep breaths. "Serenity now. Serenity now. Serenity now," I mutter fast. My eyes flutter open, and I can see Rafe's lips twitching. "What?"

"I don't think it quite works like that, sis."

"Whatever."

"So, what do you care if he's got a work call?"

"He's always working. I mean, it's the middle of the night. We're meant to be having fun, and he's working. Can't he just let it go for one night?" I shrug. "Whatever. He can do what he wants."

"Um, are you okay?" He presses the back of his hand to my forehead. "Well, you're not burning up, so you don't have a fever."

"It's fine. I'm fine. I'm totally fine. I'm having fun. I'm drinking strawberry daiquiris. I'm here with my friends, and I'm here with Luke, my boyfriend, the love of my life, my—"

"Are you sure you're not rushing this?"

"What are you talking about?"

"I'm just saying, there's obviously a reason why you didn't tell me, Mom, or Dad, or the grandparents. I don't know if you told Juniper, but I know you, sis. When you're in a relationship, you want to scream it from the rooftops, and the fact that you've kept this secret …" He frowns. "It's not a good sign."

"It's fine, Rafe."

"I'm just saying, you like to go fast sometimes, and I don't want to see you hurt."

"It's not like *that* time." I press my lips together.

"I just worry about you, sis. You know that."

"I know, and I'm grateful to you."

"I love you, and you could have been seriously hurt that summer. You—"

"I don't want to talk about it," I say quickly. "Okay?"

"Just know, if you ever need me, I'm here for you." He holds his hands up.

"Thank you."

"You're welcome." He gives me a kiss on the forehead. "Well, I should be heading home soon. I've got an early morning tomorrow. Animals that are waiting on me."

"You ever thought that the animals would want to see you happy too?"

"What are you talking about?"

"The animals want you to find love as well. You haven't dated anyone in a while, unless you're also hiding something from me."

I feel slightly guilty about lying to my brother, but the simple fact is that he's so honest that he will tell everyone in the family—even in Luke's family—that we're not really together if he knows the truth, and I just can't have that. That will make everyone think I'm even more pathetic than I already am.

"Obviously, I date, but that's not my priority right now. I'm trying to build my practice. Plus, I haven't met anyone who strikes my fancy." He looks around the bar. "It's just the same old, same girls in Coconut Beach, and maybe my girl's not here."

"Really? There's not one woman you've ever seen or met on the island that you think could be the one?"

"Not a one," he says, his tone stiff.

"There you are, Mia." Juniper races over to us. "Hey, Rafe."

"Hey," he says, his voice almost a grunt.

I watch as he stares at her, and there's something in his expression that shifts slightly. There's a curl to his lips that wasn't there before.

"Are you having fun tonight?"

"Yeah, you know. It's always fun at Cocktails & Chaos. Cal makes the best drinks, and I just love the music and dancing and having fun. And who knows? Maybe I'll meet someone tonight."

"Yeah." The small smile has gone from his face, and he turns back to me. "Well, like I said, I've got to be going. I have to be at work early tomorrow. I'll catch you girls later. Bye."

"Bye, Rafe," she says, then leans over at me. "Was it something I said?"

"No, he was on his way out anyway. He's just in a bad mood—I think because of me and Luke."

"What's up with that? I noticed he kind of had an attitude."

"I think he feels really overprotective about me, and I think he thinks I don't make the best decisions in relationships because of ..." I stare at her, and she nods slowly.

"Yeah, I know." She reaches over and squeezes my hand. "So, what's up with you and Luke?"

"What do you mean, what's up?"

"That kiss earlier ... it looked real."

"It was real," I say, laughing.

"I know it was real, but it looked *real*, real, like passionate."

"Oh, no way," I say quickly. "I saw Rex and Andi and Talia were here. He saw them as well, so we put our all into it. You know we're good at this. I was in the drama club in school, and, well, Luke can just follow my lead. You know he's good at stuff like that."

"Yeah, I guess." Her eyes narrow, and she leans closer to me. "You're not catching feelings for him or anything, are you?"

"Are you joking?"

"No." She shakes her head. "I'm just wondering if—"

"It's just an act for the summer. It's just for two weeks for the wedding. You know this, girl. We're doing this because Rex is a jackass." My voice is slightly too high, and I'm not sure why.

"Yeah, sure." She nods slowly. "I get it, if that's what you're saying."

"Yeah, that's what I'm saying." I sigh suddenly, not able to keep it in any longer. "Okay, do not tell anyone this."

"Who am I going to tell?" She grins. "You're my best friend."

"He's kind of cute, right?" I whisper. "Like sexy cute."

"Who?"

"Luke, duh. That's who we're talking about."

"I know." She giggles. "I was just joshing you."

"This is going to sound crazy, but has he always been this cute?"

"I don't know. He looks the same to me." Juniper shrugs. "Not to be mean, he's not my type, but I guess I can see why women would find him attractive."

"He used to be all skin and bones and lean and gangly and zitty. Shit, I remember when his face was like a washboard." I start laughing. "But now he's freaking tall and muscular, and he's got those deep blue eyes and that silky, dark hair, and have you seen his abs? And, yes, I saw his abs today."

"Ooh. He's so built. You must have noticed that."

"It's hard not to." I groan. "Of course I would never act on that. For one, he's my best friend, aside from you, of course."

"I know I'm your female best friend, and he's your male best friend." She smiles, her eyes searching mine. "So, you're into him?"

"No, I just … it's complex. I just think that there's no point in us doing anything or exploring anything because he lives in New York and I live here, and it would totally ruin our friendship if we were to go any further than we currently have."

"I don't think it would ruin your friendship. Iit's not like you guys have done anything. A kiss is just a kiss."

"Yeah, exactly. I kiss men all the time, and it means nothing." I don't explore intimately with men all the time though, but I decide not to share that information with her.

"Exactly."

"There y'all are." Josie comes running toward us. "I've been looking for you, girls."

"What's going on?" Juniper turns to her, offering her a side smile.

"We're all going to go down to the beach and play Twister. You want to come?"

"Yeah, that sounds fun," I say. "Come on, Juni."

"Oh, I don't know," she says, shaking her head. "We were just chatting about—"

"I'm done talking about it. Let's have some fun."

"Fine. Let's see if we can get Wendy to join."

"I don't know if Wendy's going to join," Josie says. "I think she's chatting with Carter. Oh, look, there she is. Let's see if she wants to join. Come on, girls." We follow Josie to the side of the bar, pushing through laughing girls and the guys who are trying to get their numbers.

"Hey, Wendy, Carter, you want to join us? We're going to play Twister down at the beach."

"That sounds like fun," Carter says, staring at Wendy with twinkling eyes. "You down?"

"No way," she says, shaking her head quickly. "I do not play Twister."

"Come on, Wendy. It'll be fun." His voice is deep, and the look he's giving her makes me feel like I'm witnessing some private moment. "Josie, convince Wendy to play."

"Come on, sis," Josie says, laughing.

"Nah, I'll watch, but I'm not playing."

"Has anyone seen my man?" I ask as we head out of the bar to the beach. "Luke?" I call out as I down the last of my drink.

"Did someone call?" Luke's voice sounds from behind me, and I spin around. He's standing there with his phone in his hand. "Sorry, I was just—"

"I know you had a work call," I say sharply, and he flinches slightly.

"Sorry, it was important. The deal I'm in, there's another company that—"

"I get it. I get it. It was important."

"Yeah, I was just trying to explain."

"It's nighttime, and we're trying to have fun, Luke. You know what that is? F-U-N?"

"I think so."

"We're going to play Twister. Do you want to join us?" Juniper says, trying to break the awkwardness between us.

"If Mia wants me to play …"

"If you don't have to take another work call."

"I don't have to take another work call."

"Then let's play."

We all head down to the beach and join a group of four others. Luke and I stand to the side as the game gets set up. I watch as Josie spins the dial and then puts her hand on red.

"Are you really mad at me?" Luke whispers.

"I just think it's weird that you're taking work calls when we're at the bar, and we're trying to show everyone that we are in love and having a good time, and you're not even around."

"I'm sorry. I didn't think a quick twenty-minute call would—"

"You didn't even tell me," I cut him off. "Plus, that was far longer than twenty minutes."

"You're mad."

"I'm not mad. I'm just saying."

"Are we going to play Twister, or are we going to argue?" He reaches over and brushes some loose tendrils of hair away from my face. "Your hair's grown really long. I like it like this," he says softly.

I look around and frown when I don't see Rex, Talia, Andi, or Rafe.

"Who are you looking for?" He looks around as well.

"I was just wondering why you were saying that."

"What do you mean, you were wondering why I was saying that?"

"You don't normally compliment me."

"I always compliment you, Mia."

"I guess." I shake my head.

He grabs my hands and pulls me closer to him. "You think I don't compliment you?" His tone is low, and my heart skips a beat.

"Do you want the truth? I haven't seen you in a while, so I guess I can't really remember."

"I tell you all the time when we have phone calls that I'm proud of you for starting your business and that you and Juniper are really killing it."

"Yeah, you tell me lots of things on the phone."

"Do you not enjoy our phone calls?"

"They're fine. I love speaking on the phone." I pause. "All the time."

"Why do I feel like you are trying to tell me that you don't like speaking on the phone?"

"Maybe, sometimes, it would be nice to see each other in person."

"You can come to New York, you know? You've never visited me. You've never been to my place. You've never seen the Empire State Building. You've never seen the Statue of Liberty. I haven't taken you out to the bar I love in Greenwich Village. I haven't taken you to the Upper West Side to grab—"

"You've never invited me," I say softly.

His expression changes. "What do you mean by that?"

"Really Luke, you've never invited me to come visit you."

"I didn't think I needed to invite you, Mia. Since when have I needed to invite you? That's so formal."

"Maybe because that's the polite thing to do."

"But we're best friends," he says, shaking his head. "Since when are we polite with each other?"

"You don't have to take our friendship for granted."

"Wait, what?"

"It would have been nice if you had said to me, *I'd love for you to come to New York and see my place.*"

"Is that why you've never been to visit me?"

"Maybe, but what's your excuse?"

"What do you mean?" He frowns.

"Why haven't you been back home?"

"You know I've been busy with work. You—"

"Yeah," I say, my voice trailing off.

I'm starting to feel annoyed and upset, and I don't want to. I don't want to have this out with him now, and I don't want to seem insecure because as much as I love Luke and our friendship, I've been dissatisfied in ways that I haven't even expressed to myself.

"You guys playing?" Josie calls out. "It's your turn, Mia."

"Okay, I'm coming."

I head over and spin the dial and put my hand on blue. I see Luke standing there, just staring at me, his face illuminated by the moon. He looks thoughtful, handsome, worried. He looks like the Luke I've always known, the guy I've depended on my entire life, and yet he also looks like a stranger. My heart pounds as he spins the dial, and he stands next to me on the board.

"Don't be mad at me," he whispers.

"I'm not," I say.

"You sure?"

"I'm sure." I give him a warm smile because the truth is, I could never be mad at him for long. He's Luke, and Luke is just someone who fills a part of me that can never be filled by anyone else.

"Oh boy," Luke says as he spins again, and he comes up behind me. "Sorry, I didn't mean to get in your space."

"It's okay," I say as I realize that my ass is now up in the air, right in front of his crotch. "I think you planned this."

"This could be dangerous," he says as he shifts slightly, his eyes laughing at me.

There's a twinkle in his eyes that makes me flush. He reaches down and lightly taps me on the ass, and I shake it back and forth. I laugh as I see his expression widen. He didn't think I knew how to twerk.

"Like what you see?" I say, teasing him.

He doesn't answer. Instead, his eyes darken, and he licks his lips, and suddenly, I'm taken back to the previous night and the way he touched me, the way his fingers gently and easily caressed me.

Shit. I'm lusting over Luke. I want him to touch me again. I want to feel him.

"Oops," Josie says suddenly as she goes falling and takes all of us down with her.

I fall to the ground, and Luke falls to the side of me. He rolls over and grabs me and pulls me on top of him. I straddle his lap and laugh as I look down at him. My skirt rides up slightly, and he grabs my hips to steady me. I slowly grind back and forth, my panties gliding across the top of his pants. As I continue to move, I feel his cock stiffening, and heat radiates into my increasingly wet panties. Finally, he pushes me back into the ground and kisses the side of my face. I am unable to look at anyone as we lay there because I'm sure everyone is wondering what is going on. No-one is used to PDA by Luke and I.

"I've been waiting to do that all night." His voice is a growl.

"What? Kiss the side of my face?"

"No, just touch you."

He runs his fingers down the side of my face and through my hair, down my arm, and then along the inside of my thigh. My breath catches as he trails his soft touch up my dress toward my hidden spot. My breath catches as I debate allowing him to caress me here and now.

"We're on the beach, Luke," I hiss at him, and he throws his head back and laughs. "And other people are here."

"So, you're saying if we weren't on the beach, it would be a yes?"

I stare at him and just shake my head, but he knows that if we were in private ... I don't know what would happen.

"Stop thinking," he says suddenly. "You're always in your head, Mia. Get out of your head."

"I'm not in my head. I'm just—"

"You are," he says. He leans over and gives me a kiss on the lips and then pulls me up. "Come on. Let's go back to the hotel. I think we both could do with some sleep tonight." He grins. "And when I say sleep, I mean just sleep."

"Pillow fort again?" I ask him.

"If you think you need it, handsy Mia."

"Ha-ha, very funny, Luke."

"I'm just saying, you might not be able to keep your hands off of me."

"Well, you might not be able to keep your tongue off of me."

"No, I think what you meant to say is, I might not be able to keep my tongue from being inside of you."

I gasp as I look over at him.

His eyes are dancing with merriment. "Got you."

"You're so bad, Luke. That's not a funny joke."

"Who says I was joking?" He's teasing me, and yet the air between us is filled with tension.

The jokes and the touches are confusing me. I'm having a hard time deciphering what's real and what's not.

chapter fifteen

Luke

"Are you tired?" I ask her as we make our way into the hotel room in companionable silence.

She stretches her arms out and shakes her head as she gazes at me. I close the door behind us and start to unbutton my shirt. "You hungry? Do you need me to get you some room service or anything?"

"No, I'm fine," she says, giggling slightly and then hiccuping. "I might need to drink some water though. I'm just a teensy-weensy bit drunk from all those strawberry daiquiris."

"Not too drunk, I hope. I don't want you to be hungover in the morning."

"I'm fine, Lukey." She yawns loudly. "By the way, I just want you to know that as much as I'm frustrated by the fact that you have to work, I'm still glad you're here," she says sleepily.

"Well, I'm glad to hear that, Mi-Mi," I say as I pull off my shirt, fold it up, and then place it on the couch. "I wish I could have been here and not had to work, but—"

"I know you need to make your billions."

"You'll be happy about it one day when I can buy a private island and fly you in my private jet."

"I think you have enough money that you could do that now."

"You may be right about that," I say, laughing. "You need help with the zip?"

"No, I can just pull the dress off. It's not that tight."

"If you say so. I'm just going to head into the bathroom and brush my teeth and get ready for bed."

"Sounds like a plan. Do you want me to get the pillow fort ready?"

"You do whatever you need to," I say, though disappointment courses through me.

I don't really want to have to sleep with another pillow fort between us tonight, especially as it didn't last very long the night before, but then maybe it would be good. I don't want to fall into temptation again.

"You want to watch a movie tonight?" she asks as she yawns slightly. "We meant to watch a movie last night, and we didn't."

"I think you're too tired for that."

"I know, but we only have a finite amount of days together while you're in town, and I just want to do all the things that we used to do when we were young."

"You mean younger?"

"You know what I mean."

"I know," I say.

My breath catches as she pulls her dress up and throws it onto the couch. She stands there in front of me in a black push-up bra and a very slinky pair of pink panties. My stomach tightens as she runs her fingers down the side of her body.

"What PJs should I wear tonight?" she asks as she heads toward her suitcase and starts unpacking it. "It's kind of warm. Should we turn the AC down?"

"If you want to," I say, unable to keep my eyes off of her.

She spins around and gazes at me. "I guess I'll just wear a T-shirt and shorts. That seems like the most sensible thing to wear. That's what I wear at home."

"Sounds like a plan. I'll just wear my boxers."

"Good. For a minute, I thought you were going to say you were going to sleep naked or something." Her voice is silky.

"Why would I do that, Mia?"

"I don't know. Maybe you would if you thought Rex might barge into our room in the morning, and you might want to be naked so that he'd believe us that this is real. So then you might think you had to sleep naked."

"If I was worried about Rex sneaking into the room in the morning, I'd make sure we didn't have a pillow fort," I say dryly.

"That's true." She giggles and then runs up to me. "I'm so glad you're here."

She wraps her arms around me and holds me tight. I wrap my arms around her and give her a hug in response. The feel of her warm body next to mine is driving me crazy, but I can't let her know that. Mia loves touch. She's always been a woman who loves to give hugs, and I've always enjoyed receiving them from her, but this is different. We've never hugged with her in her underwear and me just in pants.

"Well, I'm just going to brush my teeth, and then I'll come back and we can choose what we want to watch."

"Are you yawning, Luke?"

"Nah, I've got plenty of life left in me for the rest of the night." I grin at her. "You're the one who should be worried. You're the one who always falls asleep when we watch movies."

"Only when we watch your boring movies, as you very well know."

"Okay then. So, tonight, you're saying you're going to stay up all night?"

"I'm going to try my best." She giggles. "Okay, let me find my PJs, and you can brush your teeth, and then I'll brush mine."

"Sounds like a plan." I head into the bathroom and unzip myself so that I can pee before I brush my teeth. I stand there, relieving myself, and all I can think is what sweet torture I have gotten myself into.

"Did you know Andi and Rex weren't even—oops," she says as she walks into the bathroom and looks down.

"What are you doing?" I say as I quickly zip myself up.

"Sorry. I didn't realize you were peeing. It's not like I saw anything."

"I don't care if you saw anything," I say, shaking my head and turning toward her. "I just want to make sure that I didn't burn your eyes out or anything."

"Oh, I'm okay."

"Anyway, what were you going to say?" I say, trying to extinguish the fire that I'm feeling as she just stands there in her bra and panties.

"Did you know Andi and Rex weren't dating for very long before they got engaged? Wendy was telling me that she heard that Rex was actually not even that interested in Andi."

"No, I did not hear that. Who would I have heard that from?"

"I don't know. That's just the gossip in town right now."

"They're getting married now, so I suppose it's for a good reason."

"Yeah, I suppose so."

"Wait, are you asking me this because you still have—"

"Do not ask me if I still have feelings for Rex. Really, Luke? You know I don't."

"I'm just saying this whole farce is because you didn't want people to think that you were jealous that he was getting married."

"No, this is because he left a rude note on my invitation, basically saying I was incapable of getting a date. And, yes, the fact of the matter was, I didn't have a real date, and it was unlikely I was going to find one in that short amount of time, but I don't want to be known in Coconut Beach as the loser whose unrequited love married someone else, and she was going to all the wedding festivities as some sort of sad sack."

"No one would have thought that. Plus, what would they be thinking about me? I got a note as well."

"I know. Let's not talk about it anyway. You know what I was thinking?"

"I don't know, but you seem to be doing a lot of thinking."

"Really, *Luke*?"

"Really, *Mia*?"

"I was thinking that we should go on a night walk tomorrow."

"A night walk?"

"Yeah, like we used to back when we were younger."

"You mean to watch the stars?"

"Yeah, I miss those days. You always knew every constellation, and it was just cool, lying back in the sand and staring up at the sky and thinking about the universe in its entirety."

"There's something about thinking about other galaxies that makes you feel quite small, doesn't it?"

"I can't believe you would ever feel small, Luke, what with all your money."

"You know, I don't do it for the money, Mia."

"I know why you do it." She grabs my hand and squeezes. "You do it to prove to your family that you are capable, that you're brilliant, that you're the best Haverbrook that ever lived."

"How did you get to know me so well?"

"Maybe because I've known you for so long and we're just always in tune with each other, aren't we, Luke?"

"Yeah, we are." I wrap my arm around her shoulders and bring her in close to me. "I'm not going to lie. It hurts, what my dad did. He still doesn't really look at me. If I didn't know better, I'd think my mom had an affair, and I wasn't really a Haverbrook, but—"

"You are. Of course you are."

"I know I am," I say. "I look just like my dad. How could I not be?"

"Exactly," she says softly. "And, hey, who cares that you weren't on the football team and that you didn't go to UF? UF is not the only good school in the country."

"Try telling my dad that. If I'm not a Gator, I'm nothing."

"You're not nothing, Luke. You're not nothing to me."

"Thanks. I've missed you, you know, Mia."

"What do you mean you've missed me? I thought you loved our phone calls."

"You're right. Phone calls aren't everything."

"Wow, you're actually admitting that I'm right?" she says softly.

"I am, but let me brush my teeth and you should put on some clothes because—"

"Because of what?" she says, leaning back slightly, giving me a sexy little smirk.

"Because if you don't put on some clothes, I may just have to remove the ones that you currently have on."

"Oh, yeah? And how would you do that?"

"What do you mean, how would I do that?"

"What don't you understand, how would you do that?" She puts her hands on her lips and juts her chin out. "You would undress me?"

"I've undressed you before. I'd do it again."

"Is that a challenge?"

"I don't know. Do you want it to be?"

"I don't want it to be anything," she says, giggling. I don't quite know what's going on between us, but I'm not hating it. In fact, I'm very intrigued by it.

I grab my toothbrush and pick it up and then grab the tube of toothpaste and squirt it on. I start brushing my teeth, and she just shakes her head and sashays back out of the bathroom into the main hotel room. I stare at her pert little ass as she walks away, and for a few moments, I'm disappointed.

I wish she had pulled off her clothes. I wish she'd stood there naked in front of me. I don't know why. I shouldn't be having these thoughts about her. I shouldn't be lusting over my best friend. I didn't want to make this more complicated for myself or for her.

I finish brushing my teeth, put my toothbrush up, and head back into the bedroom. Mia's standing there in a long T-shirt and boy shorts. She grins as she looks up at me, one sleeve half off her shoulder.

"I'm going to brush my teeth now," she says as she walks up to me. "And then I'll meet you in bed, and we can choose the movie."

"Sounds good," I say.

"Yay." She bounces up and down.

It's then I notice that she's taken her bra off and her breasts are pressed against the thinness of her T-shirt. I can make out her nipples through the material, and I try not to groan.

Shit. What is she doing to me? Why is she so sexy? She's so effortlessly sexy, and she's going to drive me crazy. The next two weeks are going to be the most intense of my life. I know it. I can feel it in my bones.

I get onto the bed and grab the remote control and start scrolling through the channels, waiting for Mia to get out of the bathroom. She comes back with a slightly wet face, and I watch as she dries it. She grabs a hairbrush and brushes her hair, and I stand up and head toward her. I lightly touch her on the shoulder, and she looks back at me in surprise.

"What is it, Luke?"

"You want me to brush your hair for you?"

"Sure. I'm not going to say no."

We head back to the bed, and she takes a seat. I sit behind her and grab the hairbrush and brush her silky locks.

She moans slightly as she leans back. "I love it when you brush my hair. It's so relaxing."

"I love brushing it," I say, "though I'm not sure why. I don't even really like brushing my own hair." There's something about just being close with Mia that makes me feel warm, that makes me feel at home.

"What are we going to watch?" she says as she turns around. "Are you done, by the way?"

"I'm done." I chuckle as I put the hairbrush on the side vanity, and she scooches up the bed next to me.

"I was thinking we could watch *FBI*," I say to her.

"Huh?" She doesn't look impressed as she crosses her legs and leans back.

"*FBI*. It's a TV show. I think you'd—"

"That sounds so boring, Luke. I do not want to watch a show about the FBI."

"It's not a real FBI show. It's just fictional."

"Same difference. It's about the FBI. I don't care if it's real FBI cases or not." She shakes her head. "That's not a rom-com."

"Does everything have to be romance-related?"

"Seeing as I have no real romance in my life, it's kind of nice to see fictional romance, have something to aspire to."

She leans back, and I turn to her.

"So, that's something you really, really want in your life?"

"You know this, Luke. I've always wanted a romance for the ages." She taps her fingers against her calf. "Why? You don't want that?"

"I've kind of thought about it, but not really anything seriously. So, okay, no *FBI*. Something else?"

"Sure. What are the other options?" she says softly, her thighs rubbing against mine now as we lean back in the bed.

"I don't know. Let me see. There's *Blue Bloods*. It's about—"

"That doesn't sound like a show I'd be interested in," she says quickly, and I laugh.

"Really?"

"Luke, you know me well enough to know that I'm not interested in FBI, CIA, Blue Bloods, Red Bloods, Green Bloods, Purple Bloods."

"Really, Mia?"

"What? I like cop shows sometimes, but I don't want to watch one right now. I'm kind of tired and—"

I notice that her eyes are on my chest. There's a slight tension in the air as we just stare at each other.

"Tonight was fun," Mia says softly.

"I think so."

"It was interesting when we kissed."

"It was," I say. "I bet you Rex was super jealous."

"You think?" she asks, giggling slightly.

"Yeah. I think he had to have noticed that it was pretty intense."

"I wasn't sure if I was too weird or uncomfortable-looking," she says, pressing her lips together.

"What do you mean?"

"I mean, when I was trying to press my body against yours, I wasn't sure if it was right."

"Did you want to practice?"

"Practice what?" she says, blinking rapidly.

"I don't know … how we sort of fit together. You know, in case we're around people, and they're looking and—"

"I guess we can practice." She nods. "How?"

"Well, why don't you lie flat on your back?" I say.

"Huh?" She looks at me with a frown. "What do you mean? Explain"

"Lie flat on your back, and I'll lie flat on my back. It's a test. I want to see how you curl into me, how I curl into you. It has to be natural, right?" I ask her softly. "If you're naturally able to curl into me and touch me without feeling self-conscious, then that's the first step in making it seem real."

"Oh, I guess," she says. "You should do the same thing too though."

"Well, we'll both practice then. You first."

I watch as she unfolds her legs and lies flat on her back. I lie flat next to her and stretch my arms out.

"Now roll into me like we're really together."

"Okay," she says, giving me a weird look as she shifts next to me.

I feel her hand lightly on my chest as she places her head in the crook of my arm.

"Really, Mia?"

"What?"

"If I were your boyfriend and we were madly in love, you'd be this far away from me?"

"I'm touching you."

"Your head is in the crook of my arm, and your hand is on my chest and that's it."

"Yeah, and that's how we normally snuggle. What's wrong with that?"

"If you were my girlfriend and we were in love, do you really think that's how you'd be touching me?"

"I guess not." She shifts awkwardly. "Well, what should I do?"

"What would you do if I were your boyfriend for real?"

She thinks for a second, and I watch as she licks her lips. My heart thuds as I wait to see what she'll do next. She shifts over slightly more and lifts her right leg. She places her right leg over mine and moves closer toward me. Her head is now on my chest, and her hand is cradling the side of my face. I feel her breasts crushed into me, and she looks up at me with a dimple in her smile.

"Is this better?"

"Now this is something I could believe," I say as I reach down and stroke her leg. She gasps slightly and shivers at my touch. "You see, you can't act like that. You can't recoil every time I touch you."

"I don't recoil every time you touch me. I just—"

"It's not natural yet, right?" I say.

"Yeah, I guess I'm just not used to those familiar touches."

"Well, we've got to make sure that you don't recoil like that every time I touch you slightly more intimately."

"That's something I guess we need to practice, huh?"

She looks up at me, and I nod slightly.

"Yeah. Okay, my turn," I say.

"Your turn?" She looks at me in confusion.

"To practice how I would snuggle next to you."

She rolls off of me and lies flat on her back. I lie flat and then move over to her. I place my hand at the bottom of her T-shirt and slide it up under her shirt on her stomach. She takes an inward breath as she gazes at me, eyes wide.

"When two people are in love, they have a familiar touch," I say as I run my fingers across her skin. "You can't gasp every time I touch you."

"I know," she says, licking her lips. "I just—"

"You just what?" I say as I slide my fingers up further under the curve of her breasts, then stop.

She bites down on her lower lip. "I just … nothing."

I grin as I pull my hand back from under her T-shirt. She looks slightly disappointed, and I wonder if she wanted what I wanted—to play with her nipples, to pull her T-shirt up and suck on her breasts—but that would be taking this way too far. It's not like I am going to be sucking on her nipples in front of our family and friends.

She looks over at me. "Should we watch your movie?" she asks softly, and I nod. "Shall we turn out the lights?"

I jump off the bed and turn the lights off. When I get back, we get under the sheets, and she snuggles into the crook of my arm again as I find a Kate Hudson movie that she loved when we were younger.

"This one is so funny," she says, staring at the TV screen.

"Oh, yeah?" I run my fingers down the side of her face casually.

"Yeah, she has to convince him that she's crazy to get him to dump her."

"Oh, yeah, I kind of remember this movie," I say, staring at her, not the TV screen.

Mia starts laughing at some of the antics on the screen, and I delight at the sound of her voice. It's really nice, being here with her, having her next to me.

"I wanted to just see something."

"What's that?" I ask her.

"Well, I was thinking that when we go out next time, I should sit in your lap."

"Oh?" I freeze suddenly.

"Yeah."

She rolls over, and all of a sudden, she's on top of me, straddling me. She slides back and forth, her panties grinding on top of my cock. I look up at her innocent, wide eyes.

"I feel like I should know how to sit in your lap properly."

"Well, right now, you're doing more than sitting in my lap."

"What do you mean?"

"Right now, I'm lying flat on my back, and you're straddling me, Mia."

"Yeah, otherwise known as sitting in your lap."

"Well, I'm not sitting, and I think you need to stop that," I say, grabbing her hips.

"What?"

What does she mean, what? I reach up and pull her down toward me so that her face is next to mine. Her ass sticks up in the air, and I slide my fingers down her shorts and squeeze her ass cheeks.

"What are you doing, Luke?"

"I'm doing what any man who's just had a beautiful woman grinding on him would do," I say through gritted teeth, my voice a whisper.

"I wasn't grinding on you. I was—"

"You were what?" I say.

I see her breasts hanging through the V of her T-shirt.

"I was just—" she says breathlessly as I run my fingers up the small of her back and then around to the front and squeeze her breasts.

"Luke, what are you doing?"

"Nothing," I groan as I gently rub my thumb against her nipple.

She gasps as she looks down at me, placing her hand right against my hardness. She shifts back and forth slowly now. Her movements subtle, but I know she's feeling something because I am as well. My cock grows thicker between her legs.

"Mia, you're playing with fire," I say.

"Would that be so bad?" She lets her hair hang down across my chest and across my face and leans down to give me a peck on the cheek, then a peck on the lips.

"I think we don't want to go down this road without fully understanding where it could lead," I say, gazing at her.

"What's wrong with—" she says softly.

I grab her, push her down to the side of me.

"Mia," I say, glancing over at her.

We're both panting slightly now.

"Yes, Luke."

"I think we should go to sleep."

"What if I'm not ready for sleep?"

"I think you're ready," I say.

"What if I'm not?" She reaches over and touches my abdomen and runs her fingers along the length of my cock.

"Mia," I gasp.

"Yes, Luke."

"Fire."

"Fire's burning, huh?"

I grunt and grab her hand and pull it away from me. "Mia, once we go down this road, we can't stop it."

"Who says I want to stop it?" she says, breathing faster and faster.

I touch her bottom lip, running my thumb against it gently. She bites it slightly and then giggles.

"I'm not playing."

I grunt, and then because she's giving me a seductive look, I roll over and grab the bottom of her T-shirt and yank it up. She stares at me in surprise, and I grin down at her like a hungry wolf.

"Is this what you want?" I say as I kiss her on the lips and run my thumb against her nipples.

She moans slightly as I play with her breasts and then kiss down the side of her neck.

"Is this what you want?" I repeat, feeling like I'm spinning out of control.

I take her right nipple in my mouth and suck and tease it gently as I play with her other nipple. Her entire body is shaking as I squeeze her breasts and then kiss down her stomach. My tongue trails along the valley between her breasts and then down toward her belly button. I grab her panties with my teeth and tug down slightly. Her entire body stills, and I feel her fingers on my shoulders. I grab her panties and pull them down, looking up at her. She looks dazed. She looks beautiful.

I spread her legs and stare at her beautiful pussy.

"I didn't shave," she says.

"I don't care."

I grin at her and slide an index finger up between her slit and rub her clit. She moans slightly as her back arches.

"My goodness," she says in a low voice, sounding and looking like she's about to faint.

I stare at her. I'm about to go down on her when I realize what I'm doing. This is Mia, my best friend.

"We can't," I say as I pull my fingers from between her legs.

She moans as she looks over at me. "What do you mean, we can't?"

"It's not a good idea, Mia. Remember what you said when we were younger?"

"What?"

"We said we didn't want to go down this road. It could ruin our friendship."

"But—"

"But nothing. I don't want to lose you. You're the best friend I've ever had."

"And you're the best friend I've ever had, Luke."

"So, then let's just remember the rules."

"The rules?" she blinks at me in confusion.

"The rules we put in motion when we decided to fake date. Remember, we weren't going to cross the lines, and we've already gone way too far over them."

"Fine," she says, licking her lips. She grabs her T-shirt and pulls it back on. "You're right. We shouldn't cross any lines." She rolls away from me. "I'm tired. I think I'm going to go to sleep now."

"Mia, you're not mad at me?"

"I'm not mad at you," she says, shaking her head. "I'm just really horny right now, and I can't even look at you."

"You can take care of yourself, you know."

"What?"

"I wouldn't mind watching you."

"Luke, really?" She turns back to look at me with wide eyes.

I give her a wicked grin. "In fact, I'd quite like to look at you. I could even help you if you wanted."

"Are you saying what I think you're saying?"

"I think so." I grab her hand and slide it between her legs. Her eyes widen. "You're wet." I place my hand on top of hers and slide it up along her clit.

"Really, Luke?" She whimpers.

"What?"

"We're going to do this?"

"Don't best friends do everything together?"

I wink at her, and she just laughs.

"This is something that I've never heard of best friends doing all the time." She moans slightly. "But I'm willing to give it a try. What do I do?"

"I think you need to rub your clit a little bit faster," I say as I move her finger back and forth.

She spreads her legs a little wider, and I try not to groan as my fingers glide along her clit, along with hers.

"You're so wet," I say.

"I'm so horny," she breathes out and whimpers.

"What are you thinking about?" I ask her softly.

"Thinking about you touching me."

"Is that what you want?"

Our fingers move faster now, and all I want is to slide inside of her.

"I don't even know. I just want to come," she says softly.

I rub her for a couple more seconds, and then I pull her top up again and start playing with her breasts.

"Luke?" She's breathing loudly now, almost panting.

"Continue playing with yourself," I say.

She nods slightly, and I watch as she rubs herself faster and faster as I play with her nipples.

"Oh fuck, I'm going to come," she calls out, her voice cracking.

"Come for me, Mia."

Her body starts shaking as she rubs herself into an orgasm. I lean down and suck on her nipple, and she grabs my head and plays with my hair. She's breathing heavier now, and I can tell she's close. I slip my finger back between her legs and grab her hand and guide her into ecstasy. She screams, her body shuddering as she comes on my fingers.

"Fuck," I say as I press my lips against hers. "That was hot."

"You think so?"

She kisses me back urgently, and I nod as I pull away, hard as hell. It was absolutely amazing, and even though I know, inside, we've crossed a line we shouldn't have crossed, I just don't care. That was the hottest moment I'd ever had in my life, even hotter than sex, and I couldn't imagine what it would feel like to actually be inside of her. I know if that time comes, it has to be about more than her just feeling horny or wanting to be in a fake relationship. It has to be because she wants me with her mind, body, and soul. It has to be because she's falling for me in the same way that I've already fallen for her.

As her eyes flutter and she drifts off to sleep, I wonder if we've crossed a line that we shouldn't have.

How far can we go and convince ourselves it's for the plot of our story?

chapter sixteen

Mia

Boy, the lines are blurring, I think to myself.

Actually, that's not exactly correct. The lines are blurred.

They are already fucking blurred.

Luke helped me masturbate into one of the best orgasms of my life.

That was not on my playlist for the summer.

Shit! I don't even know how I got myself in this position, but all I can think about is the way that Luke makes me feel when he touches me.

We resisted for so many years from ever being physical with each other. We certainly didn't even contemplate being friends with benefits, and yet here we were, three days into a fake relationship, and we were already intimate. In ways I'd never even dreamed about.

How did this happen?

I swallow hard as I rub my forehead and stare at my face in the mirror. *You are going to get yourself in trouble, young lady.* I point at my reflection. My hair sits at the top of my head, and my eyes look tired. I have to head down to work, but I'm not sure exactly what I'm going to tell Juniper.

All the other girls knew that we had kissed, of course. We were going to do that in front of them for the show, but what we were doing late at night, when the lights were low and no one was around, had nothing to do with our pretenses. It wasn't like Rex had a secret camera in the hotel room, spying on us.

We were doing it because we wanted to do it, and I wasn't sure just how far it was going to go before we realized we were making a huge mistake. I hear a knocking on the door, and I freeze.

"Hey, Mia, are you nearly ready?" Luke calls out.

"I'll be out in just a moment," I say.

"Actually, I need to send some emails, so I was going to head down to the conference room and just have a seat and do some work."

"Okay. Are you not going to come with me to the beach to see the bookmobile and get some amazing books?" I call out.

"I'll have to do that later if you don't mind."

"Not at all," I say quickly. "Not at all."

Thank God. I don't really want to look into his eyes right now and think about the way he sucked on my breasts.

Like he'd enjoyed it. Like my nipples were tasty morsels. Fuck, we were in trouble.

"I'll see you later, Mi-Mi."

"Bye, Luke." I take a deep breath and grip the marble countertop of the vanity.

I am actually grateful that he's not coming with me directly to the bookstore. I just need some space to think, to ponder, to ask myself what the fuck I'm doing. While a part of me is slightly irritated that he's choosing to work again instead of spending time with me, I'm not going to look a gift horse in the mouth.

When I hear the door slam, I slowly open the bathroom door and head out into the hotel room. My eyes spy the rumpled sheets on the bed, and my body grows warm with heat and desire. Luke made me come on that bed not eight hours ago.

"I—oh my gosh, what did I do?" I cry out.

I know I should feel disgusted with myself, but it was just so hot. I'd never done anything like that before in my life. Not even with a boyfriend, which wasn't saying much because all my boyfriends sucked. But still, it was Luke!

I pull on a floral dress, brush my hair quickly, grab my bag, and head out of the hotel. I need to speak to Juniper. I need to find out from my friends if I'm making a big mistake.

As I walk along Main Street toward the beach, I start to jog. I'm not really much of a runner, but I can't wait. I'm so incredibly grateful when I see Wendy, Juniper, Summer, and Silvie all standing by the bookmobile.

"I've never been happier to see a group of girls in my life," I say as I run toward them.

"Everything okay?" Juniper gives me an odd look. "You look like you've been running. Your face is flushed."

"I *was* running. Last night was crazy. Crazy, I tell you," I say dramatically, about to fall to pieces.

Silvie stares at me for a couple of seconds, looking concerned. "Does this have anything to do with you and Luke?"

"How did you guess?"

"I was just speaking to Cal earlier this morning, and he mentioned that you guys were there last night and had some interesting interactions."

I wonder how early they were speaking and if it was in bed, but I don't ask.

"What do you mean, interesting interactions?" I stare at her. "What was Cal saying?"

"He was just saying that he thought he saw you guys arguing at one point and that it seemed like a couple's argument. So, he was asking me if I was sure that your relationship was fake like ours is because, shit …" Her voice trails off. "Well, he thought it looked kind of real."

"It's not real, okay? Is your marriage to Cal real?"

"No, of course not. We are getting married so I can get the inheritance from my family because my sister is a slut and she slept with my fiancé." Her lower lip trembles. "And I know I look like I'm sad right now, but I'm really not. Did I think he loved me? Yes. But did I really want to marry him? No."

"It still sucks that your sister did that to you."

"It's just reprehensible." She sniffs.

"It was abominable," Juniper adds. "So, what's going on, Mia? Why were you running? Because you never run."

"Okay, girls …" I look around the beach. "I need to tell you something, but this has to stay between us."

"Of course," Wendy says. "Everything we tell each other stays between us."

"Good. Last night got kind of intense."

"When you were dancing on top of the bar?" Juniper giggles. "We always dance on top of the bar."

"No, not then. I mean, when we got back to the hotel room."

"What happened?" Wendy asks with wide eyes.

"Luke and I ... well ..." I lick my lips slowly. "We might have kind of—"

"Did you guys have sex?" Juniper's jaw drops. "You guys were definitely looking overly friendly, and when you kissed, I could have sworn I saw tongue. But sex, Mia? Really?"

"No," I say loudly. "No, of course we didn't."

"Phew, because, girl, I was about to say, remember, this is just meant to be an act, not for *real*, real."

"We didn't have sex, but we kind of touched—or he kind of touched me."

"Ooh, tell us more." Summer grins. "I want all the juicy details."

"Me too," Silvie says, nodding.

"Look, he might or might not have pulled off my top, and I might or might not have had a bra on, and he might or might not have kissed my breasts and touched me somewhere else."

"No way," Juniper says. "Did he go down on you?"

"No, but he—we kind of just fooled around. Very hot and very heavy, and, yes, I orgasmed, and, I am out of my mind, girls, I don't know what to do. He's Luke. He's my best friend, and we are totally doing things we should not do. It's totally going against rule number two, which is no physical intimacy, no touch that crosses any lines, and, oh, we've crossed so many lines."

"I can tell you from my experience that entering into a fake relationship or marriage is not for the faint of heart," Silvie says softly. "I know Cal and I—well ..." She blushes slightly. "It's kind of complicated for us as well."

"Oh?" I turn to her with narrow eyes. "In what ways is it complicated?"

"I don't want to talk about it now," she says quickly. "I'm just saying, I think something complicated is just happening to all of us this summer."

Wendy nods. "Carter and I—well ..." She goes a deep red. "Let's just say, he's not *just* a guest at the bed-and-breakfast."

"Wait, did you and Carter fuck?" I ask her.

She gives me a look. "No, but …" She grins. "Let's just say, that man knows how to work his tongue."

"Whoa." We all look at Summer next and I can tell she's nervous about what question we're going to ask her.

"What about you, Summer?" I ask.

"Me?" She blushes a light shade of pink. "I have zero men. Dayton might or might not have seen some naughty pics of me, and, well, it's a little intense there, but *nothing* is going on."

Oh shit, something is definitely going on.

"What about you, Juniper?" she says, changing the subject quickly.

"Well, I definitely have zero men, and you all know that." Juniper lets out a deep sigh. "That's why I run a bookstore selling mainly romance books because I don't get romance in my real life, so I need it from my books."

"I'm there with you, Juni. We own the bookstore together, and I love a romance book."

"Yeah, but you have Luke."

"I don't have Luke though. He's my friend—emphasis on F-R-I-E-N-D."

"If you say so," she says.

"Anyway, I don't know. What should I do? Should I tell Luke we can't continue down this path?"

"Do you want to continue down this path?" Wendy stares at me. "Did you enjoy whatever went down last night?"

I nod slowly. The truth of the matter is, I more than enjoyed the previous evening. In fact, even though it is still morning, I am looking forward to this evening because I want to see what is going to go down next.

"I just feel like we've been friends for such a long time, and this is kind of a slippery slope, and I know many friends don't recover when they're intimate like this."

"It'll be fine," Juniper says. "He's Luke. He's always going to be there for you. Plus, he lives in New York. Who cares? Even if it doesn't go well, you'll stop speaking for a couple of weeks, and then you'll FaceTime him, and it'll be all good again."

"I suppose," I say, nodding slowly.

My phone beeps, and I look down at the screen. I laugh when I see Luke's name—speak of the devil. I quickly open his message.

"Luke says he's going to come join us after lunch and that he'll bring my swimsuit if I want him to so we can go on an afternoon dip."

"Ooh, ooh," Silvie says. "I think the man wants to see you in a bikini."

"I think he doesn't really care about seeing me in a bikini when he saw me with nothing on last night." I laugh, and all the girls join in cackling alongside me. "I'm feeling so tired," I say, wiping sweat from my forehead as Juniper and I sort through a new stack of books that was just delivered. "It's so hot already."

"Well, Luke should be here soon, right? He'll cool you down." Juniper winks, and I just shake my head.

"I am definitely going to go for a swim. I told him to bring my white bikini with the pineapples on them."

"Really, Mia?"

"What? It's cute."

"Isn't it, like, a thong bottom?"

"Well, I want Luke to see what he can't have."

"What do you mean, what he can't have?" She giggles. "He can totally have it."

"Well, maybe. Maybe not." I wink at her.

The fact of the matter is that I want him to appreciate my body. I want to tease him, and I have no idea why.

"Hey, girls. How's it going?" Luke strides up with a *Living the Sweet Life in Coconut Beach* tote bag over his shoulder. He looks over at Juniper and then at me and holds up a hand. "I've got some towels in here and your bikini. Are you hungry? Do you want to swim first or eat?"

"I am actually not hungry. We had fish tacos from the new Loco Moco food truck, and now I would love to swim. I'm so hot and sweaty right now. I want to get these clothes off and put on my bathing suit and submerge in the water."

"Are you going to go for a proper swim, or are you just going to float and pretend to swim?"

"Luke, do I ever pretend anything?"

"I hope not," he says in a soft voice as I gaze at him. "Especially when it comes to getting wet."

I know the double entendre to his comment, and I blush a deep red.

"I didn't fake it," I say, and he chuckles.

"We really can read each other's mind, can't we?"

He moves closer to me, and I forget that there is anyone else in the world as we gaze at each other.

"I think you two should have a cold swim, Mia," Juniper says quickly with a teasing smile. "I really do not want to be a witness to your sexual flirting."

"Hey, we weren't sexually flirting," I whisper at her, jaw dropped.

"You forget that I am also one of your best friends, Mia, and I can also read your mind, and I know exactly what you were both saying just now. Like, after last night, who wouldn't know?"

"She knows about last night?" Luke looks at me, surprised.

"She knows. All the girls know." I make a face. "I, um, well ..."

"I guess maybe you will grow up to be one of the busy Bees."

"What's that supposed to mean?"

"It means that you like to gossip."

"Hey, I was just telling my friends because—"

"Well, what? You were telling them how good I was in the sack?"

"No, I was not, and it's not like we had sex, so I don't know how good you are in bed."

"But I'm good with other things, right?"

He waves his pinkie finger at me, and I just shake my head and groan. Luke needs to grow up.

"I'm gone," Juniper whines. "Come on, Wendy, Josie, Summer, Silvie. We do not have to listen to their X-rated conversation." She tuts at me as they all head into the bookmobile.

"See what you did, Luke?"

"What did I do?"

"You scared off Juniper and the girls."

"I think we both scared them off." He grins at me. "You want to change, and then we'll go into the water?"

"That sounds great." I beam at him, trying not to laugh. "No more wet or hard talk."

I give him a look, and he just wiggles his eyebrows.

"Let me go and get ..." My voice trails off as his phone beeps.

He hands me the tote bag. He frowns as he stares down at the screen. "Shit," he mutters under his breath.

My heart stills. I already know what's coming.

"What is it?"

"Nothing." He stares at me for a couple of seconds, and I can see him doing some mental calculations in his brain. "Do you mind if I join you in the water in thirty minutes?"

"What do you mean? What are you talking about?"

"I have to take a call. It's for work."

"It's—let me guess. It's really important."

"But I promise it will be thirty minutes, an hour at most." He nods.

"How did you just go from thirty minutes to an hour? This is the middle of the day, Luke. I'm working as well. I can't just take off endless amounts of time. Juniper would not be happy about that."

"Well, I'm in the middle of a really big deal, Mia. It requires my focus."

"You're always in the middle of a really big deal."

"Not big like this."

"Whatever. Whatever you have to do. I'll just find some cute surfer who wants to swim with me instead."

"What's that supposed to mean?" He frowns, and I watch as he puts his phone in his back pocket. He takes a couple of steps toward me. "What are you saying, Mia?"

"What am I saying? What do you think?"

"You're going to find a really hot surfer to swim with?" His lips thin. "Really?"

"Well, maybe a hot surfer on the beach will have time for me and my itty-bitty white bikini with the pineapples on them."

"It's a cute bikini. I want to see you in it as well."

"Maybe you will. Maybe you won't. Guess it depends on how long your phone call is."

"Mia, I don't think it's a good idea for you to go and flirt with some random surfer. I'm sorry that I have to take this call, but it will be quick."

"Rex and Andi have gone to taste wedding cakes today," I say, "so it's not like they're going to see me on the beach. You're safe. Our cover won't be blown."

"I don't give a fuck about our cover," he says. "I think it's highly inappropriate for you to go looking for some hot surfer to flirt with."

"Why is it highly inappropriate? Why do you care, Luke? It's not like any of this is real."

He stares at me for a couple of seconds and just shakes his head. I watch as he pulls his phone out of his back pocket and walks away.

"I'm going to work. Enjoy your swim, Mia."

"Fuck you," I whisper under my breath as I stand there, watching him leave me.

I'm absolutely furious. I can't believe he just walked away from me. I can't believe that he didn't even respond to my concerns about him prioritizing work again. I can't believe he didn't even answer when I said this wasn't real. He could have said last night was real, or our friendship was real, but nothing. Not even an apology, like, *I'm sorry that I have to work, but our friendship means a lot to me, and that's really what matters.*

All he could do was walk away. Just like when he'd left for New York and never come back. Luke would rather ignore something than deal with it head-on, and it is annoying as hell.

"Hey, you okay?" I see Juniper peering at me through the door at the top of the bookmobile. "We heard you arguing. No longer swimming?"

"I'm fine. He had to work."

"That sounded like a hell of an argument," she says softly. "It sounds like you guys are experiencing the ups and downs of a real relationship. You went from hot to cold so fast."

"I guess it means we're really great actors." I shrug. "We're pulling it off well."

"Maybe you should go to a boutique and find a really great evening dress, Mia, because if that was an act, then maybe you're going to win an Oscar soon."

"Funny, Juni. Not. I'm going to go change and swim by myself. I'll see you later."

I know I'm being a bitch, and I know I'm taking my anger out on her, but I can't stop myself. I hurry to the restroom so I can change into the bikini and take a couple of deep breaths. I don't know why I'm so upset, why I'm so angry. I just know I'm disappointed. I was really looking forward to swimming with Luke. I was really looking forward to seeing how he would like my bikini on me, but yet again, I was second in his life to work.

"I'm fed up with this bullshit," I whisper to myself. "When I get a real boyfriend, I'm going to be one hundred percent certain I'm with a man who puts me first because if I'm not first, then what's the point of the relationship?"

This isn't a relationship though, Mia.

Then why do I feel like I'm on a roller coaster?

Why do I feel like Luke and I are finally having to face issues that neither one of us has brought up before?

This summer romance is fast proving to be an unraveling of a friendship I know so well, and I'm not sure if faking it with Luke to get back at Rex is going to be worth the price we'll end up paying to come out on top.

chapter seventeen

Luke

It's times like these when I wish that I also had a male best friend. I need someone to talk to about Mia. I saw the anger in her eyes when I told her I wasn't able to swim with her right away, and a part of me wondered if it was because she was feeling tense due to our physical intimacy. It wasn't like I could go to her and ask her if she was upset with me because I knew she wouldn't tell me the truth, and I had no one to speak to. I had male friends, of course, but none that I was especially close to. None that I could tell about my situation with Mia.

I think about Rex and how different our relationship could have been if we'd been like real brothers and had a bond. What would it have been like if we hadn't always been competing?

I look down at my phone, and I see that I have missed calls from my mother and my father. They were both annoyed that I hadn't told them about Mia and the fact that I had not spent any one-on-one time with them. Nor have I asked to visit their home yet, but I just didn't want to. It had never felt like my home. Not like Mia's parents' house or my grandparents'.

Who can I speak to? I think to myself.

There is only one person I can call and ask for advice, but I know I'll have to be really careful. I can speak to my grandma. Bitsy is a gossip, and she is a busy Bee, but she loves me, and she's always been there for me throughout the years. She is the only one who knows about just how much I cared about Mia back in the day. I decide to call her because I know I'm going to go crazy if I don't speak to someone about what's going on.

"Hi, Luke. What are you doing?" She answers the phone right away. "Grandpa wants to know if you want to play golf later today."

"Hey, Grandma. I was just calling to see if everything's going well. I can't play golf today though."

"Grandpa will be disappointed, but he will understand. Lucille and I just got back from crochet, and we're going to go to bingo tonight."

"Wow, busy."

"It's always busy on the beach."

"I suppose that's why you'll never leave."

"It's my home, Luke. Of course I'll never leave. I just hope that, one day, you'll move back." Her voice softens. "I do miss seeing you weekly."

"I know, but I wouldn't count on it, Gran."

"But what about Mia?"

"What about her?" I say before I think about the fact that we're supposed to be in a relationship. "I mean, she and I haven't gotten to that stage in the relationship yet where we're talking about where we're going to end up."

"Even though you've been dating for a year? Now, now, Luke, I hope you're not just wasting her time."

"No, I would never do that to Mia."

"So, why are you calling? Is everything good?"

"I just … it's actually about Mia."

"What's going on? Do you want to meet for coffee or—"

"No, I'm actually headed down to the shoreline to meet up with her and talk, but I think she's annoyed with me, and I just don't know how to address the situation."

"Why is she annoyed with you?"

"I'm not really sure," I lie because there are three reasons in my mind why she could be upset.

One, she could be upset because we'd been extremely physical. Two, she could be upset because I hadn't gone to the beach with her, which I thought was unlikely because we went swimming in the ocean all the time. Or three, she was just cranky because she was worried about something else. Maybe she was still heartbroken over Rex. The thought makes me distraught.

"Luke, you don't have any clue?"

I realize then that my grandma can't help me because there's not much information I can share with her. No one can help me unless I'm fully honest with them, and the only people I can be fully honest with are Mia's friends, and they are her friends first and foremost.

"Actually, I think it's probably just a stupid minor argument. I think I see her. I have to go."

I hang up and just stand there in the grainy white sand. I don't know what to do. I can head down to the water and search for Mia or just leave it until later. When I spy the tiki torches outside of Cocktails & Chaos, I think about Cal and his own situation. He knows this relationship is fake. He is also in a similar situation with Silvie. Maybe he'll have some advice for me. I hurry down toward the bar and walk past the palm fronds that decorate the front pole, along with several colorful flags.

"Hey there, Luke. You want a beer?" Cal says as I enter and make my way to him.

It's still quite early, so the tourists haven't flooded the place yet. I notice two older men playing darts toward the back and a single lady sitting at the bar, reading a book. I wonder if it's a romance. I know if Mia were here, she'd ask the lady what she was reading.

"No thanks. Actually, I was wondering if you had five minutes so we could have a quick chat."

"Sure. We're not very busy right now. What's going on?" He heads toward the front with a rag towel and starts drying the stack of cups.

"I'm kind of flustered and frustrated about this situation with Mia." I lower my voice and look around. I definitely don't want anyone to hear me.

"Oh no. Is the fake dating situation not going well?"

"It's not going poorly. I just think we've crossed a couple of lines that maybe we shouldn't have, and I think maybe she's mad about it. I don't know. She's just been really grumpy today, and I'm trying to navigate that without having her blow up at me."

"You think it's got to do with the kiss from last night?"

"That's the least of it, dude. We've done a bit more than kiss, Cal."

"I got you," he says, nodding, his eyes twinkling as he pours me a beer and sets it in front of me. "Just in case you need it. I understand how complicated these fake relationships can be." He grimaces. "These women know how to drive us crazy."

"I'm guessing you and Silvie have also crossed a couple of lines?"

"I will not say if I've sampled the goods or not." He winks. "Luke, I'm a gentleman."

"I'm a gentleman as well. How's it going with you and Silvie though? Is it super complicated?" I want to hear it's not just me who is going out of his mind.

"Aren't these things always super complicated?" He grabs a bottle of whiskey. "You want a shot?"

"Sure, thanks." I nod.

At the end of the day, I'm starting to realize drinking with him may not have been my finest decision. Nor sharing the same room. Nor flirting. Nor touching. Nor kissing. Nor getting to know each other intimately.

"You know, I figured Mia and I had been best friends for so long that this would be fine, to pretend we were dating, but I guess I didn't predict the fact that she would be sexy as hell and I couldn't resist her."

"She's a good-looking girl," he says with knowing eyes. "A lot of guys try to get with her."

"They do?" The thought doesn't please me.

"Yeah, she and the girls come by maybe once a week, and there's always a local tourist asking me if I know who she is and if she's in a relationship and if she's looking for some fun."

"Well, great. That's always good to hear," I say sarcastically.

"It doesn't bother you, does it?"

"No, of course not. She's free to do what she wants. Obviously not right now while we're in this fake relationship, but once this is done, she can date as many tourists who are asking about her as she wants. Like I care."

I'm not about to admit I've been in love with her for over a decade and I'm finding it hard to navigate fake dating without getting my real emotions and wants to surface.

"If you don't care, then what's the big deal? Just go back to being as platonic as possible when it's just the two of you and just hold hands or something when you're around your family."

"I suppose so." The thought doesn't settle well in my mind. I don't want to go back to just being friendly with Mia in the bedroom, but then I don't know if our current friendship can handle any more lines being blurred.

Don't even go there, Luke. Do not try and sleep with her.

"So, how's business? I heard you're doing amazing in the city." He hands me the shots, and we down them. "No chance of you coming back?"

"Business is great, and it's unlikely I'll move back."

"And your parents' business?" he asks. "I assume it's going well also?"

"No idea. Why do you ask?"

"Between you and me, I've noticed Rex has seemed a little anxious the last couple of times he's come in, and I've overheard him arguing on the phone, and the calls seemed to be about money. I was just curious if it was business-related or wedding-related."

"I'm sure it's wedding-related," I say, shaking my head. "My brother is the last person I thought would ever get married and settle down, and I'm sure he's probably having second thoughts."

"Yeah, he's not exactly a monogamous sort of man, is he?"

I lean forward and look at Cal. "What does that mean?"

"It means that I might or might not have overheard him having a conversation a couple of nights ago, talking about wanting Mia Bishop and how gorgeous she was looking and how he would hate to have to ruin your relationship by having her want him again."

"He said fucking what?" I clench my fists and stare at Cal. "You're joking, right?"

Cal shrugs. "I wasn't going to say anything because what's the likelihood of Rex really making a play for Mia when he's about to get married? But I just wanted to make you aware. I know there was some history with Mia and Rex."

"It's fine. Thanks. I should get going though. I know Mia is probably huffing and puffing, waiting for me."

"Okay, cool. Well, you let me know if you want to chat any more."

"Thanks, Cal. And you let me know if you need to chat about Silvie."

"Will do."

"What do I owe you?"

"It's on me today. I'll catch you later." He grins as I head out of the bar.

I notice Carter walking in, head down deep in thought as I made my way out.

"Hey, Carter. How are you doing?"

"Oh, hi, Luke. Good to see you again."

"How's it going at the bed-and-breakfast? It's a really nice place that Wendy and her family have, right?"

"Yeah, it is quite pleasing." He smiles a wide smile and runs his fingers through his blond hair. His eyes are twinkling. "Very comfortable and relaxing."

"The bed's that good, huh?"

"Yeah, something like that."

He offers me a wink, and I nod knowingly. These women have gotten their hooks into all of us.

"Well, I'm out of here. Got to go and meet Mia. Enjoy the afternoon. It's a beautiful day."

I head out of Cocktails & Chaos and down to the beach. I see Mia standing there, running her fingers through the sand. Her bikini is small and tight, and my jaw drops as I notice it's a thong at the back. I try not to stare at her beautiful ass, but I'm finding it hard not to. She looks up and sees me and waves, her bangles shaking from side to side as she offers me a small smile. Her long hair is wavy as it hangs down her back, still wet from the water.

"Finally finished with work?" she says, offering me a wry smile.

"Yeah, for now. Are you still mad at me?"

"Could I stay mad at you for long, Luke?"

"I guess not. Look at my handsome face," I tease as I look at her feet and notice that she's painted her toenails an aqua-blue color. "When did you do that?" I say. "I didn't even notice before."

"Yeah, I did them earlier today when we had some downtime. Juniper did a hot pink."

"It looks nice."

"Thank you."

"Your bikini also looks very nice."

"Oh, yeah? I was wondering if you were going to say something."

"Showing a lot of skin, I see."

"I don't want to have tan lines."

"Then shouldn't you go to a nude beach?"

"Is that an offer, Luke?"

She winks at me, and I just shake my head.

"You wouldn't dare go to a nude beach with me."

"You think?" She grins and presses her finger against my lips. "You think you know me so well, Luke Haverbrook, but you don't know me at all. I would one hundred percent go to a nude beach."

"Then it's a pity that we don't have any nudes on the island, isn't it?"

"We could always go up to Hidden Cove," she says, and her

expression changes. "Or we just wait until nighttime and we go skinny-dipping in the ocean, like you and Talia did."

"It wasn't just me and Talia," I say. "It was me, Talia, and some other people, and it's not like anything happened."

"So, you did or you didn't see her naked?"

"I might have seen her naked."

"And she did or didn't see you naked?"

"Well, I was nude. She obviously—"

"Exactly. So, you guys went skinny-dipping together."

"Is this why you're mad at me? Are you jealous?"

"No, I'm not jealous," she interrupts me quickly. "I just thought we were best friends, and best friends tell each other everything." She stops. "You know what? Whatever. Have you thought about the treasure map yet and what the clues might mean?"

"I have actually," I say, gazing at her, "and I think I am onto something."

"What do you think?"

"I kept going through the lines of the poem that were on the map."

"Yeah?"

"It said: A treasure awaits an island. / The island is big; the island is small. / A treasure awaits somewhere rocky. / Don't trip, or you'll fall." I stare at her as I stop talking. "Gold, silver, bounty aplenty. Do your very best to come and find me."

"Where's the clue there?"

"Don't trip, or you'll fall," I say, gazing at her.

"What does that mean?"

"Where are people constantly tripping on the island?"

"I don't know." She shakes her head. "Oh, wait. Down by the pier, where the rocks are. Tourists love to climb on them, and they always end up slipping. That's why we locals call it Slippery Rock Beach."

"Exactly. Tourists are always going down the pier to the beach and tripping over the rocks. They don't see the moss on them at first."

"You think that's it?"

"All I know is, that is what my brain is telling me. We're here, we're at the beach. We could go and check now."

"Shoot, do you think I'm going to find a bucket of gold right now?"

"No. There were several clue numbers on the map. I think there are going to be several clues until we get to the end."

"Then we'll find a bucket of gold?" she asks hopefully.

"Maybe. I don't know who set this up." I very much doubt it, but I don't want to burst her bubble.

She looks at me through narrowed eyes and grabs my hand. "Lukey, you would tell me if it was you, right?"

"What do you mean?" My heart pounds as she traces her fingers across my palm.

"Did you create this treasure map so that we could spend more time together, so that we could practice being a couple? Because you knew I was upset that you didn't come early, like you were supposed to."

"I wish I could say that I did"—I pause—"but I didn't."

Her eyes narrow, and she gazes at me. She takes another step forward, and I feel sand brushing from her toes onto my legs. She reaches up and touches the side of my face and gazes deep into my eyes. My heart races as she touches me. I can smell sun tan lotion on her skin and see remnants of salt on her body. She's got a golden glow from her time in the sun and rosy-pink cheeks. She looks absolutely beautiful.

"You know I can tell if you're lying, right?" She leans forward. Her lips graze against mine as she studies my eyes. "Tell me again."

"Tell you what?" I say, barely breathing.

"Did you create the treasure maps?"

"I didn't," I say.

She steps back slightly and frowns. "I can't tell if you're telling the truth or not."

"I thought you could always tell."

"I thought I could always tell as well, but maybe I'm losing my touch."

"I don't think you are."

I grab her around the waist and pull her into me. She looks around quickly.

"Who's here?"

"What do you mean, who is here?"

"I just assumed that—"

"You just assumed what?" I say as my hand slides down the curve of her waist and then her hip to her ass.

I squeeze gently, and she moans as she presses herself against me.

"I just assumed that this sort of touch was reserved for when people were around."

"Maybe we should make sure that we do it all the time because we don't know when people will be around. Someone could be spying on us right now," I say, grinning at her.

"You don't really believe that, do you?" She looks around quickly. "Rex is not that crazy, is he?"

"I don't know. I was speaking to Cal earlier, and he said that Rex has had a lot of anxious, frustrated-sounding phone calls. I don't know what he might do, knowing that he lost you to me."

"He didn't lose me," she says sharply. "He never had me, and I'm not yours. Remember?"

"I know, but he doesn't know that. Men always want what they can't have. He probably assumed you still wanted him," I say quickly, though my heart is pounding.

I want her to be mine, and I want her to want to be mine. Fuck. I'm still in love with Mia. I've always been deeply, endlessly in love with Mia, and this has all been a mistake.

I should not have come back to Coconut Beach for this wedding. I should not have been in a fake relationship with her, and I should not have agreed to share a hotel room with her. All the feelings that I've held down for so long are rising in me like lava in a volcano that's about to erupt. I feel hot, and I feel anxious, and I feel the way I felt when I was eighteen and she told me she was going to prom with William Setta, a guy from the tennis team who, frankly, was a nice guy, but he wasn't me. And if he hadn't asked her, she would've gone with me because we were going to go as friends.

I can still remember seeing her in her pink gown, twirling so happy as she laughed. Then he gave her a corsage, and she thanked him by giving him a kiss on the cheek, and his eyes lit up because he thought she would fuck him that night. But there was no way I was going to let that happen, even if I was just the third wheel on their last-minute date.

It stung. It stung then to know she would never be mine, and it stings now because my feelings are deeper and more invested than they have ever been. When I finally get off the island again, I will have to stay away for a much longer time. I'll have to stay away until she finds someone she loves, until she finds someone she wants to give her life to. I just hope I can survive through the pain that will awaken in me.

"Hey, Luke," she says, touching my face softly. "Shall we go and check by the pier? What are we looking for?"

"I don't know," I say. "I guess another postcard, but it would get wet. I think we'll know it when we see it," I say softly, grabbing her hand and squeezing. "Don't you?"

"I guess so," she says, nodding slowly, her expression changing as she gazes over at me.

I'm really glad she can't actually read my mind. I'm really glad that she doesn't know I love her, that this is beginning to feel real to me. I'm really glad that she doesn't know this fake summer romance is burning me up inside because I don't want it to be fake.

We walk down toward the pier, and we both stop as we notice a bunch of surfers in the water.

"Wow, they're good," she says, admiring them, and I wonder if she's talking about their skill at surfing or if she's admiring their bodies or how she wants to be with them.

"You really love surfers, don't you?"

"They're okay," she says, looking at me. "They're not the be-all and end-all of my world."

"Why don't you know how to surf, Mia? I've always wondered that."

"I'm scared of sharks. I'm definitely not going that far out in the water. The sharks abound."

"I know," I say, "but you don't have to be scared. You shouldn't live your life in fear."

"I know, and I try not to. I mean, it's hard sometimes, right?"

"Yeah," I say, nodding slowly because I, more than anyone, know how hard it is to be open and honest about everything. I haven't ever told Mia that I love her because I was in fear that once she knew that information, our relationship would be forever changed, and I was not willing to risk that. Not at all.

Though a part of me wonders if I already have.

chapter eighteen

Mia

"Do you really think that the next clue is going to be here?" I ask Luke as we carefully clamber around the rocks and look around. I just can't imagine how another clue could be planted here and not be destroyed or taken out to the ocean with all the waves that keep coming up and then receding.

"I didn't write the clue, so I don't one hundred percent know if they're here, but I just have a feeling that something is going to be around here. We just have to know what we're looking for. Keep your eyes peeled for anything that looks like it shouldn't be here."

"But that's the thing. We don't know what we're looking for." I run my fingers through the sand and pick up shells and then head back toward the side of the water again. "Maybe there's a message in a bottle or something."

"That would be cool."

"That would be really cool. One of my favorite books when I was younger was about this guy who put a love letter in a bottle, and he said that the woman who found it was likely to be his wife, and then—"

"Focus, Mia. Not time to talk about your romance books."

"I know, it was just a really good book. That's all. I don't know what I would do if I found a message in a bottle. It would be so …" I continue to survey the area when I freeze. "Help," I scream. "It's a shark. It's a shark. Run." I point to something gray in the water and fall back as I try to get away.

Luke stills and then heads slowly toward the mini Jaws, and he just confirms what I already knew. The man is half crazy.

"Whatcha doing?" I bellow as I jump up from the water. I'm completely soaked again.

"Sharks wouldn't be this close to the rocks," he says, his eyes watching me as I stand there, wringing the water out of my hair. "Where do you see it?"

I point to the side, and he hurries over. I watch him kneel down and grab something and pull slowly. It looks like a shark head, and I think I might faint.

"Is that a baby shark?"

"No, it's an inflatable shark. It was attached to a rock with some rope to weigh it down."

"What, you think a tourist put it there?"

"I don't," he says, giving me a wicked grin. "If I am not mistaken, it looks like there's a ziplock bag inside of this shark with a note in it. Come on. Let's go up, and I'll open it."

"Did we just find the next clue?" My heart races.

"I think we did," he says, his eyes glowing. "Let me open it. Let's see what it says."

We walk back up the beach, and he rips open the shark as we stand next to the bright yellow lifeguard hut.

"Rest in peace, Sharky," I say as he tears it to pieces with the sharp end of a shell he picked up from the sand, and he just laughs.

He opens the Ziploc bag carefully, and there's another white note card. My heart races. We've officially found the next clue.

"You listening, Mia?"

"No, I'm floating in the air."

He gives me a look and continues, "*Lawyers and judges spend their days here. / Convicts and jurors don't want to be near. / You don't have to go inside. It's a hot day, I fear. / Cool your mouth down and enjoy the ice. / That much is clear.*"

"Say what?" I stare at him for a couple of seconds, my mind scrambling to decipher a code that means absolutely nothing to me.

"Come on, Mia. I know you got this. You think you already know it. Listen to it again."

"What are the first words again?" I ask him.

"Lawyers and judges spend their days here," he says.

"Wait, the courthouse. Lawyers and judges spend their days at the courthouse, right? You think it's at the courthouse?"

"No, I don't." I feel slightly deflated. "But listen again, Mia. *Lawyers and judges spend their days here. / Convicts and jurors don't want to be near. / You don't have to go inside."* He pauses. "So, I think it says we don't have to go inside the courthouse. We just have to be in the vicinity."

"Okay, that makes sense. And what's the rest of it?"

"It's a hot day, I fear. / Cool your mouth down and enjoy the ice. / That much is clear."

"Enjoy the ice. That is clear. Say what?" I stare at him and rub my forehead. This feels like some sort of puzzle or brain teaser, and then it suddenly clicks in my brain. "Enjoy the ice. That is clear," I repeat again.

"What are you thinking?"

"The shaved ice cart that's near the courthouse."

"Bingo," he says with a grin. "I'm almost positive it's there."

I immediately jump into his arms in excitement, and he laughs as he grabs ahold of me. I suddenly remember I'm in a skimpy bikini, and I'm wet. His hands are positioned under my ass, and I feel them sliding inward, into dangerous territory, and I freeze and push back slightly.

"Oh, sorry, I forgot I was wet."

"And we're not even in the bedroom."

I lick my lips and adjust my thong, trying to not think about how easy it would be to slip it to the side.

"Shall we go now?" I need to change the subject, fast.

"I don't know that we have time. We have dinner with Rex and Andi and the grandparents in an hour or so."

"Oh, yeah," I say. "This is going to be interesting."

"It's going to be very interesting and boring." Luke groans.

"You still haven't made up with Rex, have you?" I say as we walk back up to the bookmobile so I can grab my clothes.

"He's a douche, and he's rude, and he thinks he runs the world, so, no, I am kind of over him."

"I'm sorry. It's really unfair how your parents have treated you."

"It's fine. I don't want to talk about it right now. Shall we head back to the hotel and get ready?" he says as we see the bookstore. "I need a shower and a little break before we head out again."

"Okay, so is everyone enjoying the oysters?" Bitsy beams as we all sit at the large, oversize table, eating our hearts out.

"Yeah, I love oysters," I say, licking my lips nervously.

I feel like I am being examined by everyone around me, and they're just waiting for me to mess up and give away that Luke and I are not really in a relationship.

I look over at Luke for encouragement and smile.

"Do you remember the last time we were here at Tide and Table?"

"I do," he says, "and I remember that you accidentally ordered a two-hundred-dollar steak, and you were panicking because you didn't have two hundred dollars, but you didn't want to tell me that, and so we spent thirty minutes just staring at the bill."

"I thought it said twenty dollars. In my mind's eye, I could never have imagined that a steak would cost two hundred dollars."

"Well, you don't have to worry about tonight. I'm sure it's on my parents."

"I know, but I'm definitely not going to get the two-hundred-fifty-dollar steak." I grin at him.

"Yeah, you wouldn't want to do that and blow my parents' bank account."

"Exactly." I start laughing.

I notice that Luke has been staring at me often throughout the evening, but I don't know if it's because Rex is here or if it's because he just wants to look at me.

He reaches over and grabs my hand and squeezes.

"Mia, to love you is to—"

"What are you saying?" Rex booms from the other side of the table.

"I'm speaking to Mia, my girlfriend," Luke stresses.

Rex just rolls his eyes. He turns to Andi and starts laughing.

"Do you think it's weird that my brother keeps going on about his girlfriend? Like, Luke, is this the first girlfriend you've ever been able to get?"

Andi looks uncomfortable as she sits there. Bitsy gives Rex a stern look, as does my grandmother.

"That's enough, Rex," Bitsy reprimands him, and he looks taken aback.

"This is supposed to be my celebration. I dunno why we're always focusing on Luke," he mutters under his breath loudly.

I just stare at him with a blank expression on my face. What did I ever see in that blowhard?

I turn to Luke and ask him if he knows what he wants to eat, but I realize there's a weird expression on his face.

"Hey, what's going on?" I asked him. "Why are you looking at me like that?"

"I just saw the way you were looking at Rex," he says in a low voice. "Do you still like him?" There's suspicion in his tone.

I frown. What on earth is he talking about?

"I know you're not seriously asking me that question."

"Mia, you were just staring at Rex, and there was a sort of nostalgic look on your face."

"No, there was not any nostalgic look on my face. I was—"

"If you say so," he cuts me off and turns away grumpily.

"I am saying so, Luke, but let's not have this conversation here because I don't want to have to cuss you out in front of everyone."

"You want to cuss me out?" His lips twitch.

"You don't want me to cuss you out. How could you even ask me if I still like Rex? He's a douchebag."

"Yeah, but you—"

"Luke!"

"My bad."

"Yeah, it is your bad." I roll my eyes and look away from him and grab my glass of champagne and sip it slowly. Trying to ignore everyone around me.

A couple of seconds later, my phone beeps. I look down, and I see different shark memes from Luke in my text messages, and I try not to laugh.

I look over at him. "Really?"

"I just want you to smile again."

"I am smiling. Stop sending me shark memes. We're at dinner."

"You are pretending you're fine, but I can tell you're clearly not. I take back what I asked about Rex."

"Let's hope so. I'm fed up with this line of questioning, Luke."

"Well, what if I told you I have something really exciting for you to see?"

"What's that?" I ask him, curiosity getting the better of me.

"Do you want to see photos of the new couch that I had delivered to my apartment in New York?"

When he brings up his place in New York, I suddenly feel deflated because it's just a reminder of the fact that he will eventually be going back, and once again, there will be distance between us.

"Sure," I say, forcing a smile even though I don't really want to see right now.

He grabs his phone and places it in front of us so that we're both looking at the screen. As he's going through his photos, a text message comes through. I don't want to be nosy, but I can't help but read it. I see Talia's name at the top.

TALIA

Miss you, big boy. Want to grab dinner this week? I'm headed to New York next month. Would love to chat with you about some business. I have some ideas I want to get your feedback on.

I press my lips together. Why is Talia messaging him? I look over at him, but he quickly just moves the message off the screen. He says nothing, but I can feel all my insecurities growing larger and larger. It sucks. I know Talia fits into his new world in New York a lot better than me, and it's just a reminder of the fact that I'm part of his old life and this is just a vacation. Talia fits into his big-city dreams. She understands his world.

I suddenly feel sad.

"Hey, what is wrong?"

"Why is Talia messaging you, and why is she calling you big boy, and what the fuck is she talking about, going to visit you in New York?" I hiss.

"Hey, calm down. You're being loud," he says, giving me a look.

"Don't tell me I'm being loud," I say even louder, and everyone at the table immediately turns to look at us. "Hey, don't mind me. Just a couple too many glasses of champagne," I blurt.

I give everyone a smile, and everyone turns their attention back away from me. Luke just stares at me, his eyes curious.

"I don't know why she messaged me, Mia."

"But you know why she called you a big boy?"

"I think we both know why she called me big boy." He gives me a wink, but I don't smile or laugh at his stupid joke.

Instead, I feel searing jealousy coursing through me. I feel blindsided because Talia messaged him and he doesn't care. He's not dismissing anything. He's not saying that there's no way he's going to meet up with her.

"Do you have feelings for her?" I whisper.

"What?" He stares at me in confusion. "What are you talking about?"

"Do you have feelings for Talia? Is this why she's been acting so obnoxious to me?"

"Firstly, she's always been obnoxious, Mia, and secondly, no, I don't have feelings for her. You know this."

"Why didn't you tell me about the skinny-dipping that time? Then what else do I not know about?"

He lets out an inaudible sigh. "We cannot have this conversation here, Mia. We do not want to blow up our entire ruse."

"All it is right? Just a ruse."

"It's not just a ruse." He presses his lips together. "You know this."

"Yeah. Well, maybe I don't."

I grab another oyster, and I down it quickly, trying to ignore the anger that is coursing through me. I'm so fed up with Luke just dismissing my concerns like I don't matter. Like I am just going to accept whatever crumbs he gives me. I deserve better than this. From him as a friend, from him in a fake relationship, from him as someone who—

Stop it. Mia, you're acting crazy, the voice inside of me says, *You're not really his girlfriend. Stop acting like a jealous bitch.*

I bite down on my lower lip and turn to Luke. He's gazing at me with worry and concern.

"Hey, we okay?" he whispers, and I nod.

"You want to dance?"

"We're in the middle of dinner."

"The band's playing over there, and there are a couple of other people dancing."

"We can't."

"I can," he says as he grabs my hand. "Excuse us. We're just going to the dance floor for one dance. Mia loves this song," he says as he pulls me toward the small floor.

"Everyone is going to look at us."

"Let them look," he says.

We look away from the table, and Rex is staring over at us with narrowed eyes.

"He's so mad right now," Luke says almost gleefully as he pulls me into his arms.

"What are you doing?"

"I'm just letting everyone know that you're mine," he says.

He leans down and kisses me passionately. I wrap my arms around his neck as we sway back and forth, his lips pressing against mine. His body feels warm and hard against mine, and it's like time has stood still. I forget about my jealousy. I forget about my insecurities. I forget about everything, but being in his arms, it feels like magic. I don't want the moment to end, but finally, he pulls away from me, and we just dance.

"That kiss was everything," he says, his eyes gleaming as he stares down at me.

He turns to look back at the table, and there's a wicked grin on his face.

"What is it?" I say.

"Rex was watching the entire thing." He turns back to me with a wicked smile. "This is going exceptionally well, isn't it, Mia?"

My heart sinks. For a few moments, I thought everything was real. When he kissed me and we danced, I thought he was in the moment, like I was, that he'd sensed that I was upset and annoyed and jealous and he wanted to make it right, but this is just all about one-upping his brother and ensuring that our fake relationship is a success. It has nothing to do with any genuine emotions that he has for me. It just has to do with the fact that he has to one-up his brother because Luke has always felt inferior. He's always been trying to prove himself.

"I think today has been a success, don't you?"

I look up at him and just nod slowly. I don't really know what to say. When he kisses me lightly on the forehead, it just confirms to me that all he really thinks about me is that I'm his friend.

I'm his friend with benefits, but nothing more.

All the hopes and dreams burning inside of me, underneath the surface, are in my head, and I need to remember that. I need to remember that I can't get carried away. This isn't real. Luke isn't feeling the things that I am feeling. This isn't a romance book. This is true life, and we both know what we are doing, what the stakes are. I just need to remind myself that he is just my friend, and it is never going to be anything else.

chapter nineteen

Luke

I study Talia's text message in contemplation. I don't really know why she texted me the evening before, but I know Mia physically and emotionally reacted to the text message. A part of me hoped it meant that Mia was developing feelings for me that were more than just that of a friend, but then the other part of me was worried she was just upset because she felt I was holding things back from her. I still had no clue what Talia was up to or if she were hoping to cause drama between Mia and myself. I can still remember the comments she'd made that night, calling Mia naive and gullible. It had been one of the reasons I'd been turned off from making out with Talia. No one talked about my best friend like shit. Especially when I so desperately wanted the friendship to be more than innocent.

Mia and are walking along the line of friendship and something resembling love, and I know I am falling for her in a way that can't be undone, but I also know I am so scared of losing her friendship—that it would kill me inside to express feelings for her, have them not be returned, and then be rejected. I know our friendship couldn't handle that. And yet, I don't know how much longer I can hold back. I think a part of the reason I'd been gone from Coconut Beach for so long was because I'd known that as soon as I was in close contact with her along, it would be like detonating a bomb. I wouldn't be able to resist her. The way she smiled at me, the way she played with her hair, the way she giggled and teased me, the easy way she came in for hugs, the way her nostrils flared when she was mad, the way her feet tapped when she was bored, the secret half-smiles she gave me when she wanted to say something rude but had decided to be polite. Mia had always been the only woman that had seen every side of me and I wasn't even sure she knew that. She was so open, so trusting, so giving, and she was my one, whether or not she felt the same way.

Mia held a lock on my heart that no key could open.

But she didn't even know.

Now everything was starting to unravel because I was no longer able to keep my feelings to myself.

But I'd known as soon as I'd stepped off of that plane and back onto Coconut Beach that I was finally home and ready to claim the woman who made everything feel better in my life. I just hadn't expected that she's be so open to exploration.

"What are you looking at?" Mia says as she walks into the hotel room with a bag of fruit in her hand. There's a quizzical look in her eyes like she wants to ask me something else. Like she knows I've been holding back from her. I wait for her to ask me to declare my true feelings and intentions.

I want her to ask.

I need her to ask.

"Oh, just a message from work," I say quickly as I put my phone away. "Nearly ready for breakfast?" I ask her. I'm not going to force something that she's not ready for.

"Yeah. I just went down to the market to get some fruit as I was craving clementines and I needed to help Juniper open up this morning," she says, avoiding eye contact with me. "I also got my camera so I can take photographs of the breakfast. Andi asked me if I would mind being the unofficial photographer." Her lips twist up in irony.

"I hope they're going to pay you," I say. Though I know Mia. She hates charging friends and family for anything and I bet she don't even bring it up.

She looks at me with a smile. "I didn't ask for payment, Luke." I gloat inside. *I know my Mia so well.*

"Well, you should. I don't want them taking advantage of you."

"It's fine. I'm always taking photos. I love taking photos, and I don't mind doing it."

"I know you don't mind doing it, but ..." I pause as she gives me a look. "You know what? I'm sure they'll be very grateful."

"Yeah, I hope so."

There's an awkwardness between us I haven't ever felt, and I wonder if this is it for us. I wonder if playing fake boyfriend and girlfriend for just a matter of days already caused a rift in our friendship that will never heal.

"That text message and your reaction last night scares me, Mia." I wish I had the words to explain to her that I had a breadth of feelings for her that made it difficult for me to breath sometimes. I wish I could grab her hand and have her close her eyes and reach into my soul. There's a storm raging inside of me, and my heart is in the eye of it, scared, vulnerable and weary.

"Yeah?" She raises her eyebrows to look at me, and I watch as she twirls her fingers in her hair—a telltale sign that she's anxious or nervous about something.

"I just want you to know that I really don't know why Talia sent me that text message."

She shrugs nonchalantly. "Doesn't matter. I'm sure she sent it to you because she wants to get with you, and I think it's extremely disrespectful, seeing that she thinks we're in a relationship, but she can do whatever she wants to do if she thinks that's okay. That's her problem."

"Yeah. Well, I just want you to know it's not something I led her to believe was in the cards."

She stares at me for a couple of seconds and nods slowly. "You've dated in New York though, right?"

"Yeah. Nothing serious. I didn't care about those women, and I don't care about Talia."

"Talia's a bitch, and you can do much better than her, but if that's the sort of woman you want to go for, then you go ahead." She shrugs and I wonder if she really doesn't care. I wonder if this has been nothing but a bit of fun for her.

"Really, Mia?" I stare at her. "That's where we're going to leave this?"

"What?"

We stare at each other for what feels like an eternity. No smiles. No eyebrow waggles. No teasing smirks. Just searching eyes gazing at each other in contemplation. I wish I could really read her mind. I wish I knew what she was thinking. I wish that I knew the answers. But the silence between us was like an impenetrable wall that neither of us could scale.

I wanted to step forward. I wanted to be brave. I wanted to tell her what was in my soul. But I was scared I would be too much. That she wouldn't understand my feelings. And then what? Where would that leave us. The silence was better than answers I didn't want to hear.

"Nothing. You know what? If you don't want to talk about it, I don't need to talk about it. Let's go down for breakfast."

"I told you, I'll be ready in a couple of minutes," she says, her tone sharp. "Let me put the fruit down on the table and get it out of the plastic bag and let me brush my teeth, and then we can go down for breakfast. Or why don't you just go by yourself and I'll meet you down there? I have to take photos anyway, and that will just make it easier so you don't have to wait around for me."

"Hey, there's no need to get an attitude." I don't bother arguing with her about what information she had and hadn't given me. I didn't want to rile her up, even more.

"I don't have an attitude, Luke." She lets out an audible sigh. "Okay, maybe I have a bit of an attitude, but I just don't want you waiting around for me. Everyone knows I'm taking photographs this morning anyway, so they will not expect to see us together."

"Okay." I nod slowly. "Do you want to try to find the clue later this afternoon so we can continue the treasure hunt?"

"Yeah, we can do that." She turns around, and I watch her pull out mangoes, pineapples, oranges, lemons, and apples from the bag and place them on the table.

"Well, you really had a fruit kick," I say, walking up and picking up an orange.

"I guess so." She smiles at me and runs her fingers through her hair. Her eyes look sad for a few moments, and then she gazes at the table and starts laughing. "This cost me forty-five dollars."

"Wowser," I say, laughing. "We're not even here that long."

"I know. So, I guess we have to eat a lot of fruit, or we have to have a party in the hotel room."

I raise an eyebrow at her. "Is that your way of telling me you want to have an orgy?" I hope my light teasing will soften the mood. Jokes have always been a way for us to move on from awkwardness. Most probably not the most healthy way of us dealing with shit, but it worked for us. At least it had in the past.

"No. That's not my way of telling you I want to have an orgy." Her tone is still quite sharp, but she's smiling now, and I can tell that she's coming around.

She can never stay mad at me for long, and that's one reason why I love her. Even when she's angry at me, she gets over it pretty quickly.

"Mia, I think when all this is said and done, we should think about making plans to do something fun together that's got nothing to do with the wedding." I bring up the subject lightly, so that it doesn't sound like our entire relationship weighs on her answer.

"Okay, sure," she says. "If that's what you want to do." Her words are easy and that's all I need to feel relaxed. We had a lot of shit to talk out, but right now we were okay.

"I do. I am going to head downstairs," I say, and I pause as a clause in one of the work contracts comes to mind. I need to have the attorneys check out a statute and I know that it will be on my mind until I email them.

"What is it?" she says. "Shoot. Tell me what you're thinking." She crosses her arms and gives me a knowing look. She knows me far too well.

"I have to make a quick call." The words trip out of my mouth of their own volition.

She stares at me for a couple of seconds. There is a subtle disappointment in her eyes, and I don't know why she looks upset. Does she think I'm going to call Talia or some other woman.

"It's not like I'm going to be long, Mia. It's just a quick call about work." I wait for the understanding to hit her eyes, but she still looks pissed.

"I don't care. I'll be taking photos. It's fine." She presses her lips together. "Go take your call for work, and I'll see you down in the restaurant for breakfast." There's a coolness that permeates the air, the shift causing a chasm between us that I know can't close in the time we have available to us right now. Staring at her face makes me think of days when we'd argued and she'd said she was fine, but gave me the silent treatment. There was something about the silent treatment that felt worse than being shouted at or cursed out. The silent treatment was like an ache that couldn't be soothed.

"Okay." I nod and then walk out of the hotel room. I don't want to just leave, but I know for the sake of both of us, I need to.

For some reason, my footsteps feel like lead as I head to the elevator. There is a somberness that I feel in the air, and I don't know why.

Maybe it's because Mia and I are not connecting how we normally do—how our friendship normally is.

We are always light and funny and laughing, and now it's complex and complicated. I step into the elevator, and I'm grateful to see it's empty. I really don't want to come across anyone from the wedding party, especially not Rex or Talia. When the elevator dings and alerts me to the fact that I'm in the lobby, I step out and decide to walk outside of the hotel to take my phone call.

I call the office and wait for my assistant to update me as I lean back against a large white column. I notice that there are several couples standing there in matching outfits. I notice that one woman notices that I'm looking, and she grins.

"We made the guys wear matching shirts." She giggles. "They didn't know it was going to happen."

"That's cool. You look like you all could be related," I say.

"We're just best friends who came to Coconut Beach to relax, and it's amazing here," the girl continues. "I feel like I want to move here."

"We can't afford to move to the island," the man behind her says, and I'm pretty confident that's her husband or boyfriend, "but it's just so gorgeous. Imagine being able to watch the beach every day and go to food trucks for delicious food."

"And then that cool mobile bookstore. I would absolutely die if we had that back home," the girl adds.

"My girlfriend owns the bookstore actually," I say, smiling and walking over to them. I'm still on hold, so I don't mind carrying on the conversation.

"Oh, really?" The girl's eyes light up. "That is so cool. Your girlfriend must be amazing."

"She really is," I say.

Then it suddenly hits me I called Mia my girlfriend and not my best friend, and it didn't feel weird or unusual. There is a part of me that likes her having that moniker. There is a part of me that wishes that this weren't a pretense.

"She specializes in romance books, so if you like romance, definitely head down to see her and her best friend, Juniper. They can actually recommend books if you tell them what you like, but I know they also have quite an extensive collection of thrillers and psychological thrillers and murder mysteries, even some sci-fi and horror."

"Oh, I like sci-fi," the man behind her says. "Maybe I will go back with you later."

"Oh, yay. Thank you, Dylan." She turns around and kisses him and then looks back at me. "Thank you for convincing my husband to take me to the bookstore. I was begging him to come with me last night, and he was like, 'I don't want to go to the bookstore.' "

"Well, you were just going on about all the romance stuff," he says. "I don't care about romance books."

She looks at me and rolls her eyes. "What do you say when your girlfriend talks to you about romance books? Do you say you're not interested?"

"I can honestly say that when Mia mentions romance books to me, I listen with half my brain, and the other half of my brain thinks about work," I say honestly.

"But she can't stop loving love, right?"

"No, she can't." I nod.

"Well, I think we're going to head out to the beach now, but it was really nice meeting you."

"Nice meeting you too. You have a good day."

I walk back into the hotel lobby and stand there. My phone disconnects, and I want to curse because I waited so long. I'm about to call the office back again when I see Rex walking into the lobby. I quickly step back out of the line of sight so he doesn't see me. I really don't want to have a conversation with him.

A couple of minutes later, I see Mia step out of the elevator with her camera. She spies Rex and heads over to him. I frown as I watch them. What is this about?

"So, Mia, Mia, Mia, you are looking absolutely stunning this fine morning," Rex says to her loudly as he looks her up and down. He lets out a low whistle, and I watch as she blushes. "When we were teenagers, I didn't really notice you."

"What do you want, Rex?" Mia says, holding the body of her camera in her hands. She looks uncomfortable, but she also looks like she's still willing to give him the time of day, which annoys me.

"I just wanted to say that I regret not giving you a chance. If I had known—"

"I know. You've already mentioned this," she says.

"Well, I want to mention it again." He reaches out and touches the side of her face. "You're beautiful, Mia."

"Thank you," she says, and she blushes again.

I can feel myself growing angry as I squeeze my phone in my palm.

"I want to tell you something that I don't think you know," Rex says.

I frown as I watch Mia tilt her head to the side and look at him with a curious expression and wide eyes.

"What's that?"

"I want you to know that Luke will never marry you."

Her jaw drops, and so does mine. What on earth is he talking about?

"Sorry, I don't know what you mean," she says, frowning slightly.

"Have you ever heard that saying, *Why buy the cow when the milk is free?*'" He looks her up and down. "I'm just trying to be honest with you, Mia. He's fucking you because you've grown into an exquisite woman and you look like you have a body to die for, but he's never going to marry you."

She licks her lips nervously. "I don't really know what you're trying to say."

"I am saying, no one in my family knew he was dating you, period, okay? And if he was serious about you, he would've told us. Also, I know you're not really into him."

"What are you talking about?" she says, taking a step away from him.

"I'm just saying, I know he's the consolation prize."

"What?" She just stares at him.

"You wanted me. You couldn't get me, so you got the second-best Haverbrook brother." He shrugs. "Look, you know you would've done anything to be with me. Well, now's your chance. Don't you want a chance with the best Haverbrook brother?"

"I think you're fucking rude as hell, Rex," Mia says.

I smile at her response to him. I know I should step forward and let them know that I've witnessed the conversation, but for some reason, I want to see how Mia handles it.

"I don't know what you're talking about," Rex says.

"You think I give a shit about you? You think that you're going to send me some wedding invite with a note and be like, *Mia's a loser, and she can't get a date,* and I'm just going to take it, lying down?"

Rex frowns as he stares at her. "Look, Mia, our families are close. Of course you were going to get an invitation. Everyone got the same note."

"Everyone did not get the same note," she says. "Juniper didn't get the note. Wendy didn't get the note. Silvie didn't get the note. Josie didn't get the note. Summer didn't get the note."

"To be quite honest with you, you're listing a bunch of names, and I don't even really know half of these people, and I don't care about them. I don't even know what was written on the invitation."

"You're telling me you don't know what was written on the invitation?" She glares at him. "You're such a pig to think that I ever thought you were cute."

"You thought I was cute. You thought I was sexy. You wanted me to be your first. Remember?"

She glares at him. "Thank God that never happened," she says, shaking her head.

Rex steps forward and grabs her by the hand. "We can still make something happen."

"You're getting married, Rex!" She's practically screaming at him. "You're such a jerk."

"Maybe I want to sample some other pieces of meat before I finally decide which cut I want."

It's then that I have to step forward.

"Excuse me, what's going on here?" I say.

Both Rex and Mia turn to me with shock in their eyes. She runs over to me immediately and jumps up into my arms, grabs my face, and kisses me hard and passionately. Her tongue slides into my mouth, and I run my fingers through her hair. She's breathing heavily, and I can't stop myself from kissing her back passionately. Our tongues twist together, and I feel her fingers running down my shoulders. She presses herself against me, and I wrap my arms around her waist and squeeze her ass. She's wearing a pair of shorts, and I slide my fingers up her inner thigh. She giggles slightly as she steps back.

"There. You are my knight in shining armor yet again," she says.

I kiss her on the lips and turn to Rex, giving him the most disdainful glance I can muster. "Don't you ever hit on my girlfriend again. Do you hear me?"

Rex stares at me in shock, saying nothing.

"She's mine."

Rex just shakes his head and walks away.

Mia looks up at me and takes a deep breath. "I can't believe I ever thought he was cute. Why was I such a fucking fool? He's horrible. I'm sorry. He's really, really horrible."

"I know. I really do. Did you kiss me because he was there and you wanted to prove to him that we were together or—"

"I kissed you because as I was speaking to him, all I could think was that Luke would never talk to me like this. He would never shame me like this. And then you were there, and you were coming toward me, and I could see the anger in your eyes, and, yeah, maybe I thought you were going to hit him—but when I ran up into your arms and kissed you, it was because I wanted to feel your lips against mine." Her voice lowers. "I wanted to just be in your arms. You're so much better than he is."

At that moment, I feel chosen. I feel validated. I feel hope. Maybe this can actually go somewhere for real.

"There's something I want to tell you, Mia, something you need to know."

"What is it?" she says. "Oh shit. I need to go though because I need to take the photos."

"Listen to me," I say, grabbing her hands and squeezing. "It's something I've wanted to tell you for a long time, and I don't want to not reveal this anymore."

"What is it?" She looks nervous now.

"Remember when we were teenagers, and you got drunk at that party, and you got carried home by a guy in a bear costume who took care of you, and you always thought it was Rex, and you were like, *This shows me he's a really great guy*?"

"Yeah. That was the only redeeming factor he had. Sure, I thought he was cute, but he had always been a jerk. Until that moment."

"It was me," I say.

"What?" She looks at me as if she doesn't quite understand what I just said.

"It was me in the bear costume."

"It was you?" She stares into my eyes for what feels like forever and just shakes her head. "What do you mean, it was you?"

"It was never Rex. I was the one in the bear costume. I saw you were drunk. I saw guys were looking to take advantage of you, and I wanted to make sure you were safe, so I took you home, and I tucked you in, and I got you water and soup and let you sleep. I don't even know if you remember the chicken noodle soup I got." I stop and survey her face, but she says nothing. "And I'm sorry if you think I'm a creep or a liar for not telling you. I just didn't know what to say. You really were convinced it was Rex, and it seemed to mean so much to you, and I didn't want to take that away from you. And when I realized that you were giving him far too much credit, I felt shitty to then tell you the truth. But I can't keep this to myself anymore. It was me, Mia."

I stare at her as she silently watches me, processing the information. I know if she takes this poorly, our entire relationship is down the drain. If she thinks I'm a liar, if she thinks I deliberately held this from her, I know I've lost her.

She lets out a long sigh and shakes her head.

I feel my heart drop. This is it. Just when I thought we finally had a chance, this is where it is all going to end.

"It was you," she says softly. "My darling. I should have known it was you."

She smiles a wide, happy smile, and her eyes light up as she leans forward and gives me a quick peck on the lips. I feel exposed but hopeful because she's touching me.

"Are you mad?"

"Why do I feel like you've said that many times on this trip?" she says, laughing. "You're someone I don't want to hurt, and it makes sense, obviously. I feel like a fool for ever thinking it was him."

She groans as she buries her face in her hands. "Tell me why, I'm such a fucking fool. How could I have ever thought that Rex took care of me that night? Nothing else he's ever done in my time of knowing him would lead me to believe that he was sweet and lovely like that."

She lets out a long sigh and looks up at me again. "Of course it was you, Luke." She touches the side of my face. "You've always been amazing."

"I hope that's good."

"It's not bad," she says, shrugging. "Okay, later this afternoon, after you've taken your work calls and I've taken the photographs, let's go look for the second clue. I'm really hoping to win a pot of gold at the end of this so I can change my life and go traveling."

"And where would you go traveling to?" I ask, my heart in my throat as I wait for her response.

"I don't know. Europe or Australia or something."

Disappointment floods through me. I hoped she was going to say she would come to New York. I hoped she was going to say that she would come and see if we could make a real relationship work, but she isn't there yet. She doesn't hate me, but I think, in her eyes, I am still just her best friend—the best friend who has always been there for her, the best friend who takes care of her, the best friend who doesn't let her down.

"Well, I've heard Australia's really fun to visit," I whisper, not wanting her to know just how morose I feel.

"Yeah." She nods slowly. "I think it would be an epic trip, but I should go take photos because I said I would." She leans back and tucks her camera to her body. "I'll see you later."

"Yeah," I say.

I watch as she walks away, and I know I should follow her. I'm a part of the breakfast as well, but I'm not ready to go in yet. I'm not ready to deal with Rex. I'm not ready to see Mia.

I just need to process everything that I'm feeling. I need to figure out where I'm going to go from here. Because there's a morose feeling in my stomach that tells me she will never be mine.

chapter twenty

Mia

I finish taking the photographs and head back upstairs to the hotel room. When I walk in, I'm surprised to see Luke sitting on the bed. He looks up, and there's a serious expression on his face.

"Hey," he says, gazing up at me. "You doing okay?"

"I'm fine. The photos went well. Everyone was really nice. To be honest, I didn't even really see Rex. He went to do something with some of his football buddies from high school, and I guess that was more important than the breakfast with his fiancée. But that doesn't really surprise me because he doesn't really seem like he's going to be an amazing husband."

"Yeah, he seems like he's going to be a bit of a jerk. I just want to see how we are."

"We're fine, Luke," I say, putting my camera down on the table and going to sit next to him on the bed. "We're still going to go and look for the clue at Kona Ice, right?"

"Yeah. I figured we could go in an hour or so. There is something I wanted to speak to you about."

"Is it about the bear costume again?"

"No, unless you wanted to speak to me about it."

"No, I'm not mad at you or anything."

"I know."

"Maybe I should be because I acted like a fool, going on and on about how Rex was such a great guy when it was really you. But it doesn't surprise me that you did that for me because you've always been a stand-up guy and you've always looked out for me, and I guess … thank you."

"I appreciate it. I was worried you would be mad at me. I was worried you would think I was a liar or that I deliberately held it back from you, and—"

"Hey, I know you better than that. You're not ill-intentioned."

"I know, but I couldn't help but think that you might be upset."

"I'm more surprised, and I feel slightly foolish. Thank you, Luke. You are one of only two men in my life who has really been there to protect me." He smiles one of those breathtaking smiles that makes my heart stop. "Don't tell my dad or grandad that I said that, though."

"Who's the other one?" he asks me, and I see a flash of what appears to be jealousy in his eyes.

"Rafe," I admit.

"Oh." He looks at me in confusion. "I didn't know Rafe had ever protected you. What happened?"

"I don't know how to tell you this," I say softly.

He shifts suddenly. "What is it?"

"I haven't told you because I didn't want you to get upset, but a couple of summers ago, I had been hanging out with this tourist who was in town. One night, he wanted to go dancing at Cocktails & Chaos. We were dancing, and we were having fun, and he asked me if I wanted to go on a walk on the beach. Rafe saw us about to leave, and he kind of made some comments to me, like 'I don't really think this guy is good,' and I just sort of brushed him off. Anyway, we went down by the ocean, and the next thing I knew, this guy was pushing me to the ground."

"What?" Luke sounds pissed. "What happened, Mia?"

I sniff, remembering that night. "It was horrible," I admit. "He wouldn't let me up. He was trying to pull my skirt up. I was telling him no." I close my eyes in remembrance. "I don't really like to think about it or what could have happened."

"But did he hurt you? Do I have to find him and kill him?" The steel in Luke's voice is venomous, and I know in my heart that he would do exactly that if he had to.

"No, it was fine. Nothing happened." My eyes fly open, and I reach over and grab his hand. There's such care and concern in his expression that it melts my heart. "Rafe had a weird feeling, so he followed us, and basically, he ran up, and he grabbed this dude and punched him and told him to get out of town or he'd make him. And then he told me off for ignoring his advice and said I was his sister, and he loved me, and he didn't want to see me get hurt, and that I should listen to him because he knows better than me." I roll my eyes. "He thinks because he's my brother, he knows everything."

"Is that why he's been such a jackass about us?" Luke says, nodding slowly. "Does he think I'm going to break your heart or something?"

"He thinks that I don't meditate and deliberate things through properly or rationally, and he's worried about me. He's nervous for me, and he's nervous because he loves me and he wants to protect me. He's my older brother, and I love him for always looking out for me, but I'm also so aggravated. I'm not a kid anymore."

"I know, but I'm glad he was there for you when I wasn't." Luke frowns. "I'm fucking pissed that I wasn't there to help you."

"Luke, you don't even live in town anymore. What would you have done from New York?"

"Why didn't you tell me?"

I shrug. "Maybe the same reason you didn't tell me about Talia and skinny-dipping."

"I doubt it was the same reason," he says, "but I guess there are things that we just aren't able to share when we're so far away."

I nod slowly. "Yeah, I guess so."

"I have an idea," Luke says, his eyes intense, and he grabs my hands. "What if we get engaged?"

"What are you talking about?" My voice rises. Has he finally lost it? "We can't get engaged. Are you crazy?"

For a few moments, I wonder if this is him trying to tell me that he likes me. Is this real?

Hope expands in my heart as I gaze into his eyes, and he grins.

"Imagine Rex's face if he thought we were engaged." He gets serious suddenly. "Look, I didn't appreciate how my brother spoke to you. I didn't appreciate what he said to you about me never committing to you, and I just want to show him you are special. And I realize I want him to know that he can't get away with—"

"No," I say, grabbing Luke by the arm and squeezing. "We will not keep doing this, Luke."

"What do you mean?"

"We will not keep letting our relationship be defined by Rex. We got into this fake dating situation because we didn't want Rex to think we were single and couldn't get dates for the wedding. Now we're going to get fake engaged just so we can prove something else to him? No. We will not act defensively because of him anymore. You hear me?"

Luke stares at me and nods slowly. "I guess I understand, but it would be so cool to just see that smirk wiped off his face."

"But we come first, Luke. Who cares what he thinks? I don't want our relationship to be affected by him anymore. I don't want you to constantly be fighting that battle because your brother is a jerk."

"I get it," he says.

He reaches over and brushes hair away from the side of my face. His fingers trail down the side of my cheek and across my lips. He runs his fingers down the side of my arm and leans forward and kisses me softly. Time seems to stand still as his lips press against mine.

I can smell his musk as I hold him to me, and we fall back onto the bed. I run my fingers down his arm as he murmurs against my lips, as he slides his fingers up my top and caresses my breast through my bra. His tongue slowly enters my mouth, and I suck on it as if it were candy. He tastes so sweet.

We roll around on the bed until I'm on top of him, and I kiss him with passion. I feel like my body is on fire. His eyes gaze into mine, and he slowly pulls off my top. I unbutton his shirt, and we're both touching each other gently and more and more intensely. He slides the straps of my bra down and unclasps it and throws it to the floor before kissing down and sucking on my nipple. I close my eyes and cry out as he kisses down toward my belly button.

He stops and looks up at me with hooded eyes, and I run my fingers through his hair.

"You've got such beautiful, silky hair," I say, and he just laughs as he kisses back up and touches my lips gently.

"Did you know that when I was about to go to college, I nearly canceled?" he whispers.

"What do you mean?"

"I don't know if you remember, but there was one night we went out to the beach to stare up at the moon, and then you started falling asleep. And I remember you whispered, 'I wish you weren't going to Harvard. I wish you would stay,' and I was going to cancel my admission package. I was going to tell them I wasn't coming. I was going to stay in Coconut Beach. I didn't want to go. I didn't want to leave you. I didn't know what that was going to mean for our friendship. And you have always been the closest person in my life.

"Then, the next day, Rex came into my room, and he made fun of me, and he called me a loser, and he said that I shouldn't worry because he'd always make sure that I had a job, working for him."

"And I remember thinking to myself, *I don't want to work for you, Rex. I don't want you to be in charge of me. I want to prove to you and I want to prove to our parents that I have what it takes to be better than you.* And I knew I couldn't do that, staying in Coconut Beach. I knew I had to go to Harvard. I knew I had to leave town, and so I decided not to reject my acceptance.

"And you know what, Mia? You're right; I did that because of Rex, because of how he defined our relationship. And I've been doing so many things in my life defensively and not offensively, and I don't want to do that anymore. I don't want us to do that anymore.

"I love being with you. I love spending time with you. I miss the us that was in each other's life every day. I miss laughing with you, and going to lunch with you, and playing games with you, and practicing guitar, and just lying in the sand, staring up at the stars and wondering how this universe was so uniquely and beautifully made, and watching the crabs as they crawl on the sand, and watching the fish as they swam and the dolphins as they jumped, and just staring at you as you swam like a mermaid in the water." He smiles at me as his fingers lazily trace down the side of my arms. "I miss just being us." He takes a deep breath and his nostrils flare. "Who knew I could talk this much at once?"

My heart races at his words because, as I stare at him, I realize there is no one in my life even close to Luke, in any way, shape, or form, and I love that. I love him in ways that are deeper than our friendship. I love him in ways that are deeper than my own understanding of what it is to love. I love him because he is simply him. I love him because that's what's in my heart and my soul. To know him is to love him and I realize that this feeling of adoration and calm has always existed in me when it came to him.

I want him. I want him to stay, and I want to beg him to not leave. I want him to tell me he doesn't want to leave, but I'm scared to ask him for answers because I don't know if he can ever choose me because I know he is still fighting that battle with Rex—perhaps for the rest of his life. Perhaps his job will always mean everything to him I know I don't mean anything, but I still don't quite come first. I still am not enough, and I don't want to not be enough, and I don't want to ask him and find myself secondary to a subconscious battle that he is not completely aware that he carries.

"I want to tell you, Luke, that I know in your mind's eye, Rex has always been the golden son, the one that everyone looks at, but you've always been that to me."

"I know," he says, smiling at me and brushing my hair with his fingers. "You've always made me feel good about myself, Mia. You've always made me feel like I was enough. You've always made me feel like I was more than enough, and I love how honest and open you are. And I'm so sorry I didn't tell you it was me in the bear suit, and I'm so sorry I didn't tell you that I went skinny-dipping with Talia, and I'm just so sorry about all of it—that I got you embroiled in this crazy plan and we're lying to our friends and family members, and I just wanted us to be the winners for once. I didn't want to be the loser in Rex's story anymore."

"And you're not," I say. As I push him back slightly, I sit on his lap, and I hold him close to me. "You are so much more than the loser in Rex's story."

I can feel his hardness between my legs, and I rub back and forth gently at first and then with more pressure. He pushes me to the side and then he reaches up and unbuttons my shorts, and I feel his fingers slip inside my panties, pulling them down. I reach down, and I unzip him. He looks up at me with a question in his eyes, and I just grin at him as I pull his shorts down.

I sit back down on his lap, his briefs the only two things between us, and I stare down at him and rock back and forth. The feeling of desire is overwhelming and heady. I have not known a man in this way before. Not so wantonly. Not so heavenly. Not so delightful. I have never wanted a moment to last forever with anyone else. Only him.

"What are you doing?" he says breathlessly as he reaches up and cups my breasts with his hands.

He squeezes my nipples, and I close my eyes as I arch my back and continue to grind on him.

"Mia," he says.

"I'm just pretending that I'm a stripper." I laugh. "You can pretend this is your bachelor party, and I'm the entertainment."

"Fuck," he says. "You do not want me to pretend that you're a stripper."

"Why?" I say, giggling.

"Because that's a fantasy I've always had," he says.

He slips his fingers between my legs and slides my panties to the side. I watch as my hand reaches down and my fingers grab his cock, loving the feel of its hardness, and it's between my legs. Suddenly, I'm rubbing back and forth with it between my folds. I can feel his head gliding against my clit, and I'm growing wetter and wetter. We're so close to actually having sex, and a part of me thinks all I have to do is grab ahold of him and slide down, and I could be riding him and fucking him. But then he pauses suddenly.

"Are you doing this because you don't want to get fake engaged to me?" he says.

I stare at him for a couple of seconds, feeling angry and annoyed at his question. "What?"

"I just want to make sure this isn't some sort of pity lap dance because you feel bad about how Rex has made me feel and—"

"Of course not. Really, Luke? How could you think that?"

I'm so upset. I'm so frustrated. I feel like every time I try to show him how I really feel, what I really want, he misunderstands me.

I wonder if he just doesn't see me as more than just his friend, if he doesn't see me as more than just a fun time and a laugh. Maybe I'm not good enough for him. Maybe he doesn't see me in his world as more than his best friend. Maybe he's moved on from ever thinking of us as more, and maybe that's the lesson I have to learn.

I slide off of him and roll over onto the side and jump off of the bed.

"Wait, what did I say?"

"Nothing. It was just a bad idea," I say quickly.

"No, but—" He stares at me, dismay in his eyes. "I didn't mean to say that I thought you wanted to be with Rex or anything. I hope you didn't misunderstand me."

I let out a deep sigh. "I know you don't think I want to be with Rex, but the fact of the matter is, you thought I was doing things to you because of you feeling bad about Rex. What sort of woman do you think I am, Luke?"

"I didn't ..." He pauses. "Fuck. I'm just fucking this up." He clenches his fist and his face contorts as his chest heaves. I've never seen this side of him before.

"I don't know," I say, shrugging. "Maybe we've both fucked it up. Maybe this was just all a terrible idea. I'm just going to grab a drink with Juniper or something." I don't want to deal with this right now. I can't deal with this right now.

"But I thought we were going to go on the treasure hunt," he says, reaching out to stop me. "Mia."

"I think I'm going to go to Kona Ice by myself." I know I'm running away, but I don't know what else to do. This has all gotten so complicated so quickly. We'd crossed so many lines that I'd thought we'd never cross and it had all been fun and games until everything started to feel too real.

"Oh." That one word made my heart pound. His expression made me want to throw up. I couldn't read his eyes, but I could sense that he, like me, wanted to say so much more than we were saying. How had we gotten here? How were we not able to communicate properly with each other.

"I think that makes sense." I don't really think it makes sense, but I don't know what else to say.

"But don't you think that we—"

"I don't think that we should do anything right now, Luke. You just enjoy your time in the hotel room. I'm going to spend the afternoon and evening alone."

"I'm sorry, Mia."

"You have nothing to apologize for, Luke. This is not on you."

It's on both of us. We have equal parts in fucking this up.

chapter twenty-one

Luke

It's been two nights since Mia left the hotel room, and she hasn't been back since. I don't really care what anyone else thinks or has to say about the fact that she hasn't spent the night. I've been easily able to explain that she's just been busy working, and I've been busy working as well—because I have been. But the fact of the matter is, I miss her like crazy.

I haven't even been able to sleep without her. I feel restless and pissed off and angry and guilty. I realize I've been so consumed by Rex and our relationship that it has dictated so much of my life, and I am a fucking idiot for bringing him up right when beautiful, sweet Mia was rocking back and forth on me. I can still feel my cock between her legs, so wet and eager. I was about to pick her up by her hips and bring her down on top of me when I fucked up, and I still can't believe that I did it.

I look over at the clock, and it's eleven at night, and I'm missing her. She hasn't returned any of my text messages, and it's driving me crazy. I decide to call her, hoping that she'll pick up. It rings out and goes to voicemail, but I call her again. I'm nothing if not insistent.

"Yes, Luke," she says, answering.

I'm hurt by her tone, but happy to finally hear her voice again.

"Finally. I can't sleep without you," I say honestly, not even caring if she knows.

"Take a sleeping pill or something."

Cold.

"Are you going to come back to the hotel room?"

"Why? Are you scared Rex is going to think we're no longer in a relationship?"

"I don't give a fuck about Rex, Mia. I just—I'm sorry, okay? I fucked up."

"It's fine. I've been working, and I just needed space."

"I don't know what to say, Mia. We talk every day, and you haven't been speaking to me. I speak more to you when I'm in New York, and I'm here now, and I want to see you. I want to spend time with you before I go back."

"Well, just pretend you've already gone back. We both know it'll probably be another five years until I see you again anyway." She sounds bitter, and I sigh.

"I know. We should have been better about trying to see each other. The time went by so quickly, and we would FaceTime. We chat all the time."

"It's not the same as hanging out in person though."

"I know it's not the same, but I didn't realize just how much I'd missed you." Which is a bit of a lie. I realized; I just didn't want to open myself up to heartbreak and emotional turmoil, but I am not going to tell her that.

I am not going to tell her that I've loved her since we were teenagers because the fact of the matter is, I don't think Mia feels that way about me. I think I'm just some fun for her, and while I'm enjoying every moment, I don't want to scare her away with the intensity or the realness of my feelings. Because I am very much in love with her, and I don't want to let her go.

"What are you doing?" I ask her softly.

"If this is you asking me if I'm masturbating while talking to you on the phone, that's a no, Luke. No."

"Have I ever asked you about that before, Mia?"

"No, but it's late at night and—"

"Meet me," I say. "You don't have to come to the hotel. Meet me."

"Meet you where?"

"At the beach."

"What?"

"Let's go look at the stars. Let's look at the moon. I think it's a full moon tonight, right? And that's our thing."

"Fine. I'll meet you in thirty minutes." She lets out a low laugh.

"Thank you." My heart soars.

We hang up the phone, and I quickly get ready and head down to the beach.

I see her standing next to a coconut tree. Once I get there, she turns to look at me, but she doesn't wave, and she doesn't smile. She just stands there, looking like the Mia I remember from our teenage years, the Mia I remember from endless nights of hanging out at the beach.

"Hey," I say. "I brought two Cokes."

"I brought two Cokes as well."

We both start laughing because that was our thing. We'd go down to the beach and drink Coke and eat chocolate and just stare at the stars. We both take a seat in the sand, timidly at first, like this is a first date or a breakup meeting.

"Do you know that I have not gone stargazing in forever, not since you left town?" she says, gazing over at me.

"Well, I guess I was the one who always told you the constellations," I say, laughing.

"Yeah, you were." She lets out a long sigh, and we just stare at each other.

"This feels really nice, being here with you. Thank you for meeting me."

"I think we're stuck in the past," she says suddenly. "I think we have such a beautiful friendship, and we are so close, and we've spent so much time together through the years. I think we've both spent too many years reminiscing about how great and how perfect everything between us was, and I think we're stuck. I think we need to move past that." She looks down, as she plays with her fingers. Her foot taps in time to a song that I can't hear. I can feel her fading away from me. It feels like she's describing a memory of another lifetime. Like we no longer exist. Like we're no longer Lukey and Mi-Mi.

My heart sinks because it feels like the end of something. It feels like I'm losing her, and I'm losing her friendship, and I'm losing the part of me that makes us, us, and I don't want to lose it.

I can't lose it. I will fight for her.

I will fight for us.

I will fight for the melody that has provided the soundtrack to our lives.

I don't say anything. Instead, I watch as a crab crawls along the sand and digs its way into a hole. I look over, and I see that she's staring at me—her face beautiful, innocent, kind, angelic. I want to grab her hand and just hold it. I just want to touch her. I just want to feel that connection with her, but I don't know what to say. Words will not come because a part of me agrees with her. Those years were the best in my life. She was the best part of my life, and yet I didn't know how to tell her that.

"You want to go for a swim?" I say, standing up, needing to move, not wanting to remain stagnant, not wanting the feelings to build up—to make me upset, to make me hurt, to make me lash out.

"Swimming? It's night," she says.

"So? Let's do it."

"I don't have a bathing suit."

"We don't need a bathing suit."

"You want to go skinny-dipping?" She grins at me, her eyes light as she shakes her head. "You really are asking me to go skinny-dipping."

"Well, I'm not asking you to fuck in the ocean for the first time," I say, laughing. "But, yeah, let's go skinny-dipping."

She stares at me for a couple of seconds without saying anything.

"I dare you," I say, and her eyes narrow. "I double-dog dare you."

"You can't double-dog dare me, Luke. That's not fair." She shakes her head. "You're really not going to say anything to what I just said?"

I shrug. "Maybe I'll know what to say after I dip in the water."

"Fine," she says.

I watch as she rips her clothes off quickly and drops them to the ground, then goes running to the water. I quickly peel off my clothes as well and go running in behind her. I stare at her ass as she runs away from me, and I can't help but laugh as I jump into the water.

It is cold. I'm almost freezing, but I swim out. I feel alive. I feel so at one with nature, and I float on my back for a couple of moments and then look over at her. She's swimming next to me. Her hair is plastered to her face, and her eyelashes are wet, and she's gazing at me. The moon illuminates her, and she looks like some beautiful mermaid or sea creature—magical and mystical—and I just want to hold her.

"It's freezing," she says, and all I can do is laugh.

"It is cold," I say, "but your body will acclimate. I promise."

"I hope so," she says, and she lies on her back and starts floating. She bumps into me and giggles slightly. "Sorry."

"It's okay." I float on my back as well.

We just lie there in the water—in the calm water—naked, thinking, silent. But it's not an awkward silence. It's a companionable silence. It's a silence where a million different things are said in the beauty of the night.

I feel her fingers lightly touching mine, and I look over. She's staring into my eyes, and she smiles.

"Those were the best years of my life too."

I just smile back at her because, of course, she was able to read my mind.

"I know. I just don't want to let go of them," I say.

"I think we have to, Luke. I think, for us to move forward in life, we have to let go of the past."

"I know," I say.

I swim away from her because it hurts, and I don't want her to see the pain in my eyes. I look over and see that she's still floating. She's far away enough from me now that she can't hear me if I whisper.

"I love you," I say to the wind, even though I know it won't carry the words to her ears.

She can't hear me, and I'm glad for that because I'm too scared to tell her the truth.

"I love you," I whisper. "I've always loved you, and I wish you would love me too."

I realize then that I can't continue like this. My heart belongs to her, and now we're in some crazy standstill. My entire life feels like it's not mine. I'm here, back in Coconut Beach, and I feel like I never left. I've got a job waiting for me in New York City, and I can barely remember what my apartment looks like. I can't remember not waking up beside her. I can't remember not spending at least some part of the day with her, and I don't know that I can go back, and yet I don't know that I can stay.

"We should swim back," I say loudly, shouting as I swim over to her. "We don't want to stay here too long."

"Okay," she says, nodding slowly.

We swim back to the shore together and step out of the water. We take a couple of steps and then just look at each other. I stare at her naked body—her beautiful and large breasts, her curvy stomach, her wide hips, her long legs. She's absolutely beautiful. And I see her staring at me—my chest, my thighs, my cock—and there's awe in her expression.

I step forward and grab her hands, giving her a questioning look, and she nods slightly as she looks up at me. I grab her around the waist and pull her into me, my lips meeting hers, and she melts into me. Her breasts press against my chest. My cock twitches against her stomach, and she murmurs against my lips, a low moan.

"Are you still mad at me? Are you still angry?"

"I could never stay mad at you for long," she says.

I grin as I pick her up, and she giggles slightly as I carry her a little further along the beach. Then I place her down on the sand. She's gasping for air as I grab her hands and squeeze and then kiss her lips. The breeze brushes past our cheeks, caressing us as we tease each other.

My fingers play with her nipples, and she moans. She runs her fingers down my back and then my chest. She squeezes my ass, and I grunt as I stare down at her. She stares at me and kisses the side of my face and then my bites my shoulder before she pushes me back. Her lips trail down my stomach and my breath catches. The feeling of her lips against my skin is like the most satisfying touch of my life.

I stare at her as she continues to kiss me softly and then more passionately, and I know this is our moment. We are one with nature. We are one with each other. I slide my fingers between her legs, and I rub her gently. She lets out a whimper, and I grin to myself. I love the sound of her when I'm pleasuring her.

"You're so wet," I say, teasing her.

"It's the water from the ocean," she says, giggling, and then she freezes as I slip a finger inside of her, shuddering as my thumb gently rubs her clit.

As I finger her, she moans loudly, and I watch her breasts jiggle.

I roll over on top of her and kiss her, running my fingers down the side of her body. I place my cock between her legs, and I rub gently against her. She screams as she holds me and runs her fingers down my back, her nails digging into my skin. I lean down and kiss her, and she sucks on my lip eagerly.

"Fuck me, Luke," she whispers against my mouth. "Fuck me."

And because I can't resist her, I gently guide my cock inside of her.

She wraps her legs around my waist, and I thrust into her slowly, loving the feel of her pussy as it clenches against me. Then I slide in a little bit harder, a little bit deeper, and she sobs in pleasure as she whispers against my ear.

"Ooh, Luke."

The sound drives me crazy, and I pull out and thrust into her again—faster and harder. This time, her eyes are wide open as she gazes up at me, and I kiss her lips and then move in and out of her. It feels like my body's on fire. Her pussy feels tight and warm, and I cannot believe that it's finally happening. It feels like she was made for me and this moment. We are making love, and it's been something I've wanted my entire life. I've been waiting for years. I feel like we were destined for this moment. I feel like we were made in the stars for each other.

I whisper into her ear, and all she does is moan.

As I continue thrusting, I can feel myself building up. I've been waiting for this so long that I'm ready to explode, so I pull out and stop because I don't want our first time to be something that she laughs about or doesn't think is good enough. She looks over at me with parted lips, moaning as I wait a couple of seconds.

"What are you doing?"

"I was about to come," I say, staring into her eyes and touching her lips.

Her eyes flicker back, "So was I."

I rub my fingers between her legs and rub her clit gently.

"You can come for me now," I say as I slip two fingers inside of her.

Her body arches, and she shivers slightly, and I can feel that she's close to coming. My thumb rubs her clit faster and faster.

"Luuuke," she cries, "I'm nearly there."

I quickly slide my fingers out of her and thrust my cock into her hard and fast, loving the feel of her wet pussy on me.

"Fuck, Luke."

"Yeah, baby."

I grab hold of her and hold her tight to me as I let her enjoy every inch of me. And when I feel her coming hard and fast on me, I go faster and faster so that her breasts are slamming against my chest, and I kiss her hard and passionately while I hold her to me.

Then I explode inside of her because I can't resist. I pull my cock out slowly, and we both just lie there on the sand, looking at each other.

"Wow," she says, gazing at me with wide eyes.

She runs her fingers lazily down my chest, and I turn to her with a smile.

"Wow indeed," I say, laughing. "I think I might really like you, Mia."

Her eyes are wide and bright, and she giggles slightly. "I think I might really like you as well, Luke."

I reach over and grab her hand and squeeze.

This was our first time together, and it felt like the first time I'd ever really experienced what it was to make love. This was sex, but it was so much more. I felt connected to her in a way that could never be broken.

I want to tell her I love her. I want to tell her I adore her, that I never want to let her go, but I can't tell her that. I don't want to make too much of this. I don't want to scare her. I need her to always know that whatever we have, whatever she wants, will always remain the same.

I reach over and pull her into my arms, and she rests her head against my chest. I kiss her forehead, and she closes her eyes as she runs her fingers down the side of my body. This is the feeling that makes a life worth living. This is the cocoon I would chose for myself every lifetime over.

"I missed you so much, Mia." I whisper the words to the universe, hoping the intensity and depth of my comment can be felt in her heart.

"I missed you too," she says, whispering against my skin.

"You did?" My heart skips a beat I know it shouldn't skip. Since when did I become such a sap?

"Yeah," she says, looking up at me. "I had a really hard time falling asleep."

"Well, I guess you needed time to think, huh?"

"I guess." She giggles. "I didn't think we'd be apart for two nights and then we'd be having sex."

I want to correct her. I want to say *making love,* but I can't. I chuckle slightly and play with her hair.

"I hope you're ready for session number two in a little bit."

"I am," she says, but she suddenly looks around. "We're still on the beach, and anyone could come and find us. And, well, I think that sex on the beach is still against the local laws and ordinances, so maybe we should make our way back."

"You're going to come back to the hotel with me?" I ask hopefully.

She nods. "Yeah, I think I will." She grins as she touches the side of my face. "That was amazing, by the way."

"I think so as well."

"So, does this mean we're officially friends with benefits?" she asks me.

All I can do is laugh because the truth of the matter is, I want us to be so much more than that.

chapter twenty-two

Mia

The sound of birds singing outside the window wakes me up, and my eyes fly open with a smile on my face. My body feels warm and satiated, and I roll over to look at Luke and whisper good morning to him. I frown slightly when I see his side of the bed is empty, and I wonder if he's in the bathroom.

I lie on my back and just stare at the ceiling, smiling. We finally slept together, and it was amazing. He was the best lover I ever could have hoped for, and it felt special. The way he looked at me felt special. The way he made me feel felt special, and I was going to tell him that. I was going to tell him that it was the best thing that had ever happened to me and that, as upset as I had been at receiving Rex's invitation, I was glad that I had. I was glad that he'd written that horrible note because if he hadn't, then this wouldn't have happened between Luke and me, and what had happened was special. I could feel it in my bones. I could see it in his eyes that he felt the same way.

"Are you coming, Luke?" I say, laughing. "Did you drown in there or something?"

I wait for him to respond, but I realize the room is silent—almost deathly silent. I frown slightly as I roll out of bed. I grab the sheet and huddle toward the bathroom. The door's wide open. There's no one in there.

Luke's not in there.

For a moment, I think maybe he's gone to get me breakfast, but then I spy the note card on the table with my name on it. I grab it and pick it up, frowning.

Hey, Mia. Don't wait for me for breakfast. Had to do some work, but I'll see you later.

"What the fuck?" I throw the note card down on the table and go and sit on the edge of the bed.

I'm emotional, and I'm upset, and I feel like I want to cry.

This is not how you want to spend the moment after first sleeping with your best friend. I expected him to hold me, to cuddle me, to possibly make love to me again in the morning, tell me he couldn't wait for me to wake up—but he already went to work.

I hate the feeling of abandonment that I feel, but I have to be honest with myself. I'm disappointed. He still chose work first after I gave myself to him. I thought I'd been clear that I wanted to be his number one, that I wanted him to choose me, and he still didn't. Hadn't. Was it too much to ask?

Now I'm confused. Was any of it real? Was it just physical? Was it really just sex?

He'd been upset. He'd been messing with me. We'd argued. Maybe this was his way of trying to make up for the failed lap dance the other night.

I touch my skin softly and think about the way he loved me, the way he felt when he climaxed inside of me, and I shiver because I've never felt a connection like that before in my life.

I grab my phone and call Juniper because I don't know what to do. I want to cry so badly, but I can't. I need to be strong. I want to be strong.

"Hey, girl, you on your way to work?" She sounds chirpy, and I'm glad because I need someone happy. I need someone positive.

"Juni," I say, my voice cracking.

"What's wrong, Mia?"

"We slept together. We slept together, and it was amazing, but I woke up, and he wasn't here in the bed, and I don't want to say I feel used because I don't feel used, but I just don't feel loved and special, and I don't know what to do. What does this mean?"

"Okay, Mia. Deep breaths."

"I'm trying. I'm really trying."

"Did you enjoy it, first and foremost?"

"It was magical, Juniper. It was, like, the best sex of my life—and not just because he's got a really nice body and a really nice cock, and he knows exactly what he's doing, but it just felt like my body had been made for him. He fit in all the right spaces, and every single touch did something to my erogenous zones." I sigh. "Let's just say, it was great, but maybe it wasn't great for him. Maybe he has sex like this with everyone."

"Mia, focus. Calm down."

"I know, I'm going crazy."

"It's okay. Have you spoken to him?"

"He went to fucking work, Juniper. He got up while I was still sleeping and he left, and he left me a stupid fucking note card. What are we, roommates or something? Who does that?"

"Oh shit. I'm sorry, Mia, but it doesn't necessarily mean that he didn't also enjoy it. It just means maybe he had to work."

"We had sex for the first time in our friendship. We're best friends. We literally are in a fake relationship, and we had sex. We had sex, Juniper. You more than anyone know how much something like that means to me. I don't just sleep around, and he knows that. He knows that it had to have meant something to me, and he couldn't even be here in the hotel when I woke up."

"I hate to say this, Mia, but he's a guy, and sometimes, guys don't really think things through. I bet you were sleeping, and he was like, *Ah, she's sleeping. I need to do some work. I'll speak to her later.*"

I take a couple of deep breaths. "I know you're right, but it still really stings. He knows me better than that."

"I know, girl. I know. You want me to close up the store and come over, or—"

"No, it's okay. Thanks though for offering. I think I'm going to go shower, and I'm going to cry. Then I'm going to order myself room service, and I'm just going to move on with my life. You know what? Lots of people have sex with their best friends. Lots of people have one-night stands. I will be one of those people, and I'll just forget it. It will mean nothing. I'm not even going to bring it up to him, and I hope he doesn't bring it up to me."

I pause as I hear the door opening.

"Oh shit, he's back. I'll speak to you later."

Juniper says goodbye before I hang up. I look over as he walks in. He has a bouquet of flowers in his hand; pink, yellow, and orange petals greet me.

"Morning, sunshine," he says, heading toward me. His eyes narrow as he stares at my face. "Why do you look so forlorn? What's going on? Wait, you're not upset, are you?" He bites down on his lower lip and looks guilty. "Please tell me I didn't take advantage of you in your emotional state or anything like that. I would absolutely—"

"You didn't take advantage of me, Luke. Obviously, I wanted it. We both wanted it, and it was hot."

"So, you enjoyed yourself, huh? By the way," he says, "I know we technically should have had this conversation before I came inside of you, but—"

"I'm on the pill, Luke." I just shake my head. "But, yeah, that is a conversation we likely should have had before you decided to orgasm inside of me. I can't believe I just said that. You orgasmed inside of me."

"My sperm filled you up?"

"Luke?" I say, hitting him on the shoulder.

"What?" He starts laughing. It's true."

"Yeah, but that sounds so—"

"So, what?" His eyes light up as he takes a seat next to me. "It sounds so sexy. It sounds like you want me to do it again right now."

"Luke, I'm mad at you."

"Why?"

He looks genuinely confused, and I just shake my head.

"Because you went to work this morning. You didn't wait for me to wake up, and I just feel you should have known that I would want to wake up with you in bed. We'd just had sex for the first time, and that's an enormous deal. It would be a big deal for any two people, let alone two people who were as close as us."

He sits there, not saying anything. "I don't know what you're talking about, Mia. Did you not see my note? I left you a note on the table."

"Yeah, you left me a note on the table. That's so cold. That's what one-night stands do. That's what men whose names you don't even know do after they sleep with you—not someone that should care about you and want to make sure you feel okay after you had sex with them."

His jaw drops. "I fucked up again, huh?" He lets out a deep sigh, and I watch as he runs his fingers through his hair. "I literally had to do some work, and I didn't want to wake you up, so I left the bedroom because I was on a number of phone calls, and this is a huge deal for me. You know this, Mia. I cannot have this project fall through. And I thought I was being respectful of your feelings by leaving, and so I came back with flowers."

"Flowers don't make up for the fact that you weren't here when I woke up this morning. And, yeah, I get that you have a job, and it's a big deal, but I just want to be chosen." My voice cracks slightly.

I don't know if I'm being unreasonable. A part of me feels like I'm being really unreasonable, but another part of me feels like I deserve that. Another part of me feels like he should have known that I would need that.

"Maybe this was a mistake," I blurt. "Maybe we shouldn't have slept together. Maybe we should forget this ever happened and just move on with our lives."

"How can we do that, Mia? I was inside of you last night." He stares at my lips. "Those lips were on my cock. My tongue was on your clit. You came on my face. I can still taste you on my lips." His fingers brush against his lips. "That sweetness, that absolutely amazing scent of—"

"Luke," I say, blushing deeply, "I do not want to talk about that right now."

"Why not? It happened, and we both enjoyed it. Or are you telling me you didn't?"

I stare at him for a couple of seconds. "You just don't get it, do you?"

"Get what, Mia?"

I rip the sheet off and stand up in front of him, naked. I see his eyes on my breasts, on my pussy, and I see them glazing over, deep with desire. I push him back onto the bed and lean down and kiss him. He reaches up and touches me softly. There is a questioning look in his eyes, but I don't care.

I run my fingers down his chest and to his jeans. I undo his belt buckle and pull it off. I unzip him and pull his pants down and pull his briefs off so that his cock is there, springing free. I get on top of his lap and rub myself back and forth on him, his thick length sliding and gliding against my wet slit.

He groans as he looks up at me. He still looks surprised and shocked. I grab hold of him and position him between my legs, and I slide down, taking all of him inside of me.

"Oh fuck, that feels so good," he calls out. "Mia."

I ride his cock slowly at first, and he reaches up and plays with my breasts. I move back and forth gently, and then I bounce up and down. He grabs my hips and moves me faster and faster. I lean down and brush my nipples against his lips, and he sucks on them as I continue to ride him.

Then I feel my orgasm coming, and I scream in pleasure as I orgasm on top of him. He groans a few times, and then he bounces me up and down faster and faster until he is exploding inside of me. I collapse down on him and then kiss his lips. I grab his face and kiss him slowly. I want to remember this moment. I gaze into his eyes, and then I roll off him and head to the shower.

"Wait, what are you doing?" he says as he sits up. "What was that about? You were just angry at me, and then you just fucked me. Mia, you're confusing me."

I look back at him and just shake my head. "This is how you made me feel," I say. "I got mine, and now I'm going to go in the shower, and then I'm going to grab breakfast and go hang out with Juniper and do some work."

"What? Mia, we need to talk. Obviously, I didn't mean to hurt you. I didn't want you to feel used in any way. I like you a lot." He stumbles over his words. "This—it means something to me."

"Does it, Luke, or was it just sex? At the end of the day, you chose your need to take a phone call over your need to be there for me this morning, knowing that we had done something shocking in our friendship, in our relationship, and we'd crossed so many lines and boundaries. I would've thought you would be there for me this morning."

"I'm here for you now, Mia."

He jumps up off the bed and heads toward me. He grabs my hand and pulls me into him, but I push away from him. Our naked bodies are within inches of each other, and I feel like every nerve cell of mine is being activated by every nerve cell of his. We stare at each other. I'm glaring, and he's looking confused and annoyed and frustrated.

"So, you're really just going to fuck me and then leave?" he says.

"Yeah. I mean, it doesn't feel so great, does it?" I breathe.

He just shakes his head. "Really, Mia?"

He reaches out and touches the side of my face, and as much as I want to hold him to me, as much as I want to make it better, I'm still caught up in my own feelings. I'm still caught up in my hurt, and I'm still absolutely confused by what I just did. My body had wanted him—wantonly, passionately—and I had him, and it didn't feel good. That didn't feel like making love. It felt like raw, rough sex, and I knew I was hurting inside.

I just want this to mean something more than it does, but I can't tell him that. I know I've already been acting crazy, and by the look on his face, he is as confused as I feel.

"I'll see you later, okay? The big party's tonight, and we need to make sure we're on for that," I say. "I think we both want to make sure of that."

"Okay, so you'll be back later, or—"

"Yeah, I'll be back by this afternoon so we can get ready."

"And we're not going to talk about any of this?" he says.

"There's nothing else that we have to say right now, Luke."

"I think there's plenty more that we have to say, Mia." He sounds angry now. "But I'm going to respect your wishes, and I'm going to let it go for now because I know this has been a lot. But honestly, Mia, it's not just been a lot for you. It's been a lot for me too. And it's not just your friendship with me that has been affected by us sleeping together. It's also my friendship with you, and I think we're both trying to figure out how to navigate this space." He leans forward and softly kisses me. "Just don't lock me out, okay? I may be the only one in this world that actually understands what you're going through right now because maybe I'm going through it as well."

"Maybe," I say, nodding slightly.

But the simple fact of the matter is, I don't think he is. If he knew how desperately and deeply in love with him I was, I don't know if he'd be able to live with himself. I know if he knew how deeply I had fallen for him, he'd feel absolute guilt—because Luke didn't feel that way about me. The only thing he truly loves more than anything else is work and focusing on being the best that he can be, and I know that. I've known that for a long time. It doesn't make him a horrible person; it just means that is his priority.

I know he loves me as a best friend. I know he will always be there for me, but I also know that I don't come first. If I did, he would've seen me in the last five years. He would've begged for me to come to New York, but he didn't. He hasn't, and I have to accept that fact, no matter how much it hurts me.

chapter twenty-three

Luke

I can't take my eyes off of Mia. She's wearing a long, slinky black dress with high heels. She's got on a thin gold necklace and a diamond tennis bracelet. She looks absolutely stunning. Her gold-blonde hair hangs in curls around her shoulders, and her big brown eyes are dazzling.

We haven't really spoken much since she got back to the hotel room, but I don't think either of us knows what to say. We are in a weird state in our relationship. We are more than friends, and yet we are less than best friends. We can no longer share every single intimate detail about our lives because the fact of the matter is, we are the biggest obstacle and concern in each other's life now.

"You look very nice," she says, beaming at me.

I'm wearing a very expensive Italian suit that I got on a trip to Milan. My crisp white shirt is open two buttons down, and Mia helped me put on my black tie.

"This is going to be a very fancy engagement party," she says, laughing. "It is really kind of weird that we're going to an engagement party for a couple that's getting married at the end of the month."

Even though, on the surface, it looks like everything is light between us, the tension is high. We've been tiptoeing around each other. We have said nothing personal to each other, and we haven't touched or kissed in that way. That drives me crazy. I don't like being in this position with Mia, but I don't know how to get out of it.

"Juniper just texted me, by the way," she says. "She said she's downstairs with Wendy, Summer, and Silvie. So, should we head down?"

"Okay." I nod. "What about the guys, or am I going to be hanging out with all the girls?"

"I think Wendy said that Carter might try and show up. He felt slightly weird about coming tonight because he doesn't know Rex or Andi, but I told her to tell him that's fine. They're not going to care. And let's see … Silvie said that Cal is going to try and make it. He got someone to cover for him at the bar. Summer said that Dayton will show up at some point, so the guys will be here at some point."

"Okay, I'm just checking. I don't care if it's just me and the girls."

"I know you don't. You love to be with all the girls."

"This isn't about Talia again, is it?" I ask, and she just gives me a look. "Okay, okay. I was just double-checking because you know I'm not into her."

"I didn't even bring Talia up," she says, staring at me. "Really, Luke?"

"I know you didn't. I just—sorry. I was making a joke, and maybe it was in poor taste."

"Luke, all I have to say is, don't quit the day job. You're definitely not going to be the next Dave Chappelle."

"Maybe I'll be the next Adam Sandler."

"You're goofy enough," she teases me.

I just laugh. I love it when we can just be light with each other.

"Shall we go, my lady?"

"We shall, kind sir."

I grab her hand and squeeze it, and we head toward the door. I open it for her, and she steps outside. As I close it, I pull her toward me.

"We okay?"

She nods slowly, but she doesn't answer. That's not really a good enough reaction for me, but it's the best that I'm going to get right now. I take a deep breath and let my feelings of annoyance and frustration go. We make our way to the elevator in not-quite-companionable silence. Everything feels like it has that slight edge to it, and I just don't know how to make it better.

We step into the elevator, and I accidentally brush against her. She almost jumps away from me, and I frown slightly. I'm about to ask her if she really is okay and if we should talk, but I decide not to. It's a big night for Rex and for Andi and for the family, and I know we cannot go to the party arguing, and we cannot step away from the party either.

I press the button to take us down to the ballroom, and we stand there in silence. It's so very different from how we normally are together that it makes me feel tense, but I don't know what to do about it.

We step out and make our way toward the ballroom. The sounds of partygoers echo through the halls. There's a live band playing '60s and '70s music, and everyone seems to be having a good time as we step into the ballroom.

I see Mia looking around with a fake, plastered smile on her face.

She grabs my hand and looks into my eyes. "Time to fake it again, Luke."

"I don't like to fake it, Mia."

"You could have fooled me," she says, and I just stare at her.

"Come on," she says. "I see Juniper."

She pulls me toward the other side of the room, and I follow behind her, not wanting to make a scene, but really wanting to have a deeper conversation with her.

"Hey, Juniper. Hey, Wendy. Hey, Summer. Hey, Silvie." Mia gives them all a quick hug.

I offer them my hellos and stand to the side, watching as she smiles and jokes with them. I can't tell if she's faking it or if she's really just happy to see them.

"Would you like a drink?" I say eventually.

She turns to me, nodding. "Yeah, a glass of wine or something, please."

"I'll be right back." I look around the room and head toward the bar.

I see my grandma standing there with Lucille and try not to groan.

"Hey there, Luke," my grandma says, giving me a big hug.

"Hi, Gran. Hi, Mrs. Bishop."

"How are you treating my granddaughter? Very well, I hope."

I give her a smile. "You know how it is. Mia and I have a really good thing going, and we're just trying not to ruin it."

"I'm glad to hear that, Luke. I've been very glad to hear that the two of you have connected." She looks over at Bitsy. "Aren't you happy, Bitsy?"

"Yeah, I think we're both very happy, Lucille."

They give each other a look that I find quite odd, but I ignore it. Both of my grandparents are slightly quirky, and I don't know if that has to do with living in Coconut Beach their entire lives, but I've learned to ignore it.

"The party looks to be in full swing," I say, looking around. "I'm sure Rex and Andi must be really happy."

"Yes, yes, I suppose so," my grandma says, frowning. "We need to talk, Luke," she says in a low voice.

"What's wrong?" I frown at her. "You're okay, Gran?"

"Oh, I'm fine. I'm fine. It's not about me. It's about something else. Something sensitive. Maybe something that should not be spoken about here because there are listening ears everywhere, but we need to talk."

She gives me a look, and then she looks over at Lucille. "Ah, shall we go and dance?"

"Of course. Let us do it. I'll leave you to get back to my granddaughter."

"Okay, thanks. You guys have a great evening," I say as I watch them walk away.

That was really weird. I have no idea what my grandma wants to talk to me about, but now I'm super intrigued. I head over to the bar and call one of the bartenders over.

"Can I get a glass of pinot grigio and a Bud Light or something, please?"

"Certainly, sir. Coming right up."

I stand there, waiting for him to get the drinks, when I see Talia heading toward me.

Here we go again.

She's wearing a sheer silver dress that leaves nothing to the imagination. When I say nothing, I mean nothing. It's very obvious that she's not wearing a bra because the gauzy metallic of her dress is see-through, and I can clearly see her nipples.

"Why, darling Luke, you look absolutely gorgeous," she says as she reaches over and gives me a big hug, pressing her breasts against me. "And you smell divine." She presses her nose against my neck.

"Well, it's nice to see you as well, Talia," I say, trying to be polite as I take a step back. "How are you doing?"

"I am absolutely loving the party. Your parents took on every suggestion that I gave them, and I think I've rather surpassed myself with this shindig, don't you?"

"Well, it looks like a lot of people are having a lot of fun. It also looks like it costs a lot of money."

"Well, well, you're a Haverbrook. You guys don't have to worry about money. At least that's what Rex said."

"He is in charge of the family business and the accounts, so he knows," I say, nodding, not even wanting to think about it.

I hate the fact that I'm still irritated by the fact that Rex had taken over the family business without even having a conversation with me about my possible role. "So, have you thought about my suggestion?" she says softly.

"Sorry, I'm confused. What suggestion?"

"Did you not get my text message? I'm going to be in New York, and I don't have a place to stay yet, and I was thinking maybe I could stay with you."

"Oh, I don't think that's a good idea, Talia," I say, trying to be polite.

"But I think we could have so much fun, Luke."

"Well, as you know, I'm dating Mia, and—"

"Oh, but she's such a Goody Two-shoes with her bookmobile on the beach and her romance books and running around the island taking photos of tourists. Do you really want to be with someone like that, or do you want to be with a woman who you can have on your arm at dinner parties and who can discuss politics and the stock market? I bet you that Mia doesn't even know what an index fund is."

"I don't care if she knows what an index fund is, Talia. She very much is the woman I need and want in my life."

"If you say so, Lukey," she says, staring at me and shaking her head. "You don't know what you're missing—you know that, right?" She runs her fingers down the front of my shirt. "All those muscles wasted on her." The disdain practically drips from her tone.

"Hi, sir. Here's the pinot grigio and the beer that you wanted," the bartender says from behind me, and I'm grateful that he's finally shown back up.

"Thank you." I take them from him and drop a twenty-dollar bill into the tip jar. "Well, it was good seeing you, Talia. I'm going to—"

"Oh, I'll come with you," she says, cutting me off. "Let me say hello to the girls."

"I'm sure you don't have to do that."

"I'd love to," she says. "I'd love to see what little dinky dress Mia picked up from the local boutique. Probably something that the girls in *Little House on the Prairie* would wear." She laughs loudly, but the sound is like a cackle to my ears.

"Okay, well, let's go," I say, walking back across the room to Mia and her friends.

Mia looks up, and I can see the way her expression hardens when she sees Talia.

"Hey, here's your drink. Talia wanted to come and say hello."

"I'm sure she did," Mia says. "Hi, Talia."

"Oh, well, look at that dress. It's so cute, Mia. Let me guess—you got it at Walmart?" She cackles again.

I see Juniper's expression change, and she looks like she wants to slap her. I watch Mia grab her friend's arm and squeeze, and Juniper looks at her. Mia shakes her head, and Juniper releases a small sigh.

"No, I didn't get it at Walmart, but thank you for admiring the dress."

"Let me guess—Target?" Talia says.

Mia just shakes her head. "Nope."

"Ooh, one more guess, one more guess. Did you get it at Marshalls?"

"No."

"You got it at Ross or Kohl's, or—"

"You know what, Talia? You're trying to insult me, but I really like those stores and shopping there."

"Oh, I can tell, darling," Talia says, shaking her head. "I can very much tell that you shop at those stores, and that's where ninety-nine-point-nine percent of your clothes are from. The other percentage is probably from thrift shops, right?"

"I don't see anything wrong with thrift shops," Mia says, and her tone escalates.

"I thought I heard your voice," Rafe says.

Both Mia and I turn to the side. Rafe takes a step toward us and then notices Talia.

"Oh, hey, Talia."

"Hello, Rafe. Fancy seeing you here." There's something in her expression that tells me that she and Rafe have had it out.

"Well, you know, the local vet does get invited to these things." He walks over to Mia and gives her a big hug. "Looking beautiful, sis."

"Thank you." He looks over at Juniper and offers her a small nod.

She smiles at him in return.

Interesting, I think to myself.

There seems to be some sort of coldness between them, and I don't understand what it is.

Finally, he turns to me and offers me his hand. "Good to see you, Luke."

"You too, Rafe."

I want to speak to him. I want to thank him for protecting Mia. I know it's weird to thank him, seeing as he's her brother, but I love her with all my heart, and anyone who is there for her is a quality guy—be it family member or not. I want to tell him I will always protect her. I want to tell him I understand why he's been cold and nervous and that I have nothing but the best intentions for her. I want to become real friends with him. It's important to me that he and I become like brothers because I hope we will be one day. Though that's not anything I dare to voice out loud.

"So, Luke, what does Mia have to say about your potential move to England?"

I freeze at Talia's words as I see Mia's expression change.

Fuck.

I haven't had the opportunity to tell her anything about the developments at work. I haven't had the opportunity to say the offer I was given by my boss to lead a new branch in England for the company.

"I—"

"Are you going to go as well, Mia? It seems to me like you never want to leave Coconut Beach."

"Yeah, well, that's something Luke and I have to discuss," Mia says, looking at me with murder in her eyes.

I know I'm in trouble, which sucks because I was already in trouble with her, and even more trouble means that this relationship is going deeper and deeper into the hole.

"Can I speak to you, Luke?" Mia says suddenly, grabbing my arm. "There's something I forgot to tell you." She drags me away from the group hastily to the side of the room.

"You're fucking moving to England?" she says through gritted teeth under her breath.

"No, I'm not—I mean, I might. And how does Talia know?"

"I just—what the fuck is going on, Luke? You've got so many secrets from me and I—"

"Mia, please. I obviously didn't tell Talia anything. I didn't tell you because the only times work has come up, you've been angry at me because I've been working."

"So, how does she know?"

"It was probably talked about in *The Wall Street Journal* or something like that."

"*The Wall Street Journal*?" Mia's jaw drops.

"What? I told you the deal I was working on was really big. The hedge fund company I work for is the number one hedge fund company in New York City, and my boss offered me a position to go to England to start up a branch there. I haven't accepted it, and I haven't had time to tell you about it because we've kind of had other stuff going on. I know you don't really care about my job, and I assumed you wouldn't care about this offer."

"You assumed I wouldn't care that you were moving to fucking England, Luke?" Her voice rises.

I can see that people are looking at us, but I know she doesn't care, and I can't really say anything to her. I don't want to make her even angrier.

"I didn't tell you, Mia, because I just thought there were more important things for us to discuss before that even came up."

"Wow, thanks for trusting me and sharing with me and thinking about me before you decided to move to England."

"What does that mean?"

"It means, you're already far enough away in New York City, and I don't see you. I'll never see you in England, and there's going to be a time difference, so we won't even get to speak on the phone. But what does that matter, right?"

"Maybe you can come to England too," I suggest.

"What do you mean, I can come to England? I don't have money to live in England. What am I going to do—have Juniper move the bookmobile over to London? Where would we even put it? That's not even something that can happen."

"I could take care of you. I want to give you security so you can follow your dreams."

"You can—I don't need you to take care of me, Luke. I'm not just some sad sack that is sitting here, waiting for some man to take care of me."

"I was just going based upon the emails, when you said we should get married if we were both single at forty."

"That was a joke, Luke. You really thought I wanted to marry you because you were rich and you could take care of me?"

I press my lips together because the fact of the matter is, I did think that she wanted that—but from the look on her face, I don't think she wants me to say that to her right now.

"I'm so insulted. I just feel like you just don't care about me or respect me at all."

"It's not true. I'm sorry if I hurt you. I'm sorry that I didn't tell you about London. It's not because I didn't care what you would think. I haven't even decided if I'll take the offer. I just felt like there were bigger things going on between us that I wanted to talk about. And you have to be honest, Mia—you've been really upset every time I've had to work. I really didn't think you would want to talk about my job."

"So, this is on me now? You're blaming me because we had sex and I got upset that you weren't in the bed, waiting for me when I woke up? And so you didn't tell me you're moving across the fucking country?"

She pauses. "Actually, it's not even the country. It's the world. You're moving to the other side of the world."

"I'm not necessarily taking the job. Look, I realize I should have told you, and I normally would have told you, but we haven't been in the most normal of circumstances recently."

"This was a mistake, wasn't it?" she says. "We fucked up. We never should have pretended that we were dating. We should have both just attended as singles and just kept our friendship."

"And what, never kissed, never touched, never made love? Do you regret it all?"

"No," she says softly. "I don't regret it. And that's the worst part. What I regret is what it's reduced us to. We've spent decades, Luke, sharing everything with each other, being there for each other, and yet now I feel there are secrets and lies between us, and I can't even really tell you how I feel because—" She chokes slightly, and I can feel my heart constricting.

"What are you saying, Mia?"

"I don't know. I don't know what I'm saying, but I think that this is not the time or the place to have this conversation. I don't want everyone to think that this was fake, right? We didn't do all this and practically ruin our friendship for us to get found out at the last moment."

"Do you think our friendship is ruined?"

I reach to grab her hand, and she pulls it away.

"I don't know, Luke. I don't know anything anymore."

chapter twenty-four

Mia

The room feels cold, like I'm in Antarctica or the North Pole or something. I can't stop my body from shivering. I don't know how long I'm going to walk around the room with this fake smile plastered on my face.

I can see Juniper darting glances at me every few moments, and then when she's not looking at me, she's looking at Rafe like there's something there, and I wonder if there is. I wonder if another one of my best friends is keeping secrets from me. I want to ask her, but I'm so caught up in what I'm going through with Luke that I don't even have the energy.

I watch Wendy and Carter dance around on the dance floor. She's laughing at something he's whispering to her, and I'm happy to see her so happy.

Cal is standing in the corner, looking slightly awkward as he chats with Silvie, and I wonder what their relationship is like—being fake married couldn't be any better than fake dating, but they didn't have the history that Luke and I had. I am curious if they are actually falling in love or if they are able to keep that distance between them. I'll have to speak to Silvie and find out. Maybe we are in closer situations than I thought.

And then there is Summer standing there—beautiful, ethereal—and Dayton is just staring at her. He is an intense man, handsome as all could be, and I can feel how much he wants her. We all can. But Summer seems oblivious. Maybe as oblivious as I was to the fact that Luke had been keeping secrets from me.

I feel like a bit of a fool. I feel like my entire friendship with him has been a farce, and I feel guilty because it isn't like he is the only one who has been holding things back. He doesn't know that I love him. He doesn't know. That's why I am probably acting crazier and more emotional than I would normally be. He doesn't know that being with him, being around him, makes me feel things I've never felt before in my life.

My heart freezes as I notice him heading back to me. There's a cautious expression on his face, like he's scared I'm going to shout at him again.

I feel slightly taken aback when he offers me a small box.

"I come in peace," he says, handing it to me.

"What is this?" I can't help but smile.

"I know you like parties and you like gifts, so this is a little gift from me to you."

"What is it?"

"Open it and see," he says.

I open it slowly, and then I stare at the most beautiful silver bangle.

"This is gorgeous."

"I bought it for you from New York. I was going to give it to you at a later date, but I figured maybe now would be a good time, seeing as you're kind of mad at me." And he shrugs. "I don't want you to be mad at me."

"I can't stay mad at you, Luke, but when the night is finished, we definitely need to have a conversation."

"We will definitely have a conversation." He grins at me. "Why don't you put the bracelet on? I had a feeling you would love it."

"It's gorgeous. Thank you."

"Yeah, I wanted to get you something that I didn't think you'd be able to get yourself."

"What does that mean?" I stare at him, blinking.

"It just means that it was a really expensive bracelet, and I knew you would love it, but you would be unlikely to buy it for yourself, so I wanted to give it to you."

"So, this is about money again? Poor me, I can't afford expensive jewelry?"

"It's got nothing to do with money. It has to do with the fact that I wanted to get you something that I knew you would love." He lets out a long sigh. "Are you really going to hold that against me?"

"I am trying not to hold it against you. I just—I'm sorry. This is just really complicated. I guess this is why friends don't normally sleep together because it does mess things up."

"It doesn't have to mess things up," he says.

He turns to the side, and we both freeze as we see Rex heading over to us. I want to let out a groan because even though we're here for Rex's upcoming nuptials, I can't stand being around him.

"Mia," he says, nodding, and I'm surprised that he doesn't make another rude comment to me. Then he looks at Luke. "Hello, Luke."

"Rex," Luke says.

There's no love lost between them.

"So, I was just telling Andi here that you went to New York because I was chosen to take over the company and you couldn't take it."

Luke stares at him. "Is this really the time and the place to have this conversation?"

"I don't know what you're talking about." Rex laughs as if he didn't just insult his brother. "Andi was just asking me why you left Coconut Beach, and that was it, right? It obviously wasn't because of your budding romance with Mia. You guys weren't together back then because she was kind of trying to bounce on my—"

"Hey!" Luke shouts and grabs Rex by the neck. "Don't you ever fucking talk about my girlfriend that way again."

Andi looks over at Rex, frowning. "What's going on, Rex? This is our engagement party."

"And you told me you were pregnant, and you're not."

"I thought I was," she says.

Rex just rolls his eyes. The air is cold and tense.

I press my lips together. I feel like this is not a conversation I should hear, and I feel like it's not a conversation they should have when they're about to get married, but it's none of my business.

"Let me go," Rex says, pushing his brother off of him.

"I will not have you disrespecting me and Mia every single time. We will just leave. We will do our own thing, and we won't come to the wedding."

Rex just stares at him and then at me. "Whatever. I don't care."

"You know what, Rex? I think you do care," I say finally.

Luke looks at me in surprise.

"Excuse me?" Rex glares at me.

"I think you are jealous of Luke. I think you're constantly putting him down because he is the man you will never be in every single way. And you know what? When I was young, I was dumb, and I had a little crush on you, and it went nowhere, and boohoohoo, but I am over it. You should get over it too. You know what? I don't care if you think I'm hot now. I don't care if you think I'm sexy. I find your comments to be extremely disrespectful to me and to your fiancée and to your brother, who I am in a relationship with. Do you think I'm going to choose you over this amazing man who has always been there for me? He is smarter than you. He is funnier than you. He is sexier than you, and he's more intelligent than you."

"I kind of think smarter and intelligent mean the same thing," Luke says, grinning. I just shake my head at him. "But continue, my darling."

I laugh and then turn back to Rex. "I chose Luke because I know his heart and I know he's a good man. And I choose to not want you in my life, Rex, because you're horrible. You're absolutely horrible. And the best thing you ever did for me was reject me. I thank God that you rejected me because how horrid would my life have been if I had been with you? We never even kissed, Rex, and I'm glad for that."

Rex looks absolutely stunned at my comments. I'm kind of stunned that I made them.

"And just so you know, Rex, Luke is an amazing lover, and he satisfies me, and he makes me orgasm like I've never orgasmed before in my life."

I look over at Andi, and I'm pretty sure that she can't say the same thing because I don't know what's going on here, but she looks miserable—maybe because she realizes she's marrying a jerk.

I take a deep breath. "But I will not let you talk to me like that again. I will not let you talk to Luke like that again. You can fuck all the way off, okay? I don't know why your parents did what they did, and that's on them, but Luke doesn't need you or your family's money. And frankly, you're lucky he took time out of his busy schedule to come and support you. You should thank him."

I hear clapping from behind me, and I turn around in shock. Juniper, Wendy, Silvie, Summer, Dayton, Rafe, Carter, Cal, my grandmother, and Luke's grandmother are all standing there, clapping.

Juniper gives me a big thumbs-up and whispers, "Well done."

"Come on, Luke," I say, grabbing his hand. "We need to talk."

He nods, and we head out of the ballroom.

When we exit the door, he turns to me. "Thank you. You didn't have to do that."

"But I had to do that, Luke. I have known you your entire life, and I know your childhood—you've always been compared to your brother. Your dad's a jackass for that, and your mom was not cool for letting it happen. And I know you've always felt inferior, and I know Rex says and does things to you, and he still gets under your skin. And I know you know you're better than him, and you always stick up for me. And I know you would've beaten his ass tonight, and I love you for it. But I can speak up for myself, and I can speak up for you, and I can put him in his place because I am fucking Mia Bishop. And, yeah, I'm just a girl, and sometimes, I cry at movies, and I cry when I see animals looking lonely, and I cry when I don't get to speak to you, and I cry when I read books that make me sad. I laugh, and I joke around, and I'm goofy, and I do all sorts of things. But I know how to stick up for myself. And your brother is a bully, and he is a jerk. He has insulted me, and he's insulted you, and I've had enough. I have had motherfucking enough, okay? From the moment I got that invitation, I should have told him where to stick it."

"I'm kind of glad you didn't," Luke says, his lips twitching.

"Oh, yeah?"

"Yeah," he says. "I'm kind of glad we both got incensed and we decided to fake date."

"And why is that?"

"I don't know. Maybe because it led us to having to share a hotel room, which led us to having to kiss ..."

"Which led us to having sex."

"Which led us to making love," he corrects, a soft look in his eyes.

"You really think we made love?"

"I know I made love to you. Did you not make love to me?"

"Oh, I totally fucked you, Luke. I bounced up and down on you like you were a cowboy. I was riding in the Wild, Wild West."

He starts laughing. "Well, cowgirl, are you ready to go again?"

"I think so. Are you ready for me to ride you all night long?"

He grabs my hand and pulls me into him.

"But we've got a lot to discuss, don't we?" I say, because this feels too complicated, too real, too emotional.

"Yeah. There's something I want to tell you."

"What?"

"I love you, Mia."

"What?" My heart stills, but I laugh because I'm not sure I heard him correctly. He doesn't mean he loves me, for real, does he?

"I love you. For real, for real," he says, gazing at me with such an intense expression that I know he's not lying. "I love you more than the stars in the sky."

"We don't know how many stars there are in the sky."

"Exactly," he says and smiles. "And I love that you are fearless, and I love that you're emotional, and I love that we just get each other. And even when we fight and we argue, we're still able to come back to each other. And you're making me really nervous right now," he adds, suddenly unsure of himself.

"What do you mean?"

"You haven't said anything back to me."

I stare at him and touch the side of his face. "You want me to tell you how I feel?"

"I kind of do," he says.

I lean in and give him a big kiss, and then I step back.

"I kind of think I love you too, Luke."

The words seem lame compared to his declaration, but there's something in me that's holding back.

"Oh, you *think* you love me?" he says, looking extremely disappointed.

"I am just scared. I don't know that we're compatible to be in a relationship together." I bite down on my lower lip. "I think you're great. You're my best friend, and I love making love to you. But your number one love in life is your job and proving yourself, and you are doing amazing at that. And I don't want to hold you back from that, but I don't want to be sitting in the wings, waiting for you to get to where you want to get in your career.

"I want to be the number one. I want to be the first choice. I want to be the person who means more than anything else. And knowing you as I know you, your career and that upward trajectory have always been the most important thing. But it hasn't been me ever.

"Remember when we were in high school and I asked you to stay? You left. You left because you needed to prove yourself to Rex. And I don't think you've finished proving yourself yet. There's still that tension between you two, and I don't want to be the person who stops you from achieving those dreams and goals."

"You're not though, Mia—"

"I'm just saying that, sometimes, love isn't enough. And you're the best friend a girl could ever have, and I don't want to lose that. And we're arguing all the time, and we're not agreeing on things. And you're not seeing my side, and I'm not seeing your side. And we've never had that before. And I think if we continue to go down this road, there's a genuine possibility that our friendship could end. I don't want our friendship to end. I don't want us to end."

"I know. Neither do I."

"And that's why I don't think we should continue."

"So, what are you saying? You want to end this fake relationship?"

"No. What I'm saying is, I want to keep this fake relationship for the summer, and then we go our own way. I don't think we should make it real—even though we love each other. I'd much rather have you as my best friend for the rest of my life than my boyfriend for a year and then we break up and never talk again. I couldn't live without being able to call you at any time of the day."

"But you don't mind being the crazy best friend?"

"I've never minded being the crazy best friend. You know that."

"What can I do to convince you this is more than friendship, Mia?"

"I just don't think that we're compatible, Luke." I step on my tiptoes and kiss him. "Doesn't mean I don't love you. Doesn't mean I don't crave you. Doesn't mean I don't want to feel you inside of me."

He groans against my lips. "You can't say things like that and tell me you don't want to be with me, Mia."

"I'm just being honest with you, Luke. I think that's what we've always had, and that's what we need to keep. We need to be honest. And the fact is, I want to take you up to the hotel room right now and sit on your face and have you make me come."

"Fuck," he says, reaching behind and squeezing my ass.

He pushes me up against the wall, and I groan as he runs his fingers down the side of my dress. He shifts next to me, and I feel him pressed up against me. He kisses the side of my neck and then sucks on my lower lip. I feel his hand on my breast, squeezing.

He stares me in the eyes. "You're not the only one that loves our intimate moments. I would fuck you right here and right now, Mia, but it's not just about the raw passion. It's about what I feel when I'm inside of you—that closeness, that magic, that connection. My cock was made for your pussy. I want to live in your pussy. Do you hear me? I love you, and I will convince you that we are meant to be and we are compatible."

He groans as he presses his lips against mine.

This is about us becoming one, and I want to believe him. I want to tell him that I want that, too, but I realize he hasn't responded to the one thing that's holding me back. He hasn't told me I come before his job. He hasn't told me I am number one, that I matter more. And it breaks my heart because I know the reason he hasn't told me is that he can't lie to me.

Because it's not true.

And I will not go the rest of my life being number two to his job. I can't. I deserve better, and he deserves someone that's okay with that.

I reach down and squeeze his cock. "Well, I think if you want to do something naughty, I can do it too."

"Are you sure?" he says in a hoarse voice.

"Well, I don't mean right here, right now because anyone could walk out—including our grandparents—and I don't really want to give anyone a heart attack."

He chuckles slightly as he pulls back away from me.

"Then let's go up to the room because I want to make love to you, darling Mia. I want to make you come a million different ways, and then I want to lick every single drop off of you."

"Keep sweet-talking me, bad boy," I say, grinning at him.

He just shakes his head. "This is absolutely insane."

chapter twenty-five

Luke

"Good morning, beautiful," I whisper to Mia as soon as she opens her eyes.

She rolls over and looks at me, a light expression on her face. As she gazes at me, I lean forward and give her a quick kiss.

"Morning," she says. "How did you sleep?"

She's almost awkward, which I find adorable.

"Well. You good?"

She nods, smiling. "Last night was absolutely insane."

Her eyes widen, and I feel like I'm on a roller-coaster ride, and I don't know when it's going to stop.

"I kind of feel the same way—and not just because you were riding me all night long."

"I was not riding you all night long," she says, but blushes.

I pull her toward me, her naked body pressing into mine. I run my fingers down her silky skin and press my lips against hers. She runs her fingers down my back, and I roll on top of her.

"What do you want to do today?"

"I don't know. What do you want to do?"

She moans as I spread her legs and run my fingers along her slit. She's wet, and I'm hard, and some morning sex is just how I want to get the day started.

"Luke," she says, feverishly as I kiss the side of her face and position myself between her legs. "I just woke up."

"Hey, and that's the perfect way to wake up, right?"

"Maybe," she murmurs against my lips.

I slide into her quick and fast, and she grunts as she wraps her legs around my hips. I move in and out of her slowly. I want to savor this.

"Ahhhhhhhhhhhhhh," she moans, arching her back, her breasts pushing against my chest. I love the feel of her breasts against my skin. I love the way she fits into me. I love the way she whimpers and shivers and holds onto me like I'm an anchor in the ocean and only I can save her. "Luke." She whines my name and it has never sounded sexier.

I hold the side of her face and kiss her softly. I continue thrusting inside of her, loving the feel of being in her—like a puzzle piece that fits just right. We are two lego pieces that just click into place.

"That Ed Sheeran song should play right now, don't you think?" I whisper against her lips.

"What do you mean?" She tilts her head slightly. "Which one?"

"Lego House." I run my fingers across her nipple and she arches her back, a loud wail escaping her perfectly pouted lips as I squeeze it.

"Why do you say that?" She can barely speak as her eyes roll back in ecstasy.

"Cos we're like lego pieces. We fit together perfectly."

"If you say so," she says, giggling slightly.

I pause, and she groans and looks at me with wide-open eyes.

"Why did you stop?"

"If you don't think we're like a puzzle piece—"

"Haha, really, Luke?"

"What?" I say, teasing her. "I don't want to give you something that you so obviously aren't enjoying."

She glares at me. "You really want to play these games? Because I will withhold sex from you forever if you don't continue."

"So, are you asking me to give you the best sex of your life?"

"I never said that," she says.

I press the tip of my cock against her entrance again, and she moans.

"Luke—"

"What is it? Or is it not the best sex of your life?"

"Fine. It's the best."

I slide into her hard, and she screams, her fingernails digging into my back.

"You want to go on a boat ride today? Maybe we can ask Juniper and Rafe if they want to come."

"I can't think about that right now," she mumbles as she bites down on my shoulder.

I feel her back arching as she holds on to me, squeezing me tighter and tighter as I move faster and faster. I love how she makes me feel. I love how being inside of her makes me feel.

I slip my tongue into her mouth, and she sucks on it as I thrust faster and harder, and then we're coming together. I'm exploding inside of her, and she orgasms. Then we lie back, panting.

I lazily stroke the side of her face, and she moans.

"That was a pretty awesome way to wake up—I'm not going to lie." She grins at me. "Feel free to do that every morning that you're still here in town."

She pauses slightly as we both realize what her words mean.

There's going to come a point when I have to go back to New York City, and she's going to be here, and I don't want that point to be the end of whatever we have. I don't want that point to be something that leaves us both feeling anxious. I want her to want to be with me. I want her to fully give herself to me in love. I want her to know that we will make it. We will defy the odds because there is no one that could have a better relationship than us.

But I'm not going to push it because I know patience is the answer. Patience is the only thing that can make this work.

I don't really understand why she's nervous. I don't really understand what is keeping her from fully embracing a life with me. I'm not sure if it's because I'm wealthy and I've told her that I'd like to support her. I'm happy for her to keep her independence. I just have to let her know that. I need her to know that I don't want to take anything away from her. I just want to give her more, show her more, be more.

But I will have to be patient because I don't want to upset the delicate balance that exists between us.

"I love you, Mia," I say as I stare into her eyes.

She smiles and stares back at me. My heart stills, frozen in time for a moment, as I fear she's not going to say anything back to me.

"I love you too, Luke."

"You love me?" My heart soars. "Or you think you love me?"

"I love you. Of course I love you." She strokes the side of my face. "I just don't know. I feel like we belong together. I feel like every moment with you is like the best day of my life. I don't know if this is just a fantasy though, Luke. We're in this gorgeous hotel room. We're getting to spend every day together. We've sort of just taken our friendship to a new level, and it's exciting and new. But I don't know if we can exist in reality, being such different people."

"I'm imagining my life with you, Mia. I'm imagining you as the mother of my kids. I want it all with you, and I know you want to get married. I know you want to have kids because we've spoken about this for years."

She strokes the side of my face. "Have you ever thought that you would be the father of my kids?"

"I don't know if you want to know the honest answer to that. I don't want you to think I'm crazy."

"I don't think you're crazy, but what does that mean?"

"It means that I can see you in New York. I can see you living with me. I can see me going to work and coming home and you being there. I can—"

"Well, that's where you're wrong, Luke," she says, pulling back from me. "I don't want to be in New York."

I can see the dismay in her eyes. I can see that she's pulling away, that she really doesn't think it can work. She's not going to push for it like I want to push for it.

"What about England? What if I choose to go to England for that job?"

"I don't want to go to England. I don't want to go to New York. I love Coconut Beach. This is my life. This is my home. My friends are here."

"But I'm your best friend."

"You are my best friend, but I need more than just you, Luke."

"My love is not good enough?"

"I could ask you the same thing. My love's not good enough for you to just stop putting that job first? You can't find another job somewhere else?"

And then, suddenly, it clicks.

This is about my job.

I stare at her. "This is about my job?"

"Of course it's about your job. I've been telling you it's about your job."

I didn't get it. I guess I heard the words, but I wasn't processing them.

"You think that the job is more important than you? Really, Mia, how could you think that?"

"You haven't been back home in five years. You haven't invited me to New York. You didn't even come early when you were supposed to because of the job. You've disappeared different times on this trip because of the job. I feel like whenever we're getting closer, you have to go because of your job, and I just don't want to be second fiddle to your job."

I stare at her, finally understanding what she is feeling, what she has been experiencing, and I'm frustrated. I'm frustrated because I've worked my entire life to get to this place, and I'm so close to getting to the next level. I'm so close to achieving all my dreams and finally showing everyone in my family—especially Rex—that I am the better brother.

And then it hits me.

It hits me that I've been living and striving for something for such a stupid, obstinate reason, and I am about to lose the love of my life for it.

"Fuck, Mia—"

"No, I'm not going to fuck you again right now, Luke. That's not what I'm saying."

"I know."

She gives me a small smile. "You don't have to say anything, Luke. It's okay. We just kind of want two different things from relationships."

"We don't—"

My phone starts ringing, and I want to ignore it.

"You should answer that."

"I can get it later."

"It could be your job. It could be something important."

"Mia, we're literally in the middle of a conversation where you said you want me to put you first. I'm not going to answer the phone."

"Please answer it."

I take a deep breath and grab the phone. I'm surprised when I see it's my grandmother's name on the screen.

"Hey, Grandma. Is everything okay?"

"No," she says. "It's not."

"Wait, what's wrong?"

"Everything is going to shit. I knew this was going to happen. I just knew it, and we need you. I need you to come right now."

"What's going on?"

"It's Rex."

"Oh shit. What has he done now?"

"He's run the business into the ground. He's overleveraged the company. We owe hundreds of thousands to different creditors. We've lost several contracts. We need your help."

"What?" I frown. "What are you talking about, Grandma?"

I can see Mia looking at me with a curious expression in her eyes.

"Please, you need to come now, Luke."

"Grandma, I can't. I'm in the middle of something."

"We just got notice that we have forty-eight hours to come up with six hundred seventy-five thousand dollars, or we're going to lose one of the stores, and your great-grandfather started that store. You're the only one who can help."

"Why can't Rex take care of it? He's the CEO. Dad put him in charge."

"Please, Luke. I need you to come now."

"Okay," I say. "I'll be there in an hour."

"Thank you. I love you, grandson."

"I love you, Grandma."

I hang up, guilt filling me as I stare at Mia.

"You've got to go," she says softly. "Is everything okay?"

"I don't know," I say. "There seems like there's some sort of family crisis, and maybe the family's about to lose the business."

Her eyes widen. "What? What's going on?"

"I guess Rex has not been doing as good of a job as he's been letting on."

"Of course not." She rolls her eyes. "He fucking sucks."

"Well, Grandma said that they owe over half a million dollars, and they might be about to lose the business. I don't really understand what's going on. I haven't been involved in such a long time, but she wants me to help."

"Then you should go."

"I don't want to go, Mia. I don't want you to think that I'm choosing business over you."

"It's your family. It's okay."

"You are my family, Mia. You're the most important person to me in my life, and I don't want to leave when you've just expressed to me that you think business comes first in my eyes—and it doesn't."

"You're helping family, Luke, and I would never resent you for that. I don't even resent the fact that you care so much about business. I just have always wanted to be number one in someone's life. I've always wanted to feel seen and noticed, and maybe that's selfish of me. Maybe it's unrealistic, but that's what I want, and that's what I need. And I love you, and I want you to be happy."

"I'm only going to be happy if I'm with you, Mia. I love you. This is not just a summer romance for me. This is forever."

"I love you, too, but I'd rather not go any further with us than risk losing myself in you and losing myself in this relationship and then getting heartbroken and losing everything. I love you enough to let go," she says softly.

"What do you mean, you love me enough to let go?"

"I'm scared, Luke. What if we don't make it? What if we fuck things up? We've never been in a situation like this before, and I just don't know."

"Trust me, Mia. Trust me that I will always put you first, that I will always be there for you. I don't have to go to my grandma's right now. I will talk through anything you want to talk through. I will do anything you want to do. I will—"

"I'll come with you," she says.

"What do you mean?"

"I'll come with you to your grandparents' house, okay? I want to be a support for you, and I want you to know I'm okay with you helping them. This situation is not about that. It's just about me being worried and nervous, and this is really new for me and for you. And what if we don't make it?"

"But what if we do, Mia? What if it's everything we could have ever dreamed of?"

"I don't know," she says. "I'm just scared that it could be everything I've ever dreamed of—and then I'll lose it."

chapter twenty-six

Mia

The room is tense. Rex is sitting on the couch, looking like a scolded child. Andi sits next to him, looking like she's lost. Luke's parents are sitting at the table. His mother is crying, and his father looks like he's had the wind taken out of his sails. Only Bitsy looks solid, staunch, resolute. Her husband is at the golf course and I wonder what he'll think when he gets back.

I look over at Luke on the couch. He's just listened as he'd learned about everything that's been going on. Rex has pretty much run the company into the ground, which I think is ironic. I kind of want to laugh if the situation wasn't so serious, but I can tell that that would be the absolute worst move to make because the entire family is in crisis control. I respect the fact that Luke hasn't laughed in Rex's face and called him a loser. If it had been me, I would have let Rex have it, but Luke is better than me. He's dignified in his takedown of Rex. Though I suppose he can't jump up and down and tell his parents off for shutting him out like they had.

I didn't know one person could fuck something up that badly, but it doesn't surprise me that Rex has.

Luke speaks calmly as he addresses his family. "This is a shit show," he says, looking up from some of the folders.

He's in business mode right now, and it's interesting to see him as a businessman. It's interesting to listen to him talk about numbers and plans. This is a Luke I'm not familiar with. I'm not in his business world. I'm not that business-savvy myself, and yet I can see that he excels, that he loves it, that this is his drive. And I also realize this side of his life really doesn't have any impact on me and his love for me and our relationship, and I feel slightly guilty and immature that I've been holding his job against him because of my own selfish need to want to come first in every situation.

The fact of the matter is, I realize I can't come first in every single situation. I just want to feel like I have no chance of losing him.

"So, what exactly is it that you want me to do?" Rex says, speaking up, sounding like a petulant kid.

"I need you to step down," Luke says, running his fingers through his hair and staring at his brother. "I need you to check your ego. I need you to stop acting like you're the fucking boss of everything and that you know everything because you obviously don't. This is our family company. Our parents rely on the income that we make. Grandma and Granddad rely upon the pension they receive. You rely upon it. Your family will rely upon it."

Andi looks nervous. "Is there a possibility that you're going to have no money, Rex?"

"It's fine, Andi," he says in a tense tone.

"Because I didn't sign up for no money and I certainly didn't sign up for you …" She pauses as Rex gives her a deafening glare. She presses her lips together and stares at me.

I frown slightly because she looks miserable. She looks absolutely miserable, which is not the way a new bride should be looking. I don't say anything though because it's not my place, and she and I aren't really friends. But I'm curious as to what is going on between her and Rex and what the conversation about being pregnant meant.

"You just had to come in and save the day," Rex says. "You just had to be Batman or Superman or whoever the fuck."

Luke shakes his head and looks over at me. I blow him a kiss, and he gives me a warm smile. I smile back at him.

I look up and notice that his grandma is staring at me, and there's a pleading expression on her face, which I find surprising, given the fact that she may have to sell her house and leave the island with no money.

"Look, I can take care of everything," Luke says. "I can pay off the outstanding loans, and I can help turn the company around, but"—he pauses—"I'm just really exhausted right now. Physically, mentally, emotionally. I want to help everyone, but I do not trust Rex to still be in charge of the company."

"You just want to be CEO!" Rex screams. "That's all you've ever wanted. You've wanted to take my place. You're probably happy that this has happened."

"Do not talk to your brother like that," Mr. Haverbrook says, and I'm shocked because I've barely heard the man speak ten words in the time I've known him. But I'm not interested in football, so we never really had much to chat about. It's a pity though.

"What?" even Rex and Luke both say in shocked tones. Neither one of them has ever heard him speaking up for Luke. I think the world is about to end because this is something that I'd never expected to see.

"What are you saying, Dad?" Rex sounds like an unsure kid. He looks confused and defeated and for a moment, I almost feel sorry for him. But then I think back to how he's treated Luke their entire lives. And how he's spoken to me. And how he's treated Andi. He's a jerk and he doesn't deserve my pity.

"I made a mistake. You don't have a head for business like your brother. I'm sorry, son."

He looks over at Luke. "I've been unfair to you, and I regret it. I've noticed that Rex has not been handling this well, and I would love your help turning this around."

"So, what, you're just giving him the company now?" Rex says. "Thanks, Dad."

"No," Luke says. "We can be co-CEOs. I can help you. I can maybe mentor you, teach you, give you some—"

"You're going to mentor me?" Rex laughs. "Are you fucking kidding? I would listen to you for advice? You loser."

"I don't think he's the loser, Rex," I say loudly, then press my lips together because this is maybe not the time and the place for me to get involved.

"It's up to you, but if you continue running the company the way you have been, there will be no company. You have to see that."

Rex looks stunned for a couple of moments, but he nods. "I can't do this anymore." He jumps up and storms to the side of the room. He looks around the room and starts laughing like a hyena. I wonder if he's lost it and is finally cracking. It wouldn't surprise me. "I'm sorry, but I can't do this shit." He stands there like he's waiting for someone to console him, but everyone in the room is too shocked to say anything.

"You can't do what?" Andi jumps up and she's looking more enraged than I've ever seen her in my life. I almost wish I could take my phone out and livestream. This is DRAMA and the girls in my friend group would salivate to watch this live. The thought immediately makes me feel guilty. I shouldn't want to share this with anyone. But man, the room feels like the set of a daytime soap right now. "What can't you do, Rex?" She screams and I look over at Luke, who's expression is as equally shocked as mine is. His lip twists up at the side and I press my lips together.

"What do you think, Andi?" His sarcastic voice would make me slap him, but she resists. She's stronger than me, that's for sure. "

"Don't talk to me like that."

"Like what?" He sneers.

"It's off." She looks over at me and I freeze. Had I caused this? Holy cow, batman, was she going to blame me for this?

"What's off?"

"The engagement is over, Rex. The wedding is off." There's dead silence in the room. You could hear a pin drop if someone happened to be sewing. My jaw drops as she walks over to him and presses her finger into his chest. "You and me are done."

"This is not happening. Are you kidding me?" Rex leans forward and grabs her hand. "So, what I thought was true, huh? You're just a gold-digging hoe? You're leaving because I'm not the CEO now?"

My loud gasp is heard through out the room and Luke inches toward me slowly. I'm glad that he's coming to my side because standing here alone is making me far too self-aware, even though I'm not even close to being the center of attention in the room.

"No, Rex, I'm leaving you because I caught you fucking Talia in our room last night." Andi looks around, voice shaking.

I need to text Juniper and tell her the gossip, but there's no way I can start texting in the middle of this. Everyone would know I was acting like one of the busy bees, plus I didn't want to miss a second of this.

"What?" Rex looks around as if deciding whether or not to deny it. I think he decides against it because he doesn't say another word. I for one believe Andi 100%.

"I'm sorry for being so crude, but I can't take this anymore. This is the second time, Rex. I can't take you cheating on me. I don't want to marry a man who cheats on me and has no money. I can't do it." A sputter escapes from my lips and I pretend to cough. "A broke cheat is not the sort of man I want to be with."

"He was sleeping with Talia?" I blurt out. I can't stop myself now. This is juicy. I also want to ask if a rich cheat was okay, but I don't dare. I think I already know the answer to that question any way.

"She said that she was going to have one Haverbrook brother, no matter what it took." Andi starts crying. "She was my best friend." She looks at me. 'She tried to fuck Luke as well, but that didn't happen, so she went for Rex, the easy Haverbrook brother."

"I'm not easy." Rex looks offended. "Plus what do you mean she wanted Luke as well? She wasn't talking about Luke when I was blowing her back out."

"Rex Haverbrook, watch your language." His father finally speaks up, as his mother starts crying. I look over at Bitsy and she looks astounded, but there's a twinkle in her eyes. I know that even though Rex is her grandson, she's going to be spreading this story far and wide on Coconut Beach,

"You're disgusting." Andi sniffles. "To think I thought you were the one."

"Let's be real here," Rex says scoffing. "I didn't even want to marry you. We had sex one time, and you told me you got pregnant, and I felt pressured into marrying you so that my kid wouldn't be a bastard. And then you weren't even pregnant, but it was too far along for us to call this shit off." Wow, he's a bigger jerk than I thought.

"Well, I thought you loved me." Her face looks miserable and my heart goes out to her.

"Yeah, I *loved* having sex with you that one time."

"That's enough, Rex." Luke shuts him down and I'm so proud of him for speaking up. "I don't know how or why you think you can be that disrespectful to women, but it's not okay. Do you hear me? I don't care what happens with the business and what you decide between us, but do not speak to Andi that way."

"Are you for real, Prince Luke. You everyone's savior now? You have a thing for her too?"

"I don't have to have a thing for a woman to be kind and decent and respectful. You should be ashamed of yourself, Rex." Luke squares off in front of his brother. "You are a horrible human being."

"What did we do wrong?" Mr. Haverbrook stands there, looking ill. "What can we do to—"

"Dad, honestly, it's too little, too late. You have let Rex become a horrible human being—and why? Just because he lived out your glory days as a football star? He's horrible. He's been horrible to me. He's been horrible to his fiancée. He's done everything in his power to dismantle our family's company. It's not cool, Dad. You didn't teach us to be this way. Granddad didn't teach us to be this way."

His dad looks down at the table. "You're right. I've failed you both."

Rex just shakes his head. "I can't believe this bullshit." He holds his hand out, and Andi just stares at him.

"What?" Her voice is light and for a moment, I think she's hoping that he will beg her to forgive him. That he will say he can't live without her.

"Well, you said it's over, right? I want the ring back. That cost me twenty grand." My jaw cannot drop any lower.

"You're not going to let me keep the ring?"

"No. Didn't you just hear? My family's fucking broke. I need that twenty grand." He looks over at Luke. "Unless you think that you're willing to lend me two hundred grand to start a new business."

"Not in a billion years." Luke snorts and his eyes catch mine for a moment and I smile at him.

"I think I'm going to go to India." Everyone looks at Rex in shock.

"What? Why India? You going to harass more women?" I say loudly, then cover my mouth quickly.

"I have never harassed a woman in my life. In fact, I've been harassed."

"Stop lying to yourself, Rex." I cross my arms. "No way you think any of us are buying that?"

"You know what? This shit is stressing me out. I've had a really long couple of months. The reason why the wedding invites and everything happened so quickly was because it was a fucking shotgun wedding," he says, looking around like he's looking for pity. I'm glad no-one is coming to his rescue. "And you weren't even fucking pregnant. You tried to trap me, but you tried to trap the wrong one, bitch."

"Enough!" both Luke and their dad shout, and Rex blanches.

Luke walks over to him and stares into his brother's eyes with contempt. "You're disgusting. You know that? You are absolutely fucking disgusting."

"I'm sorry I couldn't be the golden boy like you, Luke."

Luke stares at him for a couple of seconds, just shaking his head. I just want to laugh because his entire life, Luke thought Rex was the golden boy when it turned out that he was the golden boy all along.

I knew it. I'd always known it, but he allowed Rex and his father's treatment of him to make him feel like he wasn't good enough, when all along he was too good..

I step forward and grab Luke's hand. "You're a jerk, Rex. But I already told you that. And, Andi, I don't really know why you were marrying him, but I'm really glad that you're walking away before making the worst decision of your life."

She sniffles. "I know. I was listening to Talia because she told me it would be really great if I married him, but she's—" She shakes her head. "I think she just wanted to show me that she could have any man she wanted, and she wanted mine."

"Well, this is kind of awkward," Rex says as his phone starts beeping, "but I have to go right now." He grins as he holds his phone up. "911."

"What?" Luke just stares at him. "What the hell does that mean?"

"I just got a message, and someone needs to see me. So, you guys good?"

"You're seriously going to leave right now?" Luke sounds angrier than I've ever heard him sound in his life. *Knock him out, Luke.* I want to shout, but I abhor violence normally, plus I don't want his entire family to hate me. I can't imagine his mother crying anymore than she is now.

"It seems like I'm not needed in the family business. My engagement is over, and, well, I've given enough of my life to Coconut Beach."

"You're not going to be a grownup about this?" Luke sounds so disappointed. "You can't just leave."

"I can. I need to find some flights to India." Rex closes his eyes and hums loudly.

"Is he losing it?" I whisper to Luke, who just stares at his brother in disbelief.

"I need to take some yoga classes, man. I need to learn how to chill and relax. This stress is going to make me have a heart attack. Plus, Talia said she knows this yogi that—"

Andi bursts into tears at his words and I watch as she slides the ring off of her finger and throws it at him.

"Talia, can have this." She sobs. "You can tell her the friendship is over and I'm never talking to her again." She puts her hands on her hips and she looks self-satisfied like she thinks that's actually going to hurt Talia's feelings. I want to make a comment about Talia likely not giving a flying fuck, but I don't.

Rex stares at her and then at the ring before placing it into his back pocket. For a few moments, he looks like he wants to cry and I think he's finally going to do the right thing and apologize and ask for forgiveness. I think he's going to own up to being a shitty human being. But I'm a bigger fool than he is for thinking that because he promptly hurries to the door, a swag in his step that I'd hadn't seen since his teenage years.

"Bye, guys. Love you, fam. See you later. Oh, and, Grandma?" he calls out.

"Yes, Rex?" She sounds tired.

"Let everyone know the wedding's off, please."

And with that, he leaves.

I stare at Luke, eyes wide. "Oh my gosh," I say.

I hold Andi to me as she's still sobbing. "I'm so sorry."

"It's okay. I knew I was being a fool. I knew that it was not the best decision of my life." She looks up at me with wide-open eyes. "I wish I had friends like you and Juniper. Maybe then I wouldn't have found myself in this mess."

"Yeah, maybe," I say because the truth of the matter is, she probably wouldn't have.

"I'm going to go. It was really nice, being welcomed into your family, Mr. and Mrs. Haverbrook, and I'm sorry it came to this. I really hope you can save your business, but I have to go."

And with that, Andi runs out of the house.

Now it's just Luke and me, his grandparents, and his parents. We all stand there in awkward silence.

"So, what, we just wasted that money on a wedding?" his dad says, looking around. "Can we get any money back?"

"I very much doubt it, Dad," Luke says. "And look, it's fine. I'm worth a lot of money. I can take care of this." He looks so solid and so nonchalant that I know that he will take care of everything. Luke, who thought of himself as the black sheep of the family, was now to be their savior. There was poetry in that thought and it delighted me.

"I have an idea," Bitsy says, beaming as she heads toward us. I'm surprised that she's not more upset about Rex, but I've always known she preferred Luke. Bitsy was a gossip, but she was shrewd and smart. There was a reason why she was my grandma's best friend.

"What's your idea, Grandma?" Luke asks, a tinge of apprehension in his tone.

"Why don't you two get married instead?"

"Oh, no," I say quickly. "I don't think we're ready to take that step yet."

"Yeah, Grandma," Luke says, offering her a wry smile. "I don't even know if she's going to marry me yet." He looks over at me and there's a look in his eyes that tells me that he's going to put this all on me. Bastard!

"But you love her," his grandma says, sounding confused. "It's obvious to me and to your grandfather that you two are in love. Why wouldn't you get married?"

He turns to me. "Why won't you marry me, Mia?"

I gaze at him with wide eyes, not sure if he's being serious. "Excuse me, what?"

"You know you've always been the one," he says softly. "And you know I want you to be my wife."

I swallow hard. "I—what?"

He grins at me. "Is it too soon for me to propose to you?"

"Yes. It's too soon." I punch him in the shoulder. "Luke, what are you doing?"

He laughs and pulls me into him, kissing me hard. "Just wanted to see if you'd say yes."

He turns to his grandma. "I'm sorry, Grandma, but as much as I would love to marry Mia right here, right now—or next week or two weeks from now—I think it's too soon for us. And I don't think Mia wants to take over someone else's wedding plans. She's been waiting her entire life to get married. Trust me, I know. We've talked about it enough times, and I think when it finally happens, she's going to want to make all the plans for herself. Aren't you, darling?"

I stare at him, my heart pounding with love for him because he's so sweet and gracious and loving. And I know I will marry him one day.

I nod slowly and squeeze his hand. "Yeah. When we get married, I think I'd like to be the one to plan everything."

His grandma just nods and smiles—a secret little smile. A smile that makes me think that she knows far more about our relationship. Maybe even more than we do.

"I have to make a call," she says as she leaves the room. "You'll see yourselves out?"

"Okay, Grandma." Luke turns to me. "You want to go? I know it's been a long day."

"Okay," I nod and try not to laugh. It had been so much more than just a long day."

"Let's go to Hidden Cove. Let's see if we can find that final clue," he says, a glint in his eyes that tells me he wants to do more than search for a clue.

"Sounds like a plan to me."

"Mom, dad, let's talk tomorrow." He heads over to them and gives them both a hug. "I promise I will do whatever I can to fix everything."

"Thank you, son." His dad says stiffly while his mom holds onto his arm. I can tell from their expressions that they are thankful, but I still think it's far too little after the way they'd treated him, but I know better than to say anything. I may have a big mouth, but even I know when to keep it shut.

We walk out of the house and to his car, and I just look at him with love and awe. Luke was even more of a good guy than I'd given him credit for.

"You know what? I was wrong about something, Luke."

"You were wrong about something? No way. What?"

"I thought that your job mattered more than me, but I was wrong. Your job matters to you because you're good at it, and you're intelligent, and you like problem-solving. But I see now that it's just something completely separate from our relationship."

"So, you think we could actually make this work?"

His eyes look hopeful, and I feel my heart pouring with love for him.

"I think that I choose you, and I choose our love, and I choose this relationship—no matter where it leads us."

"Are you saying what I think you're saying?"

There's hope in his eyes, and I nod.

"I'm saying, let's make this real, Luke. Let's not just have it be a fake summer romance. Let's have it be a real summer romance."

"No," he says. "This isn't just another summer romance, Mia. This is a love story—a story for life. This is a story about soulmates."

"Am I your soulmate, Luke?"

"You're that and so much more, my darling."

And with that, he pulls me into his arms and kisses me softly.

Time really does seem to stand still. I feel like our spirits are fusing together, becoming one. I feel like our love is encapsulating us, covering us, protecting us.

"I love you, Mia. I love you for this summer and a million more."

"I love you too, Luke. You are my everything."

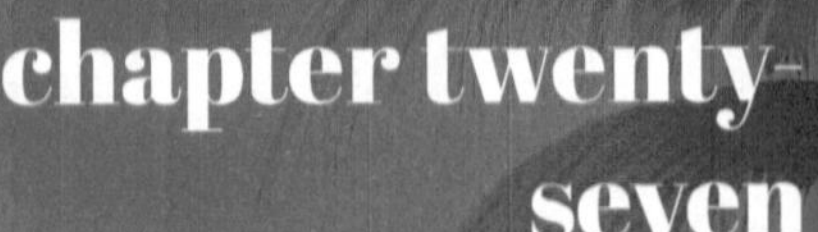

chapter twenty-seven

Luke

This is the happiest I've ever been in my life— happier than when I was valedictorian of my high school class, happier than when I got into Harvard, happier than when I got my job at the hedge fund. Happier than any other moment combined. Mia is mine, and she loves me, and she is finally ready to give me a chance.

She finally understands that while I love my job and I love my work and I love achieving everything to the best of my ability, it doesn't mean more than she does. I will ensure that she realizes that she means everything to me.

"I think that we're going to be very happy together," I say as I drive us toward the hotel so that we can pick up the last clue that she found at Kona Ice.

We can't remember exactly what it said, and though we know we have to head to Hidden Cove, we aren't exactly sure where we have to go.

"I love you so much, Luke. This is just so weird to me. Juniper is going to absolutely flip when I tell her that we are officially together." She turns to me and smiles. "By the way, do you think we should tell everyone that it started as fake and became real or not right away?"

I laugh. "I think there's been quite a lot that's gone down, especially today. I don't think anyone needs any more shocks."

"Can you believe that Rex slept with Talia?" she says in shock.

"I knew she was a hoe. I can believe it from both of them. They both kind of suck, and they deserve each other."

"Do you think they are going to get married?"

"No. They will one hundred percent not get married. I don't even think they're going to last in India together for more than a couple of days. Each of them has an ego the size of the sun. It's not going to go well for them."

"Man, I'm just in shock," she says. "I've never been in more shock in my life."

"Yeah, I can kind of say the same thing though. I'm in more shock that Rex has practically run my family's company into the ground." I shake my head. "It's kind of disgusting how poorly he's done, and I still don't really understand why he didn't come to me for help. He knows I am a good businessman. He knows I could have ensured that this didn't happen."

"But he has an ego. Remember, you just said it. He didn't want to come to you because then you would be the fixer and you would be the good son. And his whole thing over your entire life was that he was the chosen one—and, well, look how that turned out." She rubs my arm. "How are you feeling about that, by the way?"

"I don't know. There's a time in my life where I would've felt delighted, right? Rex is a screwup, a failure, and I'm coming in to save the day. But it doesn't feel like I thought it would feel. It doesn't feel satisfying. I don't like that the business is in this position. I don't like that Rex screwed up, and now he's running away, not even trying to fix it.

"I didn't want to take the company from him. I just wanted us to be brothers—to build it up together. I guess I've always just craved having that true brotherhood, and I suppose now I'm realizing that was what this was really about. It was about him seeing me not only as an equal, but as someone that he loved—someone that he wanted to go through life with. And I guess I realize that was a pipe dream. He doesn't see me as someone he wants in his life like that, and it kind of hurts.

"I think I have been chasing something that was perhaps never going to exist for me, and I don't know that I ever really realized that what I wanted more than beating Rex was actually having a relationship with him, actually having a bond with him.

"I don't think I was doing all this to prove that I was the better brother to my dad. I was trying to prove that I was his equal, that I was good enough."

I smile at her. "Really crazy, the things we figure out about ourselves, huh?"

"Yeah, it makes sense now that you put it that way. He's still your brother at the end of the day—even though he's a big jerk. India and yoga?" She raises an eyebrow. "I don't think I've ever seen him at the beach, doing yoga. Ever."

"I have no words," I say, and I can't stop myself from laughing. "I'm realizing that, obviously, he's got his own insecurities coming from somewhere, and he needs to grow up. And I think I'm going to reach out to him. I'm going to just tell him that if he ever needs to talk or if he ever wants someone, I'll be there for him. I think that's the only thing I can really do at this point."

"You're so great, Luke. How did you get to be so understanding and calm and warm? I would've been like, *Fuck you, bro. Don't bother calling me again.*"

"No, you wouldn't have, Mia."

"I know. Maybe I wouldn't have, but I would've been thinking it for at least a day."

I smile. "So, we're really going to do this, right?"

"I think we have established that we're really going to do this."

"So, it's no longer fake?"

"It's no longer fake."

"I want you to—" My phone rings, and I look down at the screen. "Shit. It's the office. It's New York. Do you mind if I take this?"

"No, not at all," she says, smiling at me.

"I'm going to put it on speakerphone."

"Okay."

"Hey, this is Luke."

"Hey, Luke. This is Johnson. We need you back in the office—like, now."

"Sorry, what?"

"The deal is about to fall through, and you've been gone long enough. Look, I know you're there for your brother's wedding, but this is a multibillion-dollar deal. It's more important than that. Throw your brother another fucking wedding next year to make up for it, but we need you back now."

"I can't do that."

"It's not a request. It's a demand. You get back now, or the deal is off."

"What do you mean, the deal is off?"

"You are part of the deal. If the deal is off, you're out. Out, as in fired, Haverbrook. So, you're on the next plane back to New York, or you're fired."

The phone hangs up.

I look over at Mia. There's a concerned expression in her eyes.

"I guess you should go," she says softly. "Do you want to drive to the airport?"

I stare at her, my heart thudding. I nod slowly.

"I'll come back in a couple of days. I'll fix this, and I will be back. And then we can discuss what we want to do—if you want to move to New York or if we want to go to England, or—"

Her expression changes slightly, but she just keeps nodding.

"I don't want to lose my job. I've been working for a really long time to make this happen. This is a big deal."

I continue driving and then make a swift U-turn.

"Okay. I'm going to go to the airport. You can stay in the hotel room. We've got it for … I don't even know how many more days. I'll give you my credit card information. You can stay there until I come back, and then we'll talk, and we'll figure out how we're going to make this work and where we'll live and if we're based in different places, how often we'll see each other." I can hear my voice escalating. Something doesn't feel right. I'm panicking.

She doesn't say anything.

"I have to leave. I cannot lose this deal. And I will figure out how to take care of the family business as well. Once I figure this deal out in New York, I'll ask for a sabbatical because I have to help my parents. I have to help our business. And then you and I will talk."

As I drive, I feel like my voice is escalating, and I'm panicking. My heart is racing, and something doesn't feel right. I don't feel right. My body is shaking and tense, and Mia is shying away from me. Her body language is off. The laugh is gone from her mouth. She's no longer smiling, and she's avoiding eye contact.

We drive past a McDonald's, and I see two kids standing outside. The little girl is giving the boy French fries.

And I smile, thinking about when we were kids—how Mia would always share her burgers and fries with me.

And that's when it hits me.

That's when everything hits me.

I pull over suddenly and stop the car.

"Fuck," I say, turning off the ignition and staring at her.

"What's wrong? Are you okay?" she asks, concern in her eyes.

I can see the tears, and I feel like a damn fool.

"I nearly did it, didn't I?"

"What?" she says.

"I nearly ruined it already."

"I don't know what you're saying."

Her lower lip trembles, and I run my fingers through my hair.

"I'm a fool. I'm not going to New York," I say suddenly.

"What? No, you have to. You'll lose your job."

"And we have literally spent a billion hours talking about the fact that you wanted me to put you first, and you were worried my job would take over, and I told you it was okay. I told you I understood.

"No. We are just figuring us out. I'm not going to rush off to New York and leave you here to pick up the pieces of everything I'd be leaving behind. You don't deserve that, and I don't want that."

"But the job—you'll—"

"I don't care about the job," I say, laughing suddenly, realizing it's true. "In every single lifetime, I would choose you over a billion dollars."

"A billion dollars?" Her jaw drops.

I smile as I reach out and touch the side of her face. "You are everything to me. You are worth every shiny silver dollar, every piece of gold bullion, every hundred-dollar note, every private island. You are my heart, Mia. I was a fool to even think about going to the airport and leaving you."

"What made you change your mind? You were dead set. You were going to go."

"Those two kids."

"What?"

"Just now, we passed a McDonald's, and there was a little boy and a little girl, and she was giving him her French fries."

"Okay … and what? You want to go to McDonald's and get fries?"

"No. It reminded me of us. Of how we've always been."

"What do you mean?" she says softly.

"How when we were younger, if you had fries, you'd give me some. If you had ice cream, you'd let me have a lick. If you had a Coke, I'd get a sip. If I was down, you'd make me smile. You'd sing to me. You'd tell jokes. You'd dance. We'd laugh. We'd stare at the sky. We'd swim. We'd read. We'd talk about our dreams and our goals. And you supported me every single time, no matter what.

"You have always been there for me, Mia. You have always supported every single selfish thing I've done, and you've never asked for anything. And I've always had you there, and I've always known I've had you there. And you've been the best friend I could ever ask for.

"And I love you. I love you to the very depths of my being. And that means I have a responsibility to show you that I will always be there for you, come hell or high water.

"You can come to me for anything. You can tell me anything. You can be anything.

"I'm not going to leave you right now. I'm not going to leave you ever.

"You are the best listener I've ever met, and you've made me a better listener, but I realize I could do better. Because I know I said you could come to New York, and you've already told me you don't want to come to New York, and you don't want to go to England.

"Coconut Beach is your home. It's our home."

I grab her hands and squeeze them. "I'm not leaving, Mia. I'm not leaving you. I'm not leaving Coconut Beach. I'm moving back." I'm not sure how I ever thought there was a possibility that I wouldn't move back. Not knowing how badly I missed being around Mia, every single day that I'd been away. Coming back to Coconut Beach had been like ripping a bandaid off. Seeing Mia every day, being next to her, laughing with her in person. It had reminded me of just how much distance had taken from me. There was no way I could go back to the friendship that had existed when I'd been in New York.

"You're moving back?" Her jaw drops and I can see the genuine shock in her eyes, but then it's followed by something that resembles hope and that makes my heart thud. Mia is excited about the possibility of me being back home. She's not hiding how happy the idea makes her. My heart soars as I stare into her open and trusting eyes. Eyes that had always been a beacon of warmth and comfort to me. "But you don't want to be here. You love New York. You—"

"I never loved New York more than being with you, Mia."

"But you left. You left me behind. You moved on with your life." My heart drops at her words. Had she really thought that? How could she think I'd moved on with my life?

"I never wanted to leave and stay gone. I have loved you since I was a teenager, and I was scared that it would break my heart, being here, not being able to have you."

"I don't understand."

"I never thought that there was even a possibility of you loving me. And if I'm being really vulnerable and honest with you, a part of me stayed away because I couldn't face the reality of loving you and wanting you and needing you and you being with someone else. It would've broken me every single day."

"But I didn't even know you had those feelings for me." Her eyes search mine and I watch as she swallows hard. There's a lump in my throat as I wait for her to process everything that I've told her. I'm glad to finally let it all out. It had been a burden carrying my love for her without being able to tell her. It had been a burden having that weight on my shoulders, wanting so much more from her and being scared to lose her if she knew the truth. In fairytales, the prince always gets the princess and they always live happily ever after. But I wasn't Prince Charming and she wasn't Cinderella. There was no guarantee that she'd love me back. There was no guarantee that I wouldn't ruin everything. There was no guarantee that I wouldn't live my life wishing I'd never told her. Though, I suppose fear had made me miss out on what could have been years of happiness. My fear had paused life.

I never wanted to pause life again.

"I know. I wasn't brave enough to tell you. I was scared. But somehow, some way, we figured it out, and we are here together, and we love each other." My words don't seem adequate. I want to explain to her that she means the world to me, that life for me doesn't exist without her, but I don't know if she would think I was being hyperbolic.

"You know you can always tell me anything, Luke." There's an ethereal softness to her words that hits me in the gut in the most beautiful way. This woman is my woman. Has always been my woman. Would always be my woman.

"I guess I'm finally strong enough to admit that it's always been you." I grin. "Who needs all the billions I make in New York, any way?"

"And who knows? Maybe if we find the hidden treasure at Hidden Cove, we'll be billionaires anyway."

"I already have a lot of money, Mia. You don't have to worry about that."

"But if I find you a treasure, I will also have a lot of money," she says, laughing. "I don't want you thinking I'm with you just for your money."

"I would never think that, Mia. You know that."

"I know," she says, reaching up to touch me on the side of the face, reassuring me that I've haven't made her feel like a gold digger. "I think I got caught up in my feelings as well."

My phone rings again and I want to ignore it, but the familiar twitch of my brain makes me look down at the screen.

"Oh no. Is it your office again?" There's a note of despondency in her voice as she looks to the side and I stroke the side of her arm as I look down at the screen.

"No, it's my grandma. I'm going to get it."

I answer the call and put it on speakerphone. "Hey, Grandma. What's going on?"

"Hi, darling. I've got you on three-way. I have Mia's grandma on the line." I look over at Mia and she shrugs. She has no idea why I'm receiving this three-way call, either.

"Hi Luke, it's me, Lucille. Mia's grandma."

"Hi, Lucille. How's it going?" I laugh at her greeting. Like I had no idea who she was. *What on earth is going on here?*

"We wanted to tell you two kids that there was just notification that a storm might be coming, okay? And we just wanted to tell you that you're not to go to Hidden Cove today, okay. The drive might not be safe."

"Okay ... did we say we were going to Hidden Cove?" I frown as I glance at Mia. Had Mia texted her grandma and told her?

"I think I heard you talking about going to get the treasure," my grandma says, clearing her throat. "From the clues, Mia's been getting."

"Oh, yeah. I guess we'll wait to go tomorrow then." I look over at Mia and mouth. "Did you tell them about the clues?" She makes a face and shakes her head.

"You don't have to go at all," Lucille says quickly. "There's no treasure."

"Wait, what are you talking about?" I demand to know to Mia takes a step closer and stares down at the screen.

"What on earth?" Mia whispers. "Grandma, what are you saying? How do you even know about the clues?"

There's silence on the other line. Which tells me that something is a brewing because Lucille and Bitsy are not known for their appreciation of quiet time.

"I suppose we should tell them now," my grandma says and from her tone, I can tell she doesn't really want to say anything.

"Tell us what?" I ask suspiciously.

"If you think so, Bitsy," Lucille must be in her kitchen because I hear the rattling of glasses in the background.

Mia frowns at me. "What are you talking about, Grandma? You're confusing Luke and I."

"Oh, just a little thing that Bitsy and I did." The voice is far too innocent. Far far too innocent.

"What did you guys do?" I ask, prodding her to actually reveal what is going on.

"Well … we might or might not have sent the treasure hunt notes to Mia so that you two could solve them together."

"What? Did you bury a treasure or something?" I am so confused. "I hope neither one of you buried any real gold or anything. That would be so irresponsible."

"No, not quite," my grandma says and giggles. "There is gold at the end of the journey, but not bullion."

"What?" I am starting to grow annoyed.

"Grandma, explain in better detail please." Mia demands.

Lucille starts giggling nervously. "Mia, darling, it was my idea."

"What, Grandma? What's going on? What was your idea? Luke and I have no clue what you're talking about right now and it's driving us both crazy."

"We wrote the notes," she admits like it's no my big deal. "Rex has no clue that you even got those notes. We wrote the notes on the back of your and Luke's invitations." She explains again. "Pity you don't have a date."

"What?" Mia looks shocked. "What are you saying?" She grabs the phone from me. "Let me get this straight," she continues without letting them speak again. "You sent that rude note to me and the one to Luke? They weren't from Rex?"

"Technically, we never said they were from Rex." Lucille sounds guilty. "We never signed any name to the notes."

"But you knew we'd think they were from him. Why on earth would Andi write us anything?"

"It wasn't intended to be malicious, darling, we just wanted to start the train to get it to the station."

"What are you talking about grandma? You made me think everyone in Coconut Beach was going to be talking about my years pining away for Rex."

"But you weren't pining away for him, Mia."

"Yes, but no-one knows that."

"I knew that and of course, Bitsy knew that as well."

"Grandma, I can't believe you did this to us. Do you know what you did?"

"Bring you both together?" She responds smartly.

"Grandma." Mia's voice is weak and she just shakes her head as she gazes at me.

"You and Luke were made for each other. We have known it since you were young, and you've just been spending too much time apart, and it felt like it was never going to happen. You are both too stubborn and so scared of being honest with each other about your true feelings. So, we thought this was the perfect opportunity."

"For you to scheme?" Mia interjects and the two ladies just laugh.

"We thought this was the perfect opportunity for you both to spend quality time together and and get closer." Bitsy adds. "We had a feeling the notes would make you both act rashly and decide to go together. Though, we never would have predicted you'd lie and pretend to have been dating for a year. That was even better than we'd hoped. What a fabulous idea."

"Grandma—" I say. I can't help laughing.

"So, you guys wrote the rude notes on the invitations?" Mia says, demanding more information. "Every single word? None of it was from Rex? I just want to make sure I'm understanding this fully."

"Yes, darling. I'm sorry. We didn't really mean them. We just wanted you both to be so infuriated that you would take some sort of action—and we hoped that action would lead you two to being together." Her grandma's voice is sweet. "We hope you both understand."

"That's all we wanted because we knew that you were made for each other, and we just needed you both to realize that," my grandma adds. "We knew if we tried to play matchmaker you'd both run from the idea, but we figured if you guys played matchmaker together, it would lead to something."

"Dang. We were set up," Mia says, shaking her head as she laughs.

"So, what is at the end of the treasure hunt, Grandma, if it's not real gold? And please do not tell me it's candy. If the gold is chocolate coins, I'm going to be mad cos you know they'll likely have melted by now."

"It's something far greater than that," Lucille says softly.

"The gold we have for you is the most valuable thing in the world," my grandma adds. "Gold everyone wishes they had."

"What's that?" Mia asks and looks at me. "Are there million dollar bills?" She asks and I just laugh as she wrinkles her nose.

"Please do tell us what awaits us." I add.

"True love," Lucille answers in a breathy sigh. "True love is rarer than any precious metal or jewel. It is the one thing money can't buy."

"You found each other, haven't you?" my grandma asks and there's hope in her voice. "You realize now that the special connection you both have is more than just friendship now, right? It's destiny."

Mia and I stare at each other, and I squeeze her hand before reaching up and touching the side of her face. My heart flows with love for her. It should feel weird feeling this strongly about her, but it doesn't. It just feels right.

Oh, so right.

"We have realized we were made for each other and I think I speak for both of us when I say we are desperately in love. Mia is my greatest treasure and you're right, she is more precious than anything else on this earth." I kiss the top of her head, then the tip of her cute little nose, and then her soft trembling lips. "I love you, Mia."

"I love you too, Luke." She lets out a dreamy little breath. "Oh, Grandma," Mia's voice softens. "Thank you."

"You can thank me when you get married and give me plenty of great-grandbabies."

"Grandma!" Mia says, laughing.

"What? A woman can wish, can't she?" Her grandma starts laughing and I lean over and whisper into Mia's ear. "Do you think your grandma would still be laughing if I told her I very much wanted to impregnate you." I tug on her earlobe. "The thought of making you pregnant fills me with joy. We can even practice right now."

"Luke." Mia blushes and grabs my bicep. "What if they hear you?"

"What?" I smile at her innocently. "Shall I tell them I want us to go and practice right now."

"Luke."

"Excuse me everyone, but I need to get Mia naked so she can ride my cock and have the best orgasm of her life…again."

"What did you say, Luke?" Bitsy says. "We didn't hear you."

"Nothing grandma," I laugh as Mia glares at me. I bring her into me and thrust into her ass as I wrap my arm around her waist. She shimmies her ass on my crotch and I groan under my breath.

"Oh are you sure."

"Yes." I bite down on my lip as I slip my fingers across Mia's stomach. "Please do not go and tell all the bees what is going on just yet, okay," I say as my fingers play with Mia's bellybutton.

"As if we would do that," my grandma says, and we all start laughing at the irony of her comment. She was most probably already texting them.

"So, remember, a storm is coming. You guys should get back to the hotel. Don't go to Hidden Cove. At least not until the storm passes," Lucille says.

"Okay, we won't," I say. The real truth is all I want right now is Mia naked, sitting on top of me.

"Oh, and if you would both do me a favor and just call your friends and tell them that the wedding is off. We're still going to have a large party, and everyone can celebrate because it's already been paid for. But it will just be a celebration of love in general. However, if you both… well, if you two decide you want to get married—"

"No, Grandma." I cut her off, as much as I would love to marry Mia, I'm not doing it at Rex's cursed event.

"Fine, fine, fine. We'll just have fun. So, Mia, you'll let your friends know that they're still to come, but we'll be celebrating something else."

"Okay, I will let them all know. I'm sure they won't be shocked."

"Great. Well, we'll see you two lovebirds, later." We hang up the phone and just stare at each other in mirth and shock. Though, I know neither one of us are mad. I know that I for one am extremely grateful.

"Can you believe that?" she says in awe. "Our grandparents set us up."

"I actually don't know how I feel about this. I'm absolutely ecstatic, but I am in shock. I feel kind of bad now that I talked shit about Rex and his notes seeing as he never wrote them."

"No, it was deserved," she says, giggling. "He must've thought I was absolutely crazy because he had no idea what I was talking about when it came to the notes, but he was a jerk in so many other ways."

"But wasn't he so self-centered that he didn't even really bring it up to you again?" I say. "You would have thought he would have questioned you to get to the bottom of it all."

"You're right. He didn't say, *I have no idea what you're talking about,* and try to get to the bottom of it."

She touches the side of my face. "I love you, but your brother really needs some work."

"I know. And maybe one day, he'll get the help that he needs, and he and I will have the relationship that I want. But right now, you're all I need and want."

I smile at her and kiss her. "Should we go back to the hotel?"

"What do you want to do?" she says, a teasing tone in her voice.

"I don't know. There are a couple of things I could think of."

"And what are those?"

"Let me see … you."

"What do you mean me?"

"I'd love to do you one time, two times, three times—"

"What about the fourth and the fifth?" she says.

"If I have energy left." I wink at her.

She laughs. "I love you, Luke Haverbrook. You are the perfect man for me."

"And you, Mia Bishop, are my beautiful angel—the love of my life, the key to my heart, the future of my being. You, Mia, are my everything. And please never forget that."

"So, I'm not just another summer romance then?"

"No, my darling. You are the rest of my life."

epilogue

Mia

six months later

"Man, it's kind of cold today," I say to Juniper as I pull on my sweater. "I feel like I need a coat and a scarf and gloves."

"It's not that cold, Mia. I suppose it's cold for Coconut Beach. That's because we're in wintertime. We don't have snow though."

"That's true," I say. "Get in any new books this morning?"

"Yeah, I'm about to start unpacking them and putting them on the shelves. You want to help?"

"Sounds good. I think Wendy, Silvie, and Summer are going to go to yoga, and they asked me if I wanted to come."

"And you're not taking up yoga now, are you?"

"No. I may have a fiancé now, but that doesn't mean I've completely lost my mind. I will never be into yoga."

She starts laughing as I grab a box of books and start putting them on the shelves outside of our bookmobile.

Even though we're no longer in the summer, the weather is still nice. It's much cooler, but the snowbirds have hit town, and they love to shop at our bookmobile. I look out at the water and smile to myself.

I'm so glad Luke decided that he wanted to move back to Coconut Beach. Ultimately, I loved him enough to go wherever he wanted to go, and if he had decided he didn't want to be in Coconut Beach, I would've gone with him wherever he wanted to go. But this is where we met, where we fell in love, and this is where we are going to raise our kids.

"So, how long is Luke going to be surfing for? I thought he was bringing us lunch." Juniper looks at her watch, and I start laughing.

"It's not like I can call him. He's in the ocean."

"I know, and I'm so happy for you. You guys are so in love." Juniper's eyes glaze over. "I've never seen two people more ridiculously in love in my life."

"Yeah, well, I'm trying not to throw it in your face or anything, Juni."

"You don't. Don't make me slap you." She laughs. "Joking. I'm joking. I would never slap you, but I'm happy that you're happy. And also, I kind of saw this coming a long time ago."

"What do you mean, you saw this coming? Are you psychic or something?"

"No, but you forget that I met you guys at a time in life where I was able to see that Luke had a thing for you, and you were always going on about him and about how great he was, and I was like, *These two are going to end up together. They just don't know it yet.*"

"Did you really think that?"

She nods slowly. "Why do you think you never found a serious boyfriend and you went after tourists and surfers and never really dated or did anything with them? Because it was always Luke. It was always Luke, Mia. You just didn't realize it yet, but you guys were practically in a relationship anyway. You were always on the phone and chatting, and it was like he lived here even though he was in New York. But it's so much better that he's here now. You love him."

"I do."

"Did I hear my name?"

A low growl sounds next to me, and I turn to see Luke standing there in his wetsuit. He's already started to peel it down. I run over to him and jump into his arms.

"Shoots, you're so wet," I say as I get ocean water all over my sweater and jeans.

"Well, you knew I just got out of the water," he says as he spins me around and gives me a big kiss. "Hey, beautiful."

"Hey, handsome. How are the waves?" I ask him.

"Pretty gnarly." He grins. "It was fun. You know, you've got to let me show you how to surf sometime."

"Yeah, when I'm one hundred percent guaranteed to not encounter any sharks, I will let you take me out to surf."

"So, that's never then?"

"Yeah, that's never."

"Okay then. Hey, Juniper." He holds up a hand. "I would give you a hug as well, but I don't want to get you wet."

"Thank you because I don't really want to get all salty wet either." She grins. "So, we're all going to play board games this weekend?"

"Yeah. I invited Rafe, Wendy and Carter, Summer and Dayton, Silvie and Cal, and we're all going to play charades and whatever other board games I can get. I think it'll be fun. We're going to grill out steaks and some burgers, and Mia said she's going to make a potato salad and an apple pie."

"Mia, you're cooking?" Juniper looks shocked.

"What? So, I'm a little domesticated now. I do it for my man."

"Really?" Luke tilts his head to the side. "You're making potato salad and apple pie for me, even though I don't really like potato salad and I requested twice-baked potatoes?"

I laugh loudly then. "Hey, you'll like this potato salad. I promise."

He kisses me on the tip of the nose. "I like and love everything you make, so I'm sure you're right."

"Oh my gosh. Gag me with a knife," Juniper says, laughing loudly. "Why are you two so sickly-sweet?"

"Maybe because we're in love."

"I guess so. Remind me when I fall in love to not act like this," she says, smiling at me. "That is, if I ever fall in love because it seems like there's no man on this island who is mature enough to date a woman like me."

"I think there's got to be at least one," I say. "Is there anyone that you fancy or have your eye on?"

"Not at all," she says, shaking her head quickly. "Not at all. There's no one."

"Wow. That was kind of a fast response." I narrow my eyes. "You mean, there's no one you've ever seen at Cocktails & Chaos that you thought, *Wow, he's cute*?"

"Nope, not at all."

"Really? What about that dude who was talking to us? What was his name? Matt?"

"Who's Matt?" Luke says, frowning slightly.

I laugh as I see the jealousy in his expression. "He wasn't interested in me. He was trying to chat up Juniper. I flashed him this absolutely gorgeous diamond ring that my fiancé put on my finger." I grin at him. "And he was not interested."

"I'm not interested in Matt. We were just talking, and he was going on and on about comic books." Juniper gives me a look. "And you know I am not interested in comic books or men who are interested in comic books."

"I know"—I laugh—"but maybe give him a shot."

"Give who a shot?"

I look behind me, and I'm surprised to see Rafe standing there.

"Oh, hey, bro. How's it going?" I head over to him and give him a quick hug.

"Why are you dripping with water?" he says as he brushes some drops off of him.

"It's my fault. I'm sorry." Luke holds up his hand, and Rafe just laughs.

"I should have known. So, what were you talking about just now?"

"Oh, I was just talking about this hot guy who's into Juniper, and I was telling her that perhaps he'll be the love of her life."

"Oh." Rafe frowns. "And who is this exactly?"

"His name is Matt."

"His name is Matthew," Juniper says, clarifying like there's some sort of big difference.

"Matt, Matthew—same difference. And he was totally trying to bang our girl. He was all over her, and she was like, *I don't know. Really?*"

"Mia, I was not saying—"

"I know you weren't saying, but you did have a high-pitched voice. Anyway, I was trying to convince her that maybe she should invite him to game night this weekend."

Rafe looks at Luke. "But don't we have an even set of numbers right now? And if we're going to play group games, we'd rather have an even set of numbers and not odds. So, I don't think that's a good idea. And plus, you don't know this guy. He could turn out to be a serial killer or a psychopath."

"And I'm not going to invite him anyway," Juniper says quickly. "So, it's okay."

"Well, that's good then. That's settled." Rafe folds his arms. "Anyway, I was just dropping by to see how everyone was doing."

"Really? You never drop by to see how we're doing." I gaze at my brother. "What's up with the shirt that you're wearing? It looks like it's brand-new and formfitting, and my brother does not wear formfitting shirts."

"Nothing. I'm just headed back to the vet clinic, and I decided to drop by to say hello."

"Well, hello."

Something about his story doesn't make sense, but I'm not even going to question him. If he's come to check up on me and find out if it's going well with Luke, I'm not going to give him the answers that he seeks. He's my brother, and I love him, and I love that he cares about me, but he does not need to be in my business.

"Luke and I are doing well, if that's what you came to ask me."

"Huh?" Rafe stares at me with confusion in his expression. "What are you talking about?"

"You came to see how Luke and I were doing, right? Because you think we got engaged too quickly and because you're being the overprotective big brother."

"No, I'm not concerned about you and Luke getting engaged after three months of dating." He rolls his eyes. "Which, by the way, lying to your family and pretending you'd been dating for a year was kind of messed up, Mia."

"You know why we did it." I shrug. "Plus that's old news."

"I know why you did it, but you didn't have to lie to me."

"I'm sorry, but I knew you would've told the parents, who would've told all the busybodies, and everyone on the island would've known we were fake dating, and then it wouldn't have fooled Rex, and that was the whole point."

"Whatever. Anyway, I should get going, but—"

"One second, Rafe."

"Yes?"

"If you didn't come to check up on me and Luke, then why did you drop by?"

"I wanted to see if you had any James Patterson books," he says quickly. "But I'll come back later."

He looks over at Juniper. "I like your earrings, Juniper."

"Oh, thanks."

"Are they new?"

"No."

"Oh, okay. Well, I'll be off. And don't invite that Matt or Matthew guy." He looks at me. "We don't want the numbers to be odd—remember that?"

"Yes, bro. See ya."

As my brother heads out, I say to Luke and Juniper, "Ugh, he's so annoying. He totally came to check up on Luke and me. Like, get a life and get a girlfriend." I giggle.

I look over at Juniper, who has a dreamy expression on her face as she watches Rafe walk away. Once again, I'm reminded of moments from the summer when they acted oddly around each other.

Does Rafe have a thing for Juniper, or does Juniper have a thing for Rafe?

"Hey, Luke, walk me to the ice cream store so we can get a quick ice cream."

"Okay. Does that mean I'm buying you an ice cream?"

"Well, duh."

"Okay. You want anything, Juniper?"

"No. Mia, didn't you just say you were cold? Why would you get ice cream?"

"Because I like ice cream, even in cold weather."

"Okay." She smiles. "No, I'm okay. Enjoy, and take a long lunch if you want. I can look after the store by myself for a bit."

"No, I don't want you to do that."

"It's fine. I know Luke doesn't always have a lot of time now that he's helping get his family business back on track, and you are newly engaged. I want you to spend as much time together as possible. I know I might have sounded like a jealous shrew earlier, but I really am so happy for you both. We've all been friends for a really long time, and to see your friendship blossom into love, well, it's really cool."

"Oh, thank you, Juni." I hurry over to her and give her a big hug. "I love you."

"I love you too. Now go and enjoy your ice cream."

"Okay. Thank you. Come on, Luke."

"Okay, I'm just finishing taking off my wetsuit," he says as he pulls it off and towel-dries himself.

My throat goes dry as I stare at his body. He's so built and still so sexy to me as he pulls on a pair of shorts and a T-shirt. I think to myself that all I want to do is get him naked, not put more clothes on him.

"Okay, let's go," he says. "See you later, Juniper."

"Bye, guys."

We walk down the boardwalk toward the ice cream store, and then I grab his hand and pull him to the side.

"What are you doing?"

"I just need to kiss you right now," I say.

I reach up and grab his face and pull him down toward me. I run my fingers down his chest and up his shirt, loving the feel of his skin against mine. He grunts as he kisses me back passionately, and I feel his hand in my hair, running down my back and squeezing my ass to him.

"Well, nice to see you too." His eyes are teasing as he holds me to him. "What was that about?"

"Just was thinking how sexy you are and how lucky I am that you're mine. And I was wondering if we could find a place to have a quickie around here."

"You want to have a quickie in public?"

"Look, we've done it in the ocean. We've done it in the sand at night."

"Mia, it's the middle of the day." He laughs loudly, though he looks excited. "But you know I can always be persuaded."

"Okay, so maybe we're not going to have a quickie right around here, but we could rush home."

"That wouldn't be a quickie then," he says, lips twitching.

"Well, Juniper did say that we could take as much time as possible."

"Okay. I'm down for it if you are. What about your ice cream?"

"We've got ice cream at home," I say, "and whipped cream, and I can think of a couple of places I would like to lick that off of."

"Oh, yeah?" he says, his tone low as his eyes darken. "And where would that be?"

"Well, one would be here." I slide my fingers down the front of his shorts, and he groans as I squeeze his cock. "Ooh. Already excited to see me," I say as I feel it hardening in my hand.

"I'm always excited to see you, fiancée."

"I'm always excited to see you too, fiancé," I say back.

He kisses me hard, and I feel his fingers reaching up the inside of my shirt and touching my stomach.

"I love you, Mia. Have you given any thought as to when you want to get married?"

"Well, I think we should date for at least a year before we get married, even though we've known each other for what feels like centuries. But we haven't been dating that long, and I don't want to be that woman who gets married six months after officially dating." I am not being quite truthful. I'd marry him today if I could, but I want everyone in my family to think I've been responsible. Darn you, Rafe.

"So, I have to wait another six months, is what you're saying? You want us to get married after one year of dating? I would marry you right now," he says. "I love you. I pick you. I choose you. I want you. And I always will. But I'm willing to wait for whenever you are ready."

"I know, and that's part of the reason why I love you so much. You care about what I want and what I need and you respect that, and you don't try to force anything out of me."

"I would never force anything out of you, but maybe I will try and convince you not to name our first son Samuel."

"What? I think it's such a cute name. We can call him Sammy."

"I do not want to call my son Samuel or Sammy."

"So, what, you're not going to let me name him even though I'll carry him for nine months?"

"I respect you, and I know it's a lot to be a mother, but Sammy? Really?"

I start laughing. "Okay, maybe not Sammy. We can come to a consensus for a name."

"When do you think you'll want to start a family?" He grabs my hand and clasps it, then kisses me softly on the lips.

"I don't know. When do you want to start a family?"

"As soon as possible." He smiles. "And by that, I mean whenever you're ready. I can't wait to be the father of your children, but we have an eternity. So, let's travel the world. Let's explore. Let's do whatever we want to do, and then we'll have kids, and we'll let them know they can be whatever they want to be, and we'll support them and love them, and hopefully, they'll find best friends like us."

"I love you, Luke. How did I get to be so lucky?"

"I don't know, but I think I'm even luckier than you because I have you by my side and you're the best woman in the world."

"If I'm the best woman, then you're the best man."

"If someone could hear us talking right now, they would absolutely gag," he says.

I grab his face and laugh. "I know. We sound ridiculously in love."

"We do."

"But that's why we're so perfect for each other. Now come on. Let's go home for that quickie. I've got three hours I think I can spare."

I laugh with abandon as we go running toward his car. I love this man. I love making love to this man, and I hope our days of joy and wonder never end. I still have to pinch myself at how life has gone. My fake summer romance with my best friend led to the love of my life and I'm so very grateful. I can't wait to spend the rest of my life with this man.

THE END

Want more of Luke and Mia?
Download an exclusive bonus scene:
https://dl.bookfunnel.com/x9p42y7xqg

Not ready to leave Coconut Beach yet?
Read the next book in the series featuring Silvie and Cal in *Just Another Summer Escape by Erin Branscom*
https://bit.ly/jasescape

Want to read Juniper and Rafe's book? Then you're in luck. Their story is coming in Next Time We'll Fall, a standalone book that you can get here.
https://amzn.to/4mmr7UG

Read the blurb for Next Time We'll Fall below!

I am the fool who accidentally entered a stripping contest, thinking I was signing up for karaoke.
Even worse? My best friend's older brother was there to witness every minute of my humiliation.
I run a romance bookstore, but I never expected to be the heroine of my own drama-filled love story. After Rafe saved me, while simultaneously telling me off, I panicked and pretended the shameful disaster was research for a book I'm writing.
Yes, that was a huge exaggeration.
But I'm paying for it now. Because he's decided I need help!
He's volunteered for the nonexistent role of my bossy bodyguard and he keeps showing up everywhere I go, including my dates.
The truth is I've had a crush on him since the day I turned eighteen when he gave me my first kiss. Back then, when I thought the kiss

meant something, a grumpy Rafe made it clear I was off-limits. I was too young and he had no interest in dating his little sister's best friend. When a local TV show casts me in a fall dating show, Rafe insists on becoming my very unwanted dating coach to help me find someone "age appropriate." However, his advice is terrible and every date ends in disaster. The show could actually boost the book I'm now writing and I'm fed up with Rafe's hot and cold behavior.

So, to get him to back off, I decide to pretend I've made it my mission to make him mine. I thought my fake, very public interest in him, would scare him off. Only he doesn't seem as opposed to the cameras nor the idea as I thought he would be.

Now Mr. Non-Committal Rafe Bishop is refusing to let me go. And I can't tell if it's because he's trying to protect me or because he finally wants me.

https://amzn.to/4mmr7UG

This series can be read in any order, so grab some sunscreen and an iced coffee, and get ready to live the sweet life in Coconut Beach!

Just Another Summer Escape by Erin Branscom

https://bit.ly/jasescape

Just Another Summer Enemy by Ariel Hendrix

https://bit.ly/jasenemy

Just Another Summer Crush by Lyra Parish

https://bit.ly/jascrush

Just Another Summer Romance by J.S. Cooper

https://bit.ly/jasromance

Each book in the Coconut Beach series is a spicy small town romcom set in summer with a happily ever after. These books are complete stand alones but you will see your favorite characters throughout the series.

acknowledgments

I am so thankful to have been a part of the project with three other wonderful authors. Thanks to Lyra Parish, Erin Branscom, and Ariel Hendrix for sharing this wonderful world of Coconut Beach with me. It was so much fun building up this world with you all.

Thanks to my friends Holly and Mara for the day we spend gallivanting from beach to beach so I could get videos.

Thanks to all the readers that took a chance on this book and have made it here. You have read a lot of pages and I hope you enjoyed all of them. I loved writing Mia and Luke's story. I loved writing about Coconut Beach, a fictional town I would love to live in.

Thanks to God for all my many blessings. I love being an author. I love being able to write stories that so many people enjoy. I am grateful every day to call this my job.

As always, if you ever want to get in touch with me, you can email me at jscooperauthor@gmail.com.

Or follow me on Instagram or join my Facebook group.

www.ingramcontent.com/pod-product-compliance
Lightning Source LLC
LaVergne TN
LVHW091111080826
845145LV00008B/1873

* 9 7 8 1 9 4 0 2 1 8 4 8 9 *